ADVANCE PRAISE

"Intimate, big-hearted, compassionate, and clear-eyed, Michelle Brafman's novel turns secrets into truths and the truth into the heart of fiction."

— Amy Bloom,
author of *Lucky Us* and *Away*

"Heartfelt and genuine, *Washing the Dead* never betrays the complicated truths of family and tradition."

— David Bezmozgis,
author of *Natasha and Other Stories* and *The Betrayers*

"From roots in one religious tradition comes a tale of emotional redemption for all of us. Michelle Brafman's astonishing compassion for all human frailty infuses this story about the need for truth and the promise of forgiveness."

— Helen Simonson,
author of *Major Pettigrew's Last Stand*

"An illuminating and intricately layered novel about the complicated legacies that pass from mother to daughter, and about the ways that understanding our own history helps make us who we are. Brafman is an insightful writer who never falters or flinches in her quest to uncover the hearts of her characters."

— Carolyn Parkhurst,
author of *The Dogs of Babel* and *The Nobodies Album*

"A rich tale of love, friendship, yearning, and forgiveness. Brafman's beautifully wrought prose quickly cuts to the heart of things: how to live, how to love, and how to care for the dead."

— Jessica Anya Blau,
author of *The Summer of Naked Swim Parties* and *The Wonder Bread Summer*

"Like a Jewish Anne Lamott, Brafman reels you in with warmth, depth, and heart. Infused with lush detail about Orthodox Jewish life in the Midwest, *Washing the Dead* is the story of three generations of women and family secrets that threaten to unravel. A charming and original spiritual page-turner about love, forgiveness, and family life."

– Susan Coll,
author of *The Stager* and *Acceptance* and
events and programs director at Politics & Prose

"Sensual and spiritual, shot with betrayals, *Washing the Dead* plumbs the destructive power of secrets across three generations of mothers and daughters. In haunting prose, Brafman offers a riveting glimpse into Orthodox Jewish life and breathtaking insight into what it means to forgive."

– Dylan Landis,
author of *Rainey Royal* and
Normal People Don't Live Like This

"With the knife blade of her prose honed razor sharp, Brafman skillfully dissects the bonds of mother-daughter relationships.... She weaves together the sacred and the profane, reverberating silences, exile and return, atonement and forgiveness with the tenderness of a mother braiding the hair of a beloved daughter."

– Faye Moskowitz,
author of *A Leak in the Heart* and
Her Face in the Mirror: Jewish Women on Mothers & Daughters

"*Washing the Dead* made me ache. Barbara Blumfield's longing is palpable on every single page: for her mother's love, for her past, and for re-admittance into a world from which she has been exiled. What a spectacular debut."

– T. Greenwood,
author of *Bodies of Water* and *The Forever Bridge*

"Brafman offers a fresh, vital narrative about guilt, love, loss, and the necessity of wrestling with the dark angel of a painful family legacy until it blesses you. June Pupnick, one of the most bewitching and problematic fictional mothers I've come across in years, makes a regular habit of escaping her life by 'gobbling up' novels 'without chewing.' *Please* resist gobbling up this novel. Slow down, savor the richness and generosity of Brafman's storytelling, and then buy a copy for your most deserving friend."

— Margaret Meyers,
author of *Swimming in the Congo* and *Dislocation*

"Throughout these pages, moving in shadow, runs the terrific responsibility of forgiveness and redemption. Brafman has done us all a true mitzvah by writing this beautiful book."

— Robert Bausch,
author of *A Hole in the Earth* and
Far as the Eye Can See

"A riveting and humane account of family pain passed from one generation to the next.... How do we begin to forgive those who injured us? Start by reading Brafman's unflinching and inspiring novel."

— Mary Kay Zuravleff,
author of *Man Alive!* and *The Frequency of Souls*

A Novel

by

Michelle Brafman

Published by Prospect Park Books
2359 Lincoln Avenue
Altadena, CA 91001
www.prospectparkbooks.com

Distributed by Consortium Book Sales & Distribution
www.cbsd.com

Library of Congress Cataloging-in-Publication Data

Brafman, Michelle.
Washing the dead : a novel / by Michelle Brafman.
pages cm
ISBN 978-1-938849-51-0 (alk. paper)
1. Jewish women--Fiction. 2. Family secrets--Fiction. 3. Jewish fiction. I. Title.
PS3602.R344415W38 2015
813›.6--dc23
2014041278

Cover design by Lissa Rivera.
Book layout and design by Amy Inouye, Future Studio.
Printed in the United States of America.

For Sally, Bertha, Rita, Lotta,
and Gabriela

WASHING
THE DEAD

THE FIRST WASHING

You don't look back along time
but down through it, like water.

— Margaret Atwood, *Cat's Eye*

December 1993

When I was eighteen weeks pregnant, I made a confession to my sonographer.

I lay on the exam table in a maternity bra and thin cotton robe, veiny belly bare, eyes fixed on the ceiling poster of a kitten with a diamond-studded collar. "This morning," I told her, "I prayed that God had spared a girl from landing in my womb."

She took off her glasses and slid them into the pocket of her lab coat. "Let's talk this out, hon," she said. Her name was Bridget, and she had an elegant neck and an impressive overbite, a Class II malocclusion—the daughter of an orthodontist notices such things.

I closed my robe and inched my rear up the table, wanting to talk. I was not a sharer by nature. I did, however, relish the company of emotional close talkers, like my friend Sheri Jacobstein, who often punctuated her sentences with "my shrink says." Last week after our birthing class, we had lunch at Heinemann's—we'd both been craving their grilled cinnamon bread—and I soaked up her description of her mother's new obsession with step aerobics. I never spoke of my mother.

Bridget grabbed the chair typically occupied by my husband, Sam, and wheeled up to the examining table. "Where's Dad today?"

"Madison. Business trip."

Sam hadn't missed a sonogram appointment yet. Bridget had

handed him a tissue when he wept after seeing the baby's heartbeat for the first time.

"I wanted him gone. He doesn't care about the gender as long as the baby is healthy, and I—" My sentence was too ugly to finish.

I stared at the feline overhead. "It's not that I don't know how to handle a little girl. I'm a teacher." I was a good teacher, too. I'd received the Milwaukee Early Childhood Education Golden Apple award two years in a row. I liked girls; I simply had too much baggage to raise one of my own.

Bridget waited for me to finish my thought.

"And I had a good mom." I paused. "For a while."

"Do you want to tell me about her?"

"I don't know." I considered what I would say. Maybe that she sang me Ella Fitzgerald to lull me to sleep and taught me how to knead challah dough. And she was a superb listener.

Bridget waited without making me feel rushed. I knew she had a packed schedule, and I felt like the person who shows up at a busy grocery checkout line with a wallet full of coupons.

"I'm keeping you from your next patient," I said.

"I'm fine."

I swallowed. "My mother baked me chocolate cakes from scratch for my birthdays and let me lick the batter off the beaters."

"To heck with salmonella," Bridget joked.

I smiled, still staring at the kitten, remembering my Saturday-morning walks to Shabbos services with my mother. She held my hand with a touch so light that it felt like her fingers were blowing mine kisses.

"Seriously, it sounds like you had a good mom," Bridget said, fishing her glasses out of her pocket.

I reached for her arm. She folded her hands in her lap.

"I can't take care of a girl," I whispered.

"Oh, get out of town. Of course you can. Look at all the things your mom taught you!"

My mother had shown me how to ditch her children when

they needed her most, to walk out the front door without so much as a glance over her shoulder after shaming them with her bad behavior.

"Yes she taught me a lot of things."

I was breathing hard now. Hot red circles were colonizing my breastbone, and my armpits were sweaty and rank, as they'd been since I woke up this morning. No matter how much deodorant I put on, I smelled like an onion bialy. Even Sam had noticed it when he kissed me goodbye, and he has no sense of smell.

"Deep breath, honey." Bridget took my hand in hers and held it tightly for a few seconds.

"Okay," I said obediently, and then waved my hand in front of my nose. "Sorry for the stench."

"Not to worry."

I tried to dry my armpits with the sleeve of my robe.

"Forget about the pits for a second. I want you to listen to me," Bridget said.

I shifted my gaze until I was staring into this semi-stranger's kind blue eyes.

"You're not the first woman to lie on this table, scared witless that you'll hurt your girl like your mom hurt you."

How did she know?

"These women go on to become good moms and love the dickens out of their daughters, and if you have one, you'll do the same."

I hope I can.

Bridget squeezed my hand hard. "Trust me, or better yet, trust you."

Trust. It was something I could think about. I shivered. My toes were icy, despite the vents blasting hot air in my direction. We sat in silence for a few seconds. Through the thin walls, I heard my OB recite his mantra to another patient: "Small meals throughout the day. Call me with any questions or concerns. You're never a bother."

"Okay, let's do this." My voice sounded gravelly.

"You don't want to wait for Dr. Mathison?"

"No." I didn't want anyone else to see me this whacked out.

Bridget got up from Sam's designated chair and walked around the table to the ultrasound cart. She gently undid my robe for me, which I liked. She squirted a glob of jelly on my stomach and spread it around tenderly. I liked that too. She detached the wand from the machine and moved it around my belly. I shuddered.

Bridget squinted into the screen. "Everything looks *real* good."

I breathed my usual sigh of relief, but I didn't let the breath entirely escape from my body.

"Mrs. Blumfield?" she said softly.

"Yes?" I answered to the cat above.

"You're having a perfect baby girl."

I stared at the screen, at the baby's heartbeat, and each pulse of light propelled me forward in time. I knew things. I knew that I would name my daughter Lili, and that after she was born, I would reach out to the mother who had left me. I knew that my mother and I would have biweekly desultory phone calls to compare the hues of the leaves falling from our elm trees or the price of unleaded gas at our respective Mobil stations. I would not sing Lili Ella Fitzgerald, even if I could carry a tune. I would choose raw folky singers like Marianne Faithfull and the Cowboy Junkies. But I too would be a superb listener.

When Lili turned two, I would run into Bridget at Sendik's, at the deli counter, but I wouldn't recognize the woman who had sat next to me and pried my fears from me as she would a sharp object from a small child's fingers. When I prayed, I would thank God for my triumph over my mother's legacy, knowing that my mother would one day need me as much as the baby now growing in my womb, and that the sour smell I'd so easily washed away after my sonogram would return with more pungency.

My glue would hold for fifteen years, until a gorgeous September day when a letter would arrive through my mail slot and blast me back to the tail end of my childhood, to the morning my mother began her final goodbye.

2

August 1973

My mother's mood hovered over us, a mist that could either turn to rain or vanish into the sunlight. During our family walk to Shabbos services, I saw her eyes honeying over, the first sign that at any moment she could dip away from us, into that place inside herself. Ever since last April, the mist had turned soupy, and I worried that we would both drown in it.

"Let's do the last block fast, Mom." If we moved quickly, we could outrun the fog.

"Okay, Barbara," she said, as if I were a small girl and had asked her to play one more game of Go Fish. I was seventeen. She appeased me, and we took off. We were both small and wiry, and we walked quickly, our heels touching the pavement in synchrony.

"Faster, Mom. They'll never catch us." I looked back at my father and my brother, Neil, both panting to keep our pace.

She slowed down, as if faltering. "I'm tired today, Sweet B."

I grabbed her hand, and she squeezed my palm with her fingers, cool and long as a concert pianist's. Then she let go. She didn't like to be touched when the mist overtook her.

"Let's let your father and Neil catch up," she said, the glaze thickening over her eyes.

Her goneness filled my chest. I wanted her back, but only if she could return as my normal mother. Her mists terrified me.

We ambled past the old beer-baron estates, with their carriage houses and panoramic views of Lake Michigan, on our way to the mansion that belonged to Rabbi Schine and his wife, the rebbetzin. Twenty-five years ago, Rabbi Schine, grandson of the great Chasidic leader Rav Isaac Schine, had been dispatched from Brooklyn to Milwaukee to ignite Jewish souls. A mysterious donor had given Rabbi Schine the mansion, which he'd converted into our synagogue, our shul. We stopped at the foot of the Schines' long driveway and faced the Tudor and its freshly cut front lawn, almost the length of a football field. The air was heavy with the scent of grass and lake. My mother, elegant in the new green hat that matched her eyes and blouse, stared beyond the house, drinking in the miles of waves fanning out behind it, as if they could absorb her. The water was unnaturally blue that morning, and its expansiveness made me feel hopeful that she would come back to us soon.

Out of habit, I glanced up at the top floor of the mansion, to the Schines' living quarters, for the signal that would tell me if Tzippy, my best friend, had already come downstairs for services. Not yet—her shade was still drawn. Our summer together was running out. Tomorrow Tzippy would go back to her yeshiva in New York to study with other Chasidic girls, and we wouldn't see each other for months and months. My mother's moods were much easier to manage when Tzippy was around.

Neil and my father caught up to us, and when we arrived at the mansion's front entrance, we took turns touching the mezuzah on the doorpost and kissing our fingers. We walked through the musty foyer, past the enormous portrait of Rabbi Schine's grandfather, whose eyes I imagined were following us as we made our way to the sanctuary, a converted ballroom with high ceilings and a real crystal chandelier.

My father and Neil sat in the front of the shul, and I trailed my mother back to the women's section. The Brisket Ladies, two women who cooked briskets for congregants who were ill or in mourning or had given birth, scooted down so my mother could take her chair next to the rebbetzin. My mother had earned this coveted seat by hosting Shabbos lunches for the nonobservant suburban Jews my parents helped recruit to the Schines' shul. My mother hated to cook, so the rebbetzin had written out four easy recipes for her on index cards. These dishes never turned out well, but it didn't matter; my mother had a quiet charisma and knew firsthand how to sell Orthodox Judaism to people brought up in synagogues with stained-glass windows and organ music. The rebbetzin and my mother spent long hours together writing and editing the talks the rebbetzin gave around town. "There would be no shul without June Pupnick," the rebbetzin said often. This was the biggest compliment she could pay to any congregant, because the shul meant everything to the Schines. The rebbetzin loved my mother like a sister and daughter rolled into one, and my mother offered the Schines all she had, except for the parts of herself that none of us could touch.

The rebbetzin leaned over to wish us a good Shabbos and kiss us hello. She was tall, exactly the same height as Rabbi Schine, and I guessed that was why she slouched and wore flat shoes with the stylish suits she sewed for herself. She was thin, too, thinner than my mom, and her skinniness accentuated the bones in her face: the bump on her nose, her tiny forehead, and her underbite, a Class III malocclusion that Tzippy inherited and my father fixed. Her eyes were round, though, and a warm, milky brown. When she looked at me, which wasn't often because she had so many people to look at, I felt important to the shul and to Hashem, God.

"Good Shabbos, Rivkah," my mother said. Nobody but my mother called the rebbetzin by her name. Ever. We all called her "the rebbetzin" like the English referred to Elizabeth Alexandra Mary Windsor as "the Queen."

My mother gave the gummy grin she used only when she was trying to act like everything was normal, but a look of recognition crossed the rebbetzin's face under her brand-new sheitel, styled into a light brown pageboy that suited her pale skin. The rebbetzin touched my mother's arm and pointed to something in the prayer book, and though my mother leaned her head into her friend's shoulder like she always did, I knew she wasn't paying attention.

Tzippy and I always sat in the far corner of the shul so that we could see everything. Mrs. Kessler, my former nursery school teacher, was sitting in the row in front of ours today. As soon as I caught her eye, she flashed me a smile so bright that it shone a light on what I liked best about myself. Her attention was different from the rebbetzin's; she was more focused on me and less on what I meant to the shul and to God. I wanted Mrs. Kessler to pull me into the cocoon of her lap and assure me that my mother would be back to pick me up from school before I knew it. Silly idea. Mrs. Kessler's lap was occupied by her baby, Yossi, and I was about to enter my senior year of high school.

My mother stopped pretending to pay attention to the rebbetzin's finger scrolling through the Hebrew words of the prayer. She excused herself and left. The rebbetzin's eyes tracked my mother but then returned to the prayer book. I checked the doorway for signs of Tzippy, whom I relied on for her sunniness and steady advice on everything from whether to tell my parents that I'd caught my brother eating a cheeseburger with his friends to which novels were appropriate for me to read.

I knew Tzippy's face better than my own, and when she showed up, I saw she'd been crying. Her lids were slightly swollen, and her chin jutted out the way it did when she was upset. She slid into the empty seat I'd reserved for her.

"What's wrong?" I mouthed.

She spoke into my ear. "My parents talked to a shadchen yesterday."

"A matchmaker?" I whispered back. Tzippy's family came from a Chasidic sect in which matches were still made and men wore long black coats and hats. My family was Orthodox, which meant that I got to pick my own husband and my father wore regular clothes.

"Yes!" Her breath warmed the inside of my ear.

"Aren't you happy?" We'd been planning our weddings since we were in third grade.

"No, petrified."

"Girls." Mrs. Kessler turned around and scolded us gently, but she could never really get mad at Tzippy or me. When we were her students, before Yossi was born, she'd given us her entire heart.

We pretended to focus our attention on the mumbled chanting of the young rabbis imported from Crown Heights to help Rabbi Schine. They bobbed up and down like ducks pecking at breadcrumbs, their long ivory prayer shawls covering their heads and flowing down their shoulders.

Yossi was growing restless, and when Mrs. Kessler stood to carry him from the sanctuary, we began whispering again.

"Let's get out of here so we can really talk," Tzippy said. "We only have one more day together." Saying goodbye to Tzippy never got easier, although I'd been doing it since sixth grade, after our Jewish day school ended and she started going to school in Brooklyn with her cousins, leaving me to fend for myself in public school.

"The nook?" I asked. That was our name for Mrs. Kessler's classroom, a warm nest in the basement of the shul.

"We'll need more privacy," she said.

Mothers were always wandering into the nook to deposit their antsy kids with Tzippy and me, and more often than not, one or more of Tzippy's little brothers would find us and we'd have to shoo them away. Tzippy didn't have any sisters, and when we were young, every time the rebbetzin got pregnant, I would secretly hope for another boy. *I* was Tzippy's sister.

"Then where?" I asked.

She cupped my ear with her hand. "Other side of the basement."

Her breath tickled. I stared at her dumbly.

"Barbara," she said, tapping my temple with her forefinger. "Use your kup. The basement has two parts with two entrances. One for the nook, and one for...."

I hoped like crazy that she wasn't thinking what I thought she was. "The mikveh?"

She nodded.

"Very funny." We weren't allowed to visit the mikveh. Men

and married women went there to purify themselves by dunking their bodies in its mixture of tap water and rainwater, and my mother came home from her monthly visits to the mikveh with damp hair and an odd calm about her, as if she'd returned from a trip to another country. Both Tzippy's mother and mine would kill us if they knew we ducked out of services to chat in the holiest spot in the entire shul.

"I'm not joking. We should go separately to avoid raising suspicion," she said. She'd leave the sanctuary first because she knew where to find the key, and I'd follow in ten minutes. She'd wait for me by the door to the mikveh. Before I could officially agree, she was gone. I let ten agonizing minutes pass, hoping either my mother or Tzippy would reappear and sit next to me, sparing me this adventure. No luck. I walked out of the sanctuary and through the social hall, swiping two mandelbrot cookies set out on a platter for the little kids. All of our meetings required a snack.

I entered the kitchen, expecting to run into Andy Noffsinger. Andy was the Schines' Shabbos goy, a Gentile they paid to turn on lights and ovens and touch anything deemed muksah, forbidden to Jews on the Sabbath. He should have been warming up the blueberry blintzes for the lunch, but today he was nowhere to be seen. I half wanted him to be there, to prevent me from having to go downstairs.

The entrance to the mikveh was off the large pantry. What if the Shabbos goy was inside retrieving a box of toothpicks or a stack of napkins? But the pantry was empty, except for the shelves lined with sacks of flour, bags of egg noodles, and bottles of juice. I opened the oak door and took a step down the stairs. They groaned under my feet. I slid off my loafers to avoid making noise; the stairwell was dark, so I held on to the railing with my free hand.

Tzippy was not waiting for me at the landing. Maybe she'd gone inside without me. I smelled cigarette smoke, but there was no way it was coming from Tzippy's lungs. Smoking was forbidden on Shabbos, and besides, a few years ago, Tzippy and I had experimented with my mother's Virginia Slims out on the bluffs behind the mansion, and Tzippy coughed so much that she swore she'd never smoke again. For days afterward, I'd craved another cigarette.

I was about to go back up the steps when a noise stopped me, a murmuring that escaped through the crack of the mikveh door like a sliver of light. I held my ear to the warped wood. My mother had told me that the mansion's original owners had built this pool so their polio-stricken son could soak his legs in it, and I swear I felt the boy's spirit talking to me. I felt sick with fear, yet a dull pressure deep inside my body, between my heart and gut, tugged at me and urged me inside. My fingers tingled as I put my sweaty hand on the brass doorknob and turned it slowly. The door was unlocked. I walked in and the whispering stopped.

The room was black, except for an ember flickering in the distance. The air shimmered, charging every cell of my body. The water was close by. I could smell it. Rain. Gallons of rain. I was too terrified to move, in case I tripped and fell into the sacred pool. My toes gripped the tiles through my socks.

A woman spoke. "Please, give me a second. I'll be up soon." I recognized the timbre of the voice, but its pleading tone was foreign to me.

Silence hung between us. My loafers shook in my hand as the tiny light moved toward me. The electricity in the air was starting to crackle, and I thought it would split me in two, like our oak tree that had been struck by a bolt of lightning last summer. My eyes followed the orange dot until the figure was standing close enough for me to touch her. I could only hear the sound of breathing. Hers and mine.

I reached out, and my fingers grazed my mother's hair. She was not wearing her Shabbos hat. Wavy auburn strands fell loosely around her face.

"Good Lord, Barbara. You scared me to death," she said, puffs of smoke escaping from her quivering lips.

I was frightened, not of the dark or the boy's ghost, but of my mother. I imagined that the smoke coming out of her body was the mist that had chased us, that could swallow us up whole. Its source was here, in the mikveh. "I'm sorry," I said quietly.

"Don't come down here again!" Her voice shook with a mix of anger and fear.

My mother and I rarely exchanged harsh words, and hers felt like a slap. "I won't. Let's go."

"First tell me that you understand me."

"I do. Please, can we leave?"

"Okay." The silkiness returned to her voice.

I followed her toward the door. She moved with ease, as if the room were fully lit. I looked around and didn't see anyone, but it was so dark that someone could easily have been hiding in here. The thought spooked me even more. "Who were you talking to?"

"Don't be silly. I was alone." She waved her hand, spraying ashes in the air.

I wasn't convinced. "Mom, you have to put out your cigarette."

"Yes." She took in a long drag of smoke. Had my mother smuggled a cigarette into the shul? She didn't carry a purse on Shabbos.

"We should hurry." Tzippy could come down any minute. I looped my elbow through hers and tried to pivot her toward the door.

She didn't budge. I pulled on her slender arm. "We've got to leave."

"I know, I know." She brought her cigarette to her mouth, and in the sparse light I could see that she looked trapped between the crook of my elbow and that spot inside herself where the mist nestled. Like a coyote, she'd have to chew off her arm to escape.

After a few seconds, she led me to a door adjacent to the entrance. I waited for her while she let herself into the changing room and flushed her cigarette down the toilet. It felt like an hour.

"Shame on us for playing hooky from services," she said lightly as we exited the mikveh.

I put my shoes back on and trotted up the steps behind her, my heart beating in my chest. She stood in the pantry, in a patch of sunlight spilling through the window, and smoothed her blouse. Her eyes were bright again, and she was smiling the way she did when she picked me up from school, as if she'd missed me and couldn't wait to hear about my day. She was back. My relief over her return always made me feel closer to her than if she'd never left at all. Today was no different.

I looked at her more carefully. Her lipstick was smeared.

"Just a second." I touched the spot on my lip that mirrored the location of her smear.

"Oh, dear. I'm a sight." She giggled, rubbing her index finger against her lip, as if she were the type of woman who didn't understand the fine art of applying lipstick.

"Where's your hat?" I asked.

She looked coyly surprised and put her hands on her head. Her hair looked more mussed in the light of the pantry. She couldn't return to shul with her head uncovered. "Oh, just a second," she said as if she'd forgotten a bag of groceries in the car.

"Do you need to go back down there?"

"Yes. Please don't follow me." She flicked one of her ashes from my shoulder before heading downstairs.

I watched her go, not entirely certain that she'd come back. The mikveh repelled me and called to me, like a ghost and a siren combined. I didn't move a muscle until my mother walked back through the pantry door, slightly winded. She didn't look at me as she wet her fingers, slicked back her hair, and bobby-pinned her pretty hat to her head.

On our way back to the sanctuary, we bumped into Tzippy, who was coming out of the bathroom. I nodded my head in my mother's direction, and without missing a beat, my mother winked at us as if she knew of our plan and had decided to overlook our mischief. She returned to the women's section to claim her seat between the rebbetzin and the Brisket Ladies, leaving the scent of cigarette smoke and Chanel in her wake.

"I'm so sorry," Tzippy said. "Mrs. Kessler needed me to watch Yossi for a few minutes." She lowered her voice. "Your mom didn't catch you in the mikveh, did she?"

"No. Luckily, I ran into her in the pantry. She was looking for a cracker because we had gefilte fish last night and it makes her stomach hurt." I was talking too fast. I'd never been so dishonest with Tzippy.

She gave me a funny look, because it wasn't like me to "prattle on," as my mother would say. "Plan B. Meet me in the nook after services," she said.

"Okay." Thankfully, she didn't suggest the mikveh again, because I wasn't going back down there. As I followed her back to our seats in the shul, Mrs. Kessler handed Yossi to me. The fine fuzz on his head tickled my neck. I patted him on the back, and we stifled our laughter when he let out a loud burp.

A few minutes later, Tzippy and I stood up and sped through the silent Amidah prayer, murmuring all nineteen blessings, our lips moving in unison. By the time the service finished, the left side of my head had started to ache mildly. As the hungry congregants began to file into the social hall, Tzippy and I snuck down to the nook, where I planned to tell her everything about discovering my mother in the mikveh. I had to or I would explode. I walked down the steps quickly, eager to breathe in the familiar scents of paint and the Jergens Cocoa Butter Mrs. Kessler applied to her perpetually chapped knuckles. I'd been volunteering for Mrs. Kessler two afternoons a week since ninth grade, and I liked having a role at the shul other than that of Tzippy's sidekick, although we both knew I felt lost without her.

Mrs. Kessler's room cheered me. Light from two high windows that gave onto the driveway splashed the blue walls she'd stenciled with a bespectacled sun and clouds that looked like the cotton balls I soaked with alcohol to dry up my pimples. Tzippy and I unfolded two rest mats, lay down on our backs with our calves hanging over the edges, and looked up at a mobile of the solar system. Saturn sagged under the weight of its loose ring, causing the other planets to dangle awkwardly.

"I have to talk to you about something." I took a big breath and searched for a way to tell her I had caught my disheveled mother smoking in the mikveh. I knew I wouldn't tell her about the mist finding its way inside my mother's body, though. My mother's moods were private, even from Tzippy.

"What?" Her chin stuck out farther now, and she was chewing on the inside of her lip, as if to keep it from trembling.

"You look like you're going to weep," I said. We'd always thought that "weep" was a funny verb, but she wasn't laughing. Neither was I.

"Trying not to." Her voice, always high-pitched and loud when she was staving off tears, almost made me cry. I wanted to cry right then anyway.

Her pain trumped my confession. "What's wrong?"

"I told you before. I'm scared," she said.

Me too. I was still reeling from standing alone in the dark, creepy mikveh, and the whole encounter with my mother was a secret lodged in my throat, growing into a ball of fear the size of a kiwi. "You were frightened the first year you went to yeshiva too." I didn't remind her that we both cried every day for months until we made new friends that we now spoke of with careful enthusiasm.

She sulked. "That was different."

"Why?"

"Because I wasn't expected to move to a strange city, much less with a man I'd only met a few times."

She told me about a cousin, Sari Levenstein, who had just found out that Rabbi Schine's father was moving her and her husband to San Diego, where they were supposed to ignite Jewish souls. The Rebbe could assign Tzippy and her groom to Duluth or Boise or Singapore.

"Let's worry about the wedding first," I said.

She started to sniffle.

"You're going to be a beautiful bride." She was. She had high cheekbones and a pretty rose tone to her skin, and she was tall and thin like her mother, but she didn't slouch.

"You're going to be there, right?"

"Like I'd miss your wedding for anything in the whole world." My head was starting to pound.

"It's going to happen a year from January."

"Then we'll have one more summer together," I assured her.

"Yeah." She wiped her nose. "What did you want to tell me?"

I looked at her blotchy face. "Just that I wish you weren't leaving tomorrow," I said. Keeping the mikveh incident from Tzippy was making me feel more alone than I'd ever felt in my life, but telling her about it would not make it go away. Our worlds were about to crack open. I could feel it.

"Hey, I see the Shabbos goy's feet." Tzippy half smiled, then bolted up and dragged me to the basement window. We scampered up onto a couple of tables to get a better view.

All summer Tzippy and I had been stealing glances at the Shabbos goy, who lived in the carriage house and had started working for the Schines last March. When I slept over at Tzippy's house, we'd stay up late, rhapsodizing about the stick-straight blondish hair he tied into a ponytail and the peace sign he wore around his neck. His bell-bottom jeans hung around his slim waist, and he had a cleft chin like Kirk Douglas. We'd listen for him to start the engine of his blue Dodge and watch him back out of the driveway. He looked about the same age as our parents, too old to be a bachelor, so we made up elaborately tragic stories about his visits to the grave of a wife we named Annette, a woman we imagined as a buxom blonde who sauntered about in gauzy blouses cut low enough to reveal a matching peace sign.

"He's going to visit Annette," Tzippy said sadly.

I could only see his work boot snuffing out a cigarette before he loped around the side of his Dodge and out of our view. "Not now. He only visits her at night," I said with authority.

We laughed too hard, grabbing onto a joke of two innocent girls, the stolen mandelbrot cookies crumbling in my pocket.

By the time I got home from services, my head ached so badly that my hair follicles hurt. I skipped lunch and crawled into bed, and when I opened my eyes, my parents were standing over me. My father held a thermometer in his hand. Dazzling waves of colored light danced across the pale pink cardigan my mother wore because she was always cold.

She sat down on the edge of my bed and put her fingers against my forehead. "What hurts?"

I pointed to my temple and reveled in the concern blossoming all over her face.

My father shook the thermometer. "Let's see if you've got a temperature, honey." He was an orthodontist, and he was speaking in the voice he used while stringing long wires through bands on his patients' teeth. He put the thermometer under my tongue, waited a minute, then removed it and read the red mercury line. "No fever, June," he said to my mother.

My mother gave me aspirin, and my parents sat on either side of my bed. I liked the way my mattress bowed at the corners from their weight. As I drifted off to sleep, I tried to piece together the filmy scraps of what had happened in the mikveh. Had there been someone with my mother? If so, who? Why had she removed her hat? Why was her lipstick smudged? And where did she get that cigarette?

In the middle of the night, I woke to the sound of my own moaning.

My mother, who was sleeping on the floor next to my bed, started. "Where exactly does it hurt?"

"Just the left side." A violent wave of nausea struck me, and I ran to the bathroom. My mother held my hair while I knelt before the toilet, but I didn't throw up.

After she helped me back into bed, she removed the pillow from under my neck and put on a fresh case. The crisp cotton felt cool against my face. "Does the light bother you?"

"Uh huh." My mouth was dry, and my spit tasted like I'd been sucking on dirty socks.

"I got my first migraine when I was about your age."

Normally, I'd gobble up the few details of her childhood that she parceled out. I didn't find out that my grandparents were dead until I was six and asked if my bubbe and zayde could visit like Tzippy's did every May, and then it was my father and not my mother who told me that I didn't have any living grandparents on either side. Whenever I'd press my mother for information, she'd say that her childhood home didn't exist any longer. I didn't understand exactly what she meant, but when she did speak of her past, her voice would grow small and distant and her eyes would lose focus. I needed her to stay put, so I stopped asking her questions and tried to forget what I'd seen in the mikveh.

My headache had disappeared by morning. I found my dad in the kitchen, slurping milk from his bowl of Raisin Bran, his shoulders hunched over the *Milwaukee Sentinel*, a roll of stomach hanging over his pants. He looked up. "Welcome back to the land of the living, Bunny."

He hadn't called me Bunny in years. I smiled, remembering the blanket with the pink bunnies that I'd carried around until it was in tatters. I poured myself a bowl of Cheerios.

"What's on your docket for today?" he asked as he folded up the sports page.

"Not sure." I grabbed the comics and immersed myself in "Doonesbury," which was "lampooning Richard Nixon again," as my dad said.

My dad wasn't the type to push, so he kissed the top of my head and went upstairs into my parents' bathroom. I thought of him sitting on the side of the tub while my mother performed her weekly task of trimming his nose hair, which grew from his nostrils like the fur on a chipmunk's tail, an unfortunate physical trait for an orthodontist. Maybe he'd been the one who had messed up my mother's lipstick. No. My father in the mikveh? He would never have skipped out of shul in the middle of services.

I loafed around the house all day. Tzippy had left early in the morning for Brooklyn, so I had nothing to do. I wasn't used to being home, because Tzippy and I spent our summer at her house, helping the rebbetzin with her cooking or babysitting a child of a congregant who had come to talk to her or Rabbi Schine about a problem. Tzippy said that I made the work fun, and even if we were peeling potatoes, the rebbetzin made us feel like we were part of something big and important.

In a few days, Neil would be leaving for college. I joined him out on the back stoop, and while he read his *Sports Illustrated*, I stared down the alley at a neighbor who was painting his garage yellow, wondering why he would bother. Nobody ever used this alley. I shrugged and turned my thoughts to the letter I'd write Tzippy once I felt better. Right now, she'd be settling into her aunt Ruthie's cramped apartment. In our next exchange of letters, we'd take a break from the wedding talk and return to griping about the summer ending and her spinster aunt's grumpiness and smelly gas.

The air was starting to reek of alewives—the bad part of living so close to Lake Michigan—so I went inside and up to my room. My parents' bedroom door was open, and I could smell cigarette smoke, which meant my mother was alone. My father hated it when she smoked in their room. I thought about her face in the dark mikveh, the smoke floating out of her nose and mouth, and I darted toward my room.

"Barbara? Is that you?"

My room was right across the hall, so I couldn't very well lie. "It's me."

"Come on in. I want to look at you," my mother said, an exhalation of smoke cloaking her voice.

I walked through her door toward the chaise longue where she was reclining primly in her weekend denim skirt and cotton blouse, her legs crossed at the ankles. She took another drag of her Virginia Slim, and when she put it out in the saucer of her coffee cup, a cluster of black ashes fell onto the shag carpet. I blinked away the memory of the ashes dusting the mikveh tiles.

"Better clean those up or your father will have my head." My mother winked. My father worshipped my mother, but she liked to pretend he suffered her. She gave me what my father had dubbed her "June smile." Her lips curled spontaneously, but slowly, as if I were the sudden cause of her happiness, and then halfway through the smile, she looked right into my eyes, her gaze direct, yet shy. The June smile made people do nice things for her, so I spent hours in the mirror trying to mimic it, to no avail.

I knelt down to help her clean up the ashes, and as she bent over, I could see the top of one of her full slips, cream-colored silk with a built-in lacy bra and a pink rose with a green stem sewn between the small cups. My mother bought her lingerie from a fancy boutique in Whitefish Bay. Once when she wasn't home, I tried on one of her slips. It fit me perfectly, and I felt like a bony Sophia Loren.

She sat back on the chaise longue and folded the corner of a page of *The Winds of War.* My mother and I gobbled up fiction without chewing. We went to the library once a week and came home with our arms full of books. "I was just going to sneak in a chapter, but I guess I got a little carried away," she said impishly, patting a spot next to her. The phone rang.

"Do you mind?" she asked. She hated talking on the phone so much that we had only one phone and it was in our kitchen.

I ran downstairs, breathless by the time I answered.

"Barbara?" Instantly I recognized the rebbetzin's voice. She and Tzippy pronounced my name "Barb-a-ra," with an accent that was a mix of Brooklyn and Yiddish.

"Hello, rebbetzin."

"How's your head?"

I wrapped the curly phone cord around my finger. "I'm fine, thank you."

"Good. Please tell your mother that I'm home and that she can come by now."

I thought of all the congregants who waited patiently for their time with the rebbetzin, and here she was summoning my mother to the shul. My mother would go eagerly, regardless of her mood. Of all the places in the world, she was at her most peaceful when she was sitting at the Schines' kitchen table, her foot tucked under her opposite leg, dropping sugar cubes in her tea, listening to the rebbetzin explain a Jewish law and scrawling notes furiously on one of Rabbi Schine's legal pads. Then she organized the rebbetzin's thoughts into chewable nuggets and transferred them to index cards just like the ones the rebbetzin used to write down recipes for my mother. The rebbetzin got nervous when she had to speak in front of a group, but she could do it if she had her cards and a chance to practice in front of my mother. My pride in my mother's role in the shul was a life raft that I clung to at school when the kids either teased me about my long skirts or looked right through me. Yesterday, my mother had poked a hole in that raft, a thought that turned from unpleasant to scary and then evaporated inside me, all within in a matter of seconds.

I returned to my mother's room and sat down where she had patted the cushion. "That was the rebbetzin, she wants you to come over."

"Okay, but first you. Feeling better?" She traced my hairline with her fingertips, and I could smell nicotine and her lavender soap.

"Just a little tired, that's all." I was still knocked out from my migraine.

"Too tired to come to the Schines' with me? I'm going to help the rebbetzin with the Rosh Hashana and Yom Kippur talk she's giving next week." Her eyes were bright. "We're expecting a big group at the shul."

"No, thanks."

"No fun without Tzippy, huh?" She patted my knee.

She was one hundred percent my mother again: inhaling novels that the rebbetzin might not approve of, smoking while my father was out of the house, and putting asidc hcr book and cigarettes to assist the rebbetzin, all the while making me feel like I was her accomplice.

"You going to be okay, Sweet B?" She squeezed my hand and held it.

"I think so." I was going to be more than okay. The sound of my nickname on her lips felt like a gift, the wrapping paper her voice, as soft as the cloth she used to clean her silver. Her eyes radiated love as she picked up her dirty coffee cup, roused herself from her chaise, and prepared to go off and help the rebbetzin reach out to women who relied on the Schines to show them the way back to Hashem.

The four of us ate an early supper that night so we could watch Walter Cronkite together. Over my mother's leftover Shabbos chicken, my father started ranting about Nixon and Agnew and the whole lot of liars. They should all resign, like Haldeman, Ehrlichman, and John Dean, he said. When my mother politely pointed out that John Dean had been fired, Neil winked at me, and we laughed until my father told us to pipe down. I told myself that things had returned to normal, that whatever had happened in the mikveh was over and my old mother was here to stay.

Later, in bed, I was fretting about the mikveh again when my parents' door opened and I heard my mother's light tread on the stairs. I wanted her to assure me once and for all that we were okay. I pulled back the covers, leaped out of bed, and ran down the steps, practically tripping over the hem of my nightgown. I looked for her in the den, assuming I'd find her tucked into a corner of the couch, smoking. She'd take my hand, lead me to my room, sit at the foot of my bed, and listen to my worries about her smudged lipstick. She'd rub my feet until my whole body felt like mush. She'd soak up my fears like a paper towel on a juice spill.

She wasn't smoking in the den. She wasn't in the kitchen or sunroom either. "Mom?" I called quietly as I moved toward the back of the house, stubbing my big toe on the hall coat rack. I opened the door, and the strong lake breeze sent a shiver through me. I ran barefoot down the steps into the deserted alley, past the freshly painted garage, my feet slamming against the pavement, my toe throbbing.

"Mom!"

The word was swallowed up by the familiar grumble of the blue Dodge idling in the alley, five houses past ours. I watched my mother walk to the car and glide into the Shabbos goy's arms as if she were his Olympic figure-skating partner. I watched the Shabbos goy open the passenger door and the wind blow my mother's hair wild.

3

The night I caught my mother sneaking off with the Shabbos goy I was afraid that she'd never come home. She did. For the rest of the week, I lay awake every night waiting for her to creep out of the house. She stayed put until the following Tuesday, and when I heard the faint creak of the steps, I put my hands over my eyes, mouthing the words of the Shema prayer—*Hear, O Israel, the Lord is our God, the Lord is One*—into my palm, begging God to please send her to the den to smoke. Then I heard the back door shut. I sprang out of bed, went over to my window, and watched her drive off.

I turned on my lamp and opened my nightstand drawer, where I kept Tzippy's letters. I wanted to reread the one that had arrived earlier today.

September 3, 1973 *B"H*

Dear Barbara,

I'm sorry about your horrible headache. Your mom probably told you that I came over to say goodbye. I took our usual walk on the bluff while my parents had their Shabbos nap, and then Mrs. Berger came over to talk to my mother about a problem, and I played with her baby, Dovid. He's not as cute as Yossi, but Yossi only likes you and Mrs. Kessler holding him.

Aunt Ruthie didn't get much happier over the summer. As scared as I am to get married, I think it would be worse to wind up like her, alone at thirty. Now I worry that the shadchen might not find someone for me either. You're lucky you get to pick your own husband.

School starts tomorrow. I'm going to wear the new maroon skirt my mom sewed for me. I miss you more than ever. My cousins are nicer than they used to be, and I don't mind sharing a room with them anymore. But they're not you. I wish we hadn't lost our last afternoon together.

Love,

Tzippy

I wrote Tzippy two letters. The one I mailed was in direct response to hers and contained a newsy account of my week. The other letter I kept. Writing it made me feel like Anne Frank, calling out to a best friend who lived outside of her crazy world, one who would never read her words.

September 6, 1973 *B"H*

Dear Tzippy,

My mother is the Shabbos goy's Annette! She has been sneaking off with him while my dad snores in their bed. He picks her up in the alley, and I saw them one night.

It's so obvious now. My mother's moods got worse back in the spring when the Shabbos goy started working for your parents. Your last Shabbos here, when we were supposed to meet in the mikveh, I found my mother smoking there, hatless and her lipstick a mess. She was deep into one of her mists, and I just wanted to run away from her and the spooky mikveh. I knew she wasn't alone because before I walked in, I swear I heard her whispering to someone. I replay that morning over and over in my head, and I can only come to one conclusion. The Shabbos goy was hiding somewhere in that dark mikveh. Writing this spooks and shames me at the same time.

I don't know what to do. I want to tell your mom about it, but if I do she and your father will have to kick my mom out of the shul. If I don't, I will betray my father, your parents, the shul, and God. Sometimes I worry that I will crumble under the weight of this secret.

Love,

Barbara

Tuesday became my mother's designated evening with the Shabbos goy, like bowling night or her Thursday-morning beauty parlor appointment. Her lie was like the ugly orange sofa that came with our house. My parents had sworn they'd replace it, but they grew accustomed to the pall it cast over the entire living room.

Mrs. Kessler saved me during the months of my mother's affair. My high school classes ended at one o'clock, and I'd rush to the Schines' and go straight to the nook, where I'd sweep scraps of felt from the floor, sit quietly next to Mrs. Kessler and help her sort and staple, or watch Yossi whenever his babysitter called in sick.

On the first Tuesday in October, I found a distressed Mrs. Kessler in the corner of the nook, trying to engage the Isen twins with Yossi braying and fussing in her arms. Six months before, their father, a founding member of the community, had run off with his Gentile paralegal. Mrs. Isen was likely upstairs crying her eyes out and talking with the rebbetzin.

Mrs. Kessler looked up at me, and the gratitude in her eyes made me feel like Superwoman. I looked at the sullen Bini and Liba Isen and flashed on a memory of the two of them giggling as they played cat's cradle in the hallway of the shul.

"It's my lucky day!" I marched over to the supply closet and grabbed a ball of green yarn and a pair of scissors. I felt all eyes on me as I cut a long piece of yarn and tied it tightly at the ends. I sat on the floor across from the girls, huddled together on a beanbag chair, and threaded the yarn through my hands. Tzippy and I used to play hours of cat's cradle when we were in second grade, the Isen girls' age. I extended my hands to Liba first. "Go ahead."

A smile began to form on her lips. I had her. She grabbed the crossed strings, and within seconds the three of us were pinching and passing while a mesmerized Yossi looked on. After we'd played a dozen rounds, Mrs. Kessler cupped my shoulder. "Well, girls, your mother is here."

I looked up to see Mrs. Isen standing at the door. The pale green scarf she wore to cover her hair made her skin look sallow, and her blouse hung loosely. Only months ago, she was so plump that the zipper on her new Shabbos dress threatened to burst. My throat closed up. What would my father look like if he ever found out about my mother and the Shabbos goy? Bini tugged on my arm, snapping me out of my thoughts.

"Can we play again with Barbara?" she asked, her face bright and relaxed.

"I hope so! In the meantime, you two practice." I handed her the yarn, hugged her, and then Mrs. Kessler and I walked the girls to the door.

"Thank you," Mrs. Isen said to Mrs. Kessler.

Mrs. Kessler deposited Yossi in his stroller and slid her arm through mine. "It was all Barbara. She's a magician with kids." In Mrs. Kessler's presence, I could fly.

I didn't want to part with Mrs. Kessler or Yossi or my powers, so I offered to accompany her home.

"You have a gift with children," Mrs. Kessler told me as we stopped at a grocery store. "Maybe one day you'll have your own classroom."

I blushed from my chest to my forehead as I followed her back to her cramped apartment, which, like our house, was only four blocks from the Schines, but in the opposite direction.

"Let me." I removed Yossi and the grocery bag from the stroller and carried them up the skinny stairway to the apartment.

"You saved me a trip," Mrs. Kessler said when she arrived at the front door, flushed and winded from lugging the enormous stroller up the steps. Yossi's diaper was warm and full, and I took him to his room. When I returned from changing him, Mrs.

Kessler had removed her sheitel and was running her fingers through her cropped hair, which she'd worn in a fat braid twisted around her head before she married. Mr. Kessler, a PhD student at UW-Milwaukee, and according to my dad a math genius, wouldn't be home until late because he was teaching a night class, so Mrs. Kessler thanked me when I offered to play with Yossi while she prepared macaroni and green peas.

"You don't need to call your mother?" she asked.

I hated Tuesday nights at home; the smell of my mother's peanut butter cookies, my father's favorite, made me sick. She'd give half the guilt-batch to my father to take to the girls in the office and the other half to the rebbetzin to serve at her teas.

I dialed my number, and my father answered on the second ring. "I'm going to help Mrs. Kessler, see you later, okay?" I said quickly, not giving him time to say no.

"Wait a second, Bunny. How are you getting home?"

"Mr. Kessler is going to walk me," I lied and got off the phone. I could picture him in his study. His sleeves would be neatly rolled up, the weekly Torah portion and books of commentary splayed open in front of him. He would slide his reading glasses up his nose and return to learning. My mother probably wouldn't bother to ask him where I was or if I needed a ride. She wasn't doing that kind of thing anymore.

"You've got me for as long as you need me, Mrs. Kessler."

I set the table while she put Yossi to bed, and then we ate the food she'd prepared. "So, what are your plans for next year?" she asked, spearing a pea.

"Tzippy's getting married."

She chewed for a second. "I know that, but what about *your* plans?"

"I'll go to Madison, like Neil."

"They have a good teaching program." She raised an eyebrow.

I couldn't help but smile. "I have to get in first."

"How is school going?"

"Okay, except for calculus." I didn't tell her that I desperately missed Tzippy or that I had just one friend, a girl I liked only because she liked me. She knew that too.

"Let's have a look at that calculus." After she read my problems, she rubbed her hands together. "This is going to be fun."

She sat up in her chair, shedding the tense fatigue she'd held in her shoulders, and explained orders of approximation in language I could understand. An hour later, she said, "Oy, look at the clock. I don't think Mr. Kessler will be home in time to walk you to your house." She bit her nail.

"I walk home from Tzippy's at night all the time. My parents are fine with it." Actually, I'd only walked home from her house during the summer when it was still light until practically nine o'clock, and now it was dark and the walk four blocks longer.

She looked tentative. "You'll call me when you get home?"

I was seconds away from asking if I could move into her tiny apartment to escape my mother, who sometimes acted enough like her old self to tease me into thinking that I'd been imagining the whole thing with the Shabbos goy. In my heart, though, I knew that I couldn't pull her back to us.

I left Mrs. Kessler's apartment feeling fed and cared for, but by the time I entered my house, my mood had blackened. My dad was studying in his office, and my mother was sitting at the kitchen table in her pink cardigan, smoking and reading the paper. Soon she'd excuse herself for her Tuesday evening bath, and after we were all tucked into bed, she'd take off with the Shabbos goy.

"Do you want a peanut butter cookie?" she asked absently, lighting a cigarette.

I stared at her. She wasn't in one of her mists anymore, but she was different, distracted but happier than I'd seen her in a long time. Couldn't she be happy and still not pull away from us?

"You're doing such a mitzvah by helping Mrs. Kessler. Doing good deeds brings us closer to God, the rebbetzin reminds us." Each of my mother's syllables was plump with pride.

I lapped up her praise despite myself. "Well, it was really Mrs. Kessler who did me the mitzvah by helping me with my calculus."

She nodded through a haze of smoke. "Don't you have a test coming up?"

"Tomorrow." I was surprised that she'd remembered my weekly test.

"You'll ace it, Sweet B."

If she was going to remember my calculus tests and call me Sweet B, I supposed it wouldn't hurt to eat one of her cookies, her only recipe that turned out well. I took a bite, sweet, but so crispy that it practically nicked the sides of my mouth. "The trick is to use Crisco for the shortening," my mother had told Tzippy and me once when we'd helped her bake for Shabbos.

"Good night, Mom," I said.

She yawned. "I'm tired."

"So you're going to sleep?" I asked too quickly.

"After my bath." She lit another cigarette.

"To bed? You're going to bed?" My voice was high and squeaky.

"Of course," she lied. "And before I forget, I put a letter from Tzippy on your dresser."

I thanked her and took the stairs two at a time.

October 14, 1973 *B"H*

Dear Barbara,

I hope this arrives before your quarter-birthday. In a few days, you'll be seventeen and three fourths.

Aunt Ruthie isn't grumpy anymore. She hasn't been yelling at Miriam for leaving jelly on the counter or Tamar for blowing her nose too loudly. Now she's just sad. She talks about my Uncle Shlomo, the one who moved to Jerusalem, and how worried she is that he'll get killed in the Yom Kippur War. I've been making all of the dinners for my cousins and me. I'm getting to be a pretty good cook, although I did burn the noodles once. I'll get better. I have to be a balabusta if I'm going to marry and become a rebbetzin.

I worry about Uncle Shlomo too. Give my mother a kiss for me.

She's probably upset about him even if she doesn't show it. My mom's not always as strong as she looks, but that's a secret between the two of us.

Write me soon. I miss you.

Love,

Tzippy

I wrote Tzippy right back, thanking her for remembering my quarter-birthday and promising her that I would check in on her mother. I didn't tell her that last Shabbos, while Rabbi Schine had ranted on and on about the Yom Kippur War during his sermon, the rebbetzin stared absently toward the front of the shul, biting her pinkie nail. I'd only seen her act worried once before, when Tzippy got a concussion after falling off the monkey bars at school. After I finished licking the stamp, I wrote Tzippy the letter I couldn't send.

October 17, 1973 *B"H*

Dear Tzippy,

Everyone is talking about the war. My worries are small in comparison, yet they feel huge to me.

Scott Dayne, the oafish boy who draws swastikas on his biology folder, said that he hoped the Jews would lose the war because we had it coming to us. David Koppelberg, now my biology lab partner, said that most Jews were normal, not freaks like us. He said that people who belong to our shul act like Moonies. He called your dad Rabbi Moon-Schine and me Moon-Schine Girl. My father said to ignore him, that one day your dad might unveil David's neshama, but even if he had a soul, I bet it would be drab. I guess I should pity David's drab neshama and ignorance of God's 613 commandments.

Besides, I have my mother's soul to worry about. She's going to get caught soon. I know it. Writing this is making me feel worse. I miss you.

Your best friend,

Barbara

Lying under the covers, I listened to the water from the bathtub swish through our old pipes. Any good feelings I'd experienced that day were devoured by my wild obsession with the mikveh and now poor Mrs. Isen, her sad twins, and my father. I wondered what would happen to him if the Schines found out about my mother's romance. After Mr. Isen left his family, the Schines told Mrs. Isen to rip her lapel and go to shul every day for a year to recite the kaddish prayer of mourning for him, as if he'd really died. Mr. Isen moved to Brookfield, the Gentile part of town, and when my mother and I bumped into him while shoe shopping at Marshall Field's, he couldn't even look us in the eye. If the Schines wanted to erase Mr. Isen's existence for "running off with a shiksa," as my dad put it, then what on earth would they do to my mother for sneaking around with the Shabbos goy? I was sure she was bound for Brookfield. Never again would she respond to the call of Rabbi Schine's Shema or savor the sweetness of the rebbetzin's freshly baked challah. Her soul would be boarded up for good. And where would that leave all of us?

4

September 2009

The letter arrived on a Sunday. Hand-delivered. Someone could have crept up the walk and popped it through our mail slot that morning, while Sam and I were driving Lili to her cross-country meet, or when she twisted her ankle in a gopher hole and fell writhing as her rival sprinted by. It could have arrived while we sat in the emergency room, as I stroked Lili's hair with one hand and squeezed Sam's forearm with the other, or while the baby-faced doctor, an Indian fellow, taped her up and advised us to find a good orthopedist. It could have been lying in wait while we drove the five miles home from the hospital.

When you read about people who have experienced life-altering events, they often say, "Only an hour before, I was fighting with my husband over our Visa bill" or "singing along to Aretha Franklin on the radio." Me? An hour before I found the letter, I was on my cell phone ordering pizza for the friends Lili had invited for dinner, yammering on about thin versus thick crust, my words crowding out the thought of Lili's injury potentially decimating her season.

By the time we arrived home, the Mama Mia deliveryman was waiting for us in the driveway, and I settled up with him while Sam helped Lili into the house. I made a salad, and within twenty minutes Lili's girlfriends were filing onto the porch we'd recently screened in because Sam insisted, "Everything tastes better when you eat it outside." The dimming sun bathed Lili and her giggling teammates in amber light, and although she was smiling, I couldn't suppress my concern. I wanted to pull her aside and make sure she was all right, but she was too old for that, so instead I watched her play with a loose strand of her kinky auburn hair. She abandoned her first slice of pizza while the other girls demolished the four pies in minutes. They were all petite cross-country runners, yet as Sam remarked, they ate like linebackers.

"Can they hang out for a while?" Lili asked me, and I said sure even though it was a school night. I'd have agreed to just about anything to distract her from her pain. I loved that our home was the fun house. I always made sure to stock our pantry with each girl's favorite munchie—pretzels, pita chips, and whatnot—and our fridge with cut-up fruit and pop.

After dinner, the girls went off to the den, sank into our overstuffed couches, took turns playing with Lili's crutches, and texted while watching *Twilight*. They knew every line. I never could figure out the hullabaloo over vampires.

Sam sat at the kitchen table chatting on the phone with his friend and client, Felix Nezbith, the Milwaukee Bucks' orthopedist. Sam had been handling his investments for years. I walked up behind him and kneaded his shoulders the way he liked, grateful as heck for a husband who could pick up the phone on a Sunday night and score an appointment for the next morning with the best bone doctor in town. After he hung up, I leaned down and pressed my lips to his hair. Always the optimist, he tilted his head back into my breasts, wordlessly telling me to stop worrying about Lili. I couldn't help it. Only with exercise—God's Ritalin, we called it—could Lili focus enough to handle her schoolwork and maintain her equilibrium. Without her daily endorphin fix, she was a hot mess. "You're only as happy as your unhappiest child," a mother of one of my students once said. So true.

I told Sam I'd join him on the porch for a glass of wine after I tidied up the kitchen. I was wiping Italian dressing from the counter when the front doorbell rang. "I'll get it," I hollered.

That was when I saw the envelope.

I assumed it was an invoice from the tree trimmer who'd been pruning our maple that afternoon. I picked up the envelope from the rug under the mail slot and opened the door as one of Lili's friends ran in from the den to greet a new teammate, Taylor, and usher her back to the rest of the girls.

I stood alone in the foyer. It was not a bill; it was a letter, on personal stationery. The noise of Lili and her friends shouting at the vampires receded, and I could hear only my pulse thumping in my ears. I recognized the no-nonsense cursive of the address instantly. I'd seen it a thousand times on four tattered recipe cards of my mother's. I ran my fingers over the return address embossed on the thin white envelope as if I were reading Braille.

Rivkah Schine
3050 Lake Drive
Milwaukee, WI 53211

Rivkah Schine. I hadn't seen the rebbetzin in more than thirty years, not since the Schines cut my mother from the community like a brown spot from an apple. My mother had left them no choice, and while they were at it, they excised Neil and me too.

I put my thumb over the address: 3050 Lake Drive. The Schines' shul. Sam, Lili, and I lived a few blocks off Lake Drive, but ten miles north, in a suburban split-level. I avoided driving by the mansion, particularly on Shabbos mornings, so I wouldn't have to look at the men in their business suits and skullcaps, accompanied by women who covered their hair with stylish hats and held their children's hands. Four decades ago, I'd been one of those children. Back then, I belonged to the Schines' shul and my mother belonged to me, two facts that I still could not tease apart.

I held the white envelope to my nose, half expecting to smell the lemons the rebbetzin and my mother rubbed on their fingers to mute the scent of the onions they'd diced for the Schines' Shabbos feasts. I closed my eyes and conjured the sound of beef meeting hot oil, and I could practically taste the luscious cholent that simmered for a full day before the Sabbath meal.

Stop it, Barbara, I almost said aloud. This was absurd. The rebbetzin could not have forgotten that as June Pupnick's daughter, I was a pariah. Until I married Sam, the most casual mention of the Schines or my mother made me feel like no matter where I lived, there was a boisterous New Year's Eve party happening two houses down the block and I hadn't been invited. I'd gotten over all that, and I wasn't going back.

I folded the unopened envelope and stuffed it into the pocket of my capris. Its corners pricked my thigh as I walked away from the mail slot in slow motion, like in the ESPN highlight videos Sam watched on his computer after Packers games.

Mounted on the hall wall were photos chronicling the life I'd built with my family: baby pictures of Lili taken at the Sears in Bayshore; our annual artsy black-and-whites of Sam, Lili, and me in blue jeans and crisp white shirts, our feet bare, our smiles broad and backlit by our love and the late-afternoon sun; a sweet candid of Sam's parents pushing Lili on a swing. I'd paid a decorator a month of my teaching salary to frame and arrange these photos just so, but despite her efforts I'd never been satisfied with the placement of one photo: my mother, Lili, and I wearing pink birthday hats, the elastic straps cupping our chins, Lili's lips covered in chocolate. My mother is draping her arm around my shoulders, grinning as if we were a normal mother and daughter.

I went into the kitchen, the hum of the dishwasher muting the girls' chatter. I pulled the envelope from my pocket and opened the trash compactor, the paper shaking in my hands as it hovered over napkins stained with tomato sauce and an abandoned slice of pepperoni. I still had qualms about ordering pizza adorned with rounds of pork, but I did it often, perhaps to erase Barbara Pupnick, the girl who'd been kicked out of the Schines' world.

I stuffed the letter back into my pocket and went to the porch. "It's getting chilly, I'm going to grab my fleece," I told Sam, who was sitting there with two sweating glasses of white wine. I took the steps to our room, shut the door, and tore open the envelope.

September 6, 2009 *B"H*

Dear Barbara,

I am sorry to tell you the news that Mrs. Kessler has passed away, aleha hashalom, may peace be upon her. Please meet me at the Abromowitz Funeral Parlor on Monday at 9 a.m. We will perform her tahara.

Rivkah Schine

The news was a sucker punch to the heart. Mrs. Kessler. She materialized in the way the newly dead do. I am five, and she is celebrating her first Shabbos at our shul. I stare at her long braid throughout services, and afterward, during the lunch, I spear a gefilte fish ball with a toothpick and give it to her. She accepts my offering. Later I learn that she hates fish.

I read the letter again. What was a tahara? The word floated over me like the name of the Alfred Hitchcock movie I couldn't recall the last time Sam and I played Trivial Pursuit. What was the name of that damn movie?

I flipped on my laptop and typed in "tahara." Google sent me straight to a Jewish funerals site. "The tahara is the sacred and secret Jewish burial rite of washing and shrouding the dead and is the highest and purest act of loving kindness." *Vertigo*. The Hitchcock movie came to me, creating a dizzying surge in my brain. I tried to imagine the rebbetzin and myself pouring water over Mrs. Kessler, but I could picture neither the rebbetzin through my adult eyes nor a dead Mrs. Kessler.

I stowed the envelope in the drawer of my nightstand and went downstairs, pausing for a moment in the kitchen. Through the silvery mesh of the screen door, I stared at Sam's silhouette, his trim body held in repose, his full head of salt-and-pepper hair, his strong cheekbones.

"Barbara?" Sam called. "Are you there?"

"I'm here." Tahara. Tahara. I couldn't wait for the house to quiet so I could Google the word again in peace.

I could hear Lili's friends leaving. I bade them goodbye, and Sam gave Lili a piggyback ride up the steps. It felt good to hear her giggle. Sam and I fell into bed and held each other. "She's going to be okay, Barbara," he whispered into my hair. He said these words at the beginning of every crisis.

I waited for his breathing to grow regular, then untangled myself from his warm body and went downstairs. I rarely kept any big news from Sam.

I sat in the dark at my tiny desk, I needed to think this tahara thing through carefully, alone. The Schines had erased my mother's existence and by default, mine. I was nineteen. The whole shul found out about my mother and the Shabbos goy, which meant I lost Tzippy, the Schines, and Mrs. Kessler all at once. I never thanked Mrs. Kessler for keeping me company during my mother's affair and shining a bright light on my professional path. She knew that teaching preschool was my calling before I did. But it was more than that—my work had served as an oasis from the disruption in my childhood, and grounded me enough as an adult to make and sustain a brand-new life with Sam. In exchange, I'd squandered her love, closing myself off to her for all these years, years when I could have visited her and exchanged notes about our students. She could have remained a mentor, and maybe I could have become her friend.

Mrs. Kessler was the only person who could draw me back to the Schines' shul. And the rebbetzin knew it, in the way she'd known to arrange for me to volunteer for Mrs. Kessler in the first place. Despite how busy she was with the shul and raising her kids, she made time to look deep inside all of us and find what we needed and wanted most, which she'd shrewdly match with a specific Jewish custom or job in the shul. Worshiping the rebbetzin was a hard habit to break, but I'd done it. Or had I?

It didn't matter right now. I would put my feelings toward the rebbetzin aside and perform Mrs. Kessler's tahara. According to my Google research, the tahara is the purest possible act of kindness because the recipient can never pay you back. I wanted to give Mrs. Kessler this pure love. I owed it to her.

The next morning, I woke up early and phoned Theresa, my teaching assistant, to tell her that I'd have to miss our prep day because of Lili's injury and that she'd have to set up the classroom alone. Barely five feet tall, with a mop of hair dyed magenta and thick-lensed glasses that magnified her eyes, she ate ramen noodles every day for lunch and supplemented her measly pay by taking care of people's children and pets. When I apologized to Theresa for dumping so much work on her, she responded predictably, "You take good care of your girl and leave setting up the room to me." Her puppy-like response made me want to jump through the phone line and scratch her scalp the way I used to do to our late black lab, Richard.

I felt bad about missing setup. Creating a warm and cozy nest for my students was one of my favorite parts of my job, and this year Sarah, the director, had given me extra money for new manipulatives and blocks. Last Friday morning, I'd picked up some bins at Staples, and ever since I loaded them into the trunk of my car, I'd been itching to wipe them down with 409 and organize the new materials by color.

Lili hobbled into the kitchen. She was never chatty when she first woke up, but normally she'd have run miles before breakfast and would arrive at the table flushed from her workout, hungry, and cheerful. Today, she stared down at her plate, picking at her pancakes and spilling maple syrup on her T-shirt.

"Way to start the day," she said.

Sam entered the kitchen, freshly shorn and handsome in a pale pink Oxford shirt that showed off the tan he would maintain throughout the fall by playing golf with his clients. He glanced at Lili slumped over her plate and raised an eyebrow at me.

"Lil, I'll take you to school," he said.

I was glad Sam could take her because he could help her in and out of the car more easily. Sam was good with her, but we had an unspoken agreement that I would shepherd Lili's care. During the most painful and frustrating months of her academic struggles, I'd guided her, trying to echo Sam's chipper confidence. Inside, her unhappiness consumed me to a degree that I knew was unhealthy.

Lili went to the bathroom to change her shirt, and I walked over to Sam and kissed his smooth cheek, letting my face linger against his and breathing him in. He'd been wearing Polo since his fraternity days, mixed with his own clean scent, and he always smelled like sun-dried laundry.

"You're sniffing me." He laughed and stroked my hair. We both knew I did this when I was troubled.

"I am."

"It's an ankle injury. Let's not get ahead of ourselves." He drew me to him.

"What if she can't run?" I asked.

"We'll figure something else out." He paused. "Or I should say, you will." His tone was self- deprecating.

"I don't want to wrinkle your shirt." I pulled away, sniffing him again, but his scent wasn't working to allay my other big fear, seeing the rebbetzin after all these years.

Lili returned to the kitchen, and before I kissed them both goodbye, I told her I'd pick her up at noon for her appointment with Dr. Nezbith.

It was a warm day, but out of respect for the Orthodox funeral home, I dressed in a black ankle-length skirt, a matching long-sleeved T-shirt, and an old pair of sneakers. It took me only twenty minutes to drive to the west side, a part of town I rarely visited. As I neared Beckerman's Butcher Shop, I remembered how in exchange for my mother's June smile, Mr. Beckerman would give her the best cuts of meat and me a free roll filled with his specialty, pickled tongue and spicy mustard. Transactions like that made me feel as though my mother and I were gliding through her errands in a golden chariot.

An old ache for my mother seized me: I remembered her comforting me the first September that Tzippy left to study in

Brooklyn. I held in my tears until I got home, where she was waiting for me with two tall glasses of Nestlé Quik. We sipped pink milk through striped straws while I told her how the popular girls had pointed me toward the "reject" lunch table. She looked as sad as I felt. I had a good cry, and then she fixed the grammar on the English homework I'd done during lunch period to avoid socializing.

On impulse, I took out my cell phone and dialed her house. After my father died, thirty years ago, she'd moved up north, to Steven's Point. She never remarried. I waited for her to pick up, imagining her tending to her tomato plants in her oversized blue work shirt, rolled-up jeans, and straw hat, à la Katharine Hepburn in *On Golden Pond,* her cheeks rosy from the sun and her exertion. She was an excellent gardener.

"Mom." *I should hang up.*

"Hello, darling. How lovely to hear your voice." Normally, my mother's diction was so perfect that she could narrate a book on tape. Today, her voice sounded less dressed.

"Were you out gardening?" Two years ago she'd retired from her job in the university's history department. She'd started out as a secretary, but the professors had come to rely on her research skills. Her work had been a safe topic for us; now we spoke incessantly about her planting and pruning.

"The weatherman is predicting a frost tonight."

I cut off the usual small talk so I wouldn't lose the courage to share my news. "I'm calling because I wanted to tell you that Mrs. Kessler died."

"Oh, that's such a shame, dear," she said absently, as if I'd told her that Lili had overfed her goldfish.

"I thought you'd want to know." *Get off the phone, Barbara. You're not going to get whatever it is that you're looking for from her.*

"Sure I do," she said vaguely.

"Mom, do you remember Mrs. Kessler?"

My mother had a superb memory, but she paused for what seemed like five minutes.

"Mrs. Kessler was the teacher who wore that gorgeous braid around her head," she said as if she'd come up with the correct question to a *Jeopardy!* answer, which she often did when we watched the show as a family. Afterward, Neil and I would make our own game out of trying to stump my mother with arcane facts we'd looked up in the encyclopedia.

"She was a lot more than a lady with a braid to me." I wanted my mother to acknowledge how Mrs. Kessler had gotten me through calculus and taken me to buy new underpants and bras, and I wanted her to apologize for not doing these things herself. A spasm of poorly archived anger gripped me like a charley horse or a menstrual cramp.

"Darling, do you have a hat to wear to the funeral?" she asked as if she were a mother who tended to such things and we were a family welcome in the Schines' shul.

Her question shocked me. "What?"

"Do you have a hat, Barbara? You need to cover your head. You're a married woman now," she explained as if I'd gotten married just the other day.

Neil had mentioned that my mother seemed confused lately, but I hadn't paid much attention because the doctors suspected her new cholesterol medication might be the culprit.

"I have a hat."

"Good. You know, my poor little tomato plants might have a time of it with that frost coming in." Only now did the sympathy I'd sought over Mrs. Kessler's death surface in her voice. "There's no there there," Sam always said when it came to my mother's heart. I could see how he'd come to this conclusion, but then again, he'd never sat across from her and sipped fake strawberry milk.

I couldn't worry about her loopiness right now. I said a quick goodbye as I approached the funeral parlor, which was sandwiched between a Chinese takeout restaurant and a check-cashing business. We'd held my father's funeral here, and I hadn't seen the rebbetzin since a week after his death.

My armpits were growing moist, and my oniony scent drew

me back to a disturbing place I could not name. I wanted to turn around and drive home, exactly as I had the first time Sam took me to Little Switzerland, when I stood on top of the hill and prayed that a ski patrol would show up and carry me down. Had I thought through that ski trip or the call to my mother or Mrs. Kessler's tahara beforehand, I would have made different choices. Now I had to maneuver myself down the mountain with as little damage as possible when I should be scouring bins with Theresa and catching up with my colleagues about their summer vacations.

My shoulders were so tight that they hovered around my jaw. An old Toyota Camry pulled in next to me, and four women emerged. The rebbetzin turned toward me, her face brushed by the weak morning sunlight. She was foreign and familiar at the same time. The three younger women, perhaps in their early forties, all in long skirts and dark headscarves, lingered around the car as the rebbetzin walked toward me. My skin started to tingle. I'd forgotten how tall she was; she'd slouched so much of her life that her upper body had taken on the shape of a question mark. She was thinner, and her slenderness accentuated the architecture of her face. Her eyes had faded to a softer brown, but they hadn't lost their glint.

"Barbara," she said.

I wanted to say "Rivkah," but my lips protested. Only my mother was allowed to call the rebbetzin by her name. "Hello."

"I'm glad you came."

"I had to." I tried to sound neutral, but my voice trembled. "How did Mrs. Kessler die?"

"Mrs. Kessler, aleha hashalom, she had a massive stroke," the rebbetzin said.

"No warning?"

"No."

I let the news settle in for a few seconds before I asked about the funeral.

"Tomorrow morning," she said, and I remembered how after my father died, she tearily told me that my mother would no longer be welcome in the shul, informing me without words that the sight of me would make the Brisket Ladies and everyone else uncomfortable. Even now, when I said kaddish for my father on the anniversary of his death, I mourned the loss of the shul too.

"Such a shame," the rebbetzin said, and I saw a flash of sadness and something else as she looked at me. This time she wasn't peering inside me, she was taking me in as I did with old students who came to visit me, but I never looked at them with the remorse, or maybe guilt, that flickered ever so briefly in the rebbetzin's eyes. Yes, such a shame.

She started to give me a hug, but I hesitated. She patted me on the back instead. Then she turned toward the car and motioned the women to join us.

"Barbara, meet Chana Shapiro, head of our Chevra Kadisha, and two of our members, Aviva Minsky and Devora Klein."

"The Chevra Kadisha is our burial society," Chana said.

Even without my research, my old knowledge of Hebrew helped me figure out what a Chevra Kadisha meant.

"I'm sorry about your teacher, may her name be of blessed memory," Chana said, and Aviva and Devora chimed in. They all had the rebbetzin's Brooklyn accent, and I figured they were each married to one of the rabbis the Schines had hired to teach at their new yeshiva.

"Thank you," I said stiffly.

"Are you familiar with the tahara ritual?" Chana asked.

"I've never done one, but I know what it is." I knew as much about the ritual as you could discover from a thorough internet search.

"Just follow us, you'll be fine," the rebbetzin said with no trace of her earlier vulnerability.

The five of us walked into the funeral parlor lobby, and I vaguely remembered how the rebbetzin had held my mother's hand and ushered us inside to the front row, a few feet from where Rabbi Schine was about to eulogize my father.

"Hello, Yossi," the rebbetzin said as we encountered a man

coming out of the restroom.

Yossi. His round hazel eyes were bloodshot from fatigue and grief. He'd grown into a lanky man with a small pooch belly like his father's. He'd lost most of his hair, a cruel reminder of the time that had passed since his baby fuzz tickled the underside of my neck.

"I'm so sorry, Yossi," I offered.

"Thank you." His words fell from his mouth like tears. I wished he were still a baby so I could scoop him up in my arms and distract him with a cookie. I couldn't tell if he remembered me. How could he? He was barely a toddler when I left the community. Even now he might be ignorant of the shame my mother had brought upon the shul, or maybe he knew of my family's shanda and didn't see me as damaged goods but simply as a person who belonged to the burial society.

The rebbetzin walked over to Yossi. Men and women were not allowed to touch unless they were married, so she couldn't hug him, but her mere arrival seemed to relax him. The rebbetzin motioned the three women to go ahead, and they responded as if they were used to taking her cues. She remained at Yossi's side as I followed the Chevra members down a long carpeted corridor to the steps leading to the basement. An older man in a rumpled suit and yarmulke sat slouched on a comfortable chair in front of the door, reciting psalms from a prayer book on his lap. He was the shomer, and so it was his job to sit with the body.

Before we entered the preparation room, Aviva touched my arm. "Are you ready?"

"I think so."

The room was cold and quiet. The floor tiles were white and freshly scrubbed. A table lined with nail polish remover and canisters brimming with Q-tips, cotton balls, and toothpicks sat on our side of the curtain. The empty pine casket lay open near the window, waiting for Mrs. Kessler.

The rebbetzin joined us. In silence, we washed our hands, pouring a cup of water alternately over each one. We put on rubber gloves and aprons similar to the ones I wore to paint with my students. Everyone else approached Mrs. Kessler, but I stayed behind. Although I'd never smelled death, I recognized the scent, acrid and fishy at the same time. A curtain surrounded Mrs. Kessler's body, yet the cloth did not spare me from feeling her absence. It filled the room.

A sick hollowness was growing inside me. The rebbetzin turned around, and the compassion on her face loosened a brick in the wall I'd constructed between us. I stalled by fiddling with the string on my apron, knowing that she'd wait until I was ready. I'd never be ready. I looked up at her, and she gently pulled back the curtain. I walked toward Mrs. Kessler's body, covered with a sheet and stretched out on a porcelain bed with a drain that emptied into a sink at the foot.

I glanced toward the rebbetzin, who lifted the sheet from Mrs. Kessler's face. I shut my eyes for a few seconds before I looked. I recognized her cheekbones, her strong jaw and nose, but the muscles surrounding them had slackened. She looked asleep, but not in a way that suggested a nap or even a coma. I beckoned her spirit as I had done last night, but Mrs. Kessler was dead. This fact clanked against the floor of my heart. A pressure formed behind my eyes.

Mrs. Kessler was gone. Gone. Gone.

Gone. I am six years old, and I am sitting across the table from my mother, eating my after-school snack and watching her smoke. I spread peanut butter on my apple with a paring knife, wondering why she hasn't noticed that I'm using it or that I've lost my front tooth. She is looking through me. We're sitting so close that I can see her eyelashes, thicker than my doll Cassandra's, but she cannot see me. This is the first disappearance that I remember, but I now know that her leaving was gradual, an accretion of tiny moments that led to her affair and her slow exit from our lives. You don't just up and walk out on a family without preparing properly. After I've eaten most of my apple, she returns to herself and tells me to please put down that sharp knife. Later she sneaks into my bedroom and puts a quarter under my pillow, and the next morning I pretend I didn't see her and that I still believe in the Tooth Fairy. I do, and I don't. She is my fairy, sometimes make-believe, but still mostly bearing treasures.

Now I was left to mourn both Mrs. Kessler and the hole she had filled for me. My mother was that hole, scary and deep and still tugging at me. I was circling it, hovering between life and death. I touched Mrs. Kessler. Her forehead was cold. I leaned into the body that was no longer Mrs. Kessler and put my fingers to her lips, colorless and thin. They used to curl readily into an amused smile she reserved for children—a smile that I'd appropriated for my students, along with her tranquilizing voice. I wanted to kiss those lips, to breathe life back into her. Her mouth hung open stiffly, which seemed undignified, so I closed it by cupping the rubbery skin of her chin and firmly pushing it up toward her nose, as though I were manipulating a mannequin.

I put my hand on Mrs. Kessler's cheek, just as she had done to me so often. Her skin had yellowed. A line of age spots mirrored the curve of one of her sparse eyebrows. Thin gray strands had replaced the brown hair that had been too lustrous to cover with a sheitel. I brushed them away from her eyes. I wondered if I would ever be able to touch my mother with such tenderness, alive or dead.

Chana tore a white sheet into small sections and filled a bucket with warm water. She put a drop against her wrist to test the temperature, as you would with a baby's bottle. "We have to make sure that the water is warm. We treat the dead with the same respect as we do the living," she told me.

"For the sake of modesty and respect, the body remains covered at all times, except for the part we are washing," the rebbetzin said, instructing me to wash from the top down, right side taking precedence over left, front over back. She washed in and behind the ears, sealing water from the lips, a courtesy offered to lungs no longer vulnerable to drowning. I cleaned under the folds of her breasts, once so full of milk that they'd strained the buttons of her blouse. Her areolas were gray and her breasts lay flat against her skin, as crinkly as an elephant's. I lost all track of the now and the then, and I felt as though I were washing baby Lili, plump and pink and practically nippleless. Memory kindled a fire made of grief and love, and a holy heat tore through my body.

Aviva prepared three buckets of water. No more than three buckets were to be poured in a continuous stream over the body. Devora and I trailed Chana as she walked alongside Mrs. Kessler, and when Chana had nearly emptied her pail, I began pouring. Devora did the same for me so we could sustain a steady stream of water.

The rebbetzin handed me a laminated piece of paper, and I read from Ezekiel in Hebrew. My voice trembled as I spoke with the fluency of someone who had learned the language as a child. "And I will pour upon you pure water and you will be purified of all your defilements, and from all your abominations I will purify you." How many buckets of water would it take to purify my mother's defilements?

We all swayed back and forth as if we were praying at the Wailing Wall, our rocking creating the effect of a hypnotist waving a chain in front of my eyes and telling me that I was growing very, very sleepy. I was transported to my canopied bed where I'd sat in my Snoopy nightgown, instructing my mother with great authority when to bow and move her feet three steps forward and backward while she practiced reciting the Amidah prayer. My mother hadn't known a word of Hebrew before she met the Schines, but she was a quick study and practiced so hard that she could almost pass as an FFB, Frum From Birth, someone who had been born into an ultra-Orthodox home, someone like me. Standing before the body of Mrs. Kessler, I longed for the version of my mother who so desperately wanted to make the Schines' world a home for us, and my longing devoured my grief.

I hovered between my childhood bedroom and the tahara room while we tenderly patted Mrs. Kessler with a white towel as if she might grow cold from a draft. We shrouded her body, and then Aviva, Devora, Chana, and I lifted her, giving me a new understanding of the term "dead weight." The rebbetzin slid the casket under Mrs. Kessler's elevated body, and we lowered her inside. I couldn't bear the sight of her loaded into a box, so I let the other women finish up while I removed my apron, gloves, and shoe coverings. I turned toward the rebbetzin, my body humming from the godliness of what we had just done together.

"You performed a mitzvah of the highest order," she said.

I put my hand to my mouth, only to find the half smile my father had worn when Rabbi Schine asked our family to host one of his new recruits for Shabbos. After decades of exile from the rebbetzin's community, I was proud that she'd tapped me for this holy ritual and that I'd performed well.

I wanted more praise from the rebbetzin, more Hebrew words on my tongue, more synchronized washing and swaddling of my beloved Mrs. Kessler, and more time travel. I wanted to go back to the Schines' sanctuary, where I had sat with Mrs. Kessler and Tzippy and my mother, talking to God, believing that He could hear me.

I couldn't go back in time. My wants morphed into a wily rage that prickled my ears and neck. My old instinct was to quash it immediately by reminding myself that my mother hadn't beaten or abused me and that the rebbetzin had every right to protect her congregation from our family's disgrace, but my mother had torched my home, my shul, and the rebbetzin had stood by and watched, and indulging myself in the luxury of hating her for that, if only for a minute, brought me a bitter relief from my sadness. I lingered in my anger for a few moments before I started walking toward the door.

"Barbara," the rebbetzin said. "Please turn around. We don't turn our backs on the dead." She walked backward toward the door.

I followed her instructions, never taking my eyes off the pine box where Mrs. Kessler lay. We filed out to the parking lot in silence, and the rebbetzin handed me a water bottle from her purse. "Wash your hands and then put the bottle on the ground. We're not allowed to touch each other until we've washed."

I took the cap off the plastic bottle and poured the water over my fingers as the rebbetzin turned to Chana, Devora, and Aviva. "Go ahead. I want to speak with Barbara for a second."

Aviva stroked my arm before she walked to her car. "May Mrs. Kessler's name be a blessed memory."

"Thank you," I murmured, and Chana and Devora offered me their sympathies, too.

A man in dreadlocks passed us on his way to the check-cashing business, leaving a sweet smoky scent in his wake. I almost chuckled at the incongruity of the rebbetzin and the Rastafarian.

"How's Neil?" The rebbetzin smiled at her mention of his name. Everyone loved my brother. He was like my dad that way.

"Busy, happy. Good." While she didn't deserve any information about my family, I couldn't help telling her that he'd taken over our father's orthodontia practice or about his lovable wife and his three sons, one named Sheldon after our father. Neil and Jenny lived a few miles away and were a regular part of our lives.

She took in my every word, then paused for a few seconds and asked about my family.

I told her that I had a husband and a daughter, and was tempted to add that the parents of my students had deemed me some kind of parenting guru, that my daughter had lots of friends and a sparkling neshama, and that my marriage was easy and satisfying on every level. Instead, I asked after her sons.

She smiled proudly when she told me about their success in what mattered most to her and Rabbi Schine, touching Jewish souls. The least charismatic one lived in Milwaukee and would inherit Rabbi Schine's pulpit one day. The fiery ones had been detailed to Portland and Biloxi and had built thriving communities from nothing.

Then the rebbetzin volunteered an update on Tzippy without my having to ask. "She's living in Hong Kong and is quite a rebbetzin herself," she said with no more familiarity in her voice than when she'd described her boys' doings.

"I don't doubt that." Tzippy was a natural. My heart was open and raw, and the mention of her name brought back the old pain over losing the closest thing I had to a sister.

We let Tzippy loiter in the air for a few seconds.

"She's the grandmother of eleven. Kein ayin harah," the rebbetzin said.

"Eleven!" I put my hands to my cheeks and shook my head. Tzippy was married with a baby while I was student teaching and living in an efficiency apartment on the east side, convinced that I'd stay single and childless forever.

The rebbetzin broke the lightness of the moment. "How's your mother?"

Blood rushed up from my neck to my temples. Knowing the rebbetzin, she probably sensed the hateful things I'd been thinking in the tahara room. My guard went back up. "She's fine, thank you."

"She's okay?" the rebbetzin said as if she possessed some knowledge about my mother's welfare. Had they been in touch? Or was she using her superpowers?

I said what I had not yet admitted to myself. "She's having memory issues."

"Serious issues?" She used the tone she would in counseling a troubled congregant.

I wasn't some naive recruit. She was a big phony, coming back to me after all these years with her concern. I wanted to hurt her. "So serious that she thinks we're still welcome in your shul. She reminded me that I'm a married woman now and I need to cover my hair at Mrs. Kessler's funeral."

The rebbetzin looked at me as if I were a naughty child who was acting out trying to win the love that she was ready and willing to provide. I was. Fifty-three years old, and my naked need lay exposed. I still wanted to climb into Mrs. Kessler's lap, and I still craved knowing that some maternal being was watching out for me, a security I freely gave Lili and my students every day.

"Has your mother seen a doctor?"

"Neil and his wife took her to see a neurologist last week." What was I thinking sharing such personal family information with the rebbetzin?

The rebbetzin looked into my eyes, unearthing the hidden parts of me: the little girl who had taken such pride in her mother's coveted seat next to the rebbetzin in shul and the teenager who had been cast out with her mother like Hagar and Ishmael. I was no longer Barbara Pupnick, but I was losing hold of Mrs. Sam Blumfield by the minute.

"It's probably the medication." I told the rebbetzin about the cholesterol drugs, and the more I talked, the louder my inner voice insisted that her memory loss was more serious. It was the same voice that had spoken to me yesterday in the emergency room when I saw the doctor's expression as he read Lili's X-rays.

"She'll need you." The rebbetzin's words bore the weight of Jewish law, halacha that demanded that I offer food, shelter, medical care, and exquisite, relentless respect to my mother and father. Tzippy and I never dared sit in our parents' assigned chairs at the dinner table, and we rose when they entered the room.

I studied her face, searching her eyes for some trace of the hurt and humiliation my mother had caused her. They looked the same as always, full of purpose and principle. And love. She could put her old wounds aside for God and for me.

"Our relationship is complex," I said, "but things are fine between us." I tried to strain the defensiveness from my words. Despite my little lapse a few minutes earlier, I'd learned to coexist peacefully with my mother, to live without her investment or love.

The rebbetzin patted her heart with her open palm. "I will help you find your way back to her."

"What?" I didn't know whether to be shocked or angry. This made no sense at all. Why would the rebbetzin want to be a part of our lives after shunning our family? And why would I want to find my way back to my mother? She'd cost me the nook and everything good about my childhood.

"It's important, Barbara."

I stared at the rebbetzin's hand flat against her sweater and tasted something like bile in my mouth. Where had she been when my mother bailed on me? Did she think we could resume our old relationship without addressing our years of silence? I took a second now to compose myself before I said something I would regret. I said tersely, "I'm fine, but I appreciate your concern."

The rebbetzin's eyes bored into me. She knew I wasn't fine, but if I chose to let my mother back into my heart, the rebbetzin would be the last person I'd ask for guidance.

I thanked her for allowing me the honor of doing this mitzvah for Mrs. Kessler and said goodbye. She reached into her pocket and handed me a piece of paper with her phone number. She didn't need to; I still knew it.

"I have to go. I have to take my daughter to the doctor." I folded the paper, turned on my heel, walked to my car, and drove back toward my life.

5

While I was performing Mrs. Kessler's tahara, Sam had left three messages on my cell, all of them telling me that Lili's appointment had been moved up an hour, which meant that I wouldn't have time to stop home and change before I picked her up. I needed to shower badly. The taste of death lingered on my tongue, and the onion stink was back. I recalled the initial onset of this horrid odor, the morning I discovered I was carrying a girl. I'd since read somewhere that perspiration has no scent; it's the stress hormone cortisol that makes our sweat smell bad.

I pulled into the parking lot of Lili's high school, feeling both wired and sleepy, as though I'd been roused from a nap that had ventured too far into the REM sleep cycle. I ran into Sheri Jacobstein in the lobby. Sheri and I had stayed friends since Lili and her son Max were born. She was my fashion consultant and a buddy who made a place for me in her book club, on her PTA committees, and at other such adult lunch tables; she felt like home to me—well, the home I'd created with Sam. I adored her. She grinned, revealing her newly whitened teeth against her tanned skin, a contrast that resembled that of a film negative. She eyed my sneakers, the unseasonably warm shirt, and the long, frumpy skirt, and I folded my arms across my chest to ward off a hug. I didn't want her to smell me.

"You okay?" She stared at me.

"Fine." I smiled, and she looked at my outfit again, but I didn't explain. I wouldn't have known where to begin.

"Lunch next Thursday, right?" she asked, and I told her that I was looking forward to it, which I was. She'd have her live-in housekeeper poach us salmon, we'd indulge in a glass of white wine, and I'd feel pampered. I'd relax into the details of her bounty: a prohibitively expensive rug she'd just purchased or the theme she was considering for the synagogue's annual gala. Last year it was *The Brady Bunch*, and almost all the women dressed as Marcia, who was the ultimate shiksa goddess, according to Sheri's husband, Brad. I went as Alice because I admired her can-do attitude and her ability to keep the Brady household running smoothly.

"I'm sure I'll see you before then," I said as we parted. I couldn't wait to shed these clothes and return to my capris and a tank top. Sheri had advised me to wear sleeveless shirts and dresses as much as possible because my Michelle Obama triceps were to die for. My mother still had pretty arms, even in her seventies, but she never showed them off until she left the Schines' community. I'd felt self-conscious wearing sleeveless clothing well into my twenties.

Sheri disappeared into one of the offices seconds before the bell rang and the halls filled up with students. Lili came limping down the sophomore corridor with Megan, Kara—carrying Lili's backpack, which we'd joked equaled half her body weight—and Taylor, who stood on the outskirts of the triangle. Taylor had recently moved to Milwaukee from Boston, and Lili had befriended her during their summer cross-country practices. My daughter gathered people effortlessly. Like my mother and me, she had full lips that didn't quite fit over her teeth, giving the impression that she was always smiling. Although she struggled with geometry and spelling, she possessed an uncanny ability to read people. She had inherited Sam's knack for zeroing in on what mattered to people most and engaging them in conversation about their passion. Sam often reminded me of this when she was struggling in school. "You don't need to worry about that one," he'd tell me. "She can sell ice to Eskimos, and that's what matters in life."

"Thanks, girls," I said to Lili's friends.

Kara handed me the backpack, which might well have equaled half of Sam's body weight.

"How you doing, Lil?" I was so happy to see her that I put my arm around her.

"Whoa, Mom." She recoiled.

"Did you like eat a raw onion or something?"

"You don't care for my new fragrance?" I put my wrist to my nose and breathed in.

"And what's up with the shoes and skirt?"

"What's wrong with my new look?" I joked.

Lili studied me for what seemed like five minutes, and I squirmed under her scrutiny, knowing that my diversions weren't working. I feared that she'd push me further and I'd have to fib. I was a horrible liar. But then she laughed. "I mean, there's nothing wrong with it, you just look kind of Amish."

I giggled too enthusiastically, more out of relief than amusement.

During the drive to Felix's office, Lili regaled me with stories about running friends who had suffered tiny setbacks after their injuries and bounced back fast. Her voice was tinny, filled with fear and hope, as mine had been when I described my mother's memory loss to the rebbetzin. Neither one of us wanted to ponder life for Lili if she couldn't run. In seventh grade, she'd started exhibiting what the specialists called soft signs of ADHD, that—combined with a mild learning disability, a drastic increase in her homework, and the onset of puberty—made our efforts to help her with schoolwork a bloody battleground. I was so wrecked by her despondency I barely ate that year. Sam and I were just about to put her on Ritalin when a miracle occurred. One day in gym class, she up and ran a sub-six-minute mile. Boom. An athlete was born. She earned the nickname Lightning Bolt Lili, and with her new status and ability to concentrate, she turned into a solid student and peace returned to our house.

"Lil, we'll wait and see what Dr. Nezbith has to say," I offered, trying my best to sound hopeful.

She jumped on the last word of my sentence. "You mean you think he's going to bench me for the rest of the season?"

I wanted to tell her that she was going to be just fine, like Sam would, but Sam believed it because life hadn't offered him many bad surprises. He said that I was always waiting for the other shoe to drop. "Let's stay positive, Lil."

"That's what I was *trying* to do, Mom." She turned her face toward the window.

"I know you were." Once we were settled in the office, I thumbed through a *Newsweek*, but I couldn't concentrate on Sonia Sotomayor's confirmation hearing. Lili sat next to me, jiggling her good heel against the floor.

"One of the girls on the track team sprained her ankle, Rebecca Freed, and it was five times this size—" she said, her voice thin and sweet.

"Lili Blumfield." A pert twentysomething with a diamond stud in her nostril appeared with Lili's chart.

We only had to wait a few minutes for Felix, a tall man with a ridiculously narrow waist for someone his age. He greeted me with a kiss and asked after Sam.

"He weathering the economy?" Felix picked up Lili's chart.

Sam's clients had taken a hit during the recession, and he was working as hard as he had in the early days when he was building his business. "Oh, you know Sam. He always manages to keep himself afloat."

"Your dad's a financial wizard, Lili. And a damn fine water-skier."

Thanks to Sam's investment savvy, Felix had done well and had invited us to his summer home on Elkhart Lake on a number of occasions to show his appreciation. We'd become business friends with Felix and Betty Nezbith, one of the many couples in our circle of friends who had begun as clients and turned into something that teetered on the fringes of true kinship.

Lili smiled shyly. "He was first place in the Camp Manakee slalom competition five years in a row," she said, reciting a statistic

Sam rattled off frequently. She resumed jiggling her good leg.

Felix laughed. "I don't doubt that for a second." He removed his glasses from his pocket. "Okay, then. Let's see what's going on here."

He took one look at her X-rays and two looks at her ankle before he delivered the news. "You have what is called a spiral break. Now, if these bones don't move, we probably won't have to do surgery, but it means you have to stay off that ankle."

Lili bit her lip to stave off tears and mustered the wherewithal to ask the follow-up question.

"When will you know if you have to do the surgery?"

"Two weeks," Felix said gently

"If I'm okay, then I can start running again?"

"I'm afraid not, Lili. You'll need a good eight or ten weeks of rehab before you even think about running again."

Oh, crap. My breath congealed in my lungs. Relax, I told myself. I tried to pretend that I was fine, but I wasn't fine at all, and instead of imagining Maui beaches and sunsets, as Sheri's shrink had instructed her to do during moments of anxiety, I started thinking about my mother's fading faculties and Lili's inability to manage life without endorphins.

"Mom, are you with us?" Lili sounded frightened.

The room was spinning a smidgeon. "Of course, honey, I'm here. I'm here, just a little off today."

Felix called in the pert nurse to get me a glass of water. He probably thought I was one of those mothers who was too invested in her child's achievements, but that wasn't it at all. Running was Lili's medicine.

"Thank you," I said to the nurse as she handed me the glass. Lili looked both worried and mortified.

"You going to be all right, Mrs. Blumfield?" the nurse asked.

I took a sip of water. "I'm fine."

Felix picked up the chart. "Look, I know this is rough, but if Lili stays off this thing, she'll have plenty more cross-country seasons."

"Thanks, Felix, you were a doll to squeeze us in," I said.

"We'll get you fitted for a boot and talk in a few weeks. Sound good?"

"Sure," Lili said as Felix left to see his next patient.

The nurse slid a big black boot on Lili's foot. "This one seems right. How does it feel?"

Lili futzed around with the boot for a few minutes. "Okay, I guess," she said and followed me to the reception desk, where I wrote a check for our co-pay. It was painful to watch her limp to the elevator, dragging her big boot behind her. We rode down to the lobby in silence. I offered to pull up the car, but Lili said that she'd have to get used to this boot sooner or later and hobbled to our parking spot. I started the engine and waited for her to break down in tears. She didn't.

"What happened in there, Mom? You were like on another planet for a minute."

"I just felt a little light-headed. Let's not make a federal case out of it." It was alarmingly easy to lie to my daughter.

"Whatever."

I felt guilty for snapping at her. "Talk to me, Lil."

"No offense, like I know Dr. Nezbith is your friend, but that guy's a quack. I want a second opinion," she said, crossing her arms over her chest. All summer, she'd woken up at six o'clock every morning to run up and down bleachers before she met up with some of the area's top distance runners for long training runs. Last week, after she won the Menomonee Falls challenge, Coach JJ, Jill Johnson, former NCAA all-American in the mile, who barked at the girls like a drill sergeant, told her she had a shot at winning the state championship.

"I know this stinks, sweetie."

Lili pulled out her phone and started texting maniacally. After ten seconds, she looked up. "Megan and Kara have last period off today. They're hanging out at Megan's. Can you drop me off?"

"Sure. You know, if Dr. Nezbith decides you need surgery, we'll talk about a second opinion," I said.

"I'm going to find out who Rebecca Freed saw for her ankle." She resumed gnawing on her cuticle.

"Okay, honey, so tell me about your new friend Taylor," I said, trying to distract her.

"Megan and Kara don't like her. They think she's too into herself."

"Maybe they'll get to know her better throughout the season." What a dumb thing to say to Lili right now.

"That's not going to happen. She quit the team today."

I waited for her to continue. She gave me more information if I refrained from peppering her with questions.

"Kara said Taylor told her that she only joined so her parents would buy her a car."

I wasn't surprised. Taylor didn't seem to fit in with Lili's other friends, who were more sporty than stylish. Though built like a runner, she wore heavy black eyeliner that accentuated her spectacular irises, as green as those of the famous "Afghan girl" featured on the cover of *National Geographic* magazine.

"But you seem to like her," I said.

"I do, and I guess I'll need someone to hang out with now that I can't run. Besides, it can't be easy coming to a new school."

Her maturity took my breath away sometimes.

"Even if you're as hot as Taylor," she added wistfully, returning to her texting.

Megan Travinski lived in Glendale, in a modest home with her two older brothers and her mother, a trauma nurse. Dawn Travinski didn't have time for PTA meetings or long lunches prepared by housekeepers; her husband had left her when Megan and Lili were in kindergarten, and Megan frequently slept at our house when Dawn had to work extra shifts at the hospital. She knew I had her back; mothering Dawn and Megan filled some maternal emptiness inside me.

I was eager to drop Lili off. I wanted to take off these godawful clothes and shower. Lili had her hand on the door handle before I pulled into the driveway.

"Thanks, Mom. I got it," she said, and managed to extricate herself from the car and retrieve her crutches without any help. Dawn came out to say hello. From a distance, she could pass as one of Lili's friends, with what Sheri called a "gravity-defying tush" that enabled her to pull off wearing teenybopper jeans. I could fit into junior-size clothes but I felt ridiculous in them.

"Rough day?" she asked.

"That's for sure." I shook my head and filled her in on the details of Lili's injury. Then I stopped, because how on earth could Dawn Travinski begin to understand that I'd begun my day washing a corpse with a bunch of Chasidic Jewish women in the basement of a funeral parlor? I also stopped because Dawn was typically the one to unload her worries on me, and it felt weird to lean on her.

"You doing all right?" She looked at me closely, taking me in.

Although I spent more time with Sheri, I had a harder time fooling Dawn. "I think I am," I said, and tried to smile.

"You go home and have yourself a cold one. We'll keep Lili as long as she wants to stay."

I thanked her wearily and drove off. I left a message for Sam, giving him the headlines of the appointment with Felix and asking him to pick Lili up on his way home from the office.

At home, I went right upstairs and stared at myself in the bathroom mirror. Black was a hideous color on me, and my hair stuck to my head in reddish-brown clumps. I'd forgotten to cover up the large brown sunspot that was beginning to form on my cheek, and my eyes looked small and lifeless sans mascara. I stripped and stuffed my tahara clothes into an old shopping bag. I turned on the shower as hot as it would go, scrubbed every inch of my body with a loofah, and shampooed my hair three times. My skin was raw by the time I finished, but I smelled like me again.

After I dried myself off, I cupped my breasts in my hands; they weren't full, but they weren't gray and flat either. I touched the skin on my belly, still taut for a woman my age. I looked past my skin to my insides. You couldn't see the big parts of me that were missing: childhood memories that normal adults call on without hesitation, a mother's steady love, and my belief in my childhood shul, maybe even in God. As the body adapts to the loss of a kidney or a lung, I'd been functioning without these organs, failing to consider the strain I'd been placing on the surviving parts.

I was starving. I dressed and went down to the kitchen. While the toaster browned a slice of rye bread, I ran upstairs to retrieve the tahara clothes, took them down to the washing machine in the basement, and doused them with Tide, extra strength. As the machine filled with water, I walked over to my old cedar chest. I'd kept all my confessional letters to Tzippy in a hatbox of my mother's, which I'd stowed in the bottom of the chest. I missed Tzippy. Sure, I had lots of friends: Dawn, whom I took good care of; Sheri, who took good care of me; Betty Nezbith, whom I enjoyed well enough, but she was a couples-friend. All my other friends fell into one of those three categories. They weren't Tzippy. I allowed myself to fantasize about an adult relationship with Tzippy, emailing or talking over tea about the people in our lives who troubled or amused us, about our worries and hopes for our children. Eventually we might have grown apart, or I might have left the shul on my own. I never had the chance to find out.

Nothing good could come from opening the hatbox, yet it cried out to me. Hadn't I learned my lesson from my earlier phone call to my mother? God intervened. I smelled my toast burning and ran upstairs.

Sam and Lili wouldn't be home for another hour and a half. Tired as I was, I was too wired to take a nap. I needed to get out of the house and put some distance between those letters and the ghosts they would beckon. I spread peanut butter on my toast, wolfed it down, and dashed out the door with my gym bag. Zumba would do the trick. I'd have to focus so closely on the steps that I'd forget everything else.

I missed the four-thirty Zumba class, so I drove to my preschool, which was housed in an annex of our synagogue. It felt good to be back in my normal clothes, walking toward what Sheri called my "second nest." I was the only teacher who had the after-hours access code to the preschool entrance. Sarah, the director and my longtime colleague, had given it to me when she won the job. She didn't know that they'd offered me the directorship first but I'd declined because I didn't want to swap my time in the classroom for an administrative job. I still got to accompany Sarah to early childhood development conferences all over the country, and she never made a hiring decision without soliciting my opinion. We'd built this beautiful school, with a waiting list a mile long, by picking teachers like Mrs. Kessler who knew that working with kids was their calling. We could spot applicants who merely liked kids and needed something to do while their own children were in school.

As I walked down the hall, I imagined myself giving Mrs. Kessler a tour. "Here we have our rooms for our two-year-olds, the Kitten Room and the Cub Room. The student bathroom is over here, and we hold our special classes—music, movement, yoga if you can believe it, and holiday celebrations—in this larger room. These next rooms are for our threes, the Frogs and the Turtles, and I teach one of the fours, the Hummingbirds. Shirley teaches the Robins. She's the only teacher who's been here longer than I have."

I opened the door to my room and flicked on the light. It smelled like plastic from the new bins and antiseptic, but soon it would smell like paint, glue, and bread from the challah baking classes held in the synagogue's kitchen down the hall. Mrs. Kessler would have been proud of my second nest, of the mural on the wall with the flowering cherry trees, daisies, tulips, and hummingbirds, and particularly of the replica of the bespectacled sunshine she'd drawn on the wall of the nook.

I sat in the rocking chair I used to cuddle a sad child or read a book to the class. I slipped off my shoes and buried my toes in the soft carpet I'd bought on sale at Kohl's last year. I got up and examined the name tags Theresa had placed over each cubby. I knew half the children because I'd taught their siblings, and the others I'd get to know. That was the best part, discovering these children, each with his or her unique personality and sense of humor. I loved their questions. A surge of good energy shot through me.

The tour was over. I stared up at the mobiles, the array of birds Theresa had so painstakingly traced and cut. Without the breeze of the children, they hung in repose. "Aleha hashalom, Mrs. Kessler, rest in peace." I turned off the light and went home.

I made us a big spinach salad and heated up the pizza left over from the night before. Lili ate a few bites and then excused herself to go upstairs. She said six words during the entire meal: "Pass the red pepper flakes, please." My good spirits from visiting my classroom dissolved over the course of our dinner.

Sam shook his head as he reached for Lili's uneaten slice. "Life without the swing ain't gonna be pretty." The swing, Sam's term for Lili's running, referred to the electric swing a neighbor had loaned us when she was a colicky infant. Had we not discovered this sanity saver, we would have continued taking turns rocking and holding her for the nine months (not that we were counting) it took for her digestive system to mature.

"It's different now, though. She's so quiet," I said.

"She'll be back to her feisty self soon, and we'll be wishing for a little peace and quiet." He didn't believe in worrying a concern into a problem.

"She did call Felix a quack."

We didn't laugh as we usually did when Lili came out with her acerbically accurate assessments of adults, because this time she was off.

"What a doozy of a day." I took a swig of Sam's beer.

"Lili said you had a little episode in Felix's office. What was she talking about?"

I began peeling the label off his beer bottle. "Fasten your seat belt." I took one of my yoga breaths. "I got a letter from the rebbetzin."

"Oh? Probably a fundraising letter. Their yeshiva must need a new building," he said too fast, his voice disdainful at the prospect of the Schines asking for money from an exile.

"*That's* harsh." I'd always felt irrationally defensive of the Schines, though I kept quiet while our friends derided the ultra-Orthodox Jews—*frummies,* they called them—as we drove past the mansion on our way to restaurants where we'd freely order shrimp.

Sam knew to veer away from this topic altogether. We'd met when I was almost thirty, years after I'd left the Schines' world and hit rock bottom. He was content with my carefully crafted synopsis of my life with the Schines, which I weighted equally with details of my romantic history, a string of dead-end if not unpleasant relationships with men I'd met through Chrissie Janikowski, a fellow student teacher from my first job assignment. They were all Polish and Catholic, hulking men with pale mustaches and long hair feathered like Tony Orlando's, alav hashalom, may he rest in peace. If I felt the need to talk about the Schines, which I almost never did, I'd phone Neil, and we'd speak in code about the shul and our exile, if we spoke of it at all.

"Sorry, honey, but what does the letter have to do with your doozy of a day?" Sam asked with enough contrition that I began to tell him about the tahara. He was a squeamish man, and I had every intention of keeping the account brief and clinical, but once I started detailing the prayer and the careful dance of the pouring, I couldn't stop, not even when he got up to get another beer or looked at his watch or picked up the front page of the paper, eyes skimming an article about the arrest of the Milwaukee North Side Strangler, Walter Ellis.

I snatched the paper from him. "Are you listening to me?"

"I'm trying," he said.

I folded up the newspaper and kept talking. By the time I got to the end of my description of the ritual, I was practically shouting. "And then we sprinkled dirt from Israel on Mrs. Kessler's body and closed the coffin, and that was it." I took a big swig of

Sam's beer.

He studied me for a second, clearly not knowing what to make of my outburst, and then said, "Where did you park?"

"What?" I stared at him.

He looked sternly at me. "It's a dangerous neighborhood, and you never know what kind of crazies are out there." He gestured toward the article on Walter Ellis.

"In front of the funeral parlor, second spot closest to the entrance." My voice dripped with sarcasm.

He dropped his eyes. "That was a stupid question, I'm sorry. Again. I just don't understand how after all these years, the Schines write you a note and you run back to them."

"I did it for Mrs. Kessler. I've told you how much I loved her." Mrs. Kessler might have served as the bait to lure me back to my childhood, but performing the tahara conjured my feelings, warm and cold, about everyone who had mattered to me back then.

"Okay, so now what?" He didn't have much patience for such detours.

I put my napkin over my pizza and blotted up the excess oil. "I'm done, don't worry, I'm not going to go all born-again on you." My laugh came out as a grunt.

Sam stared at my hands, moving efficiently across the cheese. "There's something else bothering you."

"You know me too well." I noted the absurdity of this statement. He knew so little of my history.

"So what is it?" he asked softly.

I told him about my conversation with my mother and Neil's concern about her memory. I spoke with my hand over my mouth, an old habit from my youth, when I described how the rebbetzin had practically implored me to participate in my mother's care.

Sam's cell phone rang, and he looked at the number. "I have to take this. Hold that thought."

He walked toward his office, and I got up and started the dishes, fretting about my mother. When I'd spoken with her a few weeks ago, she'd laughed her old laugh, hearty yet feminine, the way she did when I was a girl and showed her the false eyelash I'd found in my soup bowl during Shabbos lunch at the Melnicks. Today she'd seemed out of it, and yet also less defended.

Sam returned to the kitchen while I was sweeping the floor. He came up behind me, turned me around, and rested his warm hands on my shoulders. "I'm amazed by what you did for Mrs. Kessler, and I see why you did it."

"You do?"

"Yeah, and I know you're worried about your mom, but we don't have a diagnosis yet, so for now I think we need to focus on getting Lili back to herself, which we will, I promise." He gave me his best reassuring smile.

I looked at him with fresh eyes. In the months since the economy faltered, new lines had formed on his forehead, yet I'd been the one who was scared when his business first slowed down. He'd grown up with parents who loved each other and lived comfortably off the proceeds of their car dealerships, the sale of which provided a net for us. I knew better. A home could go up in smoke like that, even ours. Poof—everything in our house could be foreclosed: the farm table we'd had custom built so that we could squeeze as many guests around it as possible, the red afghan I'd crocheted so we could cuddle while we watched movies and *American Idol*, the collages Lili had made of our lives. We could lose the big beautiful rooms that I dusted myself and filled with a citrus-and-basil potpourri I bought every summer from a candle store in Door County.

When one of Sam's best clients couldn't pay his bill, I'd quit the gym, limited my trips to Sendik's, and turned down the thermostat an extra few degrees at night. But Sam, although he was stressed from working long hours, was not afraid. I'd only seen him afraid a few times in our marriage, once after Lili's birth when he saw my clots of blood soaking the mattress and another time when our plane nearly crashed on the way to Miami for his cousin's bar mitzvah. And he was mildly frightened of leeches because at summer camp one had attached itself to his testicle and spawned babies. No, his job was to comfort me, to convince me that our sturdy little nest was safe from intruders of any sort—Walter Ellis or my mother—and my job was to be comforted and take care of Lili and the life we'd created for ourselves.

I put my arms around him, and he held me for a few seconds.

"I need to make another call," he said with apology in his voice.

I drew him closer before I let him go. "Go make your call."

I swept the same patch of floor again, wondering what it would be like to be married to a man who wanted to know the why behind my fears, who would muck about in my swampy past. Shame on me for my greediness. Maybe that was how my mother felt with the Shabbos goy. Would I ditch my family for such intimacy? No. When Lili started kindergarten and I went back to work, a handsome father of one of my students stopped by my classroom after school one day to talk about his daughter's aggression on the playground. His name was Ari, and he had a magnificent smile and waited an extra second or two after I finished talking before he responded. I found myself sharing a story about how Tzippy and I had bullied poor Margie Weinstein into eating an orange crayon. There was nothing remarkable about the story, except that I'd shared it so casually. I never uttered the name Tzippy. Too raw. Ari told me that my story brought him comfort, so I regaled him with another Tzippy story, about the time we got caught trying on her aunt Gittel's sheitel during her visit to the Schines for the High Holidays. Had Sam not phoned at that moment, I would have told Ari, with the bovine-looking eyes, every detail about growing up in the shul. He stopped by again later that week, but I politely shut him down. No way was I going to risk everything for a little extra attention. I daydreamed about him for a month, as I'm sure my mother did about the Shabbos goy, but my fantasies weren't sexual; they were much more threatening to my marriage. Ari had invited me to revisit a time when the pieces of my life—the shul, my mother, and Tzippy—all fit together. My mother couldn't have felt this pull to the Shabbos goy; their relationship was a mere affair.

I'd witnessed their kisses. The term "Shabbos goy" seemed terribly derogatory to me now, and although I couldn't bring myself to call my mother's ex-lover Andy, I allowed myself to wonder what had happened to him.

Sam came back into the kitchen. "Let's call it a night."

I took his hand and led him upstairs.

Sam's Barbara Pupnick Blumfield worked for our family, and he clearly didn't wish to excavate the parts of myself he'd helped me bury. But the subconscious has a mind of its own, and that night I dreamed an old dream. A woman is floating in the mikveh. It's too dark to see her, but I can hear splashing and whispering. A hot electric pressure penetrates the core of my body, pulling me toward the water and the whispering.

My dream was so vivid that it left a residue on my consciousness in the morning, like the grease on my fingers from the pizza. While Sam was in the shower, I left Theresa a voicemail message: "It's Barbara, I'm sorry to do this to you again, but...." I told her that we were seeking a second opinion on Lili's ankle injury. I could have easily said that I was attending a funeral, but I wasn't prepared to negotiate either her questions or her sympathy. I asked her to meet me at noon to finish setting up the room. We'd have plenty of time before tomorrow, our first day of school.

After Sam and Lili left the house, I dressed in a modest black suit. My mother's suggestion from the day before to wear a hat returned uninvited, like a garlic belch. I didn't own a hat.

I couldn't eat a bite of my yogurt or concentrate on today's article about Walter Ellis's capture. Mrs. Kessler's funeral was scheduled for ten o'clock, and I waited until half past nine to get into my car and head toward the Schines'. I ached to say a formal goodbye to Mrs. Kessler, but something more powerful was pulling me to the mansion. I avoided driving by the Schines' whenever possible, and when Sam took a route that passed it, I'd turn my head. My hands clutched the steering wheel too tightly as I drove by the palatial estates hugging the lake. The radio was still tuned to one of Lili's pop stations, and I shut it off. My nerves couldn't handle the cloying electronic drums and insipid lyrics.

As I neared the Schines', the tugging sensation from my dream heightened. Traffic was backed up for a block behind their long driveway. This was no surprise; Mrs. Kessler had taught many of us who had grown up in the shul. As I waited for the oncoming traffic to let up, I reached into the glove compartment for my big sunglasses that Sheri had convinced me to buy. She said they made me look like an auburn Jackie O.

I made the turn into the driveway, half expecting my car to implode the moment the wheels hit Schine property. The sun was starting to burn a layer of fog off the lake. My body hummed from the part in my hair to my toenails. The Tudor house looked bigger than ever to me. The Schines had converted the Shabbos goy's carriage house to an annex to accommodate their growing congregation. I'd read about the project in the *Wisconsin Jewish Chronicle*. The Schines still lived on the top floor of the mansion, though, and Tzippy's old shade was down.

A man in a bright orange vest directed me to the front lawn, to an empty space in a new row he'd marked off with cones.

I got out of the car and started walking across the lawn to the house. My high heels dug into the grass, so I had to step on my tiptoes. When we were children, Tzippy and I used to take off our shoes and socks and sprint barefoot on this grass, racing each other from the house to the driveway. I always won, even when Tzippy cheated.

The lake breeze blew strands of hair toward my face, and I self-consciously tucked them behind my ears. My mother was right; I should have worn a hat.

I was just about to put my fingers to the mezuzah at the front door when I felt someone behind me. I turned around to face Mrs. Pincus, one of the Brisket Ladies. She'd grown fatter and walked with a cane, but it was her. I hadn't set eyes on her since I was buying diapers for Lili at the Kohl's on Oakland Avenue. We pretended we hadn't seen each other, but in the second I caught her staring at me, I recognized her pity for June Pupnick's daughter. My mother had become Mr. Isen of Brookfield. I never shopped at that Kohl's again.

"Barbara," Mrs. Pincus said, and the pity had not left her eyes. I was older now than she was when we'd first met, but she clearly couldn't separate me from the girl whose mother had disgraced the community.

I dabbed at the corner of my mouth. "Hello, Mrs. Pincus."

"Are you coming inside?" she asked, and all I could hear was her desire that I wouldn't.

People were starting to form a line behind Mrs. Pincus, but I couldn't move from the mezuzah. I wanted to tell her that she wouldn't even be standing here had my mother not invited her over to our house to answer all her questions about the Schines' way of life. It had been a cold winter afternoon, and she'd gobbled up half a plate of my mother's peanut butter cookies with her tea. I eavesdropped on my mother's gripping retelling of the story of the Schines finding her in the hospital after her appendicitis attack. Now I looked at Mrs. Pincus trying to offer me a smile, and my anger dissolved. She too had made the mistake of idolizing my beautiful and persuasive mother.

"Barbara," she said gently.

"What?" Was she going to tell me to leave?

She pointed behind her to the line of mourners. I looked at their faces, and their lips, noses, chins, and hats all blurred into one. I didn't know any of them, but I knew them all. And they knew me. I couldn't go inside, and I couldn't kiss the mezuzah. "Excuse me," I said. "I think I left something in the car."

I walked down the driveway, blinking away the memory of the last time my feet had touched this asphalt, placing my hands over my ears so I wouldn't imagine Tzippy's voice calling after me. I walked faster, faster than I had when I was a girl and my mother and I were running from one of her fogs.

By the time I reached my car and slid into the front seat, I was out of breath. I removed my Jackie O sunglasses and rested my head on the steering wheel. The driveway couldn't accommodate two-way traffic, so I had to wait until the stream of cars stopped entering the grounds. Nice going, Barbara, I scolded myself as I sat trapped on the Schines' front lawn.

The parking attendant noticed me and walked over. "You okay, ma'am?"

I smiled at him weakly. "I'm not feeling well."

He cocked his head toward the road. "Should slow down any second. I'll cue you."

"I appreciate that."

I glanced up at Tzippy's window, waiting for her to pull up the shade, run down to the foyer, and walk toward the women's section, where Mrs. Pincus, my mother, the rebbetzin, and Mrs. Kessler would all be arranged properly in their seats.

The parking attendant knocked on my window and pointed toward the driveway, and I sped away from the mansion like I'd just taken a turn at Ding Dong Ditch. A part of me didn't want to flee, though. I was like my college roommate who suffered from both kidney disease and heroin-like cravings for the salted fatty meats that could destroy her. The filminess of my dream clung to the dead parts of me, luring me back inside.

November 1973 – May 1974

Because I lived in constant fear that my mother would get caught with the Shabbos goy, I panicked when I found the rebbetzin waiting for me in Mrs. Kessler's room the Tuesday before Thanksgiving. Maybe my mom and the Shabbos goy had been reckless and she'd found them together in the mansion. If so, the rebbetzin was here to fire me. She couldn't have the daughter of such a woman poisoning the community she'd dedicated her life to building, much less working with children. I scanned her face for the lips she pursed when she was disappointed with Tzippy. Her lips looked perfectly relaxed, but that didn't make me feel any better.

"I'm so glad you're here, Barbara." She kissed me on the cheek. "Mrs. Kessler had to take Yossi to the pediatrician, and I'm finishing a meeting upstairs. Can you handle the class alone?"

I let out a breath so big that it parted my bangs. "I'll be okay."

The rebbetzin nodded. "Listen to Morah Barbara, children. She's in charge."

"Don't worry." I wasn't afraid. This was the one place I felt confident. Nobody was sneering at my long skirts or staring at my pimples. I smiled at the twelve children, but then two of the boys began to wrestle, and one little girl started to cry. Within seconds the classroom had devolved into chaos.

"Itzik." I placed my hand on the shoulder of one of the fighting boys. "Please go sit with Rena." Then I went over to Rena, who adored the rambunctious boy. "Itzik is going to sit with you," I said, wiping a tear from her face with my sleeve.

I remembered a song Mrs. Kessler had taught me when I was about their age. "Is everyone ready for a round of 'Father Abraham'?"

I sang about the silent father of seven sons who could only move parts of his body to communicate. Each verse demanded that we wave a new limb in the air, and by the end of the song, we were dancing around the room, swinging our arms, legs, and tongues.

Rena cheered loudly and the others chimed in. "Let's do it again, Morah Barbara!"

I feigned exhaustion as I sat down against the wall, and in no time, twelve four-year-olds were clamoring for a spot on my lap. When I looked up, the rebbetzin was leaning against the door.

"Mrs. Kessler is right. You sure are a magician with these kids." She beamed, kvelling, as if I were one of her own children.

I floated home, elated that I'd impressed the rebbetzin. I couldn't wait to tell Neil, who had taken the afternoon bus from Madison for Thanksgiving break. I opened our back door to find him sitting at the kitchen table, his face ashen.

"You need to go see if Mom's okay," he said.

"She's in the tub," I said. She always took a bath on Tuesdays.

"I heard noises coming from her room," Neil persisted. His voice was tight, and he was clenching his jaw. "Crying, I think."

Maybe Rabbi Schine had caught my mother with the Shabbos goy. The thought of the great rabbi, in his long beard and black garb, finding my mother and a man who wasn't my father groping each other made me feel sick. But what if something else was wrong? My legs felt rubbery as I bolted up the steps and knocked on my parents' door. No answer.

"Mom, it's me. Open the door."

Still no answer.

I wiggled the glass knob, and the heavy door swung open. The blinds were drawn, and I heard a whimper coming from the bathroom. I burst through the door like *Hawaii Five-O*'s Steve

McGarrett during the climax of a chase scene. My mother sat slumped in the empty tub in her slip, a lacy strap falling down her shoulder. Her hair was matted, and the whites of her eyes were so red that her pupils looked green.

She was holding a sheet of notebook paper in her hands. I pried it from her gently, and she barely resisted. I unfolded the letter, my bitterness dissolving like a sugar cube in a cup of hot tea.

November 28, 1973

My June,

I'm moving to Wyoming, for you, for me, for us. I will always love you.

Andy

She sat staring at nothing, her hands resting in her lap limply, a string of mucus dangling from her nose. I'd only seen her so unkempt once before, when I was ten and she caught a terrible flu. My father saw how frightened I was by her feverish moaning and wouldn't allow me to enter her room until her temperature went down. She was even scarier now. I hadn't touched her since the day after the mikveh incident, and I hesitated slightly before I waded through her fog and climbed into it with her. Stepping into the tub, I squatted behind her and sat down, wrapping my legs around her. I wiped her upper lip with the sleeve of my sweater and rocked her as I would one of the children in Mrs. Kessler's room.

"Come on, Mom. Let's get you out of here." I maneuvered myself out of the tub.

She shook her head despondently. "I'm fine."

I managed to lift her and guide her to the bed. I covered her with a blanket and lay down on my father's side of the mattress. We were facing each other, and her smoky breath warmed my cheeks. She closed her eyes. I waited until her lids stopped fluttering before I got up, ripped the note into a dozen pieces, and threw it in the trash. I removed the bag from the basket, fixing her blanket and kissing her on the forehead before I went downstairs. I was petrified, but I also felt important coming to her rescue, and I was glad she was back, shattered and all.

Neil was sitting exactly where I'd left him. "If she's okay, I'm going over to Hank's." He was always on his way out the door. I envied his clear skin and dozens of Gentile friends.

"No, you stay here with Mom," I said, stuffing the bag in the garbage. "I've got something to do."

Before he could object, I was out of the house running to the Schines' mansion, the static of lake water buzzing in my ears. By the time I reached the long driveway, I was sweating and gasping for air. Through the Schines' window, I could see the rebbetzin standing over the kitchen sink. Tzippy's shade was down, of course. The light in the carriage house was on. I had no idea what I would say to the Shabbos goy or what I would tell the Schines if they saw me, but I marched up the driveway anyway.

I snuck around the back of the house and through the cold, empty garage, where robbers or raccoons were probably waiting to attack me. I knocked on the Shabbos goy's door. He was pulling his T-shirt over his head when he answered, and I couldn't help but notice the thin line of hair that traveled a few inches up from the waist of his jeans. Otherwise, his chest was completely smooth. My father's chest was so hairy that it looked like he was wearing a black sweater when he undressed.

"You shouldn't be here, June," the Shabbos goy said, his shirt still covering his face. When his head emerged from the collar, he said, "Oh, Barbara."

It was the first time I'd heard him say my name. Piles of clothing and packing boxes littered the floor.

"Oh yes I should be here." My anger and hurt toward my mother had morphed into something else; now I was her fierce protector.

He pulled down his shirt. I'd never seen his hair out of a ponytail before. It fell around his shoulders, which were broad for a such a stringy man.

"I don't care about you." I glared at him. I'd never seen his face up close. He had blond stubble in the cleft of his chin, a big Adam's apple, and a finely sculpted nose with delicate nostrils.

He stuffed a sweatshirt into a duffel bag.

"Did you hear what I said?" I walked over to him and kicked the duffel. "I said I don't care about you."

"I'm sorry about all this, Barbara."

"I'm sorry about all this, Barbara." I mimicked him like a six-year-old, so angry that I couldn't find my own words.

"I really am," he said lamely.

"You better be." I kicked the duffel again because it felt so good the first time. A black-and-white photo fell out of the side pocket. The Shabbos goy and I lunged for it, but I was shorter, so I got there first.

The photo was creased and torn around the border. My mouth slackened as I examined the image of a young girl, probably thirteen or fourteen, standing on a bluff, the lake rippling in the background. She was laughing, her head thrown back, her skinny arms clutching her sides. A teenage boy, maybe fifteen or sixteen, was wearing her sunhat tugged over his ears. The Shabbos goy snatched the photo back, but he was too late. I recognized the hands and smile and tilt of her long neck.

"Who's the boy in the picture?" I asked. I'd only seen a few photos of my mother as a girl.

He started gathering the other items that had fallen across the floor.

"Answer me." My breath caught in my chest, and I couldn't get it out. I started to hyperventilate.

He led me by the elbow to an overstuffed brown chair, then went to the kitchen and returned with a glass of water. "Relax, Barbara," he said in the sweetest voice, and I hated myself for seeing how my mother could love him.

After a few minutes, I could breathe again. "Please tell me why you have an old photo of my mother."

He tucked it into his pocket. "You'll have to ask her," he said in that nice way.

"Oh, so that's what adulterers do? They share pictures from when they were young?"

"It's up to your mother to tell you about this," he said, his lips set in a firm no.

We both knew that my mother wasn't going to tell me her secrets. Or maybe she would now that I had climbed into that tub and waded into the darkness that had been pulling her away from us.

"Take care of her." He walked to the door and opened it for me.

"Oh, don't you worry. I will," I answered, my voice full of accusation and love. I walked out his door and back down the Schines' driveway. The Shabbos goy had confirmed my new role as my mother's caretaker. Now I'd always know where to find her in the middle of the night.

The first week after the Shabbos goy left for Wyoming, my mother came downstairs and flitted around the kitchen filling bowls of cereal for me, pouring my father cups of coffee, and scrambling eggs for both of us. The second week, she sat at the kitchen table in a dirty nightgown and watched us fix our own breakfasts, commenting absently that I was so grown up. The third week, she took to her bed.

That Shabbos, my dad and I walked to shul without her. The rebbetzin saved a place for me, and the women looked at me with concern. I told them nothing about my mother. I'd been designated the keeper of her secrets and her pain.

Either Rabbi Schine or the rebbetzin, or sometimes both, called my father every day, and the rebbetzen, the Brisket Ladies, Mrs. Katz and Mrs. Pincus, started showing up every few days with brisket and petrified vegetables. We accepted their meals and their concern graciously, although nobody in our house had much of an appetite. One night, I overhead my father talking on the phone, his conversation sprinkled with words like "depressed" and "psychiatrist" and "emaciated." I hoped he didn't know why my mother was in such bad shape.

When I walked by my mother's door the next morning, I heard her whimpering. I didn't go into her room to comfort her, but I ditched school early and stopped at the Shorewood Library to load up on books by James Michener, her favorite author, and Jane Austen, mine. I'd figured out the perfect antidote to my mother's funk. As soon as I walked into the house, I ran up to my parents' room and knocked on the door. She didn't answer, so I let myself in. She was in bed dozing, her ivory sheets tangled around her waist. Instead of one of her pretty nightgowns, she was wearing an old Oxford shirt of my dad's, unbuttoned enough to reveal her pale skin pulled tightly over the birdlike bones of her chest. The room stank of cigarettes and dirty scalp. I emptied her ashtray, then stretched out on her chaise longue and thumbed through Michener's *Kent State: What Happened and Why*, the perfect bait to reel my mother back into life. I cleared my throat often, hoping to wake her. Finally, she stirred.

She sat up in bed and rubbed her eyes. "What time is it?"

It was one of those dark winter afternoons when the sun set before suppertime. I glanced down at my watch. "Four forty-five."

"You need to do your homework, Sweet B."

Her voice sounded hoarse and flat, but I didn't care. She'd called me Sweet B. "Are you hungry? I can heat up some soup."

"You're such a good girl." She grabbed her pack of cigarettes and lit up.

"Do you want to go to visit the rebbetzin?" I asked, hoping that the Schines' apartment would lure her out of her bed.

"I'm a little tired today."

I sat with her while she finished her cigarette, and when she got up to use the bathroom, I arranged the library books on my father's side of the bed. "I checked out some books for you, Mom."

She climbed back into bed and pulled the covers over her thin legs. "Michener," she sighed. "I'm going to pick one after I take a nap."

She went back to sleep, the books untouched. I sat on the chaise longue until I heard my father enter the house. I ran off to my room and pretended I was deeply engrossed in my physics homework when he came upstairs and stood in my doorway, still in his wrinkled white coat, which now looked a size too big. My mother had stopped ironing his coats and feeding him.

"Are you okay?" Even his voice was losing its heft. He walked over to me and lightly pinched my earlobe, like he had when I was a little girl with a mom who read me books about my hero Chaim Pumpernickel.

"Are you?" I asked.

He looked down at his shoes. I'd been so busy worrying about my mother that I hadn't noticed the defeat in the way he held his shoulders and the purple circles under his eyes. He blinked hard. I thought he might cry. I looked at him again, and I thought I might cry too. He smiled at me. Like Mrs. Isen's, his olive skin had turned sallow and his eyes were flat.

He knew about my mom and the Shabbos goy.

I stared down at my notebook and reread my study question over and over until the words started to blur. *Does a free-falling object still have weight?*

"You seem tired, Dad." I couldn't look at him anymore.

"I'm okay. I'm worried about your mom, Bunny."

I was dying inside for my father. I knew in my heart that he was too loyal to leave my mother, especially when she was sick. Once she started feeling better, maybe my parents would fall back in love. Then again, he never missed an opportunity to go on about the lies of Haldeman and Ehrlichman, so maybe he wouldn't be able to forgive my mother for hers.

"Me too," I said.

"Let me do the worrying. You need to go to school."

The school must have called him about my absence. I felt sick with guilt for making him fret about me. I pulled at the loose seams of my bedspread. "Okay."

He patted my shin. "I'll make us my specialty. We'll take a

night off from the brisket."

"Thanks, Dad."

"I almost forgot. This came for you." He reached into his pocket and handed me an envelope before he walked into the hall. I heard him open the door to my parents' bedroom. A few minutes later he was banging pots and pans around in the kitchen, making me matzoh brei, even though Passover wasn't for another few months. I opened the letter.

January 14, 1974 *B"H*

Dear Barbara,

Happy Birthday!! Did Mrs. Kessler make you skip around the room and wear the striped birthday hat? Ha, ha. I'm mailing this early so you'll get it on your big day. I'll be thinking of you all day.

Did your mom tell you that my parents found me a match? I saw a picture, and he has reddish hair, like yours. He's a Rashi scholar and comes from a family of seven girls. I hope he's not too serious. All of this talk about a wedding makes me nervous. The only thing that calms me is knowing that you will be there to catch me if I faint like you did in Mrs. Kraven's social studies class, but then it was because the room was too hot and I hadn't eaten breakfast. My mom said that this shadchen did a good job of fixing up Sari and the rest of my cousins, and they seem happy enough. What if she makes a mistake with me?

Write soon, and tell me all of the news of the shul. I miss you.

Your best friend,

Tzippy

I didn't have the heart to remind my father that tomorrow was my birthday. Eighteen. I was old enough to vote and drink and not make a fuss over a forgotten birthday. Being an adult was overrated. I couldn't stop taking care of my mother if I wanted to, but that didn't mean I didn't yearn for my chocolate cake baked from scratch. I wanted to lick the beaters and bowl clean.

We ate dinner without talking much, and while I was getting ready for bed, I noticed puffy circles under my eyes. I was catching a cold, and my head ached. I wrote Tzippy another letter I would never send. It was Tuesday, after all.

January 17, 1974 *B"H*

Dear Tzippy,

I still can't believe that you're getting married. I guess you'll set a date soon. Mira has a boyfriend. His name is Howie, and she met him at a BBYO bagel breakfast last December. He doesn't go to our school, so Mira and I still eat lunch together. We don't see each other after school anymore, but that's okay. I feel like I need to be home anyway.

Mira and I got into a fight yesterday at lunch. I asked her to please stop sucking the white part of the banana peel from the skin because everyone would laugh at her. She said that we always sat alone at the lunch table anyway, and that if I cared so much about being laughed at, then I should stop dressing like Moon-Schine Girl. I didn't even cry when I reminded her that Moon-Schine Girl was old news. Now I answer to Zitface.

My dad knows about the Shabbos goy. He looks so sad. The only good news is that he didn't leave my mother and the Shabbos goy is finally gone. He moved to Wyoming. I hated what my mom was doing, but it hurts to see her in so much pain. These two feelings are rooted around my heart like a wishbone.

I can't wait until June. Everything will be fine by then, and we'll have the whole summer to figure out our new lives.

Your best friend,

Barbara

By April, I was working for Mrs. Kessler only once a week. My mother needed me more, so I came straight home from school. She was no longer spending the days in bed, but she rarely left the house. My father never asked me to do the grocery shopping or keep her company, but I think he was relieved that someone was taking care of her.

A week before Passover, I was walking to the Schines to help Mrs. Kessler, and as I turned up the driveway, I noticed a figure wandering along the bluff. It was a gloomy day, and it was easy to spot my mother's baggy cornflower-blue coat against the gray horizon. She moved her hand to her mouth periodically to puff on her cigarette.

I stiffened. She so rarely went out that she must have come here for a reason. When she passed the carriage house, I thought she'd look toward the window for the Shabbos goy, but she didn't. She kept walking toward the bluff.

I broke into a jog as I imagined her flapping her skinny arms, cigarette between her fingers, the tiny orange ember releasing smoke into the air. A bird in a blue coat. I wanted to shout, but my throat closed up, so I ran harder until I almost reached her. She stood with her back to me, shoulders slouched and her hands hanging limply at her sides.

"Mom?" I called out softly.

She turned around, and I shuddered. I hadn't seen her outside of the house, where she'd drawn the shades in every room. In the natural light, she looked pale, but something else about her caught my eye. I recognized the tilt of her head, the distance between her body and the lake behind her. No flowered dress or hat, but this was exactly where she stood in the photo that fell out of the Shabbos goy's duffel bag.

"What are you doing out here?" She looked as though I'd woken her from a deep daydream. She took a long drag of her cigarette, dropped it on the ground, and crushed it with the tip of her boot. She turned back to the water.

"Mom? Hello? Are you here?"

"Where else would I possibly be?" she replied, not to me, but to the miles of open water in front of us.

After a few minutes, she started back toward the mansion, and I followed. Instead of heading up the driveway, though, she went to the kitchen entrance. When she opened the door, I wasn't sure if she was looking for the rebbetzin or the Shabbos goy. The kitchen smelled like ammonia. The door shut behind us, and my mother stepped toward the pantry. A surge of the electricity I'd felt in the mikveh seemed to radiate from her body.

"Mom, this isn't a good idea. Let's go upstairs to the Schines instead." Somehow I knew she was in no shape to go back down to the mikveh. She'd fall in and drag me with her. I felt exhausted from the energy I was expending to keep her out of harm's way.

Mrs. Katz popped out of the pantry, mop in hand. "June!"

"Hello, Malka." Mrs. Katz was once called Muriel; she was one of my parents' first recruits.

"I'm doing the first round of Passover cleaning." Mrs. Katz pointed to the floor and looked at my mother eagerly. A few months ago, my mother would have praised Mrs. Katz for her service to the shul. My mother never mopped our floors, much less the shul's. Once I overheard her telling my father that she'd grown up with maids and that was why she didn't know how to clean a floor properly. My father didn't follow up and ask her more about her servants, like I would have. He simply hired her a cleaning lady whom she let go after the Shabbos goy left. Now it was up to my dad and me to scrub toilets and mop floors.

My mother said nothing. Through Mrs. Katz's eyes, I saw the knotted hair and the shoulder blades poking through her coat. Mrs. Katz, with her full mouth and giant breasts, only made my mother look more anemic.

"How are you?" Pity draped Mrs. Katz's fleshy face. She looked nothing like the adoring woman who'd trapped my mother in long conversations at the kiddush lunch table.

My mother reached into her pocket and pulled out a cigarette, but she didn't light it. "I came in for a match."

I saw the outline of her lighter in her front pocket and wondered if she'd been such a skilled liar before her affair.

Mrs. Katz reached for a box of kitchen matches on one of the top pantry shelves, slid it open, and held it out to my mother.

My mother took the whole box. "I better not smoke in here."

Mrs. Katz looked down at her apron and fiddled with the string. "You take good care of yourself, June."

We filed out of the kitchen with barely a goodbye. I waited until we were on the street to say a word. "Mom, were you going to go down to the mikveh again?"

She lit her cigarette and took a long drag. "No, Sweet B. The rebbetzin has to supervise our visits," she said, as if I was a recruit and she was informing me of a Jewish law.

The wind blew her smoke into my lungs. She wasn't going to tell me more. I was relieved that Mrs. Katz had stopped us from walking into that pantry and down the steps to the mikveh, but I felt that pull, too. We walked home in silence, the tacit agreement that I'd keep what I knew of her secrets and lies between us. I let us into the house. She tossed the box of matches on the table, flung her arm around me, and drew me in, both clinging to me and comforting me. Minutes later, she disappeared upstairs, not even bothering to take off her coat and boots.

On a rainy day in May, I came home to find the rebbetzin in our kitchen. The dishes had been washed, and it smelled like chicken was roasting. Two teacups and saucers sat on the table.

"Sit down, my Barbara." She pointed to a chair.

"I should go—"

"I just came from checking on your mother," the rebbetzin assured me.

I sat down, although I wanted to dash up to my mother's room and see her for myself.

"Let's have a cup of tea." She poured hot water into the cup belonging to the saucer my mother used for her ashtray and placed a Lipton bag and the sugar bowl near my hand.

"Thank you." I stirred two teaspoons of sugar into my tea. The warm liquid ran over my tongue and down my throat. The rebbetzin sat with me until I emptied my cup. She always said that sometimes just sitting beside someone with tsuris was all they needed to start to feel better. I had tsuris, that was for sure, trouble aplenty, and I was reveling in her attention.

"I want to discuss your summer plans."

"Does Mrs. Kessler need help with Yossi?"

"No, Barbara."

"Then what?" I asked, confused.

"It would be a good idea for you to spend a summer away," she said firmly.

"Oh, I can't. My mom needs me. I'm staying home and then taking a few classes at UW Milwaukee in the fall." I'd been accepted at Madison, but I'd deferred. I'd wait until my mother was healthy. If I could help her get better, then we could all return to our old lives.

The rebbetzin studied the contents of her teacup.

"And I have to stay home because this will be my last summer with Tzippy." My words sounded stupid as they left my lips. I was no longer the girl who stole cookies or snuck off to the nook or mused about the Shabbos goy's love life.

"No. You need to go," she said as if she were giving orders to a procrastinating Tzippy to do her homework.

Her seriousness rattled me. "Why?"

"I don't think being here is a good thing for you, Barbara."

"But why?" Sweat started to bead on my upper lip.

She walked over to the sink, her back toward me as she meticulously dried the inside of the basin with a paper towel. "I know that things have been difficult here."

"What do you mean, difficult?"

"You know, with your mother." Now she was wiping down each tile under the splashboard.

And then I saw it, as clearly as I had when I looked at my dad the afternoon I skipped school. "You know?" I asked.

She stopped cleaning, but she didn't turn around.

I didn't want her to turn around. I couldn't bear to look at her face. I tried to swallow, but my saliva had dried up. This was it. I'd never considered how she was going to tell us to leave the shul, but it was just like her to do it after making us a nice chicken. I waited for her to serve up an offering from the Talmud that would accompany a long goodbye speech, but instead she said, "I'm sorry."

My ears filled with a high-pitched noise like the warning signals television stations played once a week. *For the next sixty seconds, this station will conduct a test of the Emergency Broadcast System. This is only a test.* I put my hands over my ears to stop it, but the ringing had penetrated my skull, and it was lasting more than sixty seconds. The rebbetzin came to me. She stood next to me, and I concentrated on the perfect hem she'd sewn on her skirt and the sound of our breath: mine short and broken, hers punctuated by long sighs. She walked to the sink and ran the water, ruining all her shining. I held my head between my hands.

She put a glass of water on the table and sat down facing me, her eyes focused and bright. She was back to herself, our leader who knew the perfect next move for all of us.

"I have a wonderful opportunity for you, Barbara." She asked me if Tzippy had ever mentioned her cousin Sari and her husband, Rabbi Levenstein, who were building a community in San Diego. She said Sari was newly pregnant and had such bad morning sickness that she couldn't take care of her son. "What would you think of helping her out?" she asked me with enthusiasm.

I wanted to cry, but the tears were stuck somewhere inside me. "What will happen to my mother?"

"The first thing we need to do is get your mother well."

"How can you help her? She disobeyed Hashem."

"I know *exactly* what she did, Barbara." She almost sounded as though there was a perfect explanation for my mother's choices.

"Did my father tell you?"

She smoothed her skirt over her knees. "It doesn't matter how I found out."

"Who will take care of my parents?"

"Hashem." She let out a breath. "And Rabbi Schine and I."

"Hashem? What about His 613 commandments? Number 74: That the women suspected of adultery shall be dealt with as prescribed in the Torah. Exodus 22:18: You should not permit a sorceress to live." I recited this passage as if Rabbi Lichtenberg had just called on me in Judaics class.

"This is a difficult situation," she said as if I was a child and I couldn't possibly comprehend such a grown-up matter.

None of this made any sense. How could the Schines rip their lapels for Mr. Isen and grant my mother so much leniency? As much as I'd feared the rebbetzin kicking us out of the shul, her acceptance of my mother's affair unsettled me more. She still looked like the woman who paced back and forth while advising a congregant, transmitting her wisdom through the phone cord wrapped around her fingers, but this time her fingers were busy shredding a napkin.

"Your father thinks this is best, too," she added.

"You've been plotting with him?"

"You've been so good to your mother, but this is no life for a young girl." She cupped my chin in her hand.

I picked at the wet tea bag wadded up on the saucer. "Please, let me stay."

"I'm sorry, Barbara." She bit her lip, but her voice remained firm.

"I won't get in anyone's way, I promise."

She closed her eyes and shook her head no.

"Please," I whispered.

I, not my mother, was the one being exiled to California, which was much farther away than Brookfield.

7

September 2009

During the weeks following Mrs. Kessler's tahara, I dialed the rebbetzin a half dozen times but hung up before hitting the last number. I don't know what I wanted from her, maybe an apology for shipping me off to California. Maybe I wanted an explanation for why she'd invited me to wash Mrs. Kessler or implored me to take care of my mother or even spared a thought for a woman she'd expunged from her community, albeit for good reason. I wished she'd gone about her business of saving Jewish souls and left me in peace.

My life, however, was anything but peaceful these days. Lili's bones had shifted, and she needed surgery. She had stopped telling me her friends' orthopedic-recovery stories and was withdrawn and in a constant state of unrest, partially from her discomfort, but more because her body craved exercise. One night, after struggling with a trigonometry problem, she threw her pencil against the wall. Pencils hadn't flown in our home since she was in the seventh grade. The pencils I could live with, but Lili's sullen silences were new, and when they hit, they knocked me on my rear. I'd have done anything to make her feel better, so I spoiled her with designer cupcakes, an iPhone, and an expensive little Coach purse she didn't even want.

Felix scheduled Lili's operation for the week after Rosh Hashanah. We were all counting down the days until she healed enough to start running again. I missed my old Lili, and I missed her friends sprawled out on our couches, texting and eating the collection of snacks I'd so carefully curated. Lili hadn't invited anyone over since the night of her injury. The house was deadly quiet, and I hated it.

My only refuge was my classroom, even though I had a biter, along with two boys who were exhibiting signs of a spectrum disorder, and our class hamster, Buttons, had suffered an untimely death. For the first time since I had Lili, I'd been lingering after school, chatting with Sarah and Theresa about the kids.

The morning before the first night of Rosh Hashanah, Lili's mood miraculously lifted. She stopped fidgeting and laughed at two of Sam's corny jokes. We felt lighter as we prepared for the holiday and the arrival of Sam's parents. Unlike many of my friends, I treasured my in-laws' company. Sam's brother, Paul, had never married or had children, so Lili and I received second helpings of his mother's affections. Rose brought us gift bags filled with travel-size moisturizers and trendy hair accessories, and when we visited Deerfield, she showed us off to her friends, who had known Sam since he was in diapers. Rose's shameless bragging embarrassed Sam, and sometimes Lili, but I bathed in the warmth of her spotlight, and when she had her hip replacement last winter, I happily flew down to Miami and took care of her for a week.

Lili helped me cut up melons, wash strawberries, peel oranges, and quarter grapes. Shortly before Rose and Artie were scheduled to arrive, I phoned my mother. I'd called her twice since Mrs. Kessler's tahara, but we'd gone back to our old conversations, which she kept too brief for me to discern much about the state of her memory.

"Happy New Year," I said.

She paused for a second. "Happy New Year to you."

"Have you packed for your big trip?" My mother had signed up for a senior women's bus tour of Washington DC and Philadelphia. I'd wondered about her ability to handle the trip, but the tour company was taking care of every detail.

"Oh, I decided not to go."

"But you were looking forward to it." My mother was practically a George Washington scholar.

"I know, but I can't leave my tomato plants for that long."

Yet she had no problem leaving Neil and me for good. Stop it, I scolded myself.

"Can't Greg look in on your plants?" Greg Gein was a widower who owned a Kinko's franchise and lived next door to my mother. He'd succumbed to her charms and made sure her driveway was shoveled, her gutters cleared of leaves, and her garbage disposal kept in working order.

"I'll visit Monticello this winter. It will be a good break from the cold."

"You mean Mount Vernon." It wasn't like her to confuse her historical sites, especially ones that pertained to U.S. presidents.

"I said Mount Vernon, darling." She spoke with enough authority for me to question whether I'd misheard her.

I changed the subject. "Neil's coming over to celebrate," I said with a pang of guilt. Her loneliness was a result of her choice to isolate herself, I rationalized, but I still felt rotten. For years, we'd engaged in this dance where she'd pretend that she was too busy to visit even if the holiday fell on a weekend, and I'd feign disappointment.

"How lovely, is there a special occasion?" She was officially disoriented.

The relief I'd been enjoying from Lili's good spirits vanished. "Rosh Hashanah."

"Of course, silly me. What time is Norman coming?"

Norman was her late brother, whom she never spoke of. My fingers tightened around the receiver. "Norman?"

"Is he feeling up to it?" She sounded more sure of herself when she was drifting into the past.

"Do you mean Neil?"

Now she changed the subject, telling me that Greg's schnauzer had died. After we exhausted our short list of safe topics, I handed the phone to Lili.

"Happy New Year, Grandma," she said politely, and after a few minutes of stiff conversation handed the phone back to me. "She wants to talk to you again," Lili whispered.

"Mom?" I said.

"Happy New Year, Sweet B." She sounded like she was trying to prove something to me by remembering Rosh Hashanah, but she hadn't called me by my nickname since I was eighteen. It still made me melt.

A few minutes later, Rose and Artie's Buick pulled into the driveway—Artie only bought American cars—and Lili grabbed her crutches and limped outside to greet them. The kitchen window was open, and I could hear Rose fussing over Lili's ankle and Lili reassuring "Grose," a nickname resulting from Lili's inability to pronounce "Grandma Rose" when she was a baby. Then Sam pulled up and hugged them all. He knew better than to retrieve his parents' luggage from the trunk. Artie was a proud man who worked out with a trainer twice a week and was still perfectly capable of carrying his own luggage, thank you very much. Rose looked terrific, too, in sleek black slacks she'd had shortened and taken in slightly across the hips—"because properly fitted clothes really do make you look put together"—and a slenderizing black sweater with a V-neck to minimize her large breasts. "You're lucky you have those little knishes, big breasts make you look heavy," she told me the first time she saw me in a bathing suit. Her eyebrows had been professionally tweezed into a perfect arch, and she'd expertly fleshed out the thinning outer ridges with a pencil.

When she came into the kitchen, I put my arm around her and kissed her cheek. "I'm so glad you're here," I said. And I was. Her love nourished me.

"Me too, sweetheart. Me too." She put a large shopping bag on the table and pulled out a pan covered in foil. "I made a new noodle kugel recipe. Six points per slice, not that you need to concern yourself with such things."

She lowered her voice and patted her tummy. Rose had joined Weight Watchers in the mid-1980s after her mother told her that she looked like she'd been "eating yeast" and had since built up an SRO crowd at her Monday morning meetings.

"We all have our demons," I said, perversely pondering what Rose would do if she discovered mine.

Lili returned to the kitchen with an impish smile. "Newsflash! Grandpa Artie told me that Dora Perlstein's granddaughter came home from college with an emerald stud in her eyebrow."

"Your grandpa wasn't too crazy about that idea, was he?" Rose winked at Lili.

"How do you think I'd look with a little emerald, Grose?" Lili teased, pointing to her nostril.

Rose, one of the few people shorter than me, reached up to Lili's chin, angled her face to the side, and studied her closely. "You're more of a sapphire girl, aren't you?"

Lili's phone buzzed, and she pulled it out of her pocket and read a text.

"Lili, your grandmother is talking to you," I said.

Her thumbs moved furiously across the screen. "Just let me answer this text."

I was annoyed but also happy to see her engaged with her friends.

"It's Taylor. She wants me to come over later tonight. Can I?"

"No, Lili. It's Rosh Hashanah."

"When I was Lili's age, I always wanted to go off with my girlfriends, too," Rose said.

"Grose says it's okay." It wasn't like Lili to push.

"Let it go, Lil," I said as nicely as I could. I was about to take the chicken out of the oven when Jenny, Neil, and their son Ethan arrived with a platter of homemade brownies and some chopped liver from Benji's. It was hot out, and sweat beaded on the top of Neil's head, his baldness a genetic misfortune he addressed by keeping himself so fit that he looked younger than I.

I hugged Jenny hard. I was grateful that Neil had had the good sense to marry her and break his pattern of falling in love with women who needed rescuing. They were all petite and pale, and he found their helplessness and infidelity irresistible. Sheri Jacobstein's shrink would have said that he was dating our mother over and over again. Sheri's shrink might have pointed out that Neil had rescued me, too, and she would have been right. After my mother left, he appointed himself my friend and protector.

"Your hair looks great," I said to Jenny. She had lustrous locks that she colored at home. Tonight, she was a honey blond.

"I don't know, I think my eyebrows are too dark for this color," she said. "Are people going to wonder if the drapes match the carpet?"

I laughed. "You're terrible."

"The red looked better, dear." Rose said, missing Jenny's lewd joke.

Jenny slung an arm around Rose, who fit right under her armpit. "I love this woman."

Rose was fond of Jenny, too. It was hard to resist Tell It Like It Is Jenny, a nickname she'd given herself. Nobody ever described her as sweet, as they did me, but truth be told, she clobbered me in the nice department. She knew about my complicated relationship with my mother. Her own mother had died a few weeks after she met Neil, and she frequently told me how grateful she was for the chance to spend time with mine, an arrangement that worked well for all parties, or so I told myself.

We gathered around the table. Rose had purchased two round challahs, but we didn't bless the bread or the wine. This was a more secular celebration, to which Neil and I had adapted. Still, it always felt as strange to me to take the first sip of wine or dive into the challah without a prayer as it had to attend cross-country meets on Friday nights. When Lili was in preschool and kindergarten, we lit candles every Friday and blessed the challah, the wine, and our daughter. Slowly, we began choosing races and dinners with Sam's clients over Shabbos, until it felt like an enormous effort to rally the troops. Every Friday, I felt an ache when the scent of challah wafted down the halls of the preschool, and I was grateful to teach my students about the holidays, to keep to the faint beat of the Jewish calendar.

As Jenny and Rose helped me refill platters, I caught snippets of a discussion about President Obama's ability to resuscitate the economy. The conversation heated up when Artie, a single-issue voter who had supported Bush because he thought him "better for the Jews," argued with Neil and Sam over whether Netanyahu should freeze settlements on the West Bank.

At the other end of the table, Ethan, the youngest of Neil's three sons, was entertaining Lili with a story about one of his fraternity escapades. Lili would have loved a sibling, but my uterus had ruptured during her delivery. I was crushed. I'd assumed we'd fill our house with children, maybe as many as four. I wanted a loud, bustling house. The most painful time was when friends I'd made through Lili started having their second and third kids. Sam and I had discussed either using a surrogate or adopting. He was willing to do anything I wanted, but in the end we decided against having a second child. I told myself I was happy because I had Lili and fourteen little munchkins to take care of every day, and you had to take the lemons God gave you and make lemonade. Besides, until recently, there had been no shortage of kids or noise in our house.

I stacked plates and motioned for Neil to follow me into the kitchen. We'd been missing each other's calls, and I needed a dose of him about now. "You've got KP duty tonight, big brother."

He got up from his chair and followed me. "Lili seems in good spirits," he said.

I ran the warm water and began washing while he dried. "She is tonight. May it continue." I crossed my fingers.

He crossed his fingers too. Neil was Lili's biggest fan. He called her after every meet for a stride-by-stride account of her race.

"How's Big Al?" I asked. Jenny's father, Al, was a hulking, broad-shouldered man with a booming voice like hers. He'd entered the final stages of lung cancer and now weighed less than she did.

"Sliding downhill at warp speed. He doesn't have long."

"God, that was fast. I'm so sorry."

"Hard when your only parent gets sick." He picked up the challah plate and swiped his towel over it.

"I talked to Mom before you came over," I said.

His jaw tensed. "So you know she canceled her tour."

"Probably a good thing."

"Probably."

Neil and I knew that our mother was not the type to be herded by a chirpy guide or endure countless dinner conversations with widows and divorcees who would be seduced by her stubborn beauty and interest in their lives. Unwilling to divulge anything about herself, she'd steal away to read her historical fiction and biographies of dead presidents, which would only make them vie for her attention more, but we both knew that she hadn't canceled the trip because she couldn't handle traveling with a group.

"Neil, she's not...." I searched for the word. "Herself."

"I know."

"She thought you were Norman." I could barely speak his name. Any mention of my uncle had always been taboo in our house.

"She calls me Norman all the time now."

"What does she say?" My mother's secrets still had a power over me.

"Asks me how I'm feeling, obsessively. Tells me she misses me." He shrugged. My mother was never the gushy type.

"That's weird." I told him about her instructing me to cover my head for Mrs. Kessler's funeral.

He put down a dish and stared at me. "Mrs. Kessler?"

"Long story."

"Your teacher?"

"Yes, but we can talk about that later."

"Her test results came back this afternoon," he said, concentrating on the soap cascading down a blue and yellow ceramic platter Rose had brought us from Madrid.

"Whose test results?" Lili asked. Neither Neil nor I had heard her enter the kitchen. Even with her bum ankle, she moved like a cat and often startled me with her sudden appearances.

Neil turned off the water and looked her in the eye. "Your mom and I were talking about your grandma."

"Is she okay?" Lili asked as she grabbed two of Jenny's brownies.

"She's having some memory issues, sweetie," Neil said.

"We're sorting it out," I added, using the royal "we," though I hadn't made a single phone call to her doctor.

Lili's eyes traveled from Neil to me. She looked as though she was going to ask a follow-up question, but instead she took a bite of brownie. "Man, Aunt Jenny rocks the brownie," she said, grabbing another one. "For Ethan," she told us through a mouthful of chocolate, and left the room.

I looked at Neil, my heart racing. "And? What did the results say?"

"The cholesterol medication is not the culprit."

"Then what is it?"

"Alzheimer's, dementia maybe. They don't know for sure yet, but she can't live alone."

I scrubbed brisket detritus off the bottom of the Pyrex dish until I was able to ask, "Can't Greg help her out?"

"She needs more care than a helpful neighbor can provide." I glanced at Neil and saw my father's face, the long upper lip and almond-shaped eyes. "I'm going to bring her here. I'm driving up after services tomorrow."

I felt as if he'd dropped a bookshelf on my chest. By the time Rosh Hashanah ended, my mother and I would be living in the same city for the first time in more than thirty years. I didn't like to consider that Neil wasn't just my protector, he was my mother's too. I was acting like a big baby, but I couldn't help it. During the early days of our exile from the Schines' shul, it had been Neil and me against the world, an alliance I counted on.

"Are you going to say something?" His tone was gentle.

"I ... time for dessert." After dinner, I settled Rose and Artie in the guest room and pretended to read. Last month, I'd been enthusiastic about my book club's pick, the story of a woman who travels through Africa in search of herself. Now her navel-gazing annoyed me.

Sam turned off the light. "Let's get some shut-eye, honey."

"Can't."

"What's up?" He held his arm out and I nestled against him.

"Neil is moving my mother here," I said.

He stroked my back. "We'll figure it all out."

"I wish I had your confidence." We were slipping back into our default pattern, where he consoled and I questioned.

I rolled over, and he stroked my thigh the way I liked. I kissed him, and he moved his hand over my belly and under the elastic of my pajama bottoms. I wiggled out of them and pulled off his boxers. "Come here," I said.

"Let me touch you." Sam was a considerate and efficient lover.

"Tonight I just want you close to me," I said, pulling him on top of me and inside of me, hoping he could travel up through my pelvis, belly, lungs, to caress my heart.

When we were done, he tried again to touch me, but I held his hand in mine until he told me that he loved me and drifted off to sleep.

I lay awake, imagining my mother in her house in Steven's Point, alone and scared and smoking in one of her silk bathrobes even though she quit years ago. I pictured the crisp white kitchen curtains unwashed and dingy from her cigarette smoke, the Oriental rugs that I now knew to be authentic stained with mud from her gardening boots, and her guest bathroom devoid of the lavender-scented soaps in the shapes of roses and seashells.

The next morning, we piled into Sam's Suburban and chatted breezily during our short drive to Temple Micah. We rarely went to services beyond the High Holidays. Sam and Lili were too antsy, and I'd never quite gotten over feeling like an outsider here. Nevertheless, we still couldn't walk two feet without running into a student, parent, client, or friend. Sam led us to our seats as if he were the president walking down the aisle of the congressional chamber on his way to deliver his first State of the Union address.

"He wasn't voted Deerfield High's Most Likely to Succeed for nothing," Rose kvelled audibly as she observed this outpouring of affection for her son. Sam's brother had never quite launched, and so Sam carried the burden of being Rose and Artie's golden boy, and in turn the quiet assumption that he would serve that role in every arena of his life. He did not disappoint.

We approached Sheri and her family. Sheri used to joke about Lili marrying one of her two sons, but I couldn't see her with either of them. Lili had had only one boyfriend, and she liked him because he was "out of the box." Last year for Valentine's Day he wrote an acrostic poem using her full name—Lili Rebecca Blumfield—and baked her a red velvet cake.

Sheri kissed everyone and motioned me to sit in the empty aisle seat next to her. "What do you think of the dress?" she whispered.

I examined the dress she'd bought at Anthropologie during one of our shopping trips last July. "Fantastic."

She patted her stomach. "Looks much better with the Spanx."

I loved Sheri. She'd given me no choice, with her humor and her persistent generosity and attention to our friendship.

"Hey, Debbie said you didn't respond to her evite to the break fast."

"Right, right. I'll do it later." For the past ten years, we'd been attending the same Yom Kippur break fast, consisting of friends we'd met through Sheri. We rotated hosting. I nodded toward my family, settling into their seats a few rows over, and got up to join them. "I better go."

If Sheri had her way we'd spend the entire service gossiping. Unlike the arrangement at the Schines' shul, here we sat in plain view of the rabbi, whom I saw every day in the parking lot, and I felt self-conscious if I didn't pay attention.

I walked down the aisle and slid into my open seat, with Lili between Sam and me. She'd had a bat mitzvah, so she knew to turn the pages at all the right places and inch toward the aisle when the cantor approached us so she could kiss the Torah with her prayer book. During the rabbi's sermon, she sidled up against me. The hypnotic sensation I'd felt during Mrs. Kessler's tahara returned, ferrying me back to the women's section of the Schines' sanctuary, where my mother would put her pearls against my cheek and bring them to her lips the way the men kissed the Torah with the stringy fringes of their prayer shawls.

I draped my hand over Lili's wrist, and her pulse beat against the tips of my fingers as I tried not to think about what made me uncomfortable about Temple Micah: women wearing sleeveless blouses to services, the ark designed by an elite New York artist, and the cantor's operatic treatment of the melodies. Today I succumbed to my longing for the wailing cantors and familiar melodies of the Schines' shul.

Our handsome, clean-shaven rabbi invited congregants to Doctor's Park to join him for Tashlich, the ritual of casting bread symbolic of our sins into the water. Rabbi Schine used to take us to Atwater Beach, where the odd sunbather would stare at his black hat and payis, the forelocks he curled up and bobby-pinned to his temples. "We throw our sins into a body of water containing fish. A net can catch a fish as unexpectedly as a sin can catch you," he told me before I knew what a real sin looked like.

Just before Lili pulled away from me, Mr. Rosen blew the shofar, the rich cry from the ram's horn that reverberated through our bodies with such force and wholeness that I wondered if my mother, miles away, felt it too.

8

My mother arrived in town a few days before Lili's surgery. The plan was that she would stay with Neil and Jenny until a bed opened up at Lakeline Assisted Living, a facility located only a few miles from both of our houses. This arrangement could last for days or months.

Neil phoned to check in while Lili was in surgery. I told him that I was a wreck about her undergoing anesthesia. Sam had lost feeling in his legs for three days after a routine hernia operation.

"Please distract me. How's Mom?" I thought of the old joke about getting rid of a stomachache by having someone clock you on the head.

"Disoriented from the move. And...." He was hiding something from me. "What?" I asked anxiously.

"Big Al is in hospice." He sounded overwhelmed.

"How's Jenny?"

"Not good."

In the short silence that hung between us, I could practically hear him trying to form the question that neither one of us wanted him to ask.

"I'll wait until Lili is home from the hospital, but then I want you to take Mom while Jenny and I say goodbye to her father." Without seeing him, I knew he was thrusting his tongue into his cheek, as he did when he was nervous.

"You're kidding, right?" My voice was shrill. I felt as though I was trying to get to the finish line of a marathon and he was asking me for a piggyback ride.

"No, I'm not."

"Neil, I kind of have my hands full over here. Lili is in surgery this very second."

"Guess what, Barbara. So do I," he snapped. We hadn't fought like this since we were kids.

"Okay, Neil. Okay."

"The world doesn't revolve around your drama with Mom."

His words were an openhanded slap across my face. Neil had always understood how my mother's antics affected me, and his admonishment made me feel like I'd been a big whiner all along.

"Sorry, that was shitty," he said.

"Shitty, but true." These days, my relationships with pretty much everyone felt off, and I couldn't afford to be at odds with Neil of all people.

"I better let you go. Give Lili a hug."

"Okay," I mumbled as I pondered the possibility of taking on my mother's care. I'd been an excellent nurse to Rose, and I certainly had experience with fixing my mother scrambled eggs and toast on trays and checking on her when it got too quiet so I could put out her cigarette in case she'd dozed off mid-puff. Once she almost burned the house down. But I was a little older than Lili when I'd last taken care of her, and neither Neil nor the rebbetzin had the right to expect this of me, particularly now. Or maybe Neil did. He'd carried the bulk of my mother's care for years. I couldn't think straight.

"What was that all about?" Sam asked.

I rubbed my forehead and sighed. "I'll tell you later. Let's see what Felix has to say."

Felix was walking toward us in his scrubs, smiling. I teared up when he told me that everything had gone well and that Lili had handled the anesthesia like a champ. We followed him to the recovery room, where we found Lili with her hands folded neatly over her lap, her ankle wrapped in layers of gauze and bandages. She gave us a woozy smile.

"Hi, Mommy," she said, slurring her words.

"Hi, baby. You did great." I tapped her good knee a little too hard.

"Ouch." She flinched. She wasn't paralyzed, thank God.

Sam and I sat on the chairs next to her bed.

Lili patted her stomach. "I'm starving."

"No solids for a while. Do you want me to get you some juice?" Sam asked.

Sam had talked Felix into keeping her overnight so she could be monitored for any ill effects from the anesthesia. Usually he talked me out of my fears, but given his experience, he'd felt cautious, too. Lili was assigned to a private room, and we all watched *Mama Mia!* on TV. I tried to concentrate on Meryl Streep's love triangle, but my conversation with Neil gnawed at me, and I couldn't get comfortable in the room, in my chair, in my skin. The letter from the rebbetzin had unearthed my relentless desire for my mother to show up, to comfort me in the aftermath of Mrs. Kessler's death, and now to arrive in this hospital room and tell me that Lili would return to her old self in no time.

Longing for my mother was a dangerous business. The last time I'd fully submitted to it, I was in the midst of delivering Lili, losing pints of blood and then my womb. I called out my mother's name, from instinct and memory. She came.

She took the bus from Steven's Point and arrived at the hospital with a pale yellow baby blanket she'd knitted. My head was fuzzy from the Percocet, and I almost pinched her to make sure she was real. When she asked Sam if he'd like to go home and clean up and get some clothes, he looked at me tentatively, and I nodded that it was okay. Enough time had passed. Abracadabra, she morphed into the mother who'd once known to bring me a lozenge before I told her that my throat hurt and who'd called the principal after she heard that the playground bully had shoved sand up my nose.

She held a straw to my lips while I took small sips of water. I drifted in and out of a hazy slumber, periodically flinging open my eyes to see if she was still there. She swaddled Lili in the yellow blanket, and my baby girl curled into her grandmother's boyish torso as if it were a bassinet custom made for her. "She looks just like you did, Sweet B," my mother murmured. For a second, I was her Sweet B, warm and safe in her slender arms.

"I'm glad you're here," I said, and she responded by kissing me on the forehead. She still bathed in lavender but no longer smelled of cigarettes.

My mother slipped out while I dozed off. That night I started hemorrhaging and asked Sam to call her. She promised him she'd be there in a few minutes.

She never showed.

The next morning Neil visited me, but he couldn't look at me as he told me that he'd just dropped our mother off at the Badger Bus depot, that she feared she was catching a bug and didn't want to get the baby sick. She'd call me later, he promised, fussing with the zipper on his windbreaker. She didn't call. I was finally done. Well, almost. I called her the first time Lili spiked a fever but hung up after a few rings. And maybe a few times after that, too.

A month later, I joined a Mommy and Me group, and in the musty basement of a church, over banana bread and bottled water, we shared war stories about our birthing experiences. I didn't mention the blood transfusions or my ruptured uterus; instead, I told the story of my mother standing me up in the hospital. I told it slow and cold.

My tale prompted other women to tell far worse tales of their mothers' transgressions. The raw anger and sadness in their voices stirred me, and the ultimate war story about my mother bubbled up from a place deep inside, to my tongue and lips. I opened my mouth but stopped short when I noticed that our babies were suckling, drinking in breast milk tainted with bitterness. I didn't want that for Lili.

I unlatched my baby from my nipple, held her close, and promised that I wouldn't deny her a relationship with her grandmother, no matter what. I'd always desperately wanted a grandmother. I also vowed never to tell my war stories. I'd been using them to shield myself from the temptation of letting my mother back inside. My shield was losing its armor. Now here I stood on the lip of the mikveh, my hatless mother slipping, slipping, and me both wanting her to steady me and wanting to follow her into the waters.

"Look, Mom, it's your favorite part," Lili said, returning me to the present.

Meryl Streep was singing about time slipping through her fingers as she combed Amanda Seyfried's hair, as my mother had combed mine, as I had combed Lili's. Crap. Tears gushed from my eyes.

Sam looked over at Lili, and they both laughed at my sappiness.

"I've got a few years until I flee the island, Mom," Lili said as Sam handed me a tissue.

Out of solidarity, we ate bad hospital food with Lili. From the way Sam was fondling his Blackberry, I could tell he was itchy to tend to a client who had been hectoring him all day. I waited for Lili to fall asleep, and then I grabbed my purse and pulled him out into the hall to talk.

"What's up?" Sam asked.

"Big Al is in hospice."

He put his Blackberry back in his pocket and gave me his full attention.

"Jenny's going to need to go to St. Paul to see him and my mother will—"

He pulled his phone out and started scrolling through his address list.

"Sam, what are you doing?"

"I have a client who owns a nursing home. He'll give us the name of someone to stay with your mom at Neil's."

Typical Sam. Pull out the phone and find the right people for the job.

I put my hand over his screen. "No, sweetie. I can't do that."

"What does that mean?"

"It means that my mother is going to stay with us."

He looked baffled. "But what about Lili? She's going to need care."

"I can handle it."

"Barbara," he said tentatively.

"I can, Sam. Trust me." I could do this for Neil. *The world doesn't revolve around your drama with Mom.* I didn't want to be that person My quivering lip betrayed me.

"Honey, I'm not so sure."

"Maybe it's a good idea to pop over to Neil's, give Jenny a hug, and assess the damage." His phone was vibrating, and I felt guilty leaving him here. "Are you okay with that?"

"Go. Lili's asleep, and I've got my laptop."

I didn't want to leave Lili, and I was half hoping that he'd beg me to stay. He would support me doing whatever it took to regain my bearings. "Okay, you hold down the fort then."

I kissed him and then walked down the corridor before I changed my mind. When I got out of the elevator, I heard someone call my name.

"My God, you walk fast. Didn't you hear me shouting my lungs out?" Dawn Travinski said breathlessly.

"I'm sorry, I'm a little spacey."

"Here, let me walk you out. How's Lili?"

"Hanging in there." I smiled.

"Such a bummer about that ankle." Dawn studied me.

"How's Megan? I miss that girl." I missed the girls, all so busy with cross-country practices and meets. I missed their backpacks lined up neatly in the hall and their laughter coming from the family room. I missed shopping for their favorite treats. Megan loved to dip Wheat Thins in salsa, Kara liked applesauce of all things, and Brooke was always foraging for something sweet. The list went on.

"She misses you too." Dawn looked away. "And of course Lili."

I rolled my eyes. "Yes, I'm hoping Lili loses interest in that Taylor Miller soon."

Dawn said nothing for a few seconds and then she touched my arm. Her kindness startled me, and I blurted, "My mom just moved here."

"Just in time to give you a hand with Lili, eh?"

I laughed aloud at the notion of my mother cooking meals or fussing over Lili's injury.

Dawn looked puzzled. Her mom, also a nurse, and a spark plug of a woman, stayed with her for two weeks after she had a hysterectomy.

"I'm sorry. I don't know why I laughed, because there's nothing funny about my mother right now."

Dawn reached behind her head, split the hair in her ponytail in half, and tugged. Megan tightened her ponytail the exact same way. They looked so much alike with their inky black hair and matching crossbites.

"My mom's sick," I said.

"Oh, shit. When it rains, it pours. I'm sorry."

Dawn's compassion made me want to cry, but I resisted the urge to unload on her. She was probably on a well-deserved break. "I'm going to my brother's to see her for a second."

"That will make you feel better."

"Can you check in on Lili?" I asked.

"Done."

"And Sam?"

"Double done."

I thanked her, though I preferred being the one who pitched in by picking up extra carpool duties or feeding Megan. We stood there for a few uncomfortable seconds before I went out to the parking lot.

When I got to Neil's house, he kissed me on the cheek, and I felt calmer. "You're here," he said.

"I'm here," I answered, absorbing the slight awkwardness between us.

"How's Lili?"

"Sleeping."

"Jenny took Mom to Kohl's to pick up a few things. They'll be back soon."

I pictured the two of them filling a basket with cottage cheese and canned pears, if she still ate that every morning for breakfast. "I don't have much time."

"It's Alzheimer's," he said loudly, as if I were standing in the next room.

A surge of panic ripped through my body. "How long has she had it?"

"I don't know. She covered it up pretty well for a while, but she's deteriorating at warp speed."

Neil rubbed his hand along the back of his neck, disappeared into the kitchen, and returned with a glossy brochure for Lakeline Assisted Living. He let the brochure drop on the coffee table. I told him that whatever he and Jenny had picked would be fine, but I didn't mean it. My mother had been my responsibility when she had her breakdown, and I was irrationally put out that he and Jenny were taking charge.

I heard the front door open and Jenny tell my mother that I was here for a visit.

"Oh, Barbara's here for a visit," my mother repeated.

I met them in the hallway. Her cheeks were rosy from the crisp air, but she'd stopped coloring her hair, and gray helmeted her skull, the remaining auburn fringing around her earlobes.

She sat down on the couch with her coat on.

I embraced Jenny and spoke into her hair. "Neil told me about Big Al. You okay?"

She shrugged her shoulders. "Not really."

My mother looked at us, bewildered.

"Here, Mom. Let me take that for you," Jenny said, helping my mother out of her coat. It had never bugged me to hear Jenny call her "Mom" until now.

"No thank you, darling. I'm cold."

I sat down a few cushions away from my mother, and Neil turned off the Brewers game he'd been watching.

"How's Lili doing?" Jenny asked.

"She'll be okay. I'm going to need to get back to her in a sec," I said.

"Lili's in the hospital. She had ankle surgery," Neil explained to my mother.

"Oh, she's in the hospital," my mother repeated carefully. She wrinkled her nose. "I'm not one for hospitals."

"Because of the appendicitis attack?" Neil asked.

I felt like we were kids sitting around the Shabbos table or at one of my mother's teas, waiting for her to tell one of the recruits her moving story of meeting the Schines in the hospital after her appendicitis attack.

She looked at Neil blankly. "Appendicitis?"

"When the Schines came to see you in the hospital and they took care of you, Mom," I prodded.

She looked back and forth at Neil and me, like a lost little girl we'd found in a shopping mall. "You must be confusing me with Dad. He had his appendix out."

My mother had told her appendicitis story to every recruit we'd ever hosted. Neil and I glanced at each other, and I was both scared by my mother's confusion and grateful that I had a brother to confirm the facts of our childhood.

"Lili should soak those legs. It will make the world of difference," she said with great authority.

"Thanks, Mom. That's good advice," I said.

"It sure is. Isn't that right, Norman?"

"Right, Mom," Neil said.

"All this talk of Lili. How are *you*?" I asked her.

"How am *I*?" She put her tongue over the top of her upper lip as she'd done when she was threading a needle or removing a splinter from my big toe. Then she looked at me, and her eyes clouded.

I looked away, too frozen to act on my Pavlovian impulse to

jump in and either answer or divert the question, to be that girl in the Schines' pantry who'd pointed out her mother's smeared lipstick.

Jenny came to her rescue instead. "She's doing just great. We've been getting some big shopping done, and we went to feed the ducks today."

"Oh yes, the ducks." My mother clapped her hands together.

"Well, Lili will be happy to see you after she gets better," I offered.

"I hope you don't mind, but all this fresh air has worn me out." She got up and started walking in the opposite direction from the guest room.

Again I felt the strong drive to cover for her. Jenny rose and went to her. "Here, Mom. Let me take your coat before you go to bed."

My mother turned around to face us, her eyes revealing her gratitude that she'd been spared the embarrassment of getting lost in her son's house. "Sleep tight, chickens." She bade Neil and me her old goodnight. He looked over at me, and I could see that his eyes were starting to water. No doubt he too was remembering how we'd waited for our mother in our beds, all cozy in our Dr. Denton pajamas. She'd ask us if we'd brushed our teeth, and if she wasn't too tired, she'd make up a story about an orphan named Birdie.

My mother unbuttoned her coat slowly, revealing the pale pink cardigan I hadn't seen since she left us. The delicate wool had pilled, and a long thin coffee stain paralleled a row of mother-of-pearl buttons.

I was back in the hospital within an hour. Lili was snoring, and Sam had muted the television and was staring blankly at a closed-captioned news report about Roman Polanski's arrest in Switzerland for an old charge of sex with a minor.

"What a creep," I muttered, and sat down next to Sam.

"Yeah," he said, dazed. He pointed to an enormous bouquet

of stargazer lilies. "Sheri."

"They're gorgeous," I said. I loved Sheri.

"She wants you to call her when you come up for air."

I walked over to the flowers. Their odor was strong and sweet, like Sheri. "Did you tell her where I was?"

"Yeah." He rubbed his eyes. "Jenny okay?"

"She's tough," I said, avoiding mention of my mother.

"I'm glad you're back."

"Did Lili wake up?"

"Nope." He got up to leave. "You snuck out without getting caught."

I felt as though he was comparing my outing to my mother's late-night adventures with the Shabbos goy. But he wasn't. He knew nothing about the Shabbos goy or the hazy force drawing and repelling me from my mother right now.

9

Big Al died in his sleep. The morning of Lili's release from the hospital, Neil called to tell me that he and Jenny were taking the next flight to St. Paul. While Sam checked Lili out of the hospital, I picked up my mother. The rebbetzin's words had been prescient. My mother's care had in fact fallen on me, albeit temporarily.

Neil's kitchen smelled like coffee and hair dye. My mother was leaning over the sink in a stained smock while Jenny sprayed her scalp with one hand and rubbed dye out of her hair with the other.

"Hey, you." I slung my arm around Jenny's shoulder and pulled her toward me. "I'm so sorry about your dad."

"Is that Barbara?" my mother called over the running water, her head facing the drain.

"Hi, Mom," I said. "Shouldn't you be getting ready to leave?" I asked Jenny.

"Soon," she said, massaging my mother's scalp with shampoo. The steady movements of Jenny's hands mesmerized me. When she finished, she blotted moisture from my mother's hair with a towel. "Ta-dah!"

My mother looked like Lucille Ball with a bad haircut. "I'm speechless," I muttered.

"Go take a peek." Jenny directed my mom to the hallway mirror and turned to me with a look that said, "I tried."

I bit my tongue. My mother was going to be upset when she

saw her hair. When Revlon modified Dark Auburn 31, she had tried four different rinses before finding the right color. So now, in the midst of taking care of Lili, I would either have to run out to Walgreens, find another dye, and redo her hair, or take her to the salon. My mother returned to the kitchen with a grin. "It's perfect."

Now I knew we were in trouble. "I think we're ready, then," she said brightly.

"Mom, you might want to give Jenny back her smock," Neil said as he entered the kitchen with my mother's suitcase.

She looked down at the blue floral polyester and laughed. "Silly me."

I gave Jenny a bear hug as Neil led our mother out to my car and settled her in.

"We'll be back in two days," he said.

"You take care of your wife." I kissed his cheek.

I'd get through this. I'd mentally hunker down as I had for the Caribbean cruise we took to celebrate Rose and Artie's fiftieth wedding anniversary, though I knew beforehand that a vat of Bonine wouldn't stave off my motion sickness. Maybe I wasn't ready yet to assume my mother's care, but I'd worry about that later. For now, I just had to survive two days. One hour at a time.

Sam headed out to the office right after we arrived. I wish he'd given me a few minutes to check in on Theresa, which I'd been wanting to do all day. I knew she could handle the class, but I wanted to call her and hear her talk to me as if I were the guru she thought I was, and I wanted my mother to go back to Neil's house so I could go back to Theresa and my kids.

Lili looked up from the television when my mother and I walked into the den. "Hi, Grandma," she said, groggy from pain medication, a blanket I'd crocheted draped over her shoulders. It was unusual to see Lili so still. She was always moving—jiggling her leg, stretching, pacing—even when she was sitting down.

"Oh, look at your foot, all bandaged up. Does it hurt something awful?" my mother clucked.

"Uh-huh." Lili's glassy eyes lingered on my mother's hair.

I sat on the ottoman and fussed with the pillows under her ankle. "Let's get you elevated."

"What are you watching?" my mother asked.

"*Titanic*," Lili mumbled.

I heard a humming noise, probably the whiny motor from our neighbor's leaf blower, but it was coming from the direction of my mother's chair. I looked over at her, and she was indeed humming, bobbing her head, eyes closed, as if she were trying her hardest to recall something.

"Mom, you okay?" I asked.

She opened her mouth, and a song I'd learned at summer camp tumbled out of her. "It was sad when the great ship went down to the bottom of the sea ... fishes and turtles, little ladies lost their girdles...."

Lili stared at my mother, her eyes large as dessert plates. We let her finish singing.

My mother was the only person in our family who could carry a tune, and I remembered how she sang to me when I was a little girl. Her illness had stripped her of her inhibitions, made her much looser. Maybe these few days weren't going to be so rotten after all. Maybe there was an opening for all of us and she'd finally let us in. Maybe I'd let her in, too. "Now, that takes me back to a very long and bumpy bus ride," I said.

"You hated that camp," my mother said.

"What camp?" Lili tore her eyes away from Leonardo DiCaprio.

"It was a Jewish camp out in the cornfields, too Jappy for your mama."

My mother never used words like that. I laughed nervously. "I'm going to show Grandma to your room," I said to Lili, assuming that Sam had discussed the sleeping arrangements with her. Lili was going to sleep on the pullout couch in Sam's office to avoid the steps.

Lili shot me a look.

"Lili would rather I not," my mother said, a perfectly lucid observation she normally would have refrained from voicing.

"Well," I said, "Lili doesn't have a vote on this. She can't handle the steps yet." Besides I wanted my mother upstairs in case she wandered.

I settled my mother in Lili's room, and she told me to go tend to my daughter. She was tired and wanted to read her new biography of FDR. I was relieved that she could still enjoy this pleasure. She pulled her book out of her suitcase and opened it up to the first page. I went back downstairs.

"Mommy, it really hurts." Lili pointed to her ankle. She had an enormous pain threshold, which was what made her such a promising endurance runner.

I sat down next to her, and she rested her head on my shoulder.

"Forty more minutes, and I can give you another Vicodin," I said.

"Good."

I could feel her eyelashes brush against my skin.

"Grandma's kind of funny this way, not so ice princessy."

"We should probably cut your grandmother a little slack right now. She was diagnosed with Alzheimer's, Lil."

"I figured," she said, picking up her head from my shoulder.

"So what do you think?" I tucked a strand of her hair behind her ear.

"That's sad."

"It's okay for you to be sad."

"I said it's sad that she's sick, but I'm not sad, because I don't really know her. Is that okay?"

No, it's not okay, and I don't know her either, I wanted to say. "It's okay, but we can wish it were different."

Titanic was over. Lili started punching buttons on the remote, and I got up and made grilled cheese sandwiches for lunch. I called up to my mother, and the three of us ate them on trays in front of the television. Lili had found a documentary about the Spanish-American War on the History Channel, a network she'd begun watching after Sam and I designated it the only television we'd allow. Now she trounced both of us in the history category of Trivial Pursuit.

My mother watched intently, and when a commercial came on, she said, "They'll talk about the Treaty of Paris next, you watch."

Lili and I looked at each other.

My mother clapped her hands together three times. "It's how we came to acquire the Philippines, Guam, and Puerto Rico, ladies."

Lili grinned for the first time since she'd been home. "That's the treaty that ended the Spanish-American War, Mom."

They started to chat easily about William McKinley and William Jennings Bryan and their opposing views on acquiring the Philippines, and I remembered the last time I'd seen them enjoy each other. My mother had visited a few months before Lili was diagnosed with ADHD along with a slight amorphous learning disability that made reading and writing difficult for her. Sam, Neil, and the boys were watching a Packers game in the den, and Jenny and I were slicing bagels in the kitchen. When the food was ready, I found Lili and my mother huddled together on the sofa with a soft tan leather scrapbook, a gift from my mother, straddling their laps. They were inspecting the empty pages as if they were silently mapping out the placement of Lili's mementos and photos. A mix of jealousy and longing ripped through me as I remembered what it felt like to languish in the warmth of my mother's undivided attention. Lili startled her by kissing her cheek, and I turned around quickly, pretending that I didn't see the surprise on my mother's face. After the brunch, I found Lili in her room, sifting through a pile of ticket stubs, photos, newspaper clippings, and party favors she'd been collecting, as if she'd been waiting for this very scrapbook to appear.

Lili's tutor had encouraged her to continue creating collages, because they gave her a nonlinear outlet to order her thoughts and perceptions. "Lili's collages reflect her great gift, a 'subliminal awareness' of the people she cares about," the tutor wrote in her final evaluation letter. I didn't completely understand the term "subliminal awareness," but I was so proud of Lili's "great gift," particularly after watching her struggle with her schoolwork, that I'd neglected to give props to my mother, who had intuited Lili's need and filled it. My mother's scrapbook was the first of dozens Lili completed throughout the years. The memory made me feel like a canoe capsizing in rapids of love and regret.

I stared at the two of them, completely absorbed in the documentary. "You ladies sure know your history," I said. I waited for another commercial to tell Lili that her grandmother practically ran the history department up at the university.

My mother gazed at the television with a nostalgic smile. "I learned about all this when I typed up a paper on the Treaty of Paris for Norman in college."

She had to be talking about her brother, because when Neil was in college, she'd been too preoccupied with the Shabbos goy to pay attention to him.

"Who's Norman?" Lili asked.

"Your grandmother's brother," I said.

Lili looked baffled. "Norman? Where is he? Did he die?"

"Shhh, let's watch this part. I'm a big McKinley fan." My mother looked at Lili and pointed to the remote. "Will you turn it up, dear? I can't figure out these buttons."

Lili turned up the volume and mouthed to me, "Norman?"

I shrugged.

"You sure have a lot of secrets, Grandma," Lili said through a yawn, but her words chilled me. I couldn't tell if my mother was engrossed in the show or just hadn't heard Lili's comment, but either way, she remained the vault, and none of us, maybe including her, had the key to open the door.

I squeezed Lili's shoulder, got up and cleared the plates, and pulled the glossy Lakeline brochure from my purse. The photos featured old people visiting with younger versions of themselves, sipping iced tea on a lovely veranda at tables covered by blue and red umbrellas. A young girl I recognized as my former student Nancy Feinberg played checkers with one of the residents. Up until a few minutes ago, I couldn't imagine Lili casually playing checkers with my mother. I'd been so careful to make sure that my mother could never hurt Lili that I'd thwarted what might have blossomed between them.

Shortly after four, Theresa and Sarah knocked on the back door, carrying an aluminum pan covered in foil and a bouquet of Mylar balloons.

"I can't believe you two," I said as I let them into the house.

Theresa put the lasagna down on the kitchen table, and we went into the den. Sarah handed Lili the balloons.

Lili grinned again. "Oh my God, these have designs on them." She pulled each one toward her and examined it with glee.

Sarah sat down next to her. "You've probably outgrown Hello Kitty by now, but we couldn't help ourselves."

Theresa walked over to my mother, who was looking on with great interest. "Hello, Mrs. Pupnick, my name is Theresa. I'm your daughter's assistant teacher."

"Mom, this is Sarah, my boss and our fearless leader, and Theresa, my partner in crime."

Sarah piped in. "Your daughter is actually my boss. She runs the place."

"Well, she certainly is lucky to work with such generous people," my mom said.

"It's our pleasure. Barbara is always the first person to organize meals when people need it," Theresa said.

"Yeah, Mom, I'm a Brisket Lady," I blurted out before I could stop myself.

Everyone looked confused except my mother. She laughed, and I warmed at the notion of our sharing an inside joke.

"So, ladies, please tell me what happened today at school," I said.

They looked at each other. "You've got your hands full, we can talk about it later," Theresa said.

I knew what they were avoiding. "Ally Cooper?"

They nodded.

"I'll call her mom tonight." Ally had been teasing and hitting another little girl. If I hadn't been so preoccupied with Lili and my mother, I would have called Ally's mother this week as a preemptive strike. I'd observed Ally in the threes, and she was a different kid this year. Something was going on, and I would figure it out. Some people took apart cars or ham radios for a hobby. I liked figuring out the puzzle of a child like Ally.

Theresa looked relieved. "You know your daughter is a genius with kids, and parents too," she said to my mom.

"Well, she's been working in a preschool since she was...." My mother paused. "How old were you when you started with Mrs. Kessler?"

My mother's acknowledgment that we were a family with a real history and real memories filleted me. "Thirteen," I whispered.

"Well," Sarah said, slapping her knee, "that makes the rest of us mortals feel a little better!"

"Mom, you're a rock star," Lili said.

"Okay, enough of this," I said, but I didn't want Theresa and Sarah to leave and take their version of me with them.

We were all in good spirits when Sam came home. Minutes later, Megan and Kara knocked on the back door, their arms filled with flowers and shopping bags.

"Look at all of this," I said, hugging them. Megan had spent so much time in our house that she felt like a second daughter to me, and Kara, a serviceably pretty girl with a widow's peak and a perfect pug nose, had pulled Lili through algebra their freshman year. They made a beeline for the den, and Lili tore through the contents of the goody bags: DVDs, cookies, and a host of trashy magazines.

"Can Kara and Megan stay for dinner?" Lili asked.

Sam and I looked at each other. "You sure you're feeling well enough?" I said.

Lili nodded. She looked high from the Vicodin. What could it hurt? I was also relieved to see her having fun with her old friends.

A few minutes later, Taylor knocked on the back door, and I ignored Lili's slight shift in demeanor—a new self-consciousness perhaps—because the house was so full and loud and happy.

I heated up Theresa's lasagna and took out salad fixings from the fridge.

"Looks like we're having a party," my mother said as she walked into the kitchen. "Put me to work."

"Sure, you can give me a hand setting the table," I said.

She roamed around the island in the center of the room. Since she'd never offered to help me in the kitchen, she didn't know where I kept anything. I pulled plates from the cupboard and silverware from the drawers and directed her to the napkins in the pantry. While I rinsed black grit from romaine leaves, my eyes began to fill with tears again. Forget the fact that my mother had no place else to go; she was here and she was acting like a normal mother. Remembering the radishes I'd purchased a few days before, I went to the fridge and saw my mother standing at the head of the table, staring at the stacked plates and silverware. Sam came in and set down the extra chair he'd retrieved from the front closet. He walked over to the table. "Let's start with the plates, June," he said in the tone he used with Lili when she was frustrated with her math. He picked up a plate and placed it in front of a chair, and she put one down next to it, and they continued setting down plates and utensils until they'd completed the task. He looked boyishly handsome in his red University of Wisconsin T-shirt. The light caught the sun-bleached hairs on his forearms, ropy from playing golf. I'd always thought he looked like a shorter, Jewish version of James Taylor. God, I loved this man.

My mother seemed tired during dinner. The more the girls prattled on about their mean trigonometry teacher, the more she retreated into herself. Her absent stare, the one that had always indicated that she was preparing for flight, rekindled the ugly thoughts I'd had in the tahara room, thoughts that had been flickering inside me but wouldn't fully ignite, like a candle wick coated with wax.

"Mom!" Lili snapped me back to the table.

"What, Lil?"

"I asked you to pass the lasagna like four times," she said. "You and Grandma are like in your own worlds."

I could feel the spacey look on my face, and worse, a current pulling me away to someplace old and dark. Lili must have felt it too.

"Yeah, like Earth to Mom and Grandma." Taylor let out a cruel snicker.

I'd heard such cruelty before. Taylor was the kind of girl who teased the fat kids and laughed instead of looking away when someone tripped or left a fly open. There was something broken about her, but not broken in the way that made me want to help piece her back together, as I'd done with some of Lili's other friends. She was broken in a way that made her mean and dangerous. Megan and Kara looked down at their plates, clearly uncomfortable with Taylor's display of disrespect and Lili's giggling at it, as though they'd received confirmation that Lili's alliances had shifted away from them.

"I'm tired. Thank you for a delicious meal," my mother said, and got up from the table, her lasagna untouched. I'd forgotten that she disliked mozzarella. She never made lasagna, and she wouldn't have mixed cheese and beef when we were growing up in the Schines' shul anyway. It still felt odd to mix the two.

Sam broke the awkwardness. "What do you say we try some of Kara's famous cookies?"

After dinner, Kara's mother picked the girls up, and Sam settled Lili into the sofa bed while I looked in on my mother. She was propped up in bed in one of her silk nightgowns, the lace cuffs frayed, the white skin of her chest exposed.

"That friend of Lili's is trouble, the one with the eyes. Watch her," she said, and then she turned her attention to her FDR biography. She was still on page one.

With Lili and my mother tucked in, I climbed into my favorite flannel pajamas and joined Sam in the den for a glass of wine. "Give me news from the outside world," I said.

He grinned with his pre-recession cockiness as he described a referral with a nice-size portfolio. "Doctor a few years younger than us with family money and no clue how to make it grow. We got to talking about his new house, and he wants to come over and see our porch."

I took a sip of wine, its acidy sweetness fizzling on my tongue. "Sounds promising."

"How about this weekend? Your mom will be back at Neil's by then."

I tensed. I didn't have the energy to cultivate a new set of business friends, something that had always made me feel important to Sam's success. I loved that our happy marriage instilled confidence in his potential clients, I loved how we looked reflected in their eyes, and I loved being the wife of a golden boy, but right now I was too tired to trot. "I think I'll need to catch my breath."

He grabbed my foot and started massaging it. "You seem to be holding up just fine."

"Hardly," I said. He could be so dense sometimes. But then again, how could I blame him for not tuning into my stress? I'd hid behind my cheeriness and made myself into a carbon copy of Rose and all those women who'd called my father's office to schedule their children's orthodontist appointments. I'd done it so Lili could have the kind of childhood memories Sam did: summer camp, Hebrew school, tennis lessons at a club whose membership consisted of Reform Jews who danced the Electric Slide at nicely catered bar and bat mitzvahs. But if I wasn't really a Rose clone, who was I?

"Come on. We're both exhausted." He got up and held out his hand.

I took it, but I stayed put. "I'm sleeping down here."

"Why?"

"I'd like to be able to hear our daughter if she calls out in the middle of the night."

He crossed the arms I'd been admiring only hours earlier. "I think that's overkill."

God, how Rose and I had spoiled this man. "Sam, you'll have to be patient for a few more days."

I read once that couples fight over the same one or two things. Sam and I rarely fought, but we'd gone through a rough patch when his persistent optimism blinded him to Lili's struggles in junior high school. "She'll be fine, she'll be fine, just like the colic, it will go away," he assured me for months, and I believed him at first because that was our arrangement. My resentment grew during the weeks it took me to convince him that we needed help. Funny how quickly you can start resenting a person for the very thing that drew you to him in the first place.

I turned out the light and listened to the tick of Sam's battery-operated clock in the shape of Bucky Badger. I listened for our neighbor's dog to bark, as he did for five minutes every night at ten o'clock, and for Lili to moan for more pain medication. But mostly I listened for my mother to wander down our steps. Sure enough, she opened the door to Lili's room just as the glow-in-the-dark small hand circling Bucky's tummy hit the number eleven, the designated time when she used to slip out of the house to meet the Shabbos goy. I walked to the back door and waited for her, my heart pounding as wildly as it had the night I caught her in our alley.

The full moon shone through the slats of the blinds, illuminating her hair and the lace of her nightgown. Her eyes must not have adjusted to the dark, because she jumped when she saw me.

"You frightened me, Barbara."

"Where are you going?"

"I can come and go as I please," she said defiantly.

I stood in front of the door, the knob digging into the small of my back. "I'm taking care of you, and I'm not having any of your late-night adventures."

She looked determined and confused, as she had when she

was trying to set the dinner table. "Let's get you back to bed." I laced my arm through hers and turned her away from the door.

She pulled me back with surprising force. The fit of her bone inside the crease of my arm and the animal desperation in her eyes yanked me back in time, to our tug of war in the mikveh.

We stood with our elbows looped, like we were about to do-si-do, neither of us letting go. I leaned into her and whispered, "I don't want to be here again."

"Where?" she whispered back.

"Here. Chasing after you, worrying about you."

"What are you talking about?" She looked at me coolly.

"The mikveh," I said, my voice starting to shake. The mikveh was a code for everything: the Shabbos goy, the mists, my complicity in her lies to Mrs. Katz and everyone else.

"You're being hysterical. I simply came down here for a smoke, for heaven's sake."

"Why did you smoke in the mikveh?" How many years had I held this question inside?

"I'm not going to the mikveh. I'm going out to the porch. Your dad doesn't like the smell of smoke."

She sounded so convincing that for a second I believed my father was alive and that she had her cigarettes with her, even though she'd quit smoking years ago after she was diagnosed with a heart condition. My father was long dead, there was no pocket in her flimsy gown, and she'd balled up her empty hands.

An intense weariness swept over me. The last thing I wanted to do was to revisit anything about the mikveh, the source of a current that could sweep us both away.

"Mom, no smoking tonight, let's go back to your room."

Her arm went limp in mine as I walked her upstairs. When we reached the top, I let her go, remembering how much she hated to be touched when she was in a mood.

I woke at dawn the next morning with a crick in my neck. The anger that had been sparking inside me bloomed into a forest fire,

Colorado style, outweighing my embarrassment over using force against a tiny woman with stupid red hair. I downed one of Lili's Vicodins to take the edge off.

I checked in on Lili, who was sleeping, but I could tell from the messy covers that she'd had a rough night. Sam was still dozing as I showered and put on a fresh pair of jeans and my favorite T-shirt. I felt better in a cute outfit and clean hair and decided that my strategy for surviving today was to keep myself busy and medicated.

Felix had warned us that Lili would be in more pain on the third day after surgery, and he was right. My mother stayed in bed most of the morning and did God knows what. I started to feel guilty around eleven-thirty, so I made her tuna salad the way she liked it, with pickle relish and lots of mayo, and called her to join us for lunch. She showed up in the same outfit she'd worn the day before and greeted us brightly. If she remembered what had happened last night, she wasn't letting on.

"Here, Mom, I made you tuna salad." I tried to sound sweet.

Lili despised tuna, so I'd made her a turkey sandwich. I was too wired to eat. Lili took a few bites and then leaned back on the couch. In an hour, she could have another Vicodin. I'd already helped myself to seconds.

"You're a trouper, Lil. Isn't she, Mom?" I said, my words slightly slurred.

My mother was absently tearing off tiny pieces of her bread.

"Did you hear what I said, Mom? Isn't Lili a trouper?"

Her eyes slowly shifted to me.

"Mom, where are you?" I snapped, right in her face. I didn't recognize my voice. The Vicodin was a bad idea. I'd lost control over my mouth.

Lili looked at us wide-eyed, but she didn't say a word. She'd never heard me talk to anyone like this, and she was clearly frightened and embarrassed.

My mother got up, but she forgot about her TV tray, and her tuna fish spilled all over the arm of the couch. She looked as stranded as she had when I found her on the bluff in her blue coat. “I made a real mess,” she said as she started to pick up the tuna chunks with her fingers, but she only dug it further into the upholstery.

“Just let me get it.” My voice shook. I felt like one of those tired mothers you see in the grocery store who after hours of tolerating a whiny toddler finally snaps in front of a shocked (and rested) onlooker, in this case my own daughter. Yes, I’d lost my patience with my sick mother—unforgivable, yet Lili had no idea of the months I’d spent taking care of her, or of what had happened afterward.

I glanced at Lili, who looked as though she was watching the kind of sad movie where you feel for everyone.

My mother stood over me while I cleaned up, folding her hands. “Barbara,” she said when I finished. I looked up at her in her stained pants, on which I was now detecting the scent of urine. I pitied her and hated her at the same time.

She leaned down next to me and spoke quietly, her fish breath mingling with the smell of her. “I can’t answer your questions.”

“It’s the illness.” I couldn’t use the word “Alzheimer’s” with her.

She tapped her head with her index finger. “It’s so hard to keep track of everyone.”

“I know, I’m sorry,” I murmured. I stood up and led her to the sink to wash her hands. Lili’s eyes burrowed into us. I felt as exposed as I had when I failed to lock the ladies’ room door at a Starbucks properly, and a teenage boy burst in while I was squatting, my slacks around my knees.

After my mother returned to her room, I sat next to Lili. “Do you need anything?”

“I’m good.” She braided the fringes on a pillow I’d recently bought for the couch.

“Lili, I’m going to apologize to Grandma.”

She undid the braid and smoothed out the orange threads. “When did you start hating her?”

Lili’s question was a punch to the stomach. I swallowed my

sigh. "Why do you think I hate her?"

"Maybe you have your reasons." Her voice was tender and protective.

I listened to our breathing, savoring this sweet moment between us, although it was coming at my mother's expense. "Lili, I don't hate your grandmother."

"Mom, I know this is hard."

I could hear my mother running water for a bath, and I went upstairs to collect the dirty laundry. First I stopped in Lili's room to empty out her hamper. My mother had made the bed with perfect hospital corners. Her suitcase was lying on the floor. I deliberated for a second before I unzipped the flap, releasing the scent of Chanel and stale urine. She'd neatly folded her yellowed silk panties. I'd wash them and return them and spare her pride. When I scooped the heap of filthy lingerie into my laundry basket, I noticed a photo face down on the torn gray lining of the suitcase. I should have walked away, but I felt entitled to violate her privacy.

I recognized the image immediately, although it took my brain a few seconds to place it. I stared at the photo of the girl in the print dress with the lake in the background, and turned it over to find two names scrawled in faded blue cursive: June and Norman, Summer, 1942. I'd always wanted to see a photo of my uncle. He was tall and lean. I wished he weren't wearing that hat. I was dying to see his face. Had Neil or I or any of our children inherited his features?

I crept downstairs to Sam's office and made a copy of the photo. I folded the paper, stuffed it in the side pocket of my purse, and hurried upstairs to return the original before my mother came out of the bathroom. I wanted to barge into the bathroom and demand that she describe Norman's face in detail. I was dying to know who was under that hat and why she kept talking about him and how in God's name the Shabbos goy had come to possess this photo.

Down in the basement, I put in a load of my mother's dirty laundry with an extra dollop of detergent. Wavy lines began to trot across the lid of the machine. I was getting a migraine, and it was coming on fast. I felt nauseous.

I dialed Sam. "You need to come home."

"What's wrong?"

"You need to come home." I'd never once called him during the first four months of my pregnancy with Lili, when I threw up all day long, or the dozens of times I was down with some nasty bug during my early teaching years.

"Is it Lili?" He sounded frightened.

"No, I'm sick." I hung up. I hadn't had a migraine since the day after the mikveh, but if this was anything like the last one, it would soon debilitate me. My body remembered my pain and confusion.

I went back up to the den. My mother was staring at her book, and Lili was playing a computer game on her iPhone. "I have a little headache, sweetie. Dad's coming home to take care of us," I mumbled, then walked upstairs and plopped down on my bed. I don't know how much time passed before I heard Sam hurrying up the steps. He sat on the bed and pulled the covers from over my head.

"Can you put the laundry in the dryer?" I asked.

"Honey, the laundry can wait."

"No, it can't. Please."

He looked puzzled, but he got up. "Okay, I'll be back in a second."

I held my head as if I could stop my brain from throbbing. Thinking of the photo made it worse, so I tried to stop, but I couldn't. I had too many questions.

After a few minutes, a breathless Sam returned. "Let me go call Feldman and see if he can prescribe something for you. Are you sure it's a migraine?"

"Yes, I've had one before."

"I don't remember that."

"I was seventeen."

"You never told me."

"Never came up." A small part of me still thought that he'd

leave me if he knew everything I'd been hiding, just as I used to fret that the rebbetzin would kick us out of the shul. Once when Sam took Lili skiing, I watched all nine and a half hours of the documentary *Shoah,* and for weeks I kept hearing Claude Lanzmann saying, "If you could lick my heart, it would poison you." Most of my heart was fine, but if Sam found the bitter spot, maybe he'd kick me out of our private shul.

He lay next to me until I fell asleep.

After a few minutes, I woke with a start. "Can you fold my mother's laundry and put it back in her suitcase?"

Sam looked mildly amused. "Barbara, why are you so obsessed with the laundry?"

"My mother used to smell like Chanel."

"Okay, sweetheart. Just get some rest," he said.

When I woke up again, it was dark. I downed a Maxalt Sam had picked up at the pharmacy and went back to sleep. Shortly after midnight, my mikveh dream awakened me as Sam slept peacefully. This time a woman floats in the water while a skinny boy in a sunhat paddles around, splashing and laughing. Her face is always hidden. Tzippy and I burst into the sanctuary to tattle to the rebbetzin, but she is reciting the Shema—"*Hear, O Israel, the Lord our God, the Lord is One*"—so loudly that she can't hear us, her hands covering her eyes so she can't see us.

My pulse pounded as if it would burst through muscle and bone. I lay still for a few minutes, allowing my breathing to return to normal. When it did, I got up and vomited, thinking in my delirium that at any moment my mother would appear from the next room to sleep on the floor in case I needed her in the middle of the night.

The next morning I woke up to find Sam sitting on the edge of my bed.

"Hey."

"How's Lili?" I asked. The Maxalt had eased some of the pain, but mainly it just knocked me out.

"She'll be fine," he assured me in the voice he used to calm his clients.

"She's probably freaked out from yesterday."

He kissed my forehead. "Let's just get you better, and we'll deal with all that later."

"She asked me why I hated my mother."

He shook his head. "This is all too much for you, sweetie."

"No, I'm fine. I can handle it." I pushed off the covers and went to the bathroom to wash my face and brush my teeth.

Sam followed me. "Why don't you just stay in bed?"

"I need to check on Lili." I stripped down and showered quickly, my scalp tender as I shampooed it. No way was I going to be the mother who lounged in her sickbed with dirty hair when her daughter needed her. I stopped at Lili's room and checked my mother's suitcase. True to his word, Sam had folded her laundry. I slid my hand under the clothes, but the photo was gone. Had I imagined the whole thing? Maybe it was the Vicodin. Maybe I'd watched too many episodes of *House*. That nasty Dr. House had hallucinations, but he was an addict. I'd only taken a few pills. Weak from losing so much fluid, I held the railing as I went down the steps. My purse was sitting on the table in the foyer. I opened the side pocket to find the copy of the photo safely tucked away.

Ashamed of my outburst the day before, I didn't want to face Lili and my mother. I loitered for a minute in the hallway, growing more nervous by the second. The longer you stand on a diving board, though, the harder it is to take the plunge, so I stepped into the den.

They were sitting exactly where they were while we ate our lunch yesterday, before my tantrum. My mother held a book on her lap, and Lili was staring at the television, slack-jawed. They both looked up at me when I entered the room. Lili's eyes welled up at the sight of me; fear had settled in the tightness around her mouth and forehead.

"Can I make you some toast?" my mother asked feebly.

God help me, but I wanted to ask her why she was so

concerned about me all of a sudden. I didn't. "Thank you, but I don't think I'm quite ready to eat. When was the last time you took your medication?" I asked Lili.

"This morning. I'm not going to take any more. It's making me weird."

Me too, I thought, but now the Vicodin was out of my system, and my feelings were still out of control. "You sure?"

"I'm good," she said, and returned her attention to the television, some talent show featuring a young girl who was scream-singing, the sound a drill to my eardrum. Tomorrow she'd have to start in on her homework.

I went into the kitchen, where Sam was grabbing an apple out of the fridge to stick in his briefcase. He was a loving caregiver during a crisis, but now he was eager to return to his S&P Index analyses and his racquetball game.

My head started to throb. "You need to stay until Neil gets here tonight."

"But you said you were fine. I saw traces of the Sam who had offered me his hearty encouragement when I called him at the office in tears over one of Lili's homework meltdowns.

"What about me seems fine?" I whimpered. I'd never used this tone of voice with him, and I could tell I'd startled him. I couldn't stop myself from piling on. "I don't ask for much."

He raised his hands in surrender. "I get it, honey. Go back to bed."

"I think I will," I said. Lili had turned the television off, and she and my mother had been sitting in the den listening to our conversation. Perfect, now I'd unveiled myself to Lili as both a lame daughter and a lame wife.

I crawled under my covers with my clothes on and within seconds fell into a dreamless sleep. I awoke with creases on my cheek from the sheets. Voices traveled up the steps, but I couldn't make out the words. I got up and splashed cold water on my face before leaving the bedroom. When I passed Lili's room, my mother was sitting primly on the bed, staring out the window at the darkening sky. Her shoulders, always narrow, were the size of a child's, and she hadn't combed the back of her hair. She was a vulnerable old woman. Yet as badly as I wanted to forgive her, I couldn't do it.

Sam made his special spaghetti sauce and pasta for dinner, but we talked little over the meal. I could tell that Lili was in less pain, but we were all tentative around each other. Nobody wanted to upset the crazy lady, me.

I was sleepy from napping too long, so I went back to bed after dinner and dozed until I heard a car door slam. I got up and walked to the window. Neil had his arm around my mother and was guiding her to his car, while Sam carried her suitcase. I tapped on the window. My mother turned around, and I waved at her, something I'd always fantasized about doing all those nights I watched her walk down the alley toward the Blue Dodge. She raised her hand as if to say, I'm okay. I'd never felt so alone in my entire life. Well, that wasn't entirely true, but not since the day I kept her secret from Tzippy. I recalled that Caribbean cruise with Rose and Artie, and how after a few days of sea sickness, I'd almost jumped off of that ship, not caring that I'd never learned to swim well.

Sam and Lili liked to sleep in on weekends, but I woke up early, feeling relieved and guilty that my mother was gone. I made myself a strong cup of coffee and logged on to the computer. The summer between college and graduate school, I worked for a collections agency and became an expert at tracking down information on anyone, dead or alive. Technology might have changed, but I knew my way around an archive. The *Milwaukee Journal Sentinel* made it ridiculously easy to find my uncle Norman's obituary. My mother's maiden name was Fischer, one of the few facts I knew about her history. I typed "Norman Fischer" into their Legacy site. Bingo.

The obituary was dated July 25, 1949. I read it aloud. "Norman Fischer, age 21, resident of 3050 Lake Drive, the former Von Guttenstein beer baron mansion, died on July 23rd from complications from polio."

I reread the address of my uncle's home six times.

Thirty-fifty Lake Drive. The Schines' address.

I printed the obituary and held the paper in my hand, remembering the authority with which my mother had led me along the bluff and through the pitch-black mikveh, how she'd told me that the house she grew up in didn't exist any longer. I'd reached the end of a mystery novel. When I added up all the clues, they could only have lead to one place. My fingers could barely manipulate the mouse as I read on in silence.

"Fischer was born on April 5th, 1928, and after polio paralyzed him, he nearly graduated from the University of Wisconsin-Milwaukee with a degree in United States History. He was awarded the Chancellor's Research Award for his scholastic excellence, and as a polio survivor, delivered fundraising speeches for the March of Dimes. Mr. Fischer is survived by his father, Joseph Fischer, and his sister June Fischer."

I read the obituary again and then let my eyes linger on the word "polio." The owners had built the pool so the sick boy could soak his legs, my mother had told me. Norman. My *grandfather* had built the mikveh for Norman. The inside of my mouth turned dry as parchment as I pictured my mother smoking, sucking in her grief and letting it out, the air finding its way back into the cracks of my skin. Norman had been with us that morning, I'd felt him. And somehow the Shabbos goy was involved with my mother and Uncle Norman too. But how?

I found Andy Noffsinger's address more quickly than I had Uncle Norman's obituary. There were two listings for A. Noffsinger, business and home, both on the west side of town, maybe near Mr. Isen. Lili had taken piano lessons only a few blocks away when she was in fourth grade. I might even have driven past the Shabbos goy on my way to drop her off. I was glad when her piano teacher retired. The west side was only twenty-five minutes from us, but it felt like a different world, and that was before I knew that the Shabbos goy inhabited it.

I wrote Sam and Lili a note, "Went out to clear my head." I

thought about calling Neil to ask him what he knew about our uncle, but he would be overwhelmed with a grieving Jenny and my mother, and I was ashamed that I couldn't handle her presence for a few more days.

The sky was magnificently clear. I listened to classical music to soothe my nerves as I drove to see the Shabbos goy. I was again the young woman who'd marched over to his carriage house and kicked his duffel bag across the room. How had the Schines come to own my mother's mansion? None of it made any sense.

The Shabbos goy lived in a modest rambler, but the lot was large and nicely landscaped. I didn't know what I'd say or how I'd greet him, but something propelled me from the car to the walkway to his doorbell. My fingers trembled as I pressed the button. No answer. I poked my head around the side entrance to see if I could spot any movement, but the house was still. I rang the bell again. Still, no answer.

I returned to my car and punched his business address into my GPS. It only took me a few minutes to drive to his nursery, which was attached to a quaint building that looked like it had once been a house. I sat in my car and watched my mother's ex-lover arrange pumpkins on the front lawn. He no longer wore a ponytail, but he was still lithe and moved with the grace of a younger man. I got out of the car and walked toward him quickly, before I lost my nerve.

He spotted me right away. He set down a large pumpkin and gaped at me. As I drew closer, he greeted me with his eyes, grayish brown and wide-set; he must have popped a blood vessel in his left eye, because red veins spidered out from the corner to his iris. Gray stubble grew in the cleft of his Kirk Douglas chin. The bones of his face were still chiseled and lovely, but his skin was craggy from years of working outdoors.

"You look just like your mother," he said softly. "Same walk, same hair."

A man with a bushy beard came over and handed him a cup of coffee. "Here you go, boss." The Shabbos goy thanked him politely and returned his attention to me. I was grateful to have had a second to collect my thoughts. I took in a deep breath, heavy with the smell of mulch. He looked at me as he had so many years earlier, when I stormed into his apartment, or when Tzippy and I ran into the kitchen while he was putting kugels in the oven.

"How are you?" I asked. The words sounded silly, but I didn't know where to start.

"Pretty good, I suppose. You?" He was going to take his cues from me.

I smiled weakly.

"Why did you track me down?" he asked. His voice was still youthful.

"I'm not here to cause trouble for you. I have questions." The steady infusion of adrenaline over the past few days had made me reckless.

"Your mom should be the one to answer them."

"My mother has Alzheimer's," I said in a "so there" tone that made me sound like a child. A part of me still blamed him for everything that had gone wrong with our family.

His expression barely changed. Then he took a sip of his coffee. "How bad?"

"She wanders back and forth between the past and the present, but she definitely prefers the past." The air carried an autumn chill, and I wrapped my sweater around me.

He looked right into my eyes with an intimacy that came from sharing a common understanding of a loved one. We both knew that my mother had always wandered.

I pulled out the copy I'd made of the photo and handed it to him. "I want to know why she keeps this picture in the bottom of her suitcase, under...." I almost said "dirty underwear," but I could never hate her enough to offer up this tidbit about her declining personal hygiene to anyone.

The man with the beard beckoned him, and I wondered if he'd walk away and never come back. "Be just a minute, Kip."

"Why did you have this photo?" I demanded.

He lowered his voice. "I can't get into your mother's business with you."

"Do you mean that she grew up in the mansion? All these years of her damn secrets, and all I had to do was check the *Journal Sentinel* archive? Isn't that a kick?" I could taste the bitterness in my mouth.

"She never told you that her family lived in the mansion?"

"She never told me about the mansion. She never used to talk about my uncle or anyone else in her family, but now she can't stop calling my brother Norman."

He winced at the mention of Norman's name. "She never got over losing him."

Finally I was getting somewhere.

He rattled the change in his pockets. "I want to help you."

"Then please talk to me." I was practically begging.

"Go to her again. She'll tell you what she can." His lips tightened into a thin line.

"Her brain is a piece of soggy French toast."

He stroked his chin, and I waited as patiently as I could while men in green polo shirts and jeans unloaded a truckful of pumpkins.

"What do you want to know, Barbara?"

"For starters, I want to know who you are."

He looked at me carefully, as if he were considering opening up to me.

I hated that he knew my family history. I felt like smashing one of his pumpkins. "See, here's the thing. If you hadn't messed up her head, she would have been normal, and I could have gone to Mrs. Kessler's funeral. But the two of you wrecked all that."

"Go easy on your mother," he pleaded. "She's been through hell."

I stepped closer to him. "Do you think I'm not painfully aware of that? Who do you think took care of her after you took off?"

"I better get back to work." He turned toward the pumpkins.

I grabbed his sleeve. "Can you just tell me how the Schines

came to own the mansion?"

Kip walked over to us. "Everything okay here?"

"Fine, I'm just seeing the lady to her car." The Shabbos goy took my elbow.

"How do you think your mother met the Schines?"

The pressure on my elbow felt oddly reassuring. "I've heard the whole appendicitis story."

"It wasn't appendicitis."

"Oh, please. She told that story a million times."

"She was...." He paused. "Very sick."

"What do you mean, very sick?"

"Depressed."

I stopped walking. "How depressed?"

"Enough to be hospitalized."

We stood side by side for a few seconds, staring at my car.

"That's when the Schines found her."

"Why was she so depressed?" I asked hoarsely.

"She lost Norman and then her dad."

"So the Schines took care of her, and in return she gave them her mansion." The truth came out of my mouth, bypassing my brain.

A vein pulsed in his neck. "Barbara," he said quietly.

"What?"

"Be gentle." Again his voice was pleading. What had my mother meant to him? Not once in all these years had I considered his feelings. He'd merely existed as the person who had ruined our lives. He was done talking. I could see it in his lips, tight and locked. I opened the car door, my head whirling. He was protecting her, and like Neil, he was now shielding her from me. Everyone was forgetting that I'd been the one damaged by her affair, the one the rebbetzin had cast from the shul, from the mansion, from my home. And I was the one who'd lost my best friend.

THE SECOND WASHING

It occurs to me that I have not traveled so very far after all,
since I wrote my little play.
Or rather, I've made a huge digression and
doubled back to my starting place.

– Ian McEwan, *Atonement*

June 1974 – May 1975

Rabbi Levenstein picked me up at the San Diego airport wearing a long black coat and matching hat, his cheeks pasty white against his dark beard. He was only a couple of inches taller than me, and he had hazel eyes that changed color depending on the light. Rabbi Schine's eyes were dark brown, nearly black, and full of fire.

"Barbara." His voice was deep but almost apologetic, while Rabbi Schine's was high pitched but assertive.

"Hello, Rabbi Levenstein."

He strained to heave my two suitcases from the baggage carousel, and by the time we reached his Pontiac, his temples glistened with sweat. I'd never been to the West Coast, and I felt like I was stepping into a colorized postcard. Had I not been so homesick, it would have been thrilling. The cloudless sky was reflected in the bright blue harbor, where sailboats clanked against long white docks. Unlike Milwaukee's maples and elms, with their enormous trunks firmly planted in the earth, lanky palm trees swayed around us, their big leaves shimmying in the breeze.

Rabbi Levenstein slammed the car door shut and pointed to the sky. "Until today, it's been dark and cloudy. June gloom, the natives call it."

I wondered what native would engage in conversation with a man dressed like this. His car smelled like the men's section of the Schines' sanctuary, the kind of body odor that burrows deep into polyester. I wanted him to turn the car around so I could catch a flight back to Milwaukee and return to my shul, smelly men's section and all. I concentrated on the water stretching out into the horizon, trying not to worry whether my mother had gotten out of bed today.

The Levensteins had placed a large decorative menorah on a strip of grass in front of their townhouse, which looked exactly like every other home in the complex. A picture of the Rebbe hung on the wall in the foyer, and a few remaining moving boxes, along with toy trucks and building blocks, littered a beige carpet that smelled new.

A woman, thin and tall like the rebbetzin, sat on a worn couch with her arm around a little boy with strands of hair hanging down each side of his face like drapery cords. She smiled, revealing an overbite that my father would have wanted to fix.

"I'm Sari, and this is Benny," she said.

"Nice to meet you," I said. The rebbetzin must have been a young wife like Sari when she met my mother so many years ago, and soon Tzippy would become the wife of a young rabbi, cast out to some strange city to build an Orthodox community. In a few weeks, Tzippy would be home for her last summer before she got married, and I'd be here taking care of her cousin's child. A riptide of longing threatened to drown me.

Sari moved her hand from her belly, not yet swollen, and motioned to a loveseat stacked with children's books, but I sat down on the floor next to the little boy. "So you're Benny?" I stuck my hand into my bag and pulled out two Matchbox cars I'd wrapped in bright blue paper. Benny was small for a four-year-old, and his skin looked as if he rarely played outside. On his cheek he had a light brown birthmark shaped like the state of Illinois that disappeared into a deep dimple when he smiled.

He looked at Sari, and she shook her head yes. He opened the gift deliberately, his eyes widening when he saw the cars. "Thank you," he said without looking up.

"Aunt Rivkah was right, you're good with four-year-olds." I

flinched at the mention of the rebbetzin. Sari's thick Brooklyn accent sounded just like hers, although Sari's voice was softer.

I nodded, confirming myself as the expert. My gift with children was the one thing I never doubted, thanks to Mrs. Kessler.

Sari's skin took on a grayish tint, and she belched into her fist and bolted toward the bathroom. Benny and I raced his new cars. I pretended to cry when mine lost, knowing this would tickle him.

When Sari recovered, she walked me down to my room in the basement, and I made up my bed, a pullout couch with a thin mattress and a blanket that smelled like mothballs. I waited until the house was quiet before I phoned home.

"Hi, Dad," I said after he accepted my collect call. "I'm here."

"I've been waiting for this very call. How was the plane ride?"

"Good. Fine, I guess."

"California! What an adventure!" he said, trying to sound upbeat.

"I suppose. Can I talk to Mom?"

He sighed. "She turned in early."

I pictured her sitting in bed smoking, her eyes bloodshot and barely open. I started to feel panicky; she'd been my responsibility for months, and I needed to hear her voice.

"Can't you wake her, Dad?"

"Tell me about San Diego," he said.

"It's sunny. There are palm trees, and the water and sky are abnormally blue. Come on, Dad. I'm worried."

"Barbara, this is why you need to spend some time away. You're too young to worry so much."

"I don't want to spend time away, Dad." I wanted to sob until I'd exhausted myself.

"I don't want you to either." He sounded defeated.

"Then let me come home. I want to be with you and Mom. I'll help more. I won't have school, so I can help write the rebbetzin's talks to the newcomers like Mom did. I can cook too. I'm a better baker than Mom. And I could make the Shabbos meals, and Mom would only have to come downstairs and eat. And if I had extra time, I could spend it with Tzippy."

"It's okay, Bunny. It's okay. You'll be back before you know it."

It was no use. The rebbetzin had sold him on her plan. Even if I hitchhiked home, she'd just send me back to San Diego, or she'd pawn me off on another family, in Anchorage or Hagatna. After I said goodbye, I bawled my eyes out. When I finished, I was harder inside.

The next morning, I helped Sari unpack her boxes. She sat on the couch and told me where to put her things, clearly self-conscious about having to pay someone to play with her child and find places for her books and candlesticks. She spat often into a coffee cup, and when she got up to get sick, I rinsed out the cup in the sink.

I would take care of Sari and her saliva because it was my job. If we'd met during a different time, we might have become friends, but the last thing I wanted was to tether myself to another rebbetzin. I'd always assumed that if the rebbetzin found out about the Shabbos goy, we'd leave the shul as a family, but the rebbetzin had taken my place in nursing my mother, and I was living with strangers. The Rebbe's familiar eyes following me when I passed his photo, the ritual washing cup hanging from the kitchen faucet, and the hushed Yiddish falling from Rabbi Levenstein's lips when he spoke to his parents in Brooklyn served as painful reminders that the Levensteins' condo was only a pale imitation of the Schines' mansion, my real home.

Sari looked exhausted, so I took Benny for a walk around the housing development. "Children need to be run," Mrs. Kessler used to tell me.

I picked up a eucalyptus leaf and offered him a sniff.

He made a face. "Smells like medicine."

I took a whiff and made his same face, and we both laughed.

I spotted a digger on the horizon. "I see something you're really going to like," I said as he slipped his little hand in mine.

He looked up at me. "What?"

"You'll see," I said.

He was a fast walker for his size, and soon we were standing in front of a yellow truck with a claw appendage. Benny's eyes widened when the claw reached down and scooped up dirt.

"What's it doing?"

"I think it's making room for new homes," I said. The houses in my Milwaukee neighborhood were all old and made of sturdy materials like brick. I thought I could blow one of these new condos down with a huff and a puff.

For almost an hour, we watched the digger while the construction workers stole glances at his forelocks and my long skirt. When he finally got restless, we walked on a good half mile up a steep hill, and Benny pointed his finger toward what lay on the opposite side.

"What's that?" he asked.

I looked up at yellow steel forming an enormous V against the brilliant sky. "A crane, Benny."

"No, that!" He pointed toward a line of blue far off in the distance.

I put my hand to my forehead to shield my eyes from the sun. "Do you mean the ocean?"

"Yes! We saw it from the airplane."

Again he pointed toward the miles and miles of water new to both of us. Something opened up inside me, just a crack. For the first time since my mother got sick, I could see out of the well I'd jumped in to save her.

"Benny, have you been to the beach yet?"

He shook his head no.

The Levensteins had been living in San Diego for six months and Benny had never seen the ocean? I would find a way to get us to the beach. The water would bring me more of that sunlight, I was certain of it, even as I felt a flash of guilt over leaving my mother alone in the well.

For the next few nights, while I browned hamburger meat

for farfel and bathed Benny, I plotted how to convince Rabbi Levenstein to loan me his car. Because Sari was so nauseous, he and Benny dined alone, and then I ate and cleaned up the kitchen while he told his little boy a children's version of the weekly Torah portion.

One night, instead of retreating to the basement after supper, I waited for him in the kitchen, busying myself with cleaning the burners. "Rabbi Levenstein," I called before he disappeared into his study.

"Yes, Barbara?"

I'd figured out his schedule. He visited the hospital on Mondays and the college campuses on Tuesdays, but mostly he locked himself in his study to pore over the Torah.

"One day when you're studying here at the house, can I borrow your car and take Benny to the beach?" I asked.

He stroked his beard as if he were contemplating a Talmudic matter.

"Or the zoo, or Balboa Park."

"Let me think about it, Barbara." He gnawed the tip of his forefinger. The old Barbara would have said something to make him feel more comfortable because she empathized with his shyness. Exiled Barbara stared at his finger until he grew self-conscious and put his hands in his pockets. I'd established my dominance, like an alpha dog in a new pound.

"Thank you, Rabbi Levenstein," I said as if he'd already given me the key.

The next morning I was halfway up the basement stairs when I overheard Sari and Rabbi Levenstein talking. I sat on a step and eavesdropped.

"The Rebbe called to ask if I needed more prayer books." Rabbi Levenstein's voice vibrated with tension.

"What did you tell him?" Sari spoke with more energy than I'd heard from her voice before.

He sighed. "You don't need prayer books if you can't find ten men to make a minyan for a Shabbos service."

"Invite those men you met at the university, the ones with the long hair and the crosses. They'll stay for lunch."

I'd heard my parents talk about the beatniks and Werner Erhard dropouts, lapsed Jews who found their way to the Schines' table. These recruits were young and often sad-looking, and therefore, according to my father, ready to receive Rabbi Schine's teachings. They were nothing like the well-dressed young mothers who showed up at the rebbetzin's teas.

"When you're feeling better, Baruch Hashem," Rabbi Levenstein said bleakly.

"You are a learned man, Shimon," Sari reassured him. "You will find a way to touch these souls."

"By next summer, we'll be on our own." He sounded tense. "No more stipend."

Sari was stacking dishes in the sink, but I could still make out her words. "You'll touch people, and they'll want to help us build a shul, and it will all work out."

I walked up the steps and interrupted their conversation. "I'll cook Shabbos lunch for you."

Rabbi Levenstein and Sari looked at each other.

"Thank you, Barbara, for the light of your Jewish neshama." Sari smiled at me with relief.

My Jewish soul was actually feeling rather shaded. I felt a little sorry for the Levensteins, but I wasn't interested in helping Sari as my mother had helped the rebbetzin. Exiled Barbara wanted to guilt the rabbi into giving me the key to his car so that Benny and I could go to the beach already.

The next Friday, I engaged in an odd little act of rebellion against the rebbetzin while I cooked her Shabbos menu. I used a milchig fork designated solely for dairy foods while poking the beef for the cholent. Aside from one Yom Kippur when I'd forgotten I was fasting and ate a cherry Lifesaver after the Kol Nidre service, I'd never so much as broken a minor rule.

I prepared way too much food; the rabbi couldn't find ten men for his minyan. How was he ever going to fill a shul if he couldn't even fill his living room? Benny followed me around the kitchen while we listened to the anemic chanting of the rabbi and the two men he'd met during his rounds at the hospital.

When he reached the end of the service, I brought Benny out to the living room to hear the Ein Keloheinu prayer. I ducked into the kitchen, retrieved one of the lemon candies Sari sucked on to relieve her nausea, returned to the living room, and rolled it toward the rabbi. "Go get it, Benny," I said, remembering with a twinge how as children Tzippy and I had climbed up on the crowded bimah during the prayer and scrambled around the altar for candy.

The men from the hospital politely declined the rabbi's offer to stay for lunch, so he and Benny and I ate my bad imitation of the rebbetzin's cholent. A small eater, Benny went off to peruse his picture books, leaving the rabbi and me to finish our pareve nondairy coffee dessert, its icy blandness freezing the tip of my tongue. The faint sound of Sari's retching drifted down the steps as Rabbi Levenstein played with his spoon.

"You'll find a minyan if you keep trying the hospitals." Here I was, a babysitter, telling the rabbi what to do, and relishing every second of it.

He started to rise from the table.

"Rabbi Schine found my mother there," I added confidently.

Rabbi Levenstein settled back into his chair, and I told him my mother's appendicitis story, which I knew by heart because she'd recited it to the dozens of lost souls the Schines assigned to our Shabbos table. I told him about how the Schines visited my mother in the hospital after her appendix ruptured and how she started coming to services after she recovered and then met my father at one of their Shabbos lunches. I paused in all the right places, finishing up with her favorite line. "I hate to think where she would have ended up without the Schines."

"That's quite a story, Barbara." Rabbi Levenstein scratched his beard.

"Yeah, quite a story." I ached to hear my mother tell it. Since I left home, she hadn't come to the phone once during my weekly calls.

He shifted in his seat but didn't try to get up from the table again. "What about your father?"

I told him that my father had been tapped at the Wailing Wall by one of Rabbi Schine's brothers while he was traveling in Israel after he completed his orthodontics program. Thinking about my father or talking to him during our Sunday night phone calls made me feel like I'd bumped a bruised knee into the sharp edge of a coffee table. I lowered my voice. "Keep trying the college, but what you really need to do to build your shul is to find one or two suburban souls. They'll raise your money and recruit others to help them."

He started leafing through his prayer book, pretending he was looking for the Birkat Hamazon, a blessing he recited after every meal.

"Page 48, Rabbi Levenstein." I barely recognized my new sassiness.

The tops of his cheeks flushed, and I started feeling sorry for him again. Poor man, he was not blessed with Rabbi Schine's instincts or charisma. How was he ever going to spot the perfect recruit? I could smell them a mile away, the ones who would plunge themselves into the community, like the Brisket Ladies and their doctor and lawyer husbands who chipped in to buy a new hot water heater for the shul last year. Even if I brought the rabbi some live ones, eager secular Jews, would he know what to do with them?

After lunch, Sari felt well enough to play with Benny, so I retreated to the basement, content to read the books I'd purchased when I drove Sari and Benny to the mall. I was taking a break from Jane Austen. The rebbetzin would disapprove of these novels with their glossy covers featuring busty, raven-haired beauties embracing handsome men who had rescued them from Hester Street tenements, but their stories gave me hope that with a little luck and chutzpah, my life could change too.

11

On a Tuesday morning, a few days after I first prepared Shabbos lunch for the Levensteins, I found a brown bag labeled "Barbara" on the last step from the basement to the kitchen. The paper crinkled as I stuck in my hand and pulled out a map of San Diego and a long silver key with "Pontiac" inscribed on the shiny metal. Holding the key made me feel giddy.

"How about we go say good morning to the dolphins?" I asked Benny.

He looked as if I'd just surprised him with a new toy. "You're taking me to the beach?"

I could hear Sari coughing and gagging as I poured Benny's cereal and juice. Rough morning. I stuffed two towels into a grocery bag and scribbled a note to Sari, waiting until she was in the bathroom to tape it to her door. I buckled Benny into Rabbi Levenstein's Pontiac, and when I put the key in the ignition, my whole body quaked at the sound of the engine. I drove past rows of townhouses, lonely in the wide-open canyon and turned onto the windy road leading to the La Jolla beaches. Every time I rounded a corner, I caught a glimpse of the ocean. I'd always used the lake to orient myself, but now heading toward a large body of water meant I was traveling west instead of east. The country had done a somersault, and I'd come out on the other side.

I had no trouble parking at La Jolla Shores beach. It was so early that half the waterfront was still shaded. Benny and I looked at each other as if we were Neil Armstrong and Buzz Aldrin landing on the moon. I forgot my embarrassment over my long skirt, and we sprinted to the beach, my brown grocery sack in tow.

We passed a young woman and a little boy with curly blond hair who looked to be about Benny's age. They were playing in the water. The woman had long, straight hair the color of coal. The strings of her red bikini top formed a loose bow at the base of her neck, and a gauzy white dress billowed against her bronzed skin as she ran in and out of the waves, part gazelle, part dolphin.

We walked farther down the beach. When we reached the pier, I laid our frayed bath towels on the soft sand. I picked up a fistful of warm grains and let them fall through my fingers onto Benny's toes.

"That tickles," he said with delight.

I tugged at the rim of his Yankees cap, a shield to protect his pale skin from the sun and his forelocks from the secular world. We pushed the sand into a mound, and when Benny grazed it with his hand, it collapsed.

"It's broken now," he said forlornly.

He sat on my lap and rocked his little body against mine until we grew hypnotized by a cluster of pelicans that had gathered on a rock for their morning kaffeeklatsch. I'd only seen pelicans in my father's *National Geographic* magazines.

"We'll build a new sandcastle." I kissed his hair.

Benny shook his head in agreement as the little blond boy came running from the water. He approached Benny. "Hi!"

Benny looked at his blond curls and bare brown chest. "Hi."

"Ollie!" The woman in the red bikini jogged toward us and leaned down to talk to Benny. "I think my little boy wants to play with you."

I stared at her as Benny stared at her son. I'd never seen anyone so beautiful in person before. And the way she'd been playing with Ollie in the water made me think that she wasn't some summer sunbather like the types we saw back home at Atwater Beach; this was her turf. What would she want with me? We stood together watching Benny and Ollie shovel sand into a bucket, and

I felt so pale and weird-looking that I wished she'd take her son and go play someplace else.

"We were just going to get some water." I pointed to the ocean like a dunce. "For our sandcastle."

"Mommy, can we all build a sandcastle?" Ollie asked. Who could say no to that grin?

The woman looked at me. "I'm okay with it. Are you?"

"Sure," I said.

"This is Ollie." She put her hands on her little boy's bare shoulders, brown and sturdy compared to Benny's.

"And this is Benny," I said.

"I've seen Benny before." She touched the tip of his nose. Benny gave a little wave, but his eyes didn't register recognition. "I used to see him at the park with his mom." Her lazy smile revealed a mouthful of perfect white teeth. Probably in her midtwenties, she was only slightly taller than me, but more muscular.

I kicked at the sand. The fact that she'd met Sari made me feel more comfortable talking to her.

"I'm Simone Cox," she said, extending her hand.

I shook it. "I'm Barbara Pupnick."

Simone pulled a shovel and a bucket out of her bag. "Barbara and Benny, then. Let's go."

I took Benny's hand and we walked to the shoreline, giggling as the cold water rushed over our toes. Benny and Ollie sat down and dug their shovels into the sand. Simone spread out her large red and orange flowered beach towel a few feet behind the boys where it was dry. "Sit," she said. "Please."

I sat, and she plopped down next to me. Although my clothes embarrassed me, I preferred my odd outfit to flouncing around in a bathing suit, my horrifying back acne exposed to Simone and the rest of the world.

"Is everything okay with Benny's mom? I haven't seen her at the park lately." Simone adjusted her aviator glasses. She reminded me of Joan Baez, my friend Mira's favorite singer, but with an upturned nose and green eyes.

"Do you know her?" I couldn't imagine Sari and Simone together.

"Not really, just from seeing her at the park. We never talked or anything." I contemplated how much about Sari I should reveal. "Just smiled at each other a lot," she continued. "The last time I saw her she looked a little pregnant."

Well, if she already knew Sari was pregnant, there could be no harm in telling her about Sari's condition. "She's been having bad morning sickness."

Simone shook her head sympathetically. "I'm a little relieved, though. I was worried that something was wrong. I'm an RN. I've seen lots of bad stuff go down."

Benny and Ollie were running in and out of the ocean, giggling their heads off every time the cold water touched their feet. It warmed me to see Benny so carefree, but I couldn't help yell, "Don't go past your ankles!"

"So is everything okay with the baby?" Simone asked, again showing genuine concern.

"Everything's fine. She's just sick all day."

"That's hard. I was sick with Ollie. I ran my own IV before my shifts, I was so dehydrated. God, it was worth it, though." She stopped and glanced at my long skirt and sleeves, her first acknowledgment of how out of place I looked on the beach. "I'm sorry. Saying God. Did that offend you?"

"It's fine."

"Anyway, I used to lie in bed with a cold rag on my head and listen to a *Peter and the Wolf* tape my husband bought me. To this day, Prokofiev makes my skull throb."

"Sounds miserable," I said.

"Nah, I'd do it again in a heartbeat." Simone poured sand over her toes. Her nails were painted purple, and she wore a silver ring on her middle toe. "Hmmm. Sun feels good."

I watched the boys, terrified to take my eyes off Benny. He was a cautious child, but I didn't want any bad stuff to happen on my watch.

"Hey, Ollie!" Simone called.

Ollie turned around and smiled at her, and then he put an arm around Benny's shoulders, which were covered with a wet T-shirt, and the two boys grinned. Simone and I sat in silence, listening to the waves and the seagulls and the boys' laughter.

The sun was beginning to scorch my neck, and I was afraid Benny would burn. "Benny, it's time to go," I called out. The boys charged at us.

"Can he stay for just five more minutes?" Ollie asked.

"We should get going too," Simone said, "I'm taking Ollie to visit his grandparents." She stood up and shook out her towel. "Up in Laguna, or Laguma, as Ollie would say."

I laughed at her joke, although I had no idea where Laguna was. "Have a good trip."

"I'm glad I met you, Barbara." Simone was living proof that a whole world existed outside of the Schines' and the Levensteins' communities. Maybe my parents had felt this kind of excitement when they met the Schines. Maybe this was how Rabbi Schine and the rebbetzin had turned my shrimp-eating father and my mother, a Christmas-tree Jew, into their poster couple for Orthodox Judaism. I felt like a character out of the novel I was reading, a frumpy Jewish Hester Street girl (with big aesthetic potential) who gets whisked away to the Upper East Side.

We returned to the beach the next day in search of Simone and Ollie. No luck. A few young women who looked to be about my age rubbed lotion on their shoulders while their boyfriends played pepper with a volleyball. As I walked by, I caught snippets of conversation about how late they'd stayed out the night before.

"Where's Ollie?" Benny asked.

"I'm not sure if he's coming today, Benny." I wanted to see Simone and Ollie as much as he did. They made me feel free. I took his hand and walked him to the spot where he'd played with Ollie. We squealed when a cold wave surprised us.

I wrung out the bottom of my wet, sand-coated skirt, revealing my calves, white and fuzzy. I saw no need to shave the fine gold hairs since I always wore long skirts. Benny jumped in a puddle of water. I loved his laugh, full and direct.

"Now, that's a contagious laugh," Simone said as she walked toward me. I grinned involuntarily. Benny paused briefly when Ollie approached him and then the two ran off, chasing each other down the beach.

"Benny needs to be with kids his own age," I said.

"He does," Simone agreed. "It's good for Ollie too. And his mother."

I studied the design on my towel to hide my hunger for Simone's attention.

"So are you from Michigan or something?" she asked. "I had a cousin from Detroit, and he talked like you."

"Milwaukee."

"I've never met anyone from Milwaukee before. Far out." Simone adjusted one of the strings on her bikini top. Seconds later, with one hand, she intercepted a volleyball flying toward my head. She looked up at two young men with ponytails and leather ankle bracelets.

"My ball." The darker one laughed and gave Simone the once-over before his eyes shifted toward me. He stared at my skirt and my hairy ankles with what I imagined was disdain.

Simone hurled the ball at him so hard that he lost his balance. He walked away sheepishly.

"Where did you learn to throw like that?" I asked in awe.

"I played a lot of beach volleyball when I was in high school. With guys just like him." She pulled a bag of potato chips out of her tote bag and offered me some. If I hadn't been with Benny, I would've contemplated ignoring the laws of kashrut and accepting.

"No thank you."

"You sure?" She extended the bag to me.

I shook my head no.

Simone put her hand on my arm. "I'm so stupid. I saw a woman offer Benny a cookie once at the park, and his mom flipped out. Is it the kosher thing?"

"Yes." I wished this conversation would disappear.

"So what is it that you can't eat besides ham and pork?" she asked with interest. "I work with a doctor who I think keeps kosher."

She listened intently while I told her about the hechsher symbol. I described the "u" inside of the "o" and explained how it marked whether or not a food was kosher.

"I'm going to start noticing the hikshaw from now on," Simone said.

I laughed. "It's hechsher."

Benny and Ollie ran up to us, and Simone handed them shovels from her bag.

"Thank Mrs. Cox, Benny," I said.

"Thank you, Mrs. Cox," he said shyly, and ran off with Ollie.

Simone liked to talk. In what seemed like one run-on sentence, she told me about how she'd met her husband, Daniel, on an airplane to Morocco. Simone had eaten some bad egg salad in the airport, and Daniel rubbed her scalp and gave her his barf bag. He was engaged to his high school sweetheart, but he and Simone traveled through Morocco and Spain together and cozied up in single beds in youth hostels where they did "everything but." When she got home, she wanted to find out if she had a future with Daniel, so she visited a psychic named Marci whom she'd met when Marci was in the hospital visiting her sick mother. Marci lived in a little house in Hillcrest that smelled like patchouli, and she had located two missing children for the San Diego police. Marci made a believer out of Simone when she warned her about a cavity in her bottom incisor and recited obscure facts about Simone's ex-lovers.

"So what did Marci say about Daniel?" I asked when Simone took a break to breathe.

"Ollie, don't go too far in," Simone called. "That we'd get married and have one son."

"How did she know?"

"She read my palm," she said matter-of-factly, as if she were telling me that she'd had her tonsils removed.

I waited a second before I asked the next question so I wouldn't sound too interested, which I was. "So how did you two end up together?"

"I can't believe I'm telling you all this. You probably don't believe too much in psychics?"

"I've never heard of a psychic," I replied, "so I don't know if I believe in them or not." Once, one of the new Schine recruits dressed up as a gypsy for the Purim carnival, and the rebbetzin admonished her for toting around a fake crystal ball. Tzippy told me that the rebbetzin politely took the woman aside to inform her that fortune-tellers were evil and that only the goyim believed in sorcery. Simone didn't seem evil, although she did frighten me a little, but in a thrilling kind of way.

Simone smiled at me with admiration. "You're so real, Barbara." She pulled a floppy hat out of her bag and put it on my head.

"Thanks." I adjusted the hat. Real? Did she mean it?

"Anyway, two weeks after we returned from our trip, Daniel dumped his fiancée, and he just kept showing up at my house. We got married in my parents' garden." Simone looked off into the horizon. "In the rain."

I didn't ask her if she believed in rain causing bad luck.

"But Marci was wrong about one thing. We're going to have three more kids."

"Daniel must love children too," I said, assuming that a man who would rub a strange woman's scalp while she threw up egg salad would be patient and kind and want a houseful of kids and animals.

"He does. We're working hard on it," she said cheerfully, but she no longer looked like the woman who had shamed the smart-ass volleyball player with her bionic arm.

The role of confidante made me feel so important that I ignored the sun burning my ankles. I just wanted Simone to keep talking.

She covered my ankles with the corner of her towel. "Careful, this sun is stronger than you're used to back in Milwaukee."

I was pleased that she'd remembered my hometown.

She pulled her wallet out of her bag. "Wanna see Daniel?"

She smoothed the buckled plastic over a snapshot of Ollie in the arms of a man with shoulder-length wavy blond hair. His teeth were as white as Simone's, and he had Robert Redford's chiseled jawline. They were the most gorgeous human beings I'd ever seen.

Tzippy didn't come home from Brooklyn until late June because the rebbetzin flew to New York to help her shop for the wedding and to spend time with Tzippy's Uncle Shlomo, who had survived the Yom Kippur War. I didn't miss her until I knew she was back. Her first letter from Milwaukee made me cry so hard that I had to put ice cubes on my eyeballs.

July 1, 1975 *B"H*

Dear Barbara,

I hate being home without you. I keep thinking that I'll find you in all of our old spots. The bride's room. No Barbara. The bluffs. No Barbara. The nook. Nothing. Of course, I haven't looked for you in the mikveh. Ha, Ha.

There's nobody to giggle with when Mrs. Berger pulls out the goopy tissue from her sleeve and uses it to clean her glasses. This is how you must feel when I leave for Brooklyn. I'm lonely.

I still don't understand exactly why you couldn't stay home this summer, but my mother said that helping my cousins is a great opportunity for you to do a mitzvah and experience another part of the country. I shouldn't be selfish.

Please send my love to Sari. Isn't she nice? Please send my love to yourself too.

Your best friend,

Tzippy

I didn't write Tzippy back for weeks. It hurt too much. I distracted myself by looking for Simone and Ollie at the beach. July was an unusually hot month, and Benny and I went to La Jolla Shores three or four times a week. We didn't run into Simone and Ollie again until the last week of August, and when we did, Benny climbed on my lap and buried his face in my chest.

Simone knelt beside him. "There's someone who's been asking to see you," she said.

Benny picked up his head and smiled shyly at Simone while Ollie shouted, "Benny! Let's play!" The two trotted off with their buckets and waited for the water to reach their toes.

"He gets bashful," I explained.

Simone laid out her towel. "Ollie gets that way too sometimes."

I was hoping Simone would tell me more about psychics and palm readers. After our last conversation, I borrowed Rabbi Levenstein's Chumash and looked up the line from Deuteronomy that I vaguely remembered Tzippy showing me after the Purim incident: "For these nations which you inherit, they listen to fortune-tellers and diviners; but as for you, not so has Hashem your God given."

Simone pulled a bottle of coconut suntan oil from her bag. "So what's new?" She seemed tired.

"Oh, the same, you know. And you?"

She yawned. "I'm beat." She said her new live-in babysitter had decided to move up to Monterey with her boyfriend, so she was taking care of Ollie during the day and working night shifts.

I'll be your babysitter, I almost said, fantasizing about packing up my things and leaving a note for Sari, but I could never desert Benny or let the rebbetzin down, so instead, I offered Simone a sympathetic nod. She drizzled the oil on her legs and handed me the bottle, and I poured too much on my ankles. I dabbed it up with my fingers and rubbed it into my hands, grainy from the sand sticking to them.

"Sorry, didn't mean to waste your oil," I said.

"It's cool." Dark circles had formed under her eyes.

I wished I could offer to take Ollie home with me, but I didn't think Sari would approve. "I can watch the boys if you want to sleep," I said.

"I couldn't ask you to do that," Simone said, but something in her tone made me think that if I asked again, she'd say yes.

"I don't mind. You should get some sleep."

Simone leaned back on her towel and shaded her face with her arm. "You're too good to be true."

"Come on, boys." I took their gritty hands in mine. We walked down to the water, the wind blowing my hair into my eyes. I pushed it away with my wrist, and the scent of coconut, Simone's scent, flooded my nose. While Simone dozed, we built sandcastles. It made me feel important to help her, which I would do for as long as she wanted me to.

One Wednesday afternoon in October, we returned from the beach to find Sari wearing a big smile and holding a plate of cinnamon cookies she'd baked. I left Benny to his mother and went down to my room. A few minutes later, I heard laughter and splashing coming from Sari's bathroom. Her morning sickness had dragged on longer than she'd expected, and I was glad she finally had the energy to bake cookies and give Benny a bath. After I showered and dressed, I took my skirt and Benny's shorts out to the back porch to shake the sand out, thinking that it would be so much easier if we could both wear bathing suits. I was lucky, though: Many Chasidic rabbis wouldn't have allowed their children to visit a public beach at all.

When I got back to my room, I found an envelope from Tzippy on my pillow, along with a note from Sari that my mother had called. Not long after I met Simone and Ollie, my homesickness had begun to dull. It helped that Tzippy had returned to Brooklyn to help Uncle Shlomo's wife take care of their triplets, and that my mother had started coming to the phone, sounding more like her old self with each conversation. She'd even gone back to school for a degree in American history, so we had plenty to talk about.

Her recovery was a good thing, and I dared to hope that life would return to normal when I got home, but sometimes I'd find myself stewing, regretting that I hadn't attended my high school graduation because I knew my mother couldn't extricate herself from her bed to be there, or swearing to my father that I didn't want to go, or worrying that the horrible grades I'd received while she was sick would cause Madison to change their mind about accepting me.

My parents and I usually only spoke on Sunday nights, so I phoned back, worried that something might have happened. "Is everything okay?" I asked after my mother accepted my collect call.

"Yes, darling." She sounded good. "Have you heard from Tzippy lately?"

Tzippy had written me a brief note last week. I knew she was getting married in January, but it stung to read about her wedding plans that were progressing very nicely without me. My face grew warm.

"Yeah," I said.

"I'm so happy you'll be home for the wedding," my mother said cheerfully. "I'm going to send you a plane ticket tomorrow."

"Me too, thanks." I remembered the pledge I'd made to Tzippy in the nook a lifetime ago. I wasn't going to let her down for anything.

After we hung up, I reread Tzippy's letter.

October 9, 1975 *B"H*

Dear Barbara,

I'm starting to get excited about the wedding. When I was home over the summer, my mother showed me her long lace veil that my grandmother brought from Poland. I told my mother that we'd already figured out how to wear our hair at our weddings. All of those hours playing beauty shop in the brides' room will pay off!

I can't wait to see you in January. I hope we'll have a few days together before things get crazy. I miss you.

Love,

Tzippy

I wrote Tzippy about her wedding and the lace veil, and then I wrote another letter that I would tuck away in my suitcase and never send.

October 17, 1975 *B"H*

Dear Tzippy,

While you've been planning your wedding, I've been imagining what it will be like to come home. I still can't believe that your parents did not kick my mother out of the shul. I worry that they will now that my mother is healthy again.

We'll move to Brookfield, near Mr. Isen, and my mother will realize what she's done and fall back in love with my father, and he'll join us. We'll miss your parents and our old lives, but we'll all be together, in Brookfield, away from people gossiping and staring at us like we stared at Mr. Isen. There's life outside of the shul, I'm finding out. It's not that bad.

Of course, I'd hate living in Brookfield more than anything. I want our family to stay in the shul, but it's good to be prepared.

Your best friend no matter what,

Barbara

I put my sneakers on, snuck out of the house, and walked. I walked and walked until my calves burned, three miles to La Jolla Shores in the dark and home again. If I kept moving, I could forget everything I'd left behind and distract myself from wanting it all back.

12

I experienced my first Santa Ana in late December. Hot, dry winds blew so fiercely that they made my eyes burn and my skin chalky. The sun was relentless. The night after the winds passed, I took one of my long walks to meander along the shoreline and listen to the sound of the waves. It had been a gray day, but now a round patch of sunlight broke through the clouds and shone on the water like a spotlight illuminating a dark stage. I'd never seen anything like it. I was pleasantly surprised to spy Simone walking toward the light. She looked like some sort of angel, dressed in her white nurse's uniform with matching stockings and shoes, her hair out of her bun and flowing down her back. She must have stopped here on the way home from her shift.

"Where's Ollie?" I couldn't think of anything else to say.

She stretched her arms over her head. "Daniel's home with him now. Long week."

Daniel. When I read my romance novels, I imagined that the heroes looked like either Paul Newman or the photo I'd seen of Simone's husband.

"You hungry?" she asked me.

"Yeah." I was hungry, and I hadn't given up hope that we'd talk again like we had before she started coming to the beach to nap.

I followed her to her powder-blue VW bug. I'd never ridden in such a small car. Simone skillfully moved her feet between the three floor pedals while negotiating the skinny stick shift with her right hand and adjusting the rearview mirror with her left. She drove us to a little diner in La Jolla and flagged down a waitress with gold hoop earrings and bleached blond hair (it seemed like everyone was blond in San Diego). She ordered coffee for herself and a vanilla milkshake for me. I stared at an older couple sharing a hamburger, fascinated by the man, who was counting out the number of fries he put on each plate.

Simone caught me staring and teased me. "What do Wisconsin restaurant patrons look like?"

"My family rarely ate in restaurants," I said.

"Was it the kosher thing?"

"Sort of."

"Is your mom like Sari?"

I took a sip of my milkshake, wondering if they possibly could have used kosher ice cream. "What do you mean?"

"You know, does she wear a wig?"

I laughed, imagining the Shabbos goy admiring my mom's wig. "Definitely not."

"Someday maybe you'll tell me about your parents."

I couldn't imagine telling Simonc about my family. I didn't want to.

She dropped five dollars on the table. "My treat."

"You don't havc to do that."

Simone threw her keys in the air and caught them as she walked toward the door. "It's the least I can do for all the sleep you've given me."

"I didn't mind." I loved taking care of the boys.

Simone didn't need me to point out the Levensteins' house. I'm sure there weren't too many townhouses with enormous menorahs planted on the front lawn. If things went as well as they had for Rabbi Schine and his brothers, Jews would soon move into the neighborhood so they could stop driving to shul on Shabbos. Tzippy and I had watched it happen lots of times. But this was unlikely in Rabbi Levenstein's case. He had recruited a dozen men from the hospital who needed a place to say kaddish for their dead wives, but they wouldn't last. Rabbi Schine could

"Schineify" newcomers with a single glance, my dad always said. Rabbi Levenstein wasn't Levenstein-ifying anybody. Sometimes I just wanted to sit him down and tell him to find Orthodox Jews who looked secular enough not to intimidate the recruits. I'd tell him to hire an ugly Shabbos goy, though.

"You there?" Simone touched my knee lightly.

"I'm probably going back to Milwaukee soon," I said. "Sari is due next week."

"Do you want to stay?"

The option had never occurred to me. "I have to get back for my best friend's wedding."

"She's getting married now? What is she, eighteen or something?"

"Yeah." For the first time in my life, I imagined how the matchmaker arrangement would sound to an outsider. Simone would never understand.

"Are you getting married too?"

I laughed. "Me? No. I'll find my own husband somehow."

"Why couldn't you move out here after the wedding?"

"I don't know about that." I still missed home, but the thought of moving to San Diego made me feel wildly free.

Simone pulled up to the condo and turned off the motor. The menorah looked gigantic.

"Excuse me." She leaned across me to open the glove compartment. She smelled like coffee and the cloves the rebbetzin used in her gingered spice cake.

"One of Ollie's markers." She pulled off the cap and touched my knuckles." I don't have any paper. May I write on your hand?"

"Of course."

She took my hand. Her fingers were stubby and strong. "Can I read your palm first?"

I felt a rush about experimenting with what the Schines would consider sorcery. I was a little scared, too, but I opened my hand and didn't recoil when she traced the line that ran diagonally from my index finger to the edge. "What do you see?" I asked.

"This is the heart line." She held my palm up to the street light streaming through the front windshield. "Very unusual."

"Why?" I liked that something about me was capturing her attention.

She drew my palm further into the light. "Your heart line splits in two here." She pointed to the break in the line.

"What does that mean?"

She looked more closely. "I'm an amateur, so I shouldn't say."

"You have to tell me now."

She returned my hand to my lap. "I think it means that you've had a rupture in your life."

"Yes." The rupture had brought me here, to Simone's car.

"I see some tiny fractures too, but they all connect to the big split."

I bit back the tears that had been waiting for release since I left Milwaukee.

She took my hand again. "But then they come back together right here." She moved her finger further up my palm. "It's beautiful."

I laughed anxiously. "Why is that beautiful?"

She looked right at me. "It means that you will mend the big tear and all of the little ones attached to it, too."

I wanted her to tell me more about my heart line, although I found it unsettling that she'd intuited things about my broken life. "Thank you, Simone."

She held up the marker and reclaimed my hand. "Here, I'll write my phone number on the top so you can look at those lines on your palm if you want to." She spoke sweetly, in a tone she might use with Ollie or a patient.

The marker tickled, but I didn't giggle.

"You've got a job and a place to live if you want to come back. Ollie would love it."

I weakly promised to call Simone if I decided to come back to San Diego, but now that I knew I would mend this tear, my life in Milwaukee would return to normal, and the rebbetzin would let me stay there for good.

"Barbara!" I awoke to the sound of Rabbi Levenstein pounding on my bedroom door. My clock read 4:48 a.m. As Sari and the rabbi rushed out of the house, I dressed quickly, then stretched out on the couch to wait for Benny to wake up.

Rabbi Levenstein's adrenaline was contagious, and I was too restless to fall back asleep. I poured myself some cereal and doused it with milk and sugar. I ate the entire bowl and returned to the couch, sated and sleepy. Just as I nodded off, I felt Benny's warm breath on my face.

"Where are my mommy and daddy?"

"Hey." I sat up. "Your mommy is having her baby right now."

Benny started laughing and pointed to my left cheek.

"What's so funny?"

"You wrote numbers on your face."

We went to the bathroom mirror and he pointed to my cheek, where the phone number had rubbed off. I must have slept on my hand. I couldn't find a pad of paper, so I tore off a corner of a grocery bag and transcribed Simone's number. Then I returned to the bathroom and rubbed my face with a sponge until there were no traces of the marker.

Two days after Miriam Levenstein was born, I packed my things, changed the sheets, and scrubbed the floors until they gleamed. Sari's parents were flying in from New York, and as much as she appreciated my help, I could tell that she no longer wanted to share Benny. My usefulness to the Levenstein family had expired.

On the flight home, I tried to concentrate on reading *Jonathan Livingston Seagull*, a graduation gift from Neil, but I was too distracted. In a few hours, I would face my mother. If she was a normal weight and her color was good, it could mean one of two things: she'd gotten over the Shabbos goy, or he was back.

Of course it was over, I assured myself. There was no way

my mother could have accepted the rebbetzin's forgiveness and kindness and then turned around and resumed her love affair. No, she was done with the Shabbos goy. Everyone made mistakes. We would all move on and heal from this. I massaged those lines in my hand, hoping that Simone had been right.

My mother was waiting for me at the gate in the cornflower-blue coat that she now filled out and a scarf I'd given her for her birthday. It was full of blues and greens that set off her eyes, and her cheeks no longer sank into her head. New lines had formed around her mouth, but she looked happy.

"Hello, hello." She wrapped an arm around my waist and pulled me toward her.

I couldn't help but warm to her embrace. She was back! She'd returned from wherever she'd gone while she was sick.

"Let me take a look." She studied me in a way she hadn't since before the Shabbos goy stole her from us. "All that sunshine agreed with you."

"I loved it there," I replied.

"Oh, everyone should have an adventure at your age, sweetheart. I'm just glad you're back." She looped her arm through mine as we walked to the baggage claim.

Our house smelled the same: cigarettes and the Lemon Pledge our cleaning lady used to polish the floors. My father's galoshes were lined up neatly next to the back door. I dragged my suitcase upstairs and ran a hot shower. My bathroom at the Levensteins had a mirror slightly larger than my head, so I hadn't seen my naked body since I left. I cleared the condensation from the long mirrors in my bathroom. Thick strands of gold striped my hair, and new freckles sprayed the bridge of my nose. My hands and wrists were brown. I turned around to look at the back of my body. My legs and rear were taut and sinewy from walking and racing Benny down the beach. My eyes reluctantly traveled up my back. A miracle. The skin had nearly cleared. I wished my arms were miles long so I could reach over my shoulders and feel the smoothness with my own fingers. Maybe the rebbetzin hadn't exiled me; maybe she knew that I needed to grow new skin. I was home, and my mother was healthy again, and that was all that mattered.

My father greeted me when I came downstairs.

"How's my California girl?" he said, shaking his winter coat from his shoulders. His skin looked gray and his lips slightly blue, and he hadn't gained back the weight he'd lost while my mother was sick.

I walked over to him and put my arms around him. "I missed you, Dad."

He hugged me back in his awkward way, and we both waited an extra second before we let go. "Me too, Bunny."

My mother called us to the table, and over meatballs and rice, my favorite meal, I told my parents about Benny and Ollie and Simone. My dad nodded and smiled, and we talked about his patients and my mom's history paper. They told me that Tzippy would be home in a few days to prepare for her wedding. The mention of her name gave me a jolt. I mentally counted the hours until I could see her.

When my mother got up to refill the rice bowl, she put her hand on my father's shoulder, which I took as a sure sign that the Shabbos goy was out of the picture. I tried not to grin when my father's eyes, shining with love and admiration, trailed her into the kitchen.

"I ran into Mrs. Kessler a few weeks ago at the butcher, I forgot to tell you." My mother dug her fork into a meatball. "She's proud that you're going to pursue Madison's teaching program."

Yes, I could become just like Mrs. Kessler, adored by the children, respected by their parents, someone who always did the right thing. I chewed on that idea while my dad and I watched *Kojak*, his favorite show. Maybe I was imagining things, but his breathing seemed labored. I kissed his cheek and went off to bed.

"Glad you're home, Barbara," he said as he picked up his newspaper and disappeared into the front section.

It was Tuesday, and I couldn't help lying awake, alert, waiting for my mom to creep out of the house, even though the information coded onto my palm and my physical transformation gave me hope that all of life's blemishes had disappeared with a little sunshine and a glimpse of a different world. I heard nothing as I listened for my mother's footsteps.

I didn't let the bitter weather interfere with my morning walk. I trudged up and down Lake Drive, the air whistling through my cap. My ears were numb by the time I returned to our warm kitchen. My mother placed a steaming mug of cocoa in front of me and asked if I wanted to go shopping.

"I'd love to." We hadn't been shopping together in more than a year.

"First, we have a stop to make." She ran upstairs and returned from her bedroom with a canvas bag she used to tote library books. The bag was heavy and dragged on her shoulder. She set it down and signaled me to look inside. I thumbed through the pile of Michener novels.

"You read all these?" I asked.

"Every last one," she said with pride, telling me without the exact words that we were done with her illness and the Shabbos goy. I wrapped my arms around her, and she didn't feel as if her bones would break. She pulled me close and stroked my back for a few seconds. I almost started to sob.

We spoke little as we drove to the library and then to the Boston Store, but my mother looked over at me a few times and smiled. We walked into the mall like any other mother and daughter visiting a department store, shopping for an outfit to wear to a wedding. She snatched a reddish-brown wool dress off the rack and held it up to my face. "This looks pretty with your hair."

She waited outside the changing room while I glided the dress over my head. It was a soft wool, a grown-up fabric I'd never worn before, and it fit as though it were made for me. The neckline revealed a tiny bit of collarbone, and because I was short, it hung below my knees, so I could wear it to the Schines'. I pulled my shoulders back and examined the way the dress fell over my breasts. I tentatively exited the changing room and walked toward the stool where my mother sat, by the three-way mirror.

She stood beside me and put her hand on top of my head. "When did you grow taller than your mom?"

"Guess it was the California sunshine."

"So what do you think?"

"I like it." I was referring to both the dress and the feel of her hand.

My mother touched my neck lightly. "It will look nice with my pearls."

I felt like Eliza Doolittle in the dress and the pearls I imagined against my skin. She bought me the dress, a pair of nylons, and a white half-slip. It wasn't elegant or sexy like hers, but she told me that it would make my dress hang better on my body. It did. I held two large shopping bags on my lap as we drove out of the parking lot.

"You don't mind if we stop at Beckerman's on the way home?" She turned on her blinker. "I just need to pick up some sandwich steaks."

The butcher shop was small and dingy, and you could just see the back room where maroon beef carcasses striped with columns of white fat hung on giant hooks. My mother greeted Mr. Beckerman, a small man whose beard overpowered his tiny face.

"Hello, Mrs. Pupnick. Let me go and get your steaks," he said as if my mother was his best friend.

Just then, the front door opened, and a gust of cold air assaulted my ankles. I turned my head. The rebbetzin stood in the doorframe in a stylish cap and the black double-breasted coat she'd sewn a few winters back. Her nose was red from the cold. My anger toward her had been dissolving for months, and now I was just happy to be here with her and my mother. She held my mother's hands and then turned to me and pinched my chin with one of her cold fingers.

"I heard wonderful things about you from the Levensteins," she said.

I looked down at my feet, a little embarrassed but wanting to hear more about the Levensteins' compliments. "Benny was easy."

"You did a real mitzvah," the rebbetzin said. "And your mother didn't tell me how gorgeous you look. Tzippy can't wait to see you. She'll be home the day after tomorrow, early she's coming. Ten o'clock."

"I can't wait either," I said, blushing.

Mr. Beckerman returned with a brown paper bag. "Hello, rebbetzin." He turned to my mother. "Let me take this to your car, and I'll be right back."

"Take your time," the rebbetzin told him, "and then I want the news from Florida."

My mother rubbed the rebbetzin's hands. "Your fingers are like icicles, Rivkah." She gave the rebbetzin her gloves. "I got two pairs for my birthday last year."

"June, keep your gloves. I have some at home."

"I only have two hands! I don't want you to get sick before the wedding." My mother put both gloves in her palm and extended it to the rebbetzin. She paused for a second before she accepted my mother's gift, which further convinced me that my mother had ended things with the Shabbos goy. After all, the rebbetzin would never warm to my mother's touch, much less take her gloves, if my mother were still having an affair.

During the drive home, I noticed that my mother's fingernails had purpled from the cold. My hands were sweating inside my mittens, so I took one off and handed it to her. She touched my fingers to see if they were warm and then took one mitten for the hand she used to steer the car and placed her other hand in her pocket.

The day before Tzippy was due home, I filled in for my dad's receptionist, Frannie. I didn't mind answering the phones, listening patiently while the moms figured out how to squeeze my father into their children's schedules. The ones from the northern suburbs had names like Marlene and Brenda and belonged to synagogues with pews and plush red carpeting. They lived in custom-built houses and shuttled their kids to and from Sunday school in their station wagons. Sometimes I wondered what it was like to have the pieces of your life fit together so logically.

Who was I kidding? I wouldn't trade being part of the Schines' world for anything. I fantasized about helping Tzippy prepare for her wedding. I'd spend my days at the mansion, just like when we were kids. We'd retreat to the nook and she'd tell me all about her new husband, and I'd tell her all about the Levensteins and how great she was going to be as a rebbetzin.

I was so excited to see Tzippy that I couldn't fall asleep that night. The house was quiet, and I tried on my new dress. I practiced crossing my legs, smoothing the wool over my bare thighs. I sat in the dark in front of my window and watched the start of a new snowfall.

I was just about to change into my pajamas when I heard the stairs creak. The back door opened, and an engine thrummed. I peered out the window. Snowflakes danced around my mother, dotting the shoulders of her blue coat as she disappeared down the alley. I pressed my hands against the cold glass and opened my mouth to scream. Nothing came out. Inside I was shouting at my mother so loudly that I thought my skull would shatter. You're a liar and a shamer. You shamed Dad. You shamed me. You shamed the rebbetzin. I heard the blue Dodge drive off.

I threw on my boots and walked up Lake Drive to Atwater Beach. I sat down on a wet bench overlooking the black lake. Flakes of snow settled on my face and bare legs. I held my palm up to the streetlight and looked for those lines, searching for the spot where they reconnected. I wanted to believe Simone, but if my mother was still seeing the Shabbos goy, then no rupture could be mended, not now. I might have sat there for ten minutes or an hour, I wasn't sure. When I lost feeling in my toes and lips, I walked the half mile home.

My mother was sitting at the kitchen table waiting for me, an ashtray full of cigarette butts in front of her. She blew out a puff of smoke, narrowing her bloodshot eyes. Her nose was swollen from crying. "I've been worried sick about you."

I glowered at her. I didn't trust my words, so my silent rant continued. All I've done is worry about you, and you've cost us everything, and now you think I'm going to continue hauling around your filthy secret like a fifth limb. I started to hyperventilate, and then I felt as though my head was a carved pumpkin and someone was removing the lid. My mother put her arms around me and guided me upstairs to my room. I couldn't believe that I actually felt comfort in her arms, but I did.

I lay down on my bed, and she returned a few minutes later with a glass of water and a brown paper bag. "Here, breathe into this if you get light-headed again. You're having a panic attack."

I nodded my head.

She smiled sadly. "They pass quickly."

I clutched the bag and took a sip of water. "I can't be a part of this anymore, Mom." I still couldn't breathe very well. "Did you hear what I said?"

She looked down at the bag and nodded.

I felt a shift inside, as though a long chain with a silver hook was scooping me from my bed, from my physical being. I was floating, suspended over myself like my own ghost. Something steely gripped my heart.

"I'm going back to San Diego," I said as the decision came to me.

My mother looked up. "You're going to skip Tzippy's wedding?"

"I don't know." I took a deep breath. Never yet had I broken the commandment to respect my mother. I had held my tongue, but I couldn't any longer. Each word came out with force. "I will not walk into the Schines' shul with you and your lie." I paused. "Ever again."

The air crackled between us. I'd never mentioned her affair.

She rose and said softly, "Don't throw away your friendship

with Tzippy over me."

I wanted to say, You're right, you're not worth it, but instead, I spoke the vow I'd made to myself. "And I will not take care of you after he leaves you again."

I met her eyes and saw the fog rolling in, but she wanted to say something to me first. "Oh, Barbara. It's so much more complicated than that."

I was exhausted. I closed my eyes and seconds later drifted off, wondering if she'd come back and sleep on the floor next to my bed, and despite everything, wishing that she would.

My mother wasn't there when I woke up in the middle of the night, chilled, my new dress gathered in a damp heap next to my bed. I took a hot shower, whimpering like an animal. When the water turned cold, I wrapped myself in a towel and put on pajamas that my mother had washed for me that morning.

The house was still and dark. I found my wallet, retrieved the grocery-bag scrap with Simone's number, and crept into my father's study to use his phone. I almost hung up when a man answered. It had to be Daniel. His voice was inviting and distracted at the same time.

"I'm sorry to be calling so late. May I please speak with Simone? This is Barbara, we used to meet on the beach in La Jolla, and she said she needed a live-in babysitter and that I should call if I wanted to come back to California, which I do, which is why I'm calling, but I can always call back if this is a bad time, and I sure hope I didn't wake Ollie. I could also just give her my number and she can call me back. I know it's long distance, but I can hang up right away and dial her back."

There was silence on the other end.

"Um, is anyone there?"

"I'm here," Daniel answered with a smile in his voice. "Are you done?" He laughed, and I had an odd sense that he would have listened to me for as long as I rambled.

"I'm done."

"Okay, then." He paused. "Simone, for you."

"Thanks, babe," she said. I recognized her voice, confident and a little raspy.

I put it to Simone straight. "I'd like to work for you if you still need help."

I woke up the next morning to the smell of banana muffins baking in the oven. Did my mother think that making me my favorite breakfast was going to erase what happened last night? I picked my dress up from the floor and hung it in the bathroom, and then I crawled back into bed and stared out the window, watching the wind blow the snow off the branches of our oak tree. I folded my hands over my chest and lay still, but my brain was speeding all over the place, trying to figure out what to do next.

After the front door shut and my mother's car engine started, I went to my father's study and booked a flight for myself. It would cost me a chunk of my earnings from working for the Levensteins, but I didn't care. I dressed quickly and walked to the mansion to see Tzippy, the wind biting at my face as I trudged over the icy sidewalks.

Rabbi Schine was in the front hall when I entered the mansion. I greeted him without looking in his direction. I didn't want to find pity in his face, because I wanted to believe that he didn't know that my mother hadn't quit seeing the Shabbos goy.

"Barbara," he said.

I stared at my boots.

"We're glad you're home."

"Thank you, Rabbi Schine," I muttered, still not looking up.

"She's in the bride's room," he said kindly, and I hurried off. The bride's room doubled as a place for mothers to nurse their babies. There was an old couch with juice stains from when Tzippy and I were little and played here during services. Tzippy was sitting in front of the vanity, clearing crayon shavings and crumbs that had accumulated since the last wedding. Our eyes met in the mirror. Hers sparkled, and her skin glowed. This was not the scared girl who had cried to me in Mrs. Kessler's room.

She held her shoulders back, and her smile was radiant. She looked womanly.

She sprang up from her chair and ran to my arms. We held each other for a few minutes. In my reflection in the mirror, I could see the sadness making my whole body droop.

"Tell me all about San Diego." She held my hands in hers and gave me the full force of her attention.

"It's beautiful," I said.

"So isn't Sari a honey pie?"

"She is, but she was really sick, so I didn't see her that much."

"And Benny?"

I missed Benny. "He's very cute, but this is your day. What do we need to do to get ready?"

"My mother just told me that we have twenty more people coming. We have to bake." She rolled her eyes.

"Okay."

"I told her that I'm getting married in a few days, and she not so gently reminded me that I was going to be a rebbetzin and I had to put the needs of the community first."

We got to work in the shul's kitchen. I was relieved that Tzippy and I were using it because I didn't want to bake in the Schines' apartment. I couldn't face the rebbetzin after what happened last night.

"Are you going to tell me about your husband already?" I teased.

Tzippy smiled with her whole face, and we sat on the counter and dangled our legs like we did when we were little. "His name is Zev."

"Okay. I know his name is Zev. Tell me more."

She blushed and then started regaling me with every detail she knew about her fiancé. When she came up for air, I asked her if she was still scared.

"No, excited." She chattered on while we sifted flour, cracked eggs, and chopped almonds.

"You're quiet," Tzippy said.

"I'm concentrating. The last time we made almond cookies they didn't turn out very well."

We didn't talk much as we spooned the dough onto enormous cookie sheets.

"Tzippy!" the rebbetzin called down to the kitchen.

Tzippy excused herself and darted up the steps to her apartment. She seemed young to be a rebbetzin, and soon as she was out of sight, I felt the divide between us grow. Her whole life was mapped out. She would marry her prince and become a leader of her shul, just like her mother. I looked around the kitchen and then up the steps. All of this, the kitchen, the apartment, her parents, she had everything. She didn't need me to come to her wedding; her life was perfect. I could taste the bitterness in my mouth.

Tzippy came back downstairs breathless. "I have to go with my dad to pick up Zev's parents from the airport."

I'd always been allowed to tag along with her, but this time I knew I had no place with her family. I had no place with mine either. "I have to go, too."

"Can you come by tomorrow?"

"I'll be here," I said, knowing I wouldn't.

Tzippy walked me to the door and kissed my cheek. The air was colder here by the lake, and I bundled up. I was almost down the driveway when I heard Tzippy calling after me.

"Barbara, Barbara."

I turned around. She was running toward me in her stocking feet and long wool skirt, one hand holding her grandmother's veil on her head. The white lace billowed in the wind.

"I forgot to show you this," she said, panting.

She stood so close that I could feel her breath on my hair. I already missed us, who we were, who we would never be again. I wasn't jealous anymore. I loved her again, more than I ever had.

"Lucky Zev," I said.

"And you're going to catch me if I faint, right?"

"I'll be here to catch you, Tzippy."

"Good. It's freezing out here, see you tomorrow." She laughed and ran back toward the mansion, her veil trailing behind her. I watched her kiss the mezuzah on the front door and go inside. She shut the door behind her as my eyes watered from the cold.

When I got home, I went straight up to my room and packed. I decided to leave my wool dress and my other long skirts behind and take the two pairs of jeans I wore when we went sledding. I crawled under my covers and slept until morning.

The sun was just beginning to rise when the cab arrived. The wind chill must have been well below zero, but I left without a coat. I wouldn't need one in California. "Mitchell Field," I told the cabbie.

A light flicked on in my house, and seconds later my father stood on the front steps, robeless, looking old and foolish in his orange striped pajamas, his slippers covered with fresh snow. He didn't try to stop me. He just raised his hand, but I couldn't really see him, so I couldn't tell if he was waving goodbye or shooing me away from home.

I wanted to trudge back up the driveway and hug my father, not because I felt sorry for him, but because I loved him, as I did my mother. Plain and messy as hell.

13

October 2009

I decided to take the Shabbos goy's advice and ask my mother the questions that tormented me. I had to. I'd been driving by the mansion every day for two weeks and dreaming of the mikveh and my uncle's crippled legs at night and torturing myself with visions of an increasingly sullen Lili hospitalized for depression.

I phoned Jenny on my way to work to see if I could stop by and visit my mother on the way home.

"How are you doing?" I'd called to check in on Jenny a few times after her father's funeral, but we'd carefully avoided the topic of my mother.

"Oh, I'm hanging in." She sounded distant, and that hurt. After we exchanged niceties, I asked if I could arrange a time for me to visit my mother this afternoon.

"That's not such a great idea, Barbara," Jenny said with a kindness that bordered on condescension.

"Excuse me?"

"Neil called Lakeline, and we're going to move Mom tomorrow. We're not equipped to handle her," Jenny said.

So I wasn't the only one who couldn't handle my mother. I felt a rush of relief. "Okay, but why can't I visit her today?"

Jenny paused. "She's agitated."

"I'm her daughter, Jenny." Like the Shabbos goy, Jenny was protecting my mother from *me*, and this stung like hell.

Jenny sighed. "You and Neil should hash this out."

Great. Now I was fighting with Jenny, who had never flaunted her relationship with my mother and was just trying to do her best.

"I'm sorry, I'm being horrible," I said.

"It's all right," she said, but I could tell that she was grieving hard for Big Al and didn't have the energy to deal with me.

"No, it's not. You're right. Settle her in, and let me know when I can visit." I hung up so I wouldn't say, "And please stop calling her Mom."

I switched lanes and cut off a young man, and he honked at me so hard that I almost started to cry. I didn't like being at odds with anyone, be it an exasperated driver or big-hearted Jenny. As much as I hated this truth, whatever history the tahara had dug up between my mother and me needed to be sorted out and put to rest.

Breathe, Barbara, breathe. Work would calm me down. I felt like my old self when catching my students "being good" and mentoring Theresa. I stopped at Starbucks to pick up a skim latte, my new habit. I'd never understood the big whoop about Starbucks, but now I was so tired all the time that I relied on an early-morning and late-afternoon venti to power me through the day. By the time Theresa came in, caffeine was strumming the chords of my central nervous system, and I had emerged from the phone booth, Superteacher costume intact.

Daphne, a quiet little girl, arrived early, wearing leftover oatmeal on her upper lip. She carried her lovey, a tattered brown mouse she'd brought for Show and Share. I sat down next to her. She pointed to her stuffed animal. "His name is Ted."

I shook the mouse's paw firmly. "Hello, Ted. Welcome to the Hummingbird Room."

Daphne laughed and surprised me with a warm hug. The sudden sweetness of the gesture buoyed me. The room began to fill. Ally arrived, and her mother told me a long-winded story about how she had been the big girl at her sister's birthday party over the weekend. She'd helped the little ones put on their tutus and comb their hair. Joan wanted so badly for me to tell her that this meant Ally was okay, but I knew that within the next hour she would be pushing or maybe even biting one of her peers. I put my arm around Joan's bony shoulder.

"Ally can be helpful, and I'm glad the party went well. I'd still like us to get to the bottom of what's bothering her, though." I felt Joan's shoulder sag under my arm.

"Can I call you again tonight?" She looked desperate.

"You can always call me."

Josh Fader's mom, in her customary yoga pants and baseball cap, hovered behind Joan. She looked upset, so I took her into the hall, and she told me she was worried that Josh was experiencing developmental delays. I let her talk for five minutes, holding her bundle of fear in my hands, and then, without warning, I lost my usual patience when she described Josh's inability to read the Bob books, which her nephews had all done at age four.

"Yeah, yeah, yeah. You need to stop comparing Josh to his cousins," I said sharply. "What good is it doing anyone?"

Typically, after she'd talked long enough, she'd hear the silliness of her concern and the worry would vanish from her face. "This is why they call you the guru," she'd say, mistaking my silence for a mysterious wisdom that had always felt unearned. My abruptness today shocked her, and she lowered the bill of her cap with a perfectly manicured finger. "We can talk later. I can see you're busy," she said, recoiling into herself.

Damn. I'd never shut down a parent, even one of the overbearing ones who drove my colleagues nuts. That was why Sarah gave me the kids with the most demanding moms and dads.

When I returned to the classroom, Theresa had gathered the kids for Circle Time, and we sang a song about chipmunks, loudly and off key.

"Everyone's full of vim and vigor this morning." Theresa clapped her hands together. The high pitch of her voice jangled my nerves as it never had before.

By the time the last mother collected her child and I walked out to my car, my gut was churning. During the months I'd escaped into the calm of Mrs. Kessler's apartment and Yossi's adoration, my mother's mess would be waiting patiently for me when I emerged. Now the mess was seeping into my happy place.

I drove around aimlessly, manufacturing errands that I hoped would anchor me, and after I'd filled two grocery bags and picked up a week's worth of Sam's shirts from the dry cleaners, I went home. I sat down at the kitchen table and made a list of supplies I would need for our autumn unit, ingredients for the Greek salad I'd bring to book club, and people to whom we owed dinner invitations. I alphabetized my spice rack and emptied our pantry of the canned goods that had expired.

I left a message on Sheri's cell phone, but I didn't really want to talk to her. Our relationship operated under certain rules. I looked to her for sartorial and etiquette guidance, entertainment, and the nurturing she gave so readily, and I'd helped her find hospice care for her father and then arranged the shiva at her house after he died. Sharing my fears about my mother and Lili violated the rubric of our friendship. Granted, it was a rubric that I'd created.

I couldn't sit at home with my thoughts for one more second, so I left early to pick Lili up from Kara's house. Kara had invited Lili and Megan over after school to celebrate her birthday. Lili had been hanging around that unnerving Taylor Miller lately, and I was relieved that she was going to spend time with her old friends. I told her I'd pick her up and take her straight to her physical therapy appointment.

Kara's mother, Dot, answered the door in her expensive exercise clothes. Dot, a professional Clutterbuster, kept such an immaculate house that I wondered if there was any trash in her garbage pails. When the girls were in junior high, I was surprised to find that Kara was the more sought-after babysitter; Lili was more gifted with children, but Kara would load and empty dishwashers, clean and arrange condiments in the fridge, and fold laundry. Here I went again, comparing the two. I couldn't help it when it came to Kara. Dawn and I had once discussed how Dot's intensity goaded us into competition.

"The girls have been having *so* much fun here," Dot said, still winded from the treadmill.

I wanted to tell her how much more fun they always had at our house, but I bit my tongue. "Well, congratulations on Kara's birthday. Soon you'll have a driver in the house."

"I'm not worried," Dot said. "Kara's *very* responsible."

And Lili wasn't? "Well, we should get going. Lili's got a physical therapy appointment."

"That was such a shame about the season," Dot said, oozing sympathy.

Right, Dot. Kara wouldn't have made it to Sectionals if Lili had been healthy. I smiled and said in my friendliest tone, "Not a shame for Kara!"

Dot laughed nervously as my smile widened. I could not believe what had just come out of my mouth.

"Sure you don't want to stay?" she said, and took a swig from her water bottle.

God, there was no way I could stay. More ugliness would certainly escape my lips if I didn't leave. "Such a lovely offer, Dot, but we really need to run."

The girls came down the stairs right then.

"Happy birthday, sweetie." I kissed Kara's cheek and then Megan's for good measure.

"Thanks, Mrs. Blumfield." Kara smiled at me and looked me right in the eye, something Taylor Miller would never do.

"See you at school." Lili hugged her friends, but their goodbye seemed stilted, as if they weren't sure if this afternoon had reunited them or was simply a respite from Lili's withdrawal. I sure missed Megan, with her uncorrected crossbite and unspoiled appreciation for every small thing I did for her, and I missed Kara, who was lovable despite Dot. I even missed the girls I didn't like nearly as much, like Jenna, who routinely clogged our toilet, and Britt, whose iPhone needed to be surgically removed.

"Sounds like you had fun," I said as we went out to the car. Lili was now walking without crutches, but she hadn't fully recovered.

"Kind of." She teetered on the edge of sulking, which I couldn't take at that moment.

While I sat in the lobby of the physical therapy practice, I pulled out my laptop and started to catch up on correspondence. I thought about emailing Dot to apologize but decided against it. It might only draw attention to my remark. I did write a follow-up note with a distinct tone of apology to Josh Fader's mom, and I sent out the inaugural head lice memo, which made me scratch my scalp as it always did.

Lili appeared in the lobby with Susan, a marathon runner who had been specially assigned to her.

"What do you think, champ?" Susan asked her.

"It doesn't seem to be healing that fast." Lili looked so disappointed that I wanted to leap up and wrap my arms around her.

"Patience. You keep working at it," Susan assured her.

"And *you* keep saying that." I detected my own new hardness in Lili's voice.

Susan tapped her on the arm lightly with her clipboard. "See you next week, and don't forget your home exercises."

I looked at Susan apologetically. In the parking lot, Lili shut the car door too hard.

I waited for her to talk, but she didn't. When we got home, she hobbled up to her room, and I unloaded the dishwasher, one of her pre-injury chores that I'd absorbed into my routine. Then I cut up a pear and some sharp cheddar and put the slices on a plate.

I knocked on her door.

"It's open," she said sullenly.

She was in her team sweatshirt, sitting on the pink beanbag chair we'd given her for her ninth birthday. Her bad leg was propped up on a footstool, and her good leg supported her laptop. I sat down next to her, and we watched a clip of her winning the Sectionals meet last year. Sam had caught her sprinting to the finish line, auburn ponytail flopping back and forth, a feral look on her face as she passed the top seed during the last five yards. She was stunning.

She stared at the screen wistfully. "I miss running."

"I know, baby."

Her eyes started to well. "I mean like a lot."

I put my arm around her slim shoulders.

"I love everything about it, even when it hurts and I feel like I'm going to puke because I'm pushing myself so hard." She was still staring at the screen.

"You know you're going to run again." I squeezed her shoulders. "Soon."

"It's not just that. All Kara and Megan could talk about was Coach JJ and her new method of torture, or last week when the team went to Kopp's and Tricia laughed so hard that strawberry custard came out of her nose, and blah blah blah." She pulled the sleeves of her sweatshirt over her hands.

I waited for her to go on.

"And then when they'd notice that I wasn't exactly chiming in because I didn't exactly have anything to add, they'd change the subject."

"Oh, honey." I felt the familiar pinch that had always accompanied Lili's relaying of any sort of playground hurt.

"It made me feel left out." She wiped her eyes before a tear escaped.

"Lil. I know how it feels to be left out. And it's no fun."

She turned to me with interest. "Like when were you left out?"

I sighed. "Where to begin...."

"Anywhere." She looked eager for my words, and I couldn't let her down.

"High school, for starters. We were very religious growing up."

"Grandma eats shrimp now," Lili said.

"Yeah, well, I guess the religious thing didn't stick."

"Why?" Lili probed.

I wanted to offer her some words of comfort, but I didn't want to get into the Schines' story right now.

"I know, Mom. It was 'complicated'." She put air quotes around the word.

I stared at her computer screensaver, a photo of her with Kara and Megan. "Actually I was going to say lonely."

Lili shut off her computer.

"Let's go downstairs. We'll have a homework party." I needed to trace and cut fourteen pine trees out of construction paper. I carried her backpack while she followed me down to the den. She was quiet again, and when I looked over at her, she was doodling in her notebook. Her despondency cast a hook into the deepest part of me.

"Lili, what do you think of this tree?"

She scrutinized the paper and made a face. "Kind of flat."

"Well, what would you suggest?"

She put her chin on her hand and thought for a second. "I have an idea."

She got up and went outside. I knew she'd come up with something clever. Lili had a gift for making art out of objects most people would throw away, a magnet out of bottle cap, a purse from an old T-shirt, a Chanukah card artfully decorated with wax she'd dug out and saved from our old menorah. Sam and I had urged her to take art classes, but she declined. She said her hobby was private, and I respected that. She had a knack for finding disparate pieces and putting them together like a puzzle. I didn't. I loved to sew and crochet, but my ideas for art projects came from the internet and Theresa and my daughter.

Lili came back inside with an armful of pinecones, put them on the table, and hobbled upstairs. She returned with a box of her old dolls and their paraphernalia. "Look, you can make the Autumn family," she said.

"But Lili, these belong to your dolls."

"Mom, it's okay. This is going to be so cool." She dug into the box.

I could feel myself grinning as I watched her match hats and aprons to her pinecone family. We were both so consumed with her project that we didn't hear Sam pull into the garage.

"Dad, meet the Autumns," she said, and told him about the project she'd thankfully hijacked from me.

Sam kissed me. "Are you going to compensate her for once again saving your bacon?"

I shook my head. "She's got the gift, that's for sure."

Lili was hyperfocused on her pinecones, but I could tell she was listening.

"I know exactly where I'm taking you girls for dinner. Grab your sweaters," Sam said cheerfully.

"You must have sent off your newsletter?" Since the economy tanked, he'd been tense, busying himself crafting client email messages with hopeful tidbits about market trends.

"It's a masterpiece. So what do you say, Lil?" He grinned.

"Too much homework to catch up on. You guys go. I'll be fine." Her phone started vibrating, and she picked it up and read the incoming text. She smiled as she pounded away on the keyboard.

I leaned over to her and stroked her kinky hair, not wanting to leave her alone.

"You lovebirds need your smoochy-smoochy time," she said. Her whole demeanor had changed since she received the text.

I hoped it was from Kara or Megan, but I suspected otherwise. "What are you going to do?"

"Susan worked me out hard, so I'm just going to go finish my homework and go to bed early." Her phone buzzed again.

"You sure?"

"Go on, Mom. You two need a night off from me."

Sam looked at me and mouthed, "She's right." He loved being with Lili, but he'd always needed time alone with me, and took the lead on planning long weekends away at least once a season. Much of his job involved entertaining, and he said he craved his "Barbara time."

"I hate to leave you, but all right. There are a few leftover drumsticks and some rice in the fridge."

"Okay," she said.

"We won't be home late," Sam said.

"What time?" she asked eagerly.

"Ten or so," he said.

"Great, have fun." She returned to her texting.

"Lili," I said.

She looked up.

I pointed to the table. "You're really good at this."

"Thanks, Mom."

I went up to our bathroom to brush my teeth and rub cover-up over a brand-new pair of angry blemishes that had formed a few inches above my eyebrow.

Sam met me in the hallway. "You look pretty."

He moved to kiss my cheek, but his eyes lingered a few seconds on my two new pimples.

"Lucy and Ethel." I rolled my eyes up toward my forehead.

He laughed as he guided me down the steps, out of the kitchen, and into the garage.

"So where are you taking me, Mr. Mystery?" He did his Groucho Marx eyebrow-raising thing as he opened the car door for me. He popped in his favorite Bruce Springsteen CD and held my hand as he drove through the empty downtown streets toward loud polka music and the smell of lake and bratwursts and beer. Oktoberfest.

We parked and walked toward the revelry. A whistle sounded, the polka music stopped, and we followed the crowd to the mouth of a tent. A short man encased in an Usinger's sausage costume took the stage, his arms suspended over the bulky red cotton around his middle. He raised the microphone to his lips. "Welcome to the finals of our annual bratwurst-eating contest."

The whistle sounded again, and four people started cramming bratwursts into their mouths, buns included. A few looked as though they were eating their body weight in pork product. Nobody besides Sam and me found this humorous, maybe because the stakes, twenty-five pounds of Usinger's, were high. We walked away from the tent, and after we caught our breath from laughing, he asked, "Can I get you a brat?" We started all over again.

Sam stood in the brat line while I scanned the picnic area for a place to sit. Most of the patrons were college kids, but there was a group of women roughly my age sitting at a center table, one of whom looked familiar. Yes, it was Dawn.

She was contorting her face in a way that suggested she was doing some kind of impression. The rest of the table was cracking up, and one of the women, a heavier-set version of Dawn, was doubled over with laughter. Another woman reached into her purse and pulled out a pack of cigarettes, and they all lit up. Dawn must have felt me staring at her, because she turned around and waved me over. I walked toward the group feeling self-conscious in my Ann Taylor Loft sweater set and slacks.

Dawn stood up and slung her arm around me. "This is Barbara. Her daughter and Megan are best buds. And Barbara, these are *my* elementary school buddies. Trish, Pam, Mel, Kit." She pointed at each of them.

"Nice to meet you," I said, coveting her childhood friends. I wanted to sit at Tzippy's kitchen table and dunk mandelbrot in tea and laugh with Dawn and her friends' abandon. Although Sheri made me laugh, it was different. We didn't belly laugh. No strawberry custard flew out of our nostrils. Tzippy and I, we really knew how to crack each other up.

"Sam here, or did he go out of town?" Dawn asked. She'd grown up in South Milwaukee, which mean that her "Os" were double the length of those of the people who grew up in the northern suburbs.

"In the brat line." I pointed to the tent ahead of us.

She took a long drag of her cigarette. "Megan said the girls got together today after school."

"Yeah, I wish they'd do more of that." The ache from leaving Lili returned with a vengeance.

"And your mom?"

I sighed. "I'll tell you some time over a stiff drink."

"I want you to call me if I can help," she said.

"I just might," I said, and excused myself to join Sam, who had found two spots on a long picnic bench. A young girl with a T-shirt full of breasts stood up to leave.

"Careful. I got a splinter in my ass from this bench," she warned. She reached up to adjust her ponytail and revealed a belly tattooed with an image of a marijuana plant and the words "Heaven Hemp Me."

"I got you mustard." Sam put a few packets on the table.

I thanked him, and we dressed our brats and bit into them with gusto.

"Dawn's here." I looked over at her table, where she was resting her head on her hand and listening intently to the woman I remembered as Trish. I thought of Dawn standing at cross-country meets in her scrubs or jeans and a T-shirt while the other moms arrived in their yoga outfits or stylish suits if they'd come from work. Her sex appeal and single status marginalized her. I'd often wanted to march over to Dawn to tell her that I didn't fit in with these mothers either, that my childhood could top anyone's in the outcast category.

"A dollar for your thoughts." Sam put his warm hand on my shoulder.

"Lili." I'd rather talk about Lili than my existential loneliness.

"She seemed happy tonight," Sam said.

"Yes, because I was distracting her with an art project. She told me how much she missed running. She just hasn't been herself."

"Could be a whole lot worse." He nodded toward the girl with the tattoo and the breasts, her legs straddling a Harley as a fat middle-aged biker stuck his hand down her shorts.

I laughed. "I guess you have a point. Look, do you mind if we head home? I'm a little tired."

"It's barely nine o'clock."

"I know. Sorry to be a party pooper."

He wrapped his arm around me, and I put my head against his chest, one ear tuned to the Harley's motor and the drunken laughter of Dawn and her friends, and the other to his heartbeat, steady and whole.

I barely noticed the Nissan Sentra parked in front of our house, but when we pulled into the driveway, we saw specks of orange light coming from the screened-in porch.

"What the heck is going on?" I said as the garage door opened.

We got out of the car and followed the gravel path around to the porch. I heard someone giggle as we neared the screen door.

"Babs and Sam are home."

"Lili?" Sam put his hand on the door handle, but it wouldn't turn.

More giggling. And then I smelled the cigarette smoke.

"Open the door, Lili," I said sternly. "Now!"

Lili released the latch and let out a cloud of smoke. My eyes adjusted to the dark, and I could see Taylor standing behind her, holding a can of Red Bull. Lili crossed her arms over her chest without an ounce of contrition.

"Get inside, girls," I said, and followed them into the house. They must have been smoking at the kitchen table, because ashes dusted Lili's place mat. I hated the smell of cigarettes.

I pointed to Taylor's backpack. "I'd like you to leave now."

"Mom, she just came over to borrow my history book." Lili was a rotten liar.

"How dumb do I look, Lili?"

Her voice sweetened. "Should I have called you first to see if it was okay?"

"Cut the crap. We came home early, so you got caught. Now you're going to have to deal with the consequences." I was practically roaring. The sight of Lili through a haze of smoke had made me insane.

"You said you missed me having friends over," Lili tried as Sam shot her a look.

Taylor's spooky green eyes penetrated me, as if she wasn't going to let me forget that she'd seen inside me during that dinner with my mother and that she knew Barbara Pupnick-Blumfield, Kool-Aid mom and parenting guru, was an hysteric. I hated this girl.

Taylor put her empty Red Bull can on the table, flicked back her stick-straight hair, and walked toward the door.

"And one more thing before you go, Taylor," I said in my most commanding tone, trying to reestablish my dwindling authority.

She turned around and with fake earnestness said politely, "Yes, Mrs. Blumfield?"

"The trash can is over there." I pointed to the corner. I could feel Sam's eyes on me.

Taylor smile-smirked. She'd had a good orthodontist, I could tell. "Of course, Mrs. Blumfield."

Lili looked mortified and a little scared, too. Good. She should be afraid of me. I showed Taylor out of the house, through the front door, the entrance we used for perfect strangers, and locked the door behind her.

"Jesus, Lili," I said back in the kitchen.

"You humiliated me," she mumbled.

"Lili, you were smoking in our house," Sam said.

"I don't want that girl here anymore." Before I could stop myself, I added, "I can't stand her."

Lili and Sam gaped at me. I'd rarely said an unkind word about anyone. It wasn't because of my virtuousness, though; gossiping, like overeating or drinking too much, was a sign of weakness and poor impulse control. I kept my mean thoughts to myself.

"She's trouble," I said repeating my mother's assessment of Taylor Miller.

"Let's talk about this, Barbara," Sam said.

"You and Lili talk about this, Sam. And when you're done, Lili, you can clean up those pinecones."

I stormed upstairs to my room, slammed the door, and climbed under the blankets, reeling from the turn the evening had taken. A few minutes later, Sam came up and opened the door gingerly.

"It's just cigarettes," he said.

"They're foul. Never mind the cancer, I hate the smell." I hadn't minded Dawn's smoking because it was clearly a social thing; my mother used her cigarettes to facilitate her disappearances, like a girl who sucks her thumb to fall asleep. Lili needed to stay far away from cigarettes. And Taylor Miller. "You okay?" Sam sat down on the bed.

"I'm not taking back what I said about Taylor. I can't stand that kid."

"Really, Barbara?" He studied my face.

"Really, Sam. I came home on Monday, and she was sitting on the counter eating ice cream out of a carton with a spoon." The vitriol in my voice hurt my own ears.

He whistled. "That's bold all right."

"She puts her dirty shoes on our couch, and she paints her jeans on with a brush."

"Uh-huh?"

"And calls me dude."

"There's more?"

"Yes, I hate the way Lili acts around her." I'd always privately questioned moms who blamed their children's behavior on easy scapegoats like Taylor, uncomfortably pretty and precocious.

"She'll reconnect with Megan and Kara once she starts running again."

"I hope so, because I can't stand Taylor."

"So you've said." He got up to get ready for bed. "Three times now."

I followed him into the bathroom. "What? You think I'm being irrational."

"I get what you're saying about Taylor, but I have a bigger problem with the intensity of your reaction to her," he said, squeezing a line of toothpaste onto his toothbrush.

"Great. You just caught your daughter smoking, but *I'm* the problem?"

He rinsed his mouth out and looked at me.

"Okay, so maybe I *am* the problem. You cannot believe all the ways I've offended people lately." I told him about the comments that had been flying out my mouth.

"Wow." He led me to the bed, sat me down, and studied me as if he was seeing me new.

"Wow is right," I said. "I'm way off my game right now."

He pulled me toward him. He smelled like bratwurst. "You haven't been the same since your mother's visit." Sam was perceptive when he was paying attention or when he had a stake in the matter. In this case, he did. Me.

"I haven't been the same since I washed Mrs. Kessler's body."

"What are we going to do about it?" he asked, a smidgeon of fear rippling underneath his question. We were losing the me that he knew.

"I need to see my mother."

"Maybe you two just need some time apart. Let things settle down a little."

"Maybe," I said, but I knew there was only one thing to do. The idea presented itself to me as intuition. The rebbetzin could help me find my way, as my mother would have said, and how funny that my way back to my old self would be via June Pupnick.

14

Nearly forty years had passed, the amount of time the Jews wandered in the desert after building the golden calf, since I last set foot inside the Schines' mansion. I drove slowly up the long driveway and parked in one of the guest spots. My palms were hot, but the tips of my fingers were ice cold. This time I was going inside. I walked the familiar path to the synagogue, faced the arch of the front door, and raised my hand to the mezuzah. I let my fingers travel up and down the engraved metal plate, and then I put them to my lips. There was no Brisket Lady hovering, just me. I submitted to the pull I'd always felt toward the Schines, and to something else that I could now name. My legacy.

It was a Wednesday, and the shul was so quiet that I could hear the grandfather clock ticking in Rabbi Schine's den. I walked toward the back of the house, the Rebbe's eyes still following me. Keep your stare to yourself, you're a guest here, I wanted to say. I stopped at the sanctuary, which still smelled like musty prayer shawls, and looked around at the rows of brown connecting chairs and the dingy shades barely spanning the windows. I turned on the chandelier that my grandparents must have purchased, studying the long crystals of glass, imagining the room as my mother might have known it, red velvet drapes and my grandfather's guests chatting in their evening wear. The ballroom is filled with men dressed like Humphrey Bogart in *Casablanca*, lighting cigarettes in long black holders for women in silk gowns.

I walked to the kitchen and up the adjacent steps to the

Schines' living quarters. The rabbi opened the door. His once-black hair was fully gray, but there were few lines around his mouth and eyes.

"Hello, Rabbi Schine, is the rebbetzin here?" I averted my eyes out of habit.

He hadn't looked at me directly since I became a woman, but even without eye contact, I could feel his energy shift toward me, perforating my heart. Not now, I thought as sweat began to bead on my forehead and under my arms. I willed it to stop, but I was sweating onions again, and I couldn't do a thing about it.

The rebbetzin emerged from the kitchen with the phone cradled against her ear. She smiled as if she'd been expecting me and held up her index finger to signal that she'd be with me in a second. I discreetly wiped my face with the sleeve of my turtleneck as I followed the rabbi into the living room and sat down on the well-preserved couch. Tzippy and I never sat in the living room because it was reserved for their Shabbos guests, people who came to the shul to heal, to reclaim the light in their souls. Now they were me.

"Tell me about your family, Barbara." The rabbi sat down on the chair opposite me.

"My husband is a financial planner. He's from the North Shore of Chicago." I'd heard the rabbi do this to dozens of guests. He'd engage them in conversation, and then they'd melt in his interest. It was what he must have done to my father. I knew better than to succumb to his charm, but it seduced me just the same.

The rebbetzin appeared and exchanged glances with the rabbi, and I stopped talking. "Come, Barbara," she said.

The rabbi stroked his beard. "Your father, alav hashalom, I miss him." He didn't ask after my mother.

"Thank you," I mumbled.

"And we miss you too." His words touched the deepest part of me. I'd been Schinified.

I said goodbye to the rabbi and trailed the rebbetzin into the kitchen, which smelled like a Wednesday, coffee and the chopped liver she'd served the rabbi for lunch. She always had to remind him to eat because he became so lost in his studies. It wouldn't start smelling like Shabbos until tomorrow, when she'd begin preparing her cholent.

I was relieved to see that the Schines had kept their old kitchen table, with its gray marbled top and sturdy metal legs. Tzippy and I had quizzed each other on our multiplication tables here and peeled potatoes for the rebbetzin's kugels. We'd colored pictures of tulips and butterflies on the legal pads the rabbi bought to write his sermons on, the same ones my mother used to help script the rebbetzin's talks.

The rebbetzin put the teakettle on and placed a sugar bowl, saucers, and two bags of Lipton on the table. She stroked my cheek as if I were a child. Her hand was that of an old woman, bony and freckled.

"Barbara," she said.

I paused and let her name roll around inside my mouth. I wasn't a kid anymore, and I wasn't one of her congregants. "Rivkah."

She gave me a small smile of approval. "Yes, Rivkah."

"This is surreal," I blurted. "First washing Mrs. Kessler's body and now sitting in your kitchen waiting for the kettle to sing, like no time has passed."

She rested her chin in her palm and gazed at me, taking me in carefully.

"But time has passed," I said.

"Yes."

I pinched my thumb and forefinger together. "I was this close to going to Mrs. Kessler's funeral, you know."

"What happened?"

"Mrs. Pincus happened, and all my shame came back."

The rebbetzin put her hand over mine. Her fingers had always been cold, no matter the season.

"I could have reminded Mrs. Pincus that there really would be no shul without June Pupnick." I looked down as I repeated the words the rebbetzin had spoken so often during my childhood.

She smiled sadly. "A real gift for bringing people into the shul, your mother had."

"There's that. Plus, didn't she *give* you this mansion?" I looked right at her, the kettle whistling and neither of us getting up to attend to it.

After a few seconds of the ugly whine, she got up and poured water into our cups. I wondered if she'd stand with her back to me again, as she had when we sat in my childhood kitchen and I discovered that she knew about my mother's affair. She brought us our cups and sat across from me, steeping her tea, her shoulders bowed, and I felt like Dorothy facing the Wizard of Oz. She wasn't the answer lady for everyone's problems or the sensible adult who had shipped me off to California or the spiritual leader who had implored me to take care of my sick mother. She was sitting in front of me, stripped of the cloak of her status as the interpreter of God's mitzvot. The rebbetzin had paid in blood for keeping an enormous gift from someone who had violated her principles so radically. The cost was inscribed all over her body, from her sagging shoulders to the foot she was rubbing nervously against the leg of the table.

"You have questions." She sounded drained.

"I already hunted down the Shabbos goy for answers." I laughed at the absurdity of it.

She jerked her head toward me, unable to feign nonchalance at the mention of the Shabbos goy.

"He wouldn't tell me much. So protective!" I said.

She fidgeted with her tea bag. "I'm not surprised."

"And after everything my mother has put us through, somehow I've turned into the ogre."

"Your mother has struggled." I detected the same protectiveness I'd heard in the Shabbos goy's voice.

"He told me about how you found her in the hospital."

She winced. "That was an awful time."

I took a sip of my tea but could barely swallow it. "I'm scared."

"Tell me, Barbara." She looked scared too.

"My daughter's been so down in the dumps. What if she's inherited our depression gene?"

She twisted the string on her tea bag while she crafted her answer. "I'm not a psychologist, but you and your mother were depressed for real reasons. I venture to guess that Lili's home life is strong."

Had I mentioned Lili by name? I was sorry I'd mentioned her at all, because I didn't want to give the rebbetzin a chance to escape into her adviser role. "What happened to my mother? Help me put these puzzle pieces together. Please."

"She'd lost everything. Her parents, her brother." Her fingers trembled against her cup. "Her baby," she whispered.

The word hung in the air. "Her what?"

She pursed her lips, trying to hold in her tears. I'd never seen the rebbetzin cry. "Her baby."

I had no words.

"We met her in the hospital."

"For her depression," I insisted.

"Yes, and more." Pain creased the rebbetzin's face. "She'd suffered a botched abortion."

I let the news travel through my body, to my heart. "Who was the father?"

The rebbetzin was sniffling now. "I never found out."

"Oh, God." I covered my face with my hands.

She sat with me quietly.

I dropped my hands and looked around the shabby kitchen, at the chairs that needed mending and the smaller framed pictures of the Rebbe and the steel cup hanging over the sink for ritual hand washing. "This was my mother's happy place, right here in your house."

The rebbetzin smiled. "I loved it when she visited."

"And the mikveh? That was her *unhappy* place." Mine too.

"The mikveh was a sacred place for your mother. She told me that she kept your uncle company in the water and helped him with his exercises."

"Did it bother her when it became a public place?"

"She assured us that it didn't, but I know she went down there when she was...." The rebbetzin paused. "Grieving."

"I want to go there," I said, feeling that old tug.

"Come." She got up.

I followed her out of the apartment, down the steps, and through the mansion to the kitchen where Tzippy and I stole cookies while the Shabbos goy put kugels in the oven. I summoned memories that belonged to my mother: a cook, probably a big farm girl from the northern parts, preparing platters of roast beef, not kosher. If my mother's family could afford this mansion, they must have been wealthy assimilated Jews who would have eaten ham with buttered potatoes and trimmed their Christmas trees. I touched the walls and doors, claiming them as my own.

The rebbetzin waited for me in the pantry. I was just as frightened to walk into that closet as I'd been when Tzippy asked me to meet her in the mikveh to talk about her fear of marrying. The familiar scent of Lysol and cinnamon ferried me back to my childhood, and an old charge fired in my cells. I looked around at the cans of Rokeach gefilte fish and tuna stacked on the shelves. I looked toward the door leading down to the mikveh. That charge threatened to overtake me.

"I can't go downstairs. Not today, rebbetzin."

"When you're ready, Barbara."

"Can we still talk?" My voice sounded small.

She nodded and led me through the kitchen toward the front of the house. I paused at the entrance to the sanctuary. Then I walked to the rebbetzin's designated seat and the one informally assigned to my mother, and touched them both. I felt as though I was standing on an empty stage, improvising in front of a theater filled with ghosts. I could practically feel Tzippy's warm breath in my ear and Mrs. Kessler's smile bathing me with its light. The mansion had always felt holy to me, and to this day I couldn't hear the Shema without longing to sit in this very sanctuary. My mother felt it too, the pull and the desire to both escape from the dead and commune with their ghosts. Of course, we were never meant to stay here for long, which made every moment in here feel both electric and lost.

The rebbetzin rubbed my arm the way I'd seen her do with the troubled congregants who sought her out on Shabbos. Her touch unknotted the nerves that had bundled themselves around my muscles. I could no longer deny how much I'd been craving her counsel. She sat down in her chair, and I took my mother's spot.

"I heard what you said about taking care of my mother, but I can't do it." I told her about my mother's stay at our house. "She's got Alzheimer's."

"Oh, Barbara. I'm sorry." Her voice held her usual sympathy, but also a deeper sorrow for the sad news about a friend.

I was so tired. "How did we get here?"

"You're trying," she said.

"And failing miserably." I told her that I felt like Lili, who could no longer rely on her running to cope with her ADHD. Whatever I'd been using to temper my anger wasn't working anymore, not even my teaching.

"You're here now."

"My rage is leaking out of me like a poisonous gas."

"Who are you angry with?"

"Lili's friend Taylor, for starters." I folded my arms over my chest. "She's bad news."

"Who else?"

"Neil's wife, Jenny."

"Jenny?" She looked amused and curious at the same time.

"Yes, the nicest person I've ever met." I almost laughed at the absurdity of my fury, particularly given the weight of everything else that loomed.

"I want to forgive my mother for the Shabbos goy and everything else, but I don't know how."

"You've opened old wounds. You're raw." The rebbetzin was smoothing out her skirt with quick motions.

I stared up at the chandelier, its crystals hanging like icicles, and imagined it casting light on my mother and her brother as they played hide-and-seek or greeted company in matching sailor suits.

"Why was she so secretive about growing up here?" I asked.

"She gave us this gift anonymously, the highest form of a mitzvah. Nobody is supposed to know that you performed this holy deed. It's a bit like the tahara."

"But at the cost of denying her children the knowledge of their heritage?"

I didn't push further. Revealing my scandalous mother as the one who'd donated the mansion would have damaged the Schines' reputation, I knew that.

"I want to ask you something else." I reached into my purse for the copy of the photo I'd been carrying around and showed it to her.

She held it at a distance so she could see it without her reading glasses. "Hmm ... your uncle Norman?"

"Yes."

She examined the photo more carefully. "How young they were."

"The Shabbos goy had this picture when he lived here. I saw it when I went to yell at him about hurting my mom."

The rebbetzin ran her fingers over my mother's image. "We barely spoke of him."

"Barely?"

"Your mother only revealed what she wanted to."

How true. "Can you tell me what you know?"

"I wish there were more I could tell you." The rebbetzin wasn't going to say anything else about the Shabbos goy.

My leg started jiggling like Lili's had in Felix's office. I folded the photo and put it back in my purse. "I'm a mess."

"Remember what God told Abraham to do before he could lead a great and blessed nation?" The confidence was returning to the rebbetzin's voice.

My brain directed me back to fifth-grade Judaics class, in which Rabbi Lichtenberg doled out stale lemon drops to those of us who could parse Genesis. "Go forth for yourself, by yourself, into yourself," I said.

"Give this girl a piece of candy." She smiled and looked deep into my eyes.

Her acknowledgment of this intimate piece of our past made me feel less broken. I wanted her to know about all the pieces. If I handed them to her, chipped and misshapen, maybe she could put them together in a way that made sense. She put her hand on mine and listened intently as I went forth into myself and recounted the story of Simone and Daniel.

15

January 1975

When I left for San Diego the second time, I walked through the airport alone, smarter and steelier and wearing my sledding jeans. My heart had opened during my few weeks back home, and now it was tightening back up like a fist.

The plane took off, and I watched Milwaukee disappear, proud that I'd paid for my ticket by myself. I stuck my hand into my bag and pulled out a pen and a piece of paper.

January 16, 1975 *B"H*

Dear Tzippy,

I'm sorry I left town before your wedding. I was going to come; I'd even bought a new dress. I thought that everything with my mom had changed while I was working for the Levensteins, but it hadn't. My mom is still with the Shabbos goy, and your mom is still acting like it doesn't matter. Your mom was right; I'm not safe in Milwaukee.

I don't expect you to forgive me for breaking my promise to you. I won't write you any more letters. You should start your new life without carrying the shame of my family with you. I will simply drift from your life, and soon you will be so busy making a new home and then babies that you won't think of me.

My heart is aching as I write this. My planets and constellations are so out of place that I couldn't find the Big Dipper if I wanted to. You were always my Big Dipper, by the way.

Love,

Barbara

I swallowed the lump in my throat, crumpled the letter, and gave it to the flight attendant when she came around to take our drink orders. The man sitting next to me took the opportunity to introduce himself. "Hi, I'm Chip," he said. He was clean-shaven, with brown eyes and thinning blond hair. We ate peanuts and sipped Cokes from clear plastic cups while we chatted about life in Milwaukee. He described his small apartment on the east side, just a mile or two south of my father's office, a few blocks and a whole world away from my life. He spoke of cookouts and learning to sail from a "buddy" who belonged to the Milwaukee Yacht Club. He used the word buddy often and tapped my forearm to punctuate his thoughts

"How about you?" Chip asked when he finally came up for air.

"Oh, I'm taking some time off before college. I'm going to be a nanny for the cutest four-year-old ever, and then I'm going to college to study early childhood development. I'm going to be a teacher. I love kids." I'd just mapped out the next five years of my life.

"To you, Miss Teacher." Chip smiled.

"And to you, Mr. Yachtsman."

When the plane landed, Simone and Ollie were waiting at the gate holding a big cardboard sign with "Welcome Barbara!" in block letters and squiggly blue and green lines Ollie had drawn in the corners.

"My savior! I'm so glad you're here." Simone squeezed me hard as Ollie encircled my legs with his tanned little arms.

"Hi, Ollie." I picked him up and held him, grateful for the chance to take care of him and to regain my footing.

"Look at you, Barbara. I've never seen you in anything but

those long skirts." Simone unabashedly appraised me.

On the way to her car, I almost felt like a native, not the nunnish girl who had stepped off the plane to meet Rabbi Levenstein seven months earlier. The sun warmed my forearms and biceps, skin that I couldn't expose the last time I was here, and the warm wind tousled my hair. This time I had no desire to fly back home.

"I'll sit in the back with Ollie," I said.

He climbed on my lap. "When are you going home?"

Simone started the car. "That's not a nice question, Ollie."

I understood his question. Mrs. Kessler once told me that four-year-olds have no sense of time, so he was just trying to orient himself. "I'm not sure, Ollie, but I'm really happy to be here."

"Ditto on that," Simone said.

We talked all the way to what Simone had described as her modernized dreamy Spanish bungalow, tucked into the hills overlooking La Jolla Shores. The Coxes were renting it from a sociology professor on sabbatical in Bolivia, one of Daniel's steady customers at the bookstore he managed. The Levensteins only lived a few miles away, but the dull sameness of their condo complex contrasted sharply with this winding-road neighborhood where every house looked unique.

The outer walls of the bungalow were mainly glass, and the kitchen, dining area, and living room opened into a large airy space. Wooden plates with drawings of oranges, eggplants, and melons hung on rust-colored stucco walls. The house smelled like something was frying, but I couldn't pinpoint what. A tall, lean man, barefoot in a faded blue T-shirt and shorts, stood over the stove with a spatula in his hand.

"Daniel, come meet Barbara," Simone called out, and when he didn't come instantly, she went to the kitchen and led him to the hallway. "Here she is," she said as if she'd done nothing but talk about me for months.

"Hello, Barbara." He smiled at me, and I recognized Ollie's dimple in his cheek and the Robert Redford jaw. He was more handsome than his photo by far. Mira would have called him a fox. "Kind of a critical moment here with the tortillas, or I'd shake your hand!"

Simone smiled. "I wanted to invite you for dinner after all the naps I bummed off you at the beach, but I didn't think it would fly with the Levensteins." She gave me a spontaneous hug. "I'm so glad you're here."

Daniel fried the tortillas until they were gold and crispy. "Hope you're hungry, Barbara," he said with a wink as he stacked them on a paper towel.

Simone guided me to a nice-size room on the side of the house. "I wish you had your own entrance, but don't worry about using the front door if you have a late night."

I'd never had a late night in my life. Maybe I'd whoop it up with Sari, whom I could picture neither nausea-free nor unpregnant. I washed my face with pink soap that smelled like strawberries and ran a comb through my hair.

Simone had set the table with two fat candles in the center. Ollie patted a chair next to his, and I sat down.

"Daddy made toasted does," he announced.

"That's tostados, sweetie," Simone corrected him. "I hope you like Mexican food, Barbara."

"I'm sure I will." I'd never tasted Mexican food. One of Daniel's fried tortillas sat on my plate, and I followed Simone's lead by loading it up with refried beans, chicken, shredded lettuce, tomatoes, and a chunky green dip. I passed on the cheese, already feeling guilty about the non-kosher meat I was about to eat.

"Daniel cooks on Sundays," Simone explained.

"That's when we eat tostados," Ollie piped up.

Simone clapped her hands. "That's right, Ollie. Tostados. You said it perfectly."

Daniel smiled mischievously. "Now let's try 'quesadilla'."

"Kissed a lily," Ollie said earnestly.

Daniel chuckled and patted his head. "You'll get it."

Tostados, I said to myself. Tostados. Quesadilla. I'd only ever heard of tacos.

"Rosa, one of our old babysitters, used to speak Spanish to Ollie all the time, and I think he understood a great deal." Simone rolled her R when she pronounced Rosa's name.

"What happened to her?" I asked.

"She got pregnant and had a hard time with her morning sickness, like Sari," Simone said.

"And yours was bad too." Daniel touched Simone's wrist. "You were a real trouper."

"Maybe next time will be different." A shadow of wistfulness passed over Simone's face.

Daniel bolted to the fridge. "Forgot to offer our guest a beverage."

Before I could say anything, he opened two long, skinny bottles of beer and handed one to Simone and the other to me. I held it for a minute, wondering what the rebbetzin would think of me drinking alcohol and eating traif, non-kosher food, and then I put it to my lips and without ceremony sipped my first beer. It tasted like yeasty carbonation, not altogether unpleasant. I took another sip and then another.

Oil and corn melted on my tongue, and the copper-colored beans tasted better than any cholent I'd ever had. The crisp iceberg lettuce added a refreshing texture to the dish. I hadn't eaten all day, and I was starving. I wanted a third toasted doe, but I stopped after two, content drinking the rest of my beer.

I instinctively wiped Ollie's hands as he wiggled from his seat and ran off to play with his blocks. "I can put him down so you two can be together," I offered.

"You've had a long trip," Daniel said. "We won't put you to work just yet."

I marveled that I felt so at ease with Daniel and Simone. The candles burned, and a man with a high voice sang of tin soldiers and Nixon and four dead in Ohio. The beer relaxed me, and I could have sat with them forever. We lingered around the table until a few minutes after ten o'clock. It was after midnight in Milwaukee, and I had officially turned nineteen.

16

On a damp February morning, I was combing my hair in the bathroom when I heard a knock on my bedroom door.

"I have a shirt for you," Simone called.

"Thanks!" I replied, too shy to come out of the bathroom in my towel.

Simone had left a soft lime-green shirt on my bed. I slipped it over my head. My crew-neck T-shirts hid everything but my arms, but this one dipped below my collarbone, and the air felt cool against my exposed skin like it did against my teeth did after I got my braces off.

Ollie was sitting at the breakfast table drinking orange juice when I finally mustered the nerve to leave my bedroom. "You look like Mommy," he said.

I wanted to look like Simone. Heck, I wanted to be Simone.

"It looks way better on you," she said. "That shade of green is putrid on me. Now turn around."

I obeyed.

"See, it pulled around my shoulders. You're much smaller than me." Simone looked pleased with herself.

Daniel came in, and I felt red splotches blooming on my chest.

"You look pretty, Barbara," he said.

Nobody had ever used the words "pretty" and "Barbara Pupnick" in the same sentence before. This delicious spotlight was almost, but not quite, too intense. Thankfully, Ollie diverted our attention by spilling his orange juice.

"I have an idea," Simone said as Daniel mopped up the spill and she poured herself a glass of milk. She was the only adult I knew who drank milk.

Ollie's eyes lit up. "Me too. Let's show Barbara the tide pools."

"We'll pack a picnic lunch and stay out all day." Simone tapped his nose with her index finger.

"Let's stay out until the moon comes up!" he shouted.

The Coxes were spontaneous. Simone's shifts at the hospital were unpredictable, and Daniel sometimes worked nights and weekends at the bookstore. The Levensteins and the Schines followed strict edicts on when and how to eat, bathe, pray, and even nap, and their observance of Shabbos gave their weeks an unvarying rhythm of work and worship. My new freedom was fun and unsettling at the same time.

Daniel left for the bookstore, and I packed sandwiches and colored with Ollie while Simone fiddled around the house. At eleven o'clock, we piled into her car and drove south to Ocean Beach, a cute little town with a main drag and a straightforward shoreline, unlike the zigzagging, reefy beaches of La Jolla.

"There are a million tide pools under there." Simone pointed to an enormous pier jutting out into the ocean.

We rolled up our jeans and waded through the water. I hovered over a pool, studying it. Beneath the surface, an entire world of urchins and snails went about their business as if we didn't exist.

"Starfish." Ollie said, pointing. "And this is called surf grass." He tickled a thin green blade with his thumb.

"Who's hungry?" Simone's eyes darted toward our towels. If Ollie and I had been alone, we would have observed that starfish until he grew bored. Simone was always preparing for the next activity, and I found myself craving the attention she'd given me during our early meetings at La Jolla Shores.

Ollie and I fell behind as Simone walked briskly to our spot on the beach. "I always thought I was a fast walker," I said when we caught up with her, remembering my father panting to keep up with my mother and me during our walks to shul. The image of my father chasing after us, sweat beading on his mustache, chewed at me. Did he even try to stop my mother's affair? He didn't have a firm hold on her heart, and he probably hoped that she would grow tired of the Shabbos goy before she got us kicked out of the shul. Or maybe he knew that the rebbetzin, like the rest of us, couldn't resist coming to my mother's rescue. Enough.

"I probably walk fast because I grew up playing beach volleyball," Simone said. "I'm short for a volleyball player, but I have these big, strong thighs." She patted the tops of her legs proudly, the outline of her muscles visible through her tight jeans.

We polished off our peanut butter sandwiches quickly. "Can we go to the candy store, Mommy?" Ollie begged.

She mussed his hair. "Of course!"

We put our towels and picnic basket in the trunk, and Ollie started running when we neared the little candy shop across the street from the water. A long glass counter stocked with sheets of bubble gum cigars, candy buttons, and other treats monopolized the space in the tiny shop, which smelled like sugar and seawater. Behind the counter stood a tall bald man with a black handlebar mustache.

"The regular, please." Simone plunked a dime on the counter.

"Yes, ma'am." He disappeared to the back of the store and returned with a purple lollipop about half the size of Ollie's head.

Simone instructed Ollie to thank the man, and we walked along the main drag until Ollie grew tired of his lollipop. Simone wrapped it up and put it in her bag.

"I want to go back to the tide pools," he whined.

"Hey, Ollie Ollie Oop, it's time to go home." Simone knelt down and tried to kiss his cheek, but he swatted her away and started crying. She picked him up. "Do you know what you *need*, big guy?"

A nap, I thought to myself.

"You need an ice cream cone." Simone handed me a dollar and directed me to the ice cream shop down the street. "Strawberry," she said.

Maybe I was wrong. After all, she was a nurse.

They sat on a bench overlooking the ocean, and by the time I returned to them, Ollie was asleep on her lap. Simone and I took turns licking the ice cream cone, watching the surfers dance along the waves. When we finished, she scooped Ollie up, and he slept the entire drive home and another hour in his own bed.

I was thinking about a nap myself when Simone came into my room with an armful of clothes. "None of these fit quite right after I had Ollie," she said, pulling his lollipop out of her bag. "Damn, this gets so sticky." She peeled off the plastic with difficulty, gave the sucker a lick, and pointed to the clothes. "Fashion show!"

I went into the bathroom to change, mainly because I was self-conscious about my granny underwear. I had inherited my mother's tiny waist and slightly flared hips, and Simone's white jeans fit me perfectly. The jeans hung low, right below my belly button, showing a fold of dingy white cotton, and fanned out dramatically at the ankle. I put on a dashiki, which thankfully covered my waist.

When I came out, Simone saluted me with her lollipop. "Far out!"

We spent the duration of Ollie's nap on my fashion show. Almost every item of clothing fit as if it were made for me. When we finished, she tossed her lollipop into the wastebasket and called over her shoulder, "Wear the jeans to dinner."

I was peeling an avocado, my new favorite food, when I heard Daniel's car screech to a stop in the driveway.

"I thought you were going to do something about those brakes, baby," Simone said as he walked through the front door.

"There's a guy I surf with who works on Datsuns. I'll ask him the next time I see him." Daniel went to Simone and bent to kiss her.

"Don't forget," she said.

I concentrated on my avocado, shy about turning around to face Daniel in my new clothes. We drank beer with our meal, and I started the dishes while Simone put a reluctant Ollie to bed. Daniel sponged down the dining-room table, and I grabbed a clean towel from the kitchen to mop up the moisture.

"Thank you." He spread a stack of receipts across the surface.

I folded the towel. "Did you sell a lot of books today?"

"Two Gatsbys. Not bad."

"Fitzgerald is my favorite." This was the first substantive thing I'd said to Daniel. "I used to read a lot," I added, thinking of the novels I'd ploughed through as I sat on my mother's chaise longue waiting for her to emerge from her funk.

"Really?" He looked at me with interest.

"I tried reading through the stacks of the Shorewood Public Library by alphabet. I got to the Bs."

Daniel stuck a pencil behind his ear. "No kidding."

"I guess I shouldn't admit to something so square." Now that I'd captured his attention, I didn't want to let it go.

"Not at all. Why did you like Gatsby so much?"

"Well, I guess I liked Nick. I could relate to him."

"Oh?" Daniel gazed at me more intently. "How so?"

I'd never thought of myself as Nick Carraway, but once I spoke the words, they felt true. "Because he got a hold of a secret and didn't know what to do with it." What was I saying? Daniel was almost a total stranger.

He rubbed his whiskers and fixed me with his hazel eyes. His eyelashes were long and brownish, making his pupils look a greener hazel, as if he were wearing mascara. I was afraid he'd press me about what secrets I might have, but all he said was, "That's intriguing, Barbara."

"I've always loved to read," I said hurriedly. "It must be great to work in a bookstore." If we kept talking, I'd certainly find more intriguing things to say.

"Someday I want to open my own bookstore," Daniel said. "With a coffee shop in front."

"Books and coffee together?" What a concept!

"Yeah, a place where you can drink a cup of joe and find other people who love your favorite books. Simone thinks it's a crazy idea. She's not much of a reader."

"I'd go to a place like that." It thrilled me that there was something between us, a current of energy that didn't include Simone.

I left him to his work and returned to the kitchen to wash the dishes, imagining his eyes on my back as I scrubbed away the remnants of Simone's enchiladas.

That night I lay in bed listening to the ocean. My room smelled like grape from the lollipop in my wastebasket. Talking to Daniel had made me feel like Alan Shepard, floating, unmoored, in clothing as foreign to me as a space suit. In the last few minutes before sleep, I was bouncing around the moon hitting a golf ball while Simone sucked her lollipop and Daniel's eyes burned into my back. I wasn't me anymore. What a relief.

The Sunday after Simone gave me her clothes, she and Daniel took Ollie on a day trip to Julian, their little mountain getaway. I lounged in bed, a queen with a fluffy goose-down comforter. I stared at the four tall bookshelves stocked with novels and poetry mainly by Spanish authors who had never found a spot in the stacks of my public library. My world was growing larger every day, and soon I'd think of the Schines as a mere smudge on the big map of life.

This was the first time I'd been alone in the house. Without the distraction of Ollie and my chores, I started thinking about home. I hadn't spoken to my parents since I left Milwaukee, so maybe it was time to phone them and then I could return to my sunny new life. I hoped my father would answer. I couldn't shake the image of him waving at me so sadly from the front steps.

My mother answered on the second ring.

"Will you accept a collect call from Barbara Pupnick?" the operator asked. My eye started twitching the way it did when I read for too long.

"I most certainly will," my mother said eagerly.

"Hi, Mom."

"Hello, sweetheart. It's wonderful to hear from you. Your father will be so sorry he missed you."

So are you still having an affair? I wanted to ask, but I said nothing. Let her fill in the void.

"How is California life treating you?"

"Everything's fine. I just wanted to say hi. I'll call back when Dad gets home."

"Can't we talk a little?"

"I should probably go."

"Just a minute or two, Sweet B," she said. I tried not to let her woo me with her Sweet B business. "Okay, but just a few minutes."

"Tzippy and her husband are still in town. She's been asking for you."

I felt a surge of alarm. "What have you told her?"

"Not much."

Finally, I was grateful for her evasive nature. "Good."

"This is between you girls. I'm sure you'll sort it out."

I wanted to hurl the phone across the room. She wasn't going to take any responsibility for my skipping Tzippy's wedding or apologize for what her affair had cost our family. "It's about much more."

"You're right." She sounded defeated.

My eye was twitching madly. "So why did you bring it up?"

"I wanted to help. Tzippy's a good friend."

That dizzying sensation from our last argument resurfaced, usurping my anger. "If you want to help me, and *Dad,* you know what you need to do. I have to go," I said with a calm that surprised me, hanging up before she could respond.

I couldn't sit in this house alone with my anger, so I went to the mall. Daniel had loaned me his Datsun with instructions to pump the brakes to get them to work. I drove to the Mission Valley shopping center, where Sari and I had taken Benny to buy new shoes. Today I looked like the women who had gawked at Sari, Benny, and me. I bought myself a hot dog and a Sprite, sat on a bench, and chewed the salty pork with impunity. After I took my last bite, I felt a little sick, but I couldn't tell if it was from the hot dog or the guilt.

I wandered into Robinson's and made a beeline for a display of bikini underpants in an assortment of rainbow colors. I grabbed a pair of royal blue panties and found a dressing room. Though I knew I was supposed to keep on my own underpants for sanitary reasons, I stripped naked and faced the three-way mirror. I studied my back, as I had my mother's when I sat behind her on the yellow bench in her bathroom and watched her tweeze her eyebrows. Turn the clock back a few years, and from this angle you'd never be able to tell us apart.

The elastic band of my new underpants fell inches below my navel. I wanted to wear them home, so I ripped off the tag and was on my way to pay for them when a rack of lacy slips caught my attention. I let the material run through my fingers, wondering if Tzippy bought pretty slips and nightgowns now that she was married. A little boy's voice roused me from my daydreaming. "Mama, Mama, that's her."

Benny was standing close enough for me to make out the birthmark on his chin. I might not have recognized the thin woman pushing a baby buggy except for the sheitel I'd seen draped over its stand so many times. Sari now had color in her cheeks, and she moved quickly as she tucked Benny behind her.

"That's Barbara. I know it...." His voice trailed off as I turned my back to him, his mother, and his new sister and strode toward the dressing room. I yearned to embrace Benny, but I needed to spurn Sari's long skirt and wig and everything it stood for even more. I was done.

I pulled the small bench in the dressing room from the wall and lay down on it, face up, fingers grazing the carpet. I imagined Sari, the rebbetzin, my mother, and the Shabbos goy stacked on top of me. One by one, I took four deep breaths and with all my strength hurled them into the air, pretending I was one of those Olympic weight lifters who wore leotards and grunted as they heaved hundreds of pounds over their heads.

Now I was ready to return to the cashier and spend some of my first paycheck from Simone and Daniel on my new underwear.

When I got home, the house was eerily quiet. I missed Simone's wild energy and her devotion to redoing my look. I devised one-liners I'd toss off to Daniel should he ever engage me in another conversation. I'd been gobbling up the Coxes' attention as though they'd been offering me a taste of cream when I'd been drinking powdered milk my whole life.

The next Sunday, the Santa Ana winds blew in, and Simone and I took Ollie to a beach in Del Mar, a few miles north of where we met. Simone let me borrow her red bikini, and when we passed a group of college boys, I felt like I was parading around in my underwear.

"Just so you know, those guys are checking you out," Simone said.

"I doubt that." They were staring at her, but I had to admit that I'd come a long way from the girl skulking along the beach in a long skirt.

I swallowed my grin and lay back on the sand, feeling the warmth of the sun on my ribs.

"Be careful." Simone touched my stomach. "That's some virgin skin you've got there."

Daniel was home by the time we returned from the beach. He insisted on making his special paella, so I took a long shower and spent extra time making my hair look nice. I was standing in front of the mirror in my bra and underpants when Simone appeared with a shopping bag. She took out a tube of mascara and some blue eye shadow and went to work on my upper lids. Then she brushed my lashes with her wand.

"There you go. You have eyes now," she said.

She reached into the bag and produced a hot pink shirt with a brown and orange swirl design and a low neckline. "This will work." She snapped my bra playfully. "But this needs to go."

"I don't know about that." My breasts were small, but the

rebbetzin had always complimented Tzippy and me on our modesty because we dutifully hid our bodies under baggy blouses and thick sweaters. I undid my bra tentatively. Simone made it into a slingshot and flung it into my laundry basket.

"Put these jeans on and try these platforms." She tossed a shoe at me. "I think we're the same size."

The shoes felt heavy, and the heel was square and tall, maybe four inches. I wobbled around my room for a few minutes until I started to enjoy my new height.

"Let me introduce you," she said as she ran down the hall. "May I present the lovely Barbara Pupnick," she shouted from the kitchen. "Drum roll, please."

Ollie thumped his hands on the table, and I walked carefully out of my bedroom so I wouldn't trip. Daniel looked up from stirring his paella, and his eyes widened. I willed myself not to blush, but I couldn't help it. The doorbell rang.

Simone looked at me mischievously. "We have a guest for dinner. His name is Brian."

"His older brother and I were roommates at Berkeley," Daniel said over his shoulder as he opened the door and hugged Brian. Brian was lanky and wore his black hair in a ponytail.

"Hey, man," Brian said. "It's been like forever." He kissed Simone on the cheek, handed Daniel a bottle of wine, and patted Ollie on the head. "What's up, little man?"

"Meet Barbara, Brian," Simone said. "She's our angel."

"Hey, Barbara."

Simone put Ollie to bed while Brian expertly opened the bottle of wine, explaining that he'd been waiting tables since high school. Simone sat me next to him, and he asked me all about Milwaukee as if it were some exotic African village.

After two glasses of wine, I regaled the table with an animated story about Samson the ape escaping from the Milwaukee zoo. I caught Simone and Daniel looking at me twice. Brian put his hand on my shoulder and said that he'd never met anyone like me before. Truth be told, I'd never met anyone like this me before.

I'd never met anyone like Brian before either. He told me all about how he was studying anthropology at UC Santa Cruz and how he liked that the university didn't give out grades. After dessert, he yawned and said he had to "hit it." He'd borrowed a car to come to dinner, and his friend needed it back.

"Thanks everyone for everything, man," he said, shaking Daniel's hand.

"Next time, crash here," Daniel said.

"Goodnight, Barbara. 'Night, Simone." Brian kissed each of us on the cheek.

As soon as he closed the door, Simone turned to me. "I think he was into you, Barbara."

Daniel smiled. "Totally."

My whole body blushed.

Under the covers that night, I imagined what it would be like to kiss Brian. I'd only been kissed once, during a game of Truth or Dare that Mira and I played with her cousins when we were fourteen. Her cousin Freddie, who had worse acne than mine, stuck his tongue down my throat until I thought I'd gag. His breath tasted like tomatoes. He grabbed my breast, but I shoved his hand away. That was it.

I imagined that Brian's kisses would be smaller and dryer than Freddie's, and then I thought about how embarrassing it was that Daniel had watched me flirt, and then before I could stop myself, I wondered what it would be like to kiss Daniel. I felt a surprising but sweet pressure between my legs. I opened my eyes and told myself that my fantasies were as harmless as my daydreams about Robert Redford after Mira's parents took us to see *Jeremiah Johnson*, or about Grant, a dark-haired UWM student who helped my dad mow our lawn after he hurt his back. I listened to the sound of waves and Simone and Daniel giggling as they made their way to their bedroom.

17

Angie Dickinson is so fucking fearless," Simone said as we huddled together on a damp March night, our eyes glued to the latest episode of *Police Woman*. Angie retrieved her pistol from her purse just in time to knock off a big thug wearing a light blue leisure suit.

"So are you." It still gave me a jolt to hear Simone say the "f" word.

"I'm not fearless at all." She sounded weary.

"You're always so sure of yourself."

"Angie's fearless and lucky. She should have gotten knocked off by now."

"But then there'd be no show."

"True."

I adjusted the blanket we'd thrown over our legs and took a sip of cocoa, hoping she'd confide in me about her fears.

She touched her flat abdomen. "Daniel and I haven't been so lucky lately."

Something I'd overheard the rebbetzin say to a congregant popped into my head. "You do your very best, and God will take care of the rest." This seemed like the wrong thing to say to Simone, and I regretted my words as soon as they left my mouth.

"I don't know about God, but maybe I'll ask Marci to give me another reading." Simone got up to turn off the television. She was so different from anyone I'd ever met that it was no wonder the rebbetzin's words failed to comfort her. They still made sense to me in spite of everything that had happened.

I went into the kitchen and rinsed the pools of dark chocolate from the bottoms of our mugs. For the first time since I got back to San Diego, I missed home. The next evening was the first night of Passover, and my mother always made a big seder. She'd usually invite some of the Schines' recruits, and we'd drink four whole glasses of the festive wine and belt out every verse of "Dayenu." I'd lied to my father when he inquired about my Passover plans during our last phone call. I made up a story about Simone's Jewish boss inviting us to his family's seder, but truthfully, I didn't have any place to celebrate the holiday. The Levensteins were clearly not an option after I'd run away from Sari and Benny at the mall.

April 5, 1975 *B"H*

Dear Tzippy,

I live with a Gentile family. Simone and Daniel and their little boy Ollie. They eat bacon and play music on their hi-fi, mainly albums by Jefferson Airplane, Janis Joplin, and Crosby, Stills, Nash & Young. On Friday nights we watch reruns of a show called Bridget Loves Bernie *about a Jewish man who falls for a pretty blond lady, kind of like my mom and the Shabbos goy, but reversed.*

I've been someone else since I've been here, someone more beautiful and smart and useful. I still feel awful about missing your wedding. I know you'll never forgive me. I hope you like being married.

Your best friend (?),

Barbara

I crumpled up the paper and tossed it in the trash.

The next morning Ollie helped me stir batter for banana pancakes.

"Surprise, Daddy!" he said when Daniel entered the kitchen. "We're making you banana pancakes."

Daniel scooped Ollie up and nuzzled his neck.

Simone walked in and kissed Ollie's ear. "I'm working a double shift today, so I won't see you until tomorrow morning."

"Can I come with you?" Ollie asked, disappointed.

"No, big guy. I'd just want to play with you the whole time if I brought you to work with me." Her eyes were puffy, the irises a muddy green.

"How soon?" Ollie pouted.

"One lunch and one dinner without me."

"Ollie, we're going to have the specialest day ever," I said.

Ollie crawled into Simone's lap and nestled his cheek against hers.

I gave them a few minutes before I presented him my plan for the day. "First we're going to eat these delicious pancakes. Then we're going to say goodbye to your mommy. And then we're off to Point Loma to watch the surfers. You don't like watching surfers much, do you?"

He pulled his head away from his mother's neck and peeked at me with one eye.

"Nice work on the pancakes, guys," Daniel said.

Ollie ate a few bites and went off to play with his Legos. Daniel and Simone exchanged sad looks, and he went to her and held her. "Next month," I heard him whisper into her hair.

"Maybe," she said, and then hoisted her backpack over her shoulder and left.

Daniel's shoulders sagged as watched her go. "I'll ride my bike to the store. You take the car." He handed me his keys.

Remember, one lunch and one dinner without her, I wanted to say, but I just thanked him instead.

I drove Ollie to Sunset Cliffs, and we sat on a bench and watched the surfers negotiate the big waves. Every time a pelican flew over our heads, Ollie would quack and we'd laugh. We ate the peanut butter and jelly sandwiches I'd packed, and when we were done, he gave me a wet kiss, leaving a glob of strawberry jelly on my chin.

When Ollie grew restless, we drove to Ocean Beach and made a beeline for the candy store, where I couldn't resist buying both of us grape lollipops.

"Where's your mom?" the man with the handlebar mustache asked Ollie.

He looked down at the floor. "She's working. She's a nurse and she fixes people."

"Well, your substitute mommy is very pretty too," he said, and winked at me.

"How much do we owe you?" I asked, trying not to act as flustered as I felt.

"These are on the house."

I put two quarters on the glass and thanked him, wondering if he really thought I was pretty or if he was just a flirt. We walked to the pier, licking our lollipops, and we took off our shoes and socks and played in the surf until our toes grew numb. I didn't want Ollie to miss his nap, so I cajoled him into accompanying me to a grocery store that I'd noticed carried a few kosher items. I wanted to buy a couple of boxes of matzoh and some ingredients for dinner.

When we got home, Ollie danced to the Irish Rovers singing about unicorns and chimpanzees while I made my mom's honey chicken, a big salad with apples and walnuts—a cousin, albeit twice removed, to the ritual charoset—and "kosher for Passover" popovers.

I startled when I heard Daniel walk through the back door. We'd been alone in the house before, but Simone could always have arrived at any minute. This felt different.

"Hi," I said, buzzing around the kitchen. "Ollie, your dad's home."

Daniel knelt down to hug his son.

"You're sweaty, Daddy." Ollie touched Daniel's cheek with his little hand.

"Hello to you, big guy." He got up. "Something smells great."

The kitchen was starting to smell like honey and garlic.

Daniel took Ollie to wash up while I set the dining-room table with bright yellow cotton napkins. My mother wasn't a skilled cook, but she did know how to make the food look good, and she'd taught me how to garnish: red apples in the salad, parsley dressing the chicken, and the golden popovers nestled under a napkin in a basket. The presentation was so pretty that I wanted to take a picture.

Daniel came back with his wet hair grazing his shoulders. He wore a thick brown leather belt with the letters of his name etched into the back. "Excellent," he said as he and Ollie sat down.

The three of us rarely ate dinner together without Simone. Ollie had taken only a short nap that afternoon, and he was so tired his head was almost falling in his plate. After he took a few bites, the phone rang.

"Do you think it's Mommy?" He jumped out of his chair.

"Let's see." Daniel got up and answered the call in the kitchen. "Hey, babe. You're just in time to wish your boy a good night," he said. "Ollie, c'mere."

"Guess what, Mom. Barbara took me to the candy store, and the funny-looking man told her she was a silly mom."

Substitute. Substitute mom. I didn't correct him. Substitute Simone. Daniel shot me a curious look, and I shrugged as if to say, Beats me.

"Here, she wants to talk to you." Ollie handed the phone to Daniel and came back to the table. Daniel lowered his voice, and I told myself not to eavesdrop, but I couldn't help it. The kitchen opened directly into the dining area. "I'm sad too," he said. He paused to listen to Simone on the other end, and then I heard him tell her not to give up.

"Eat a few more bites, big guy," I said to Ollie, trying to drown out his father's conversation.

A moment later, Daniel returned to the table. "Now let's finish this beautiful food," he said, but Ollie's eyelids were drooping. Daniel picked him up and carried him off to bed. "Back in a minute," he said.

I cracked the hard shell of a popover, releasing a cloud of

steam that licked my cheeks. By now, our family seder would have ended.

Daniel came back and sat down. "I wouldn't have thought to put walnuts and apples together like this," he said, taking a bite of salad.

"It's fake charoset," I explained. "A ritual food for Passover."

"Passover." He smacked his head with his palm. "I forgot. I'm so sorry, Barbara."

"It's okay." I'd asked for the night off so I could do something to honor the holiday, although I hadn't known what that might be.

"We blew it. Is there something you need to do?" he asked with concern. "You know, for Passover?"

"Just have a seder," I said.

He shook his head. "Yeah, a seder. God, Barbara, I'm really sorry."

"This is close enough." I was happy right where I was.

We ate without talking for a few minutes, and then he asked, "What exactly happens at a seder?"

"You tell the story of the Jews' Exodus from Egypt," I said and went on to tell him the entire story, complete with the ten plagues and the parting of the Red Sea, and an explanation of the items on the ritual plate. When I got to the part about the four cups of wine, he stopped me.

"Hold on a sec," he said, returning with two wine glasses and a bottle of Burgundy. "Let's do this right." He poured and raised his glass.

I eyed the wine, thinking about how my parents used to drive all the way to Skokie to buy kosher wine. "No toasting on Passover," I retorted.

"Why not?" He clinked my glass, and we laughed as if we were sharing a private joke. This wine was much stronger than the Manischewitz my parents poured for me, and before long, I started to feel tipsy.

We cleared the table and went to the living room. Daniel pulled out an album and we sipped wine and read the lyrics together. We sat side by side on the Persian carpet, our backs against the sofa. He brought one leg to his chest and dangled an arm over his knee. His fingers were long and tapered. We weren't touching, but the heat of his outstretched leg warmed the side of my thigh.

"This is Lou Reed," he said and proceeded to tell me about Lou's friendship with Andy Warhol and how Andy manipulated the careers of artists who caught his fancy and how he told Lou Reed to write the song "Vicious." Daniel used his hands a lot when he spoke, and he made this exotic world come alive for me. I pictured him describing his favorite book to a female customer who would stare dreamily at his Roman nose and eyelashes, a yard long.

"Do you like his music?" Daniel pointed to the stereo.

"Not sure yet." I picked up the album and examined Lou's photo. He looked like a cooler, clean-shaven version of one of Rabbi Schine's brothers.

Daniel gazed at me. "Simone and I love that about you."

"What?" Please tell me more about what you love about me, I thought.

"You're who you are," he said softly, taking me in, making me feel both uncomfortable and treasured.

"Thanks. I should go to bed." I had to leave, or I would say something foolish. The wine had made me sleepy, and that night I drifted off to images of Daniel and Moses wandering through the desert, snacking on honey chicken and manna sandwiches.

When I entered the kitchen the next morning, Simone and Daniel were hugging and Ollie had scooted between their legs and wrapped his arms around their knees.

"Family hug," Ollie announced.

They parted, and I tried not to make eye contact with Daniel, who smiled warmly as if we'd never shared an intimate moment. Maybe we hadn't.

Simone walked over. "Barbara. I'm an idiot. We totally forgot Passover. I'm sorry."

"Don't worry about it."

"No, I've been too wrapped up in myself. I'm going to make it up to you, I swear."

"You've been so good to me. Please, forget about it."

After I went back to my room and showered, I found Simone waiting for me in the kitchen, keys in hand.

"I'm taking Barbara on an adventure," she told Daniel.

"Simone's a master at coming up with adventures," he said.

"We'll take your car, baby. Mine's out of gas," she said as we walked out of the house. "Hop in," she said, and I did. She adjusted the rearview mirror, fiddled with the radio, and backed the car down the driveway while accompanying Elton John on "Bennie and the Jets."

Halfway down the drive, she slammed on the screeching brakes.

"Shit." She turned around. "I almost hit that dog."

A bouncy black mutt had darted out from one of the two Torrey pine groves that bookended the house. A beleaguered-looking young woman pushing a buggy screamed, "Brandy, come back here! Brandy!"

Simone got out of the car and ran toward the woman. "Where's her leash?"

The woman was holding the leash in her hand. "I was just about to put it back on. I'm so sorry." The baby started crying. Simone leashed the dog while the woman knelt down and found a pacifier. She continued to apologize, but Simone just looked longingly at the baby and walked back up the driveway, waving her hand in the air.

Daniel rushed out of the house with Ollie on his hip. "Is everything okay?" He put Ollie down and held Simone, who was shaking.

"I almost hit that puppy. These brakes are shit." She looked like she was about to cry.

Daniel wrapped his arms around her. "It's okay, it's okay," he whispered.

Ollie tugged at the leg of Simone's jeans. "That was a big noise, Mommy."

"Nobody got hurt, big guy," Daniel said, and kissed Simone before he released her.

When Simone returned to the car, I patted her knee awkwardly. She said little during our drive along the coast. I stared out at the horizon, daydreaming about Daniel telling me that I was who I was. I didn't know what that meant exactly, but whoever I was seemed to be okay with him and Simone.

Her mood shifted. "You're going to love Old Town," she said enthusiastically. "It's so kitschy."

"I've loved every place you've taken me."

We drove toward the white, red-roofed, Spanish-style buildings. She parked far away from the other cars and reached into her big cloth purse for a cigarette that looked like it had been made by hand. "You up for trying something new?"

The odd cigarette made me nervous, but Simone was a nurse, and if she was going to smoke it, then I could. "I guess."

"Every once in a while, you know, I get the urge for a joint." Simone flicked a lighter in the shape of a banana and took a deep puff, eyes half closed, lips pursed as she held her breath. "You've got to wait until it goes down your lungs," she croaked.

I took the joint from Simone and pinched it between my fingers just as I'd seen her do. It burned my lips a little, and the smoke twirled down my esophagus like a lit match. I coughed and coughed until my eyes watered.

Simone pulled a thermos from the back seat. "Here." She unscrewed the cap and handed it to me. "It's a little stale from sitting in the car for two days."

The old coffee tasted bitter, but it cooled my throat.

"Small puffs this time." She demonstrated another hit.

I was determined not to disappoint her, so I took the joint back and inhaled briefly. Although I still coughed, I didn't feel like my insides were on fire.

"There you go." Simone clapped her hands as she did when

Ollie figured out a puzzle. "Come on, I'll show you Old Town."

I felt like I was Meg Murry, the space traveler from my favorite teen novel, and I'd been catapulted back to a mission in a far part of the world. The fact that I knew nothing about Christianity didn't faze me.

Simone took me to a gallery where brightly colored blankets hung on the walls. I fingered a striped blanket woven with blue, purple, and green yarns. "This is the most beautiful blanket I've ever seen."

Simone laughed. "You're stoned. We could buy that in Tijuana for about a dollar."

"A dollar?" I found this fact fascinating.

"Let's go." She led me to an old Mexican restaurant where we ate on the veranda under a big umbrella. A plump waiter with an accent and wavy black hair placed a basket of chips in front of us. Simone spoke to him in perfect Spanish, and he returned a few minutes later with a bowl of guacamole. I wanted to take a picture of the lush waves of green with little red onion bits sticking out of each crest. When I spooned half the bowl onto my plate and began eating it with a fork, Simone started laughing uncontrollably.

"It's Passover, Simone," I said in my practiced Tzippy Schine let-me-enlighten-you-about-Judaism voice. "No chips, no corn products."

"I have a lot to learn," she said earnestly.

"I'm going to take Spanish when I go to college. And then I'm going to become a teacher."

"You should apply to San Diego State. You can't go back to the cold."

"No, I can't go back, but not because of the cold."

"Why can't you go back?"

"My mother is having an affair with the Shabbos goy." What had I just said? And so casually?

"Huh?" Simone jerked her head up and stared at me.

I should have stopped talking, but I had her attention, and her interest in my story enticed me to talk more. "The Shabbos goy. The person who turns on the lights and does all the things you're not allowed to do on the Sabbath."

She waved her chip at me to continue.

"Use the oven, use the phone, use electricity, drive." I took a spoonful of salsa. "Rip toilet paper."

"Are you serious?"

"But he's not the Shabbos goy anymore. He's still seeing my mom, though."

"Where does he live?"

"Who knows? Pewaukee or someplace."

"Pewaukee?" Simone repeated, exaggerating my accent.

We started giggling so hard that she almost choked on her chip.

"Do I talk like that?" I asked.

"Sure you do," she replied, mimicking me.

She flagged the waiter and asked for something else in Spanish, and a minute later he returned with two glasses the size of Frisbees, rims salted and filled to the brim with a yellowish slush.

Simone raised her glass. "To Pewaukee!"

We both took a big gulp. "What am I drinking?"

"A margarita. A day of firsts." She took another sip. "So tell me more about the Shabbos goy. I'm way into this."

The room was starting to spin a little, and I couldn't stop talking about my fascinating self. By the second margarita, I was telling Simone every detail about the mikveh, Tzippy, my mother, and the Shabbos goy. I left nothing out. After I told her what happened before Tzippy's wedding, she drained her third margarita and shook her head.

"That's heavy shit," she said.

Why we thought that was so funny, I couldn't say, but we laughed so hard I almost wet my pants.

Simone pounded her fist on the table. "We need to eat something without corn."

"Or yeast, or legumes," I added.

She spoke to the waiter, who returned to the table with

another bowl of guacamole, two more margaritas, and a large slab of beef.

After a few bites, I asked, "What am I eating besides more non-kosher meat?"

"Carne asada," Simone said.

Everything was funny. We burst into another fit of laughter.

"Okay, so let me get this straight." Simone took a bite of her carne asada. "The Robertson knew about your mom?"

"Rebbetzin," I corrected, suddenly feeling defensive about the Schines. It was one thing for me to question or criticize them, but I wasn't so sure how I felt about an outsider attacking them.

"That's bull," Simone declared.

"It's complicated," I said, knowing that was true and that I didn't fully understand why. But hearing Simone's assessment also confirmed my own anger, and the half of me that wasn't defending the Schines and their rules was dying to echo her outrage. I got up and went to the bathroom.

When I returned, Simone had paid the bill and she left a big tip. She stood up. "I need to see Marci. She lives near here."

I opened my eyes wide. "Marci?"

"I want her to reread my cards."

"Why?"

"I want her to tell me that I'm going to have more babies." Simone took my hand. "She can confirm what I saw on your palm too." She traced my heart line, pausing for a second where it split into two. Her touch was light but firm, like my mother's. I wanted her to find some kind of reassurance from Marci, and I wanted to believe in her version of my heart line.

We walked out past the mariachi band to Simone's car. I dozed off, feeling lighter from telling her my story and also vaguely aware that sometimes it was easiest to reveal a secret to a person who didn't know you very well.

I woke up when Simone stopped the car.

"Come on," she said. "Let's go."

I'd never been in this part of town, with street after street of

Spanish-style homes like the ones I'd seen in Old Town. I followed Simone up the driveway and around the back of one of the houses to a small cottage.

A woman with big eyes and curly light brown hair greeted us. "I'm Marci," she said to me.

"The psychic," I said. My mouth felt like I'd eaten one of the long cotton tubes my father stuck in his patients' mouths to keep them from salivating while he braced their teeth. Marci and Simone disappeared behind a curtain, and I wondered if she read cards with a wizard cap on her head. The thought almost made me laugh, but then I burped up margarita and onions and carne asada.

"Oh, God. Where's the bathroom?"

Marci appeared and guided me to her bathroom, and I sat on the floor with my head over the toilet bowl, breathing in the harsh scent of antiseptic cleaner and the fresh mint that Marci must have been growing in her garden. "I'll give you some privacy, honey," she said, and returned to Simone.

I could hear them arguing in the next room. "Simone. You're putting too much weight on these cards."

"So you're not going to give me another read?" Simone sounded anxious.

"Relax, go away with Daniel alone. Eat good food and walk on the beach and *make love*," Marci said.

I got it. Marci was Simone's rebbetzin.

"How about my palm?"

"All right, Simone. I'll take a quick peek, and you can come back for a full read soon."

I didn't hear anything for a few minutes, and then Simone said, "What is it?"

"Nothing, Simone."

"No, you're seeing something, I can tell."

Marci paused. "This has nothing to do with a baby."

"What is it?"

"Just be very careful. There's danger in your midst." Her tone scared me.

A few minutes later, I felt a hand on my back. I looked up to see Marci, the light creating a halo around her gauzy lavender dress. Now she looked like the Happy Medium, another one of my favorite characters from *A Wrinkle in Time*. Yes, Simone had taken me to her cavern on Orion's Belt.

"You okay?" she asked.

I shuddered involuntarily, and Marci massaged my back in circles. "Call me if you need me." She handed me her card, which I stuffed into my pocket. Why would I need her?

"Let's go," Simone murmured, helping me up. She ushered me through the garden back to Daniel's car.

I was sad that our outing had ended so abruptly and that Simone was having such a hard time having a baby.

I didn't wake up until after ten the next morning. My head ached, and I felt like I was wearing cardigans on my teeth. I flung myself out of bed, worried that I might be sick again. I needed water. Fast. I brushed my teeth, gulping the water down and then regretting my haste as it floated back up my esophagus.

Daniel was sitting at the kitchen table reading the newspaper when I emerged from my room. I'd fallen asleep in the car, and I worried that I might have said something stupid in my half slumber.

"You'll feel better soon," he promised.

Ollie trailed Simone into the kitchen. "Are you sick?"

"I'm going to nurse you today. No Ollie duty." Simone rubbed my shoulder. "Go back to bed." I felt too ill to argue, and I returned to my bedroom, changed the sheets, drew the blinds, and slept until I heard a knock on the door. It was almost four o'clock.

"Barbara, your father is on the phone," Simone said.

Since my last conversation with my mother, I'd had two brief, strained phone calls with my parents, both initiated by them. My mother and I chatted about the weather and little else, and after a few moments of this unbearable exchange, she put my dad on the phone. My ear was permanently trained to pick up her mood. If she sounded happy, then she was likely still with the Shabbos goy. If she sounded sad, he'd left her again, which as much as I liked living with the Coxes, would have put me on the first plane back home to take care of her. My chest started to close as I picked up the phone on my night stand.

"Everything okay, Dad?" I could hear the panic in my voice.

"Can't a father check in on his little girl?"

Had he found out that I got drunk and smoked pot? Maybe Sari saw me in Old Town and called Rabbi Schine. You never know.

"I'm doing great," I said.

He sighed. "Those beatniks treating you okay?"

"Yes, they treat me like I'm part of the family, Dad."

"Don't forget your real family, Bunny."

"Is Mom okay?"

"She's just fine."

I prattled on about my applications to San Diego State, UCLA, and, of course, Madison as a backup. I told my father how much I loved Ollie and how I could stay with Simone and Daniel while I went to school.

"Live in a dorm," my father urged. "Have a normal college experience."

His resistance made me dig in my heels. "What about my life has been normal lately?"

He wasn't caving in. "You know I'll support whatever decision you make, but I worry about this arrangement. I want you to get back on track with your life."

My head still throbbed, and I didn't have the energy for this conversation, but inside I knew that I was getting too involved in Simone and Daniel's business. I wanted to wave a magic wand and give them a baby, and then I wanted them to keep me around and adore me for the rest of our lives.

"Don't forget who you are," my father said.

Since my mother's affair, I'd had no idea who I was, I wanted to say. Instead, I changed the subject by inquiring about their seder. When the conversation lagged, I told him that he was going to own the phone company, our family joke to end a call that went on too long.

"Dinner's almost ready, Shel," I heard my mother call.

I hadn't heard her use his nickname in ages. Had she dumped the Shabbos goy and rekindled her feelings toward my father? After we hung up, I rolled over and went back to sleep.

18

Simone got her period exactly a month after my seder with Daniel, and its arrival set us all on edge. She was subdued and only smiled at Ollie. She told me she was going to take Marci's advice and get away for a few days with Daniel, and that I could take a vacation too because her parents had been dying to spend some time with Ollie. She also said she was going to start taking hormone drugs and that she might get a little "bitchy."

On a sunny May morning, a few days before her body-temperature chart indicated that she'd start ovulating, Simone drove Ollie to Laguna. They'd spend a few days with her folks, and then she'd come home solo and take off for a week in Ensenada with Daniel. I wasn't sure what I would do with myself, so before she left I'd asked her to make a list of spring-cleaning chores.

"You're not the maid, Barbara," she'd said. "Daniel will leave you his car. Go explore. Drive up the coast or something. This is a break for you. You deserve it."

After she and Ollie left, I did two loads of laundry, sprayed Windex on sheets of newspaper to wipe Ollie's fingerprints from the glass in the living-room windows, vacuumed the floors, and cleaned out the fridge. While scouring Simone and Daniel's bathroom sink, I found a bottle of Simone's nail polish, a soft purple that looked good on her. I sat on the edge of the tub and painted my toenails. Unskilled in such matters, I did a sloppy job, but the polish made my toes look long and sexy anyway.

I'd once heard that dogs act funny before earthquakes, as if they can sense that something big is going to happen. I'd been feeling that way since my seder and my Old Town adventures with Simone. She and I hadn't discussed the conversation we'd shared over margaritas. She'd been working extra shifts at the hospital, which made it easy to keep things light. Her moods were also unpredictable, so I tried to stay out of her way. With Daniel it was different. We'd started a conversation that I wanted to continue. Badly.

At noon, I changed into my bathing suit—well, actually Simone's hand-me-down red bikini—laid a towel on a small patch of grass in back of the house, and began reading *My Name Is Asher Lev,* which I'd found in the living room. My mother and I had loved Chaim Potok's *The Chosen* and *The Promise,* and now I was devouring his story about the little Orthodox Jewish boy who draws crucifixes and has a depressed mother everyone dotes on. I loved this little boy. I was this little boy.

I barely heard the back door open. Daniel stood over my towel, and I sat up, flustered, adjusting my bathing suit top.

"I didn't know what you'd think of it," Daniel said, glancing at the book.

I wasn't sure how much Simone had told him about my life with the Schines. "I'd have been drawing crucifixes if I had any artistic talent." I laughed and put the book down. "Can I finish it?"

"Absolutely. I want to hear your thoughts when you're done." He slid his Ray-Bans down his nose and touched my shoulder with his index finger. "You better get out of the sun. You're looking pretty red."

My skin felt crinkly. "Too late, this is going to hurt." I patted the book. "It was worth it, though." I stood and faced Daniel. I came up to his chin.

"Let me take you to dinner," he said. "You know, to thank you for buffing out our house."

I folded up my towel, my heart beating so loudly I wondered if Daniel could hear it. I showered and took extra care with my hair, now past my shoulders, the auburn blending with more new strands of gold. I wore it loose instead of up in my usual ponytail, and when I turned my head, I could smell Flex shampoo.

I picked out the white jeans I'd worn the night I met Brian, a milk-chocolate scoop-neck shirt with white trim, and my brown sandals. My toes looked good. My cheeks were flushed from the sun, and I put a little Vaseline on my lips to make them shine. There was no harm in pretending that I was on a date.

Daniel was waiting for me in the living room. He'd changed his shirt, and he smelled like soap. Was this a date? That was ridiculous. He was just being charitable because I'd "buffed out" his house.

"Do you like Chinese food?" he asked.

"I had chop suey once at my friend Mira's house, and I thought it tasted like bad cafeteria food." I cringed at the thought of my high school cafeteria, a reminder of our age difference.

"Well, let me introduce you to some Chinese food that I guarantee tastes nothing like cafeteria food."

He told me about a little place south of downtown La Jolla as we lwalked out to the driveway. He opened the car door for me, which no man other than my father had ever done. I tried not to look at him too much as we drove down the coast.

When we passed the street that led to La Jolla Shores, I glanced toward the ocean and remembered holding pale, scrawny Benny's hand as we skipped through the sand toward the awesome Pacific. Now I chased after a sturdy sun-kissed Ollie in my red bikini, my midriff tanned and bare. I'd grown accustomed to the feel of the air on my body, and freckles had replaced the old acne on my back. Still, I would always associate Benny with my first dip into the ocean. I missed him.

"Smoke is coming out of your ears." Daniel knocked his knuckles playfully on my leg.

I rubbed my fingers against the spot he'd touched. "I was just thinking about my first time in the water."

He glanced over at me as he passed the turnoff for the La Jolla Cove.

"Simone might have mentioned that when she met me, I looked like I'd jumped out of a page of *My Name Is Asher Lev*." I felt as though I'd just told him I was half Martian.

"Go on."

"I grew up in a community like Asher's. Lots of rules," I said, and then my memories spilled out of me. "I liked knowing that every Saturday I was going to wake up and go to services. My best friend, Tzippy, would meet me in the women's section—men and women don't pray together—and when we were tiny, our moms would feed us saltines from the kitchen to keep us quiet."

"What about when you got older?" he asked.

"Tzippy and I played out on the bluff and came back in time for the last prayer where her dad would throw his prayer shawl over our heads, and the air would smell like our hair and the milk on our breath as he talked to God on our behalf. When we got too old for that, we'd spend much of the service trying not to talk to each other or helping the young moms take care of their children. After shul, we'd eat a big lunch, and Tzippy and I would spend the afternoon together while the adults took their Shabbos naps."

Daniel pulled into the parking lot and cut the engine but made no move to get out of the car. "You did grow up like Asher Lev."

"Kind of," I said shyly. "We knew who we were."

Daniel faced me. "I'm glad you told me all that."

"You and Simone know how to get me talking." I'd told Simone secrets about my background in order to entertain and engage her; with Daniel, I shared my most sacred memories of the Schines' world because I wanted him to help me keep them alive. My finger was starting to tingle where I'd been rubbing my leg, and I felt pressure building in my chest. It took Asher Lev and Daniel's rapt attention to help me name everything I'd lost. The sadness was intense but fleeting. I opened the car door.

"Okay, I'm ready to try your Chinese food."

Daniel held the restaurant door for me. Inside, a waiter seated us. "Would you like me to order?" Daniel asked as he opened the large red menu. I was enthralled when he spoke the words "moo shoo" and "kung pao."

"And to drink?" the waiter asked me.

"I'll stick with water, thanks." I wasn't going to repeat my escapade with Simone.

Daniel ordered a Coke, and we talked about his agnostic mother, who lived in San Francisco and worshiped Carl Jung. She seemed nice enough when she called on Sunday mornings.

The waiter arrived with a large tray of steaming dishes. "I'll make the first one for you," Daniel said, opening a flimsy beige pancake on his plate and spreading one side with what looked like brown coleslaw mixed with bite-size pieces of chicken. He folded the pancake into an envelope, handed it to me, and watched as I took a bite. The warm juice escaped from the dough and ran down my fingers. My teeth crunched on thin slivers of vegetables, releasing an exotic blend of flavors.

"What am I tasting?"

"Garlic, sesame, ginger," he replied eagerly. "So?"

"Delicious." I felt like we were acting the scene from the movie *Funny Girl* where Nicky Arnstein introduces Fanny Brice to her first bite of lobster.

"Phew. Glad you like it." He pretended to wipe his brow with the back of his hand. "Big responsibility."

After dinner, Daniel said, "Come on, I want to take you someplace." We crossed La Jolla Boulevard and walked down a narrow street that led to a small beach. We leaned over a railing and looked down at the waves, lit by the moonlight.

"This is Marine Street beach." I followed him down the steps to the water, listening to the shorebreakers slam into the sand. "There's a hurricane brewing in Mexico. The surf will be huge tomorrow."

I felt wildly free being out at night on the beach. I looked up at the moon, and something wet landed on my forehead. "I think I felt a raindrop."

"They're predicting record-breaking storms." Daniel turned

back toward the steps. "We should go." By the time he started his car, the sky was dumping rain. He gripped the steering wheel tightly as he concentrated on the slick roads. We got drenched on the short walk from the car to the front door, and as soon as we entered the house, we ran around shutting all the windows.

He tapped my shoulder. "Thanks for keeping me company tonight."

"Thanks for the Chinese food," I said.

When I was around Simone or Tzippy, I wanted to become them. But Daniel, like Mrs. Kessler, journeyed deep inside me and made me feel good about what he found. Mrs. Kessler spotted my gift with children, and Daniel made me feel that my ideas mattered, that I mattered.

I forced myself to brush my teeth, not wanting to rid my mouth of the new tastes of garlic and ginger. I fell asleep at midnight, only to be woken an hour later by loud claps of thunder. Sheets of rain pounded against the side of the house. The thunder grew louder, and when I got out of bed to check my windows, I felt a presence at my door. I turned around. Daniel stood in the doorway in his pajama bottoms, his bare chest lit by a fresh crackle of lightning.

"You okay in here?" he asked.

I swallowed hard. "I'm fine."

"Here's a flashlight. The electricity is out." He put it on my dresser.

"Thank you," I said.

"Good night."

"Good night."

I crawled back into bed, pulled the covers over my head, and I thought about what I would do if Daniel appeared in my doorway again.

The next morning, the sky was dark and angry. I could hear Daniel in the kitchen as I dressed. We drank orange juice and ate fistfuls of granola. When we finished the box, the power still hadn't returned, so he lit candles in the living room. He handed me my Chaim Potok book and sat next to me, perusing a publisher's catalogue and marking biographies to order for his store.

I read the same paragraph describing one of Asher's crucifixions over and over, unable to grasp the words that only a day before had mesmerized me. I was aware of Daniel's every breath, every mark of his pencil.

The sky opened up and unloosed more rain than I'd ever seen in my life. "How long do these storms usually last?" I asked.

"This one's supposed to go on for another day."

"It feels like we're inside a car wash," I said after a minute.

"It does."

"My dad used to take me with him to get his car washed. He'd buy me an orange Tootsie Pop, and I'd sit on his lap feeling like we were in a cave." I raised my arms over my head and stretched out my toes.

"I wish I'd had a father," Daniel said.

I looked at him in surprise. "What happened? I've told you so much about me. Tell me about your family."

"Not much to tell. My dad died when I was three, and I grew up with my mom, stepdad, and two stepsisters. Pretty dull compared to your history."

I spared a moment to say that I was sorry about his dad and then continued to detail the inner workings of my very intriguing life. I told him about Mrs. Kessler and how she'd saved me from my mother's craziness. "That's how I kept sane while my mother was living her lie."

He listened hard while I talked. "I'm sure Mrs. Kessler appreciated your help, Barbara."

"She was way more helpful to me," I said with a pang. I hadn't written Mrs. Kessler since I left Milwaukee.

"Plus, you're an easy person to have around. You have what my mom would call a light touch."

"A light touch, I like that a lot."

I tapped his wrist lightly. Then I grabbed his hand. I couldn't let go. I wanted to hold on forever.

"Oh, God. Sorry about that. I guess you want your hand back." I looked toward the window at the rain pummeling the trees, and my history didn't feel so fascinating any more.

"Don't be sorry. You're fine." He smiled at me.

That was all it took to unleash a torrent of tears. I cried for the innocent Barbara Pupnick who had been content following the Schines' rules and for the bitter Barbara Pupnick who alternately cursed and mourned the people who brought those rules to life. This rogue Barbara Pupnick was unpredictable, and entirely terrifying.

Daniel sat next to me and let me cry for a few minutes, and then he held up his sleeve. "Here, you can use this."

I slung my arm across his ribs. He patted me on the back in a brotherly fashion, which made me cling to him more tightly. I pressed my wet face against his cheek and his stubble chafed my skin. I'd been lost and alone for so many months, taking care of my mother, Sari, Benny, Ollie, and Simone, worrying about my father. I had no family or shul to hold me. I climbed into his lap and wrapped my arms around his neck, and he embraced me while I cried a new set of tears, not caring how embarrassed I'd be afterward. He was offering me comfort I badly needed, and I was going to seize it.

The hysterical claps of thunder blocked out the door slamming and Simone clomping through the house in her rain boots, carrying a bottle of champagne and two flutes.

"I came home early, love," she shouted. "Time to celebrate our vacation."

Daniel and I jumped up from the couch, but it was too late. She'd already seen us. She stood slack-jawed in her Mexican sweater, dropping the flutes and the bottle on the floor. The sound of glass shattering echoed throughout the house, and champagne sprayed my jeans.

I climbed off of his lap and wiped my nose with my sleeve.

"What's going on?" Simone's voice was shrill.

"Nothing. We're cool." Daniel looked at her as if to say, "I'll explain this to you later."

"Not cool. Barbara, why were you sitting on Daniel's *lap*?"

"Simone, it's okay," he said, walking over to his wife. "Barbara was upset."

"Daniel, cut the 'you're taking hormones tone.' I walk in from a trip to find my *babysitter* sitting on your lap? That's weird, even if she was upset."

"Simone." He tried to put his arm around her, but she shook him off.

"Look, I'm going outside, and we can all pull ourselves together." Now she was looking at me more with pity than anger, as though she wished she could save me from the humiliation of throwing myself at her husband.

I thought my whole body would go up in smoke and shame.

"Simone. Don't go out in this storm," Daniel said. "We're all cool here."

I wanted to agree with him, but I was paralyzed.

"Give me a minute alone." She looked at me and shook her head.

I got up and ran to my room. I had to get out of there. I threw some clothes and toiletries in my duffel, slung it over my shoulder, and headed for the front door. When I entered the living room, Simone was walking away from Daniel, glass crunching beneath her boots.

"Simone, come back here!" He went after her in his bare feet, the glass slicing his soles, leaving a trail of blood behind him.

My body hummed with adrenaline as I stood and watched him through the scrim of water pounding against the glass door. He ran out to the middle of the driveway, but Simone was gone. From my angle, I could see that she'd parked her car on the street, so she must be close by. He got into his Datsun and started it. Suddenly, Simone emerged from the Torrey pines at the foot of the driveway, drenched. And then it all happened so fast. I put my hand out to open the door and yell for her to move out of Daniel's way, but it was too late. I heard the familiar squeal of his temperamental brakes as the Datsun skidded down the driveway. Simone tried to move out of the way, but she tripped and landed on her back. The car slowed and rose slightly, plowing over her leg as if she were a speed bump. She gave a cry so primal that it didn't sound human.

I ran out of the house and escaped into the grove of trees, my duffel bag banging against my leg. I fell twice on the winding streets of La Jolla, relieved to hear sirens. I prayed that they were on their way to Simone. I kept running, darting through intersections with broken lights. I stopped when I reached the condominium with the big menorah teetering from the gales of wind.

When Sari Levenstein found me, I was rocking back and forth on her front porch, breathless, my leg bruised, my jeans reeking of champagne, my lips as blue as the San Diego ocean on a clear day, and my toes dotted with Simone's nail polish and Daniel's blood.

19

October 2009

I couldn't look at the rebbetzin as I told her my story about the Coxes. I kept my eyes fixed on the chandelier as I spoke, each syllable carrying me back to San Diego. I could almost taste my first bite of avocado and smell the little-boy sweat in Ollie's hair and the coconut oil I'd rubbed on my virgin skin. I felt Daniel's innocent tap on my leg, and was mortified by my neediness.

"Am I a rotten person?" I asked when I finished, still afraid to look in the rebbetzin's eyes.

"No. You were at sea, all alone." Guilt laced her words.

"Nobody forced me to cling to Daniel or abuse the Coxes' kindness or run away from Simone's accident."

She cocked her head. "As the prophet Jeremiah says, *God will judge us when we say we* didn't *sin.*"

"Well, before my father's funeral, I tried to tell my mother that I'd sinned, but she was…."

"Distracted." The rebbetzin finished my thought.

"Yes. And I have to confess that I never think about Simone and Daniel anymore. I've just been happy going along living my life."

"I'm not so sure, Barbara."

"What do you mean?"

"You came to see me because you were upset that you were leaking rage, isn't that right?"

"Like a Chernobyl reactor. Kaboom. Radioactive contamination everywhere."

"All right, let's say you're a Chernobyl reactor. If I'm remembering my history correctly, a power surge caused that explosion."

"So you're saying that all I needed was some kind of power surge to release all my unsafely stored toxins?"

She smiled. "It's just a metaphor."

"And now it's time to clean up the spill?"

"And to make room for Hashem's love to flow through you."

I stared out the sanctuary windows. The trees were bare enough that I could see the lake. The sky was black, and yellow lights blinked from a boat miles off shore. I listened for the bones of the mansion to creak as I contemplated God's love. On my last birthday card, Sam had written that if loving were an Olympic event, I'd take the gold. I lavished my love on Sam and Lili, and parents lined up at the door for the chance to have me nurture their children, and them for that matter. Beneath this patina of Olympic-caliber caring, however, I wasn't sure who I was at the core.

"Where are you?" the rebbetzin asked.

"Barbara, where are you?" I laughed, not needing to explain my reference to the question God asked Adam after he bit from the apple.

"Another one of Rabbi Lichtenberg's lemon drops for you." She squeezed my hand.

"He paid a hefty price for hiding his sin from God, that Adam."

"God knows we're not perfect. He only expects us to take responsibility for our actions, which you've done, unlike Adam."

"That's generous of you to say."

"You're not the only one at fault here, Barbara." The wrinkles on her forehead looked deeper to me.

Suddenly I had a feeling that she was hatching a plan that involved me and that I was going to start feeling better soon. In a way, I already did. I knew from long conversations with my students' parents what it felt like to hold someone's trouble in your palm and offer them a second of relief from the burden.

I left the mansion, floating between San Diego and my home

ten miles up the road. My cell phone rang.

"Hello, stranger," Sheri said. "Did you forget something today?"

The sound of her voice yanked me back into my life, but what had I forgotten? "Today?"

"My birthday lunch." She sounded hurt.

"Oh, crap."

"Barbara, are you upset with me?"

"God, no. Why?"

"You've been so distant lately. Like you're off somewhere else."

She didn't have to say more. I knew exactly what she meant. I knew how it felt to watch someone disappear into a mist.

"Sheri, I am so sorry. I've been worried about Lili. I haven't been myself." This was partially true.

"What can I do to help?" Her voice had warmed up.

"Just forgive me."

"I'm sorry things have been so rough."

"Listen, I'm just getting home, and Lili's here. Talk later?"

"Whenever you want."

We hung up, and I walked through the door to find Lili waiting for me at the kitchen table, primed to ignore me.

"Hi, Lil," I said.

"Hi," she grunted.

I was too exhausted to cook or deal with her sullenness. "You in the mood for Thai?"

She narrowed her eyes. "*Taylor* took me to Kopp's." Her lips curled into the beginning of a smirk.

"Glad you ate," I said, refusing to react. I didn't recognize this girl with the added layer of flesh and the new baseline mood of irritability.

"I flunked my geometry test, in case you're interested."

Her words made me shiver; I remembered throwing the same wounded accusation at my mother when she stopped tracking my schoolwork.

"Of course I'm interested," I snapped. "Haven't I been sitting with you every night trying to help you?"

"You suck at math."

Three deep breaths, Barbara. Math wasn't my strength, true, but working with Lili frustrated the hell out of me. I could tolerate the busiest four-year-old, but I couldn't help her for more than a half hour without wanting to tear my eyelashes out. Her stream of patter looped around her worries that she wasn't going to finish her assignment, that she was going to fail the test, that her ankle wouldn't heal, that she was going to miss the new episode of *Glee.* She couldn't sit more than five seconds without jumping up to fill her water glass or go to the bathroom.

"Your dad will help you tonight."

"Great, pawn me off on Dad," she snarled.

That was it. I was calling her doctor tomorrow and pursuing the Adderall prescription her academic support team had been suggesting.

"I'm going upstairs to shower, Lili. We can discuss this after we've both calmed down," I said. Her obnoxious behavior signaled that she needed me more than ever, but I had nothing to give her right now.

When I emerged from the shower, Sam was waiting for me. "What happened down there?"

"Your daughter was being a pill."

"That's my girl you're calling a pill." He held me for a second, my wet hair leaving an imprint on his shirt.

"Why does she have to be so mean?" I asked.

"She's hurting."

"Who isn't?"

He unbuttoned his oxford shirt and retrieved a sweatshirt from the drawer. "Are you still thinking about clearing things up with your mom?"

I wrapped my hair in a towel. "Jenny the warden won't let me see her."

"What's that all about?"

"My mother's visit here, or shall I say, her visit with *me*, agitated her." My lip quivered.

Sam pulled his sweatshirt over his head to avoid telling me what we both knew, that Jenny had a point.

"Let me talk to Lili, and we'll finish this up later." I kissed his shoulder, went to Lili's room, and knocked on her door.

"Come in." She sounded contrite.

She lay on her bed in an oversized T-shirt she'd sweet-talked Sam into buying her when he took her to see the Jonas Brothers for her twelfth birthday. A history book was open across her legs.

"Do you have a history test?"

She shut the book. "Yes. What's the difference if I get a C or a C-?" She handed me her last test, which was littered with red checkmarks. "See? It's not just math." Tears started streaming down her face. "I'm dumb." She looked so small in the big shirt, her nose running, her eyes red.

"Move over." I crawled into the slot between the bed and the wall. "You, my girl, are anything *but* dumb." I wrapped a strand of her wiry hair around my finger.

"I'm just smart in different ways," she said, mimicking me. She let me hold her for a few minutes before she squirmed away. "I'm *perceptive.*"

"You see things, Lili," I said. "You know that."

"Maybe things I shouldn't," she said.

I sat up. "What does that mean?"

"Nothing. Better get back to it." She opened her book.

I maneuvered myself out of her bed. "Do you want me to help you study?"

"No, I got it, Mom." She tried to sound brave.

"Let's try the Adderall, Lil."

"Do you think it will help?"

"Only one way to find out," I said, instead of what I was thinking. Can't get much worse.

That night, I dreamed about Simone Cox. She was wearing a red bikini that revealed her outie, as small as a buttonhole in the collar of an oxford shirt. Her hair shielded the face of a little boy who was whispering in her ear. I woke up panting as if the smell of smoke had seeped into my sleep. Who was that little boy? Mrs. Kessler's Yossi? Sari's Benny? Simone's Ollie? He was not Josh Fader or Brett Cooper or any of my students. They never would have been so bold as to intrude upon my subconscious.

I was afraid to revisit my dream, so I lay still and listened until the birds started to chirp outside my window. Sam, Lili, and I spoke little over breakfast. After I slogged through a morning of teaching, I put on my sneakers and went for a long walk.

I made a beeline for our kitchen computer as soon as I got home. I hit the return key and studied my screensaver, a photo of Sam, Lili, and me in Cheesehead hats, smiling after a Packers victory. Sam always looked slightly triumphant, as befitted a person blessed with an allegiance to a baseline level of happiness.

I opened my browser, and the Google welcome page swallowed up the image of my grinning family. I searched "Daniel Cox and coffeehouse and San Diego," and up popped a business address for Java Books in Encinitas. It made me happy to know that he was living his dream. I clicked on the website, which featured a photo of Daniel lounging on a big white chair, holding an oversized coffee mug. He was still beautiful, though middle-age had dulled his features. My hand shook as I dialed the West Coast.

"Java Books." Daniel sounded exactly the same.

"This is Barbara Blumfield. I used to be Barbara Pupnick." My hand shook harder. Maybe I'd made the wrong choice.

He paused, and I heard the grinding roar of an espresso machine and bustling sounds of a busy coffeehouse. I wondered if he was going to hang up on me.

"How's Ollie?" I asked.

"Ollie's a public defender up in Spokane. Got sick of the sunshine." His voice was tight.

I had a flash of the bright little boy I'd bathed and chased down the flat San Diego beaches. I put my hand to the place on my cheek he liked to kiss, half expecting to find grains of sand from his lips.

"Did you call to check in on Ollie after all these years?" Daniel asked.

I took a nervous swig of bottled water. "I called to apologize."

The espresso machine quieted. "Are you in some kind of twelve-step program?"

I laughed weakly. "No."

I could hear someone ask him if they had any raspberry scones left.

"In the back, in the pink box," he said. "Sorry, Barbara. Let me go outside so I won't be interrupted."

I listened to the din of the shop yield to the sound of the ocean and waited for him to speak.

"It was an accident," he said, sounding like he had when he and Simone were just about to make up after an argument.

"You're generous, but I should have stayed to see if Simone was okay."

He took a breath as if he was about to speak, but I cut him off. "Please don't make this easier for me."

"I just don't see the use in reliving that nightmare."

"How long did it take for her to get well?"

"Months. She ... um ... her hip and knee are still a little messed up."

I imagined Simone running through the sand in one of her bikinis, her muscular legs devouring the ground beneath her. Daniel told me about her recovery, about the two surgeries and the long rehabilitation, and I gathered my courage to ask, "Did you ever have more children?"

I could hear waves in the background.

"Yes, a girl."

"Oh, that's wonderful, wonderful. Congratulations!"

"She was born in 1977, but thanks."

I laughed out of relief that Simone had been spared the heartache of failing to conceive. I wondered if she ever got the reading she wanted from Marci.

"Barbara, we've forgiven you." He sounded like he wanted to get to the point of this phone call and move on.

"How?" I asked, thinking of the damage I'd caused.

"You were fragile."

Fragile. It was the word the Shabbos goy and the rebbetzin had used to describe my mother. "That's no excuse for hurting people."

I could tell that he was walking toward the water by the intensifying sound of the waves. "Do you know what our biggest seller is right now?" He didn't wait for me to answer. "It's a kid's book called *Zen Shorts*."

"I know that book. I'm a preschool teacher." I felt my old excitement when I learned that he was a Gatsby fan.

"Okay, Barbara, then go and reread—"

" 'A Heavy Load,' " I blurted. It was the story about two traveling monks who encounter a rude young woman in silk robes, sitting in her sedan chair, waiting grumpily for someone to ferry her across a mud puddle. The older monk obliges, and she treats him shabbily. Hours later, the younger monk complains about the woman's rudeness.

"Yes, that's the one. Remember the ending, when the older monk says something like, 'I set the woman down hours ago, why are you still carrying her?' "

It was the type of exchange that I was once young and foolish enough to mistake for Daniel's romantic interest in me. "I get it."

"I know you do," he said warmly.

"So you got your wish," I said. "A coffee shop where people can talk about their favorite books."

"Yeah, I did." I pictured his shy smile.

We mumbled a clumsy farewell, and then he spoke my name just as I was about to hang up.

"Yes?"

"Maybe I hadn't fully set down the woman in the robes until you called."

"Then I'm glad I did."

With the warm phone in my lap, I thought of my recurring nightmare of the naked woman floating in the mikveh and the man paddling around in his dirty work boots. Now I could see her face. It was mine.

I didn't sleep the night I called Daniel. Our conversation had released an energy so uncomfortably wild that I couldn't settle back into myself. I went down to the kitchen, heated some milk in a saucepan, and emptied it into my favorite mug, a Mother's Day gift Lili made when she was twelve. She'd laminated a collage of the two of us to the cup. I'd always focused on the cleverness of Lili's artwork and her conscientious gathering of mementos: the words "Benji's Deli" cut out of an old menu, a piece of thread from a disastrous sewing class we'd taken together, a dried blueberry we'd picked in Door County. But now that I examined the photos, I noticed that she'd selected images where my lips were smiling but my eyes were not.

It took me a week to digest my conversation with Daniel, but by the time November arrived, I was ready to visit the rebbetzin to discuss it. She kissed me hello, and I followed her into the kitchen where my mother and I had worked as a team, stacking dirty plates from the Shabbos table, arranging bakery platters, grinding coffee for the rebbetzin's teas. I started to giggle.

"What's funny?" the rebbetzin asked. I kept laughing, and soon she was laughing with me.

"I'm thinking about the time you asked Tzippy to get the chocolate sprinkles from the pantry." I didn't need to finish the story because she knew exactly what I was talking about. During the hot summer months, Tzippy and I used to eat big bowls of vanilla ice cream with chocolate sprinkles, or jimmies, we called them. Tzippy would have to climb up on a stool to retrieve the vat of sprinkles from the top shelf of the pantry. One time the lid popped off, and the sprinkles showered Tzippy, bouncing off her body and flying into the far corners of the kitchen. The rebbetzin was angry at first. "Tzippy, I told you to burp the Tupperware," she chided, but then my mother started laughing, a sound deep and rich and unexpected from a woman so refined. Soon we were all laughing so hard that tears fell from our eyes.

"The rabbi will think we're meshuganah," I said, my index finger circling near my temple as I repeated the rebbetzin's words from so many years ago. Another gale of laughter ensued.

"This is the first time in years when it didn't hurt to think about her." I could have been talking about Tzippy or my mother.

"Tzippy misses you too."

I looked out the window. I'd forgotten how gorgeous the lake was from this vantage point. "What happened when I left town before her wedding?"

The rebbetzin's words were measured as she described how Tzippy phoned my house and wouldn't believe my parents when they said I'd gone back to California.

Oh, Lord. Couldn't I have hung on a few more days in Milwaukee? No, I couldn't have. "Did you ever tell her why I abandoned her?"

"Not until your mother left the shul."

My mother had taught me how to walk out on someone in need, but not as she'd taught me how to tie my shoe or peel a hard-boiled egg. I'd absorbed the pain that caused me to leave and the belief in its necessity at the time. I told the rebbetzin about the confessional letters I'd written to Tzippy. "I've kept almost all of them. Isn't that strange?"

She walked to the counter and put a few of her apricot cookies on a plate.

"Maybe if I'd just sent one of those letters everything would be different," I said.

"What do you mean?"

"She would have understood why I vanished from her life." I thought about the letters Tzippy wrote me after her wedding. I couldn't bear to read them, so I threw most of them away without opening them.

I took a big breath, and the air filled me as if I'd cleared some debris from the lining of my lungs. "You're not going to believe what I did."

"Should I be worried?"

"No, it's nothing bad, it's just weird and completely out of character."

She offered me a cookie. "So are you going to make me guess already?"

"I tracked Daniel down," I said as if I were telling her that I'd just robbed a bank.

She raised her eyebrows. It wasn't easy to shock the rebbetzin.

"And I called him up." I told her about the conversation.

She blinked hard. "That was a brave thing to do, Barbara."

I made the call out of impulse, but now that I'd confided in the rebbetzin, I was amazed that I had the courage to do it. The fist that had tightened around my heart during that plane ride back to San Diego had opened when I met Sam and bore Lili, but not completely. A few more fingers had released their hold since I'd been visiting the mansion.

The rebbetzin opened a drawer and took out one of Rabbi Schine's legal pads and a Bic pen. She put them down on the table. "Now do the same thing with Tzippy."

She left the kitchen, not giving me the chance to protest.

October 20, 2009 *B"H*

Dear Tzippy,

I never imagined that I'd write you another letter, but here I am, sitting at your mother's kitchen table doodling tulips on your father's legal pad, trying to come up with the words to say I'm sorry.

I'm sorry for not showing up at your wedding, but I'm even sorrier for my larger disappearance from your life. When I found out about my mother's affair, I withdrew from you. I didn't want to put you in the middle of my trouble, and I was also ashamed, and maybe a little jealous that your life made such sense.

If it's any consolation, I actually did pour my soul out to you in letters, but I never sent them. Maybe we'd still be friends if I'd given you the chance to separate my mother's behavior from who I was. I sure couldn't, and maybe I still can't.

I hadn't allowed myself to think about you until your mom turned up out of the blue and invited me to participate in Mrs.Kessler's, z"l, tahara. Only you would have remembered that Mrs. Kessler ate orange jelly on rye bread every day for lunch and made funny animal voices when she read us stories she'd written especially for us. And only you would have remembered how as teenagers she gave us free rein of the nook so we could have a place to talk and dream after you started going to school in Brooklyn. Mrs. Kessler represents a mere fraction of what I lost when I left the shul.

I guess what I'm saying is that when I lost you, I lost the person I was when we were together. And by excising you from my life, I stole a piece of your history too. That's what I'm most sorry about.

Maybe one day we'll meet again in the nook. With your mother's help, I will face what my family's ghosts have cost me, most sadly, my friendship with you.

Love,

Barbara

When I finished the letter, I folded it in thirds and scraped my chair back noisily to signal the rebbetzin to return to the kitchen. She materialized almost instantly.

"Tea?" she asked.

"Water is fine, thank you." I handed her the letter.

"Do you feel better?"

"A little. I'm not as radioactive."

"But?" Her tone was more intense than it was when she counseled congregants.

"I'm horrible for saying this, but despite everything I've learned, I haven't let go of all of my bad feelings toward my mother yet." And with that, I told the rebbetzin the ultimate war story, the one that had bubbled up to my lips during that Mommy and Me class I'd taken with Lili, the one I'd silenced so I wouldn't poison my daughter with my breast milk.

May 1975

My father suffered a massive stroke the night Daniel and I ate Chinese food together. My mother called to tell me that he'd died, but the telephone lines at Daniel's were down from the storm, so she called Sari. When Sari found me on her doorstep, she broke the news of my father's death with the professionalism of an emerging rebbetzin. Paired with the right rabbi, she could have been a formidable player in the Schines' world.

She led me to the bathroom, where she'd spent so many hours being sick, and ran a warm bath.

"That's Daniel's blood," I said, pointing to a reddish streak on my foot.

She said nothing as she handed me one of Benny's Sesame Street washcloths.

I pulled down the waistband of my jeans and pointed to my stomach. "This tan line is from Simone's bikini."

"Shhh, shhh, Barbara," she said the way she did when Benny had a bad dream. She rifled through the linen cupboard over the toilet while I undressed and stepped into the tub.

I poked my toes out of the water. "And that's Simone's nail polish."

She pulled out a fresh towel.

I felt delirious. "See these?" I pointed to my lips.

She placed the towel on the toilet seat.

"I was going to use them to kiss Simone's husband."

She motioned toward the hallway. "Barbara, lower your voice, please. The children are sleeping."

I didn't say anything else for the rest of the evening, not when she left me alone in the bath or made me a bowl of tomato soup or dug into the tin can she stowed in the pantry, pulled out a wad of cash from her knipple savings, and stuffed it in my purse. I said nothing as she drove me to the airport and hugged me goodbye. I only spoke to the airline agent who sold me a one-way ticket to Milwaukee.

My mother picked me up at the terminal. It was an unseasonably cold May day, and she wore her blue coat, which now pulled at the seams. Her color was good, particularly for a new widow. I hadn't slept or combed my hair properly since I fled the Coxes' house.

During the drive home, we spoke of funeral arrangements and such logistics as who was going to pick Neil up at the bus station. My mother parked in the driveway, and I went around to the front steps, where my father had retrieved his *Sentinel* every morning, where he had stood and waved at me for the last time in his clownish pajamas. I wandered through the house touching his kiddush cup, his galoshes, and the white Pupnick Orthodontics lab coat hanging in the laundry room. It had been ironed. I went into my parents' bathroom to feel his toothbrush, stiff from the excess toothpaste he used when he brushed his teeth.

I heard my mother behind me. "So how did it happen?" My voice was lifeless.

"Frannie found him in his office slumped over his desk. He was in between appointments."

I picked up his metal comb and pulled out one of his fine black hairs. "He hated to keep people waiting."

"He was kind," my mother said in the reverent tone people use when speaking of the newly dead.

I mashed the teeth of the comb into my palm.

"Honey, that must hurt." She tried to pry the comb out of my hands, but I fought her.

You broke my father's heart, I wanted to say, but I wanted to tell her something more. I wanted to tell her what had happened at Simone and Daniel's house. I looked at her reflection in the mirror.

"Why don't you clean up, darling. You must be exhausted."

I studied her face. She looked relaxed, like she'd just returned from a long vacation.

I pushed the teeth deeper into my hand, the physical pain a welcome distraction.

"Give me that," she said as though my defiance over the comb was the real issue at hand. My palm throbbed, but I still wouldn't let go. This time she succeeded in taking it from me. She stood next to me for a few seconds and rubbed my back, finishing up with a firm pat.

"I did something very bad," I muttered, but she'd already left the bathroom.

My father's mourners packed the Abromowitz Funeral Home. Rabbi Schine teared up as he described how my father's radiant neshama would live on. I sat on my mother's right, my bruised leg practically touching hers. On her left sat the rebbetzin, and I allowed myself to pretend that Tzippy would appear any minute to whisk me away to the nook. I knew she could never make it home from Hong Kong in time, but that didn't stop me from wanting her. Thankfully, Mrs. Kessler sat next to me and held my hand as I whispered the mourner's kaddish for my father.

I felt that unmoored sensation I'd had when the rebbetzin sent me away to live with the Levensteins. I became a camera, recording footage in black-and-white: the rebbetzin seating herself next to my mother in the hearse, Neil staring out the window, the six pallbearers from the shul carrying the casket. I barely felt the rain as we trudged up the path to my father's plot. Heavy drops soaked through my coat and the brown wool dress I'd bought for Tzippy's wedding. Neil stood over my father's grave and stared down into the ground before he picked up the shovel and sprinkled my father's casket with fresh dirt. I grabbed a fistful of dirt from the pile, released it into the trench, and wiped my muddy hand on my coat.

We were drenched and chilled by the time we returned home. The rebbetzin had come over the day my father died to cover our mirrors. Today she put out deli platters, courtesy of the Beckermans, and cookies. People piled into our house to tell me how my father had straightened their children's teeth or how they'd joined the shul because he had invited them for Shabbos or to study the Torah. I remained the camera, recording their mouths moving, catching every fourth or fifth word, while Neil responded to each of them with my father's grace. My mother, tissue and sad smile at the ready, played the part of the grieving widow beautifully, although if my camera zoomed in tight, it would capture the faraway look that made me miss her even though she was sitting right next to me. It would also catch the rebbetzin monitoring her as she would a child at an adult dinner party.

I went up to bed at midnight. I was no longer the camera. I was me, at the center of this nightmare, and I had to know how severe Simone's injuries were. I waited until the house was quiet, having learned a few tricks from my mother, and dialed Daniel. No answer. I dialed every twenty minutes for an hour. Between the first two calls, I pulled out the last box of stationery my father had given me and wrote Tzippy yet another letter that I wouldn't send.

May 24, 1975 *B"H*

Dear Tzippy,

My father's dead, and Daniel ran over Simone with his Datsun. It was my fault. Simone caught me wanting Daniel's comfort. Badly. A certain kind of need can singe your brain, leaving you reckless and selfish. It can make you forget who you are.

Poor Ollie. Who's taking care of him? I don't have a father anymore. Who will take care of me?

How childish of me to hope to see you at the funeral. One day you'll turn up. Don't ask why, but it's about the only thing I know for sure right now.

Love,

Barbara

The rebbetzin sat with us the next day and the day after, and more people brought us food and tales of my father's orthodontic wizardry. I flipped back and forth from being the camera to being myself. My mother and I sat hip to hip as we accepted condolences. The warmth of her body felt so comforting that I could barely tear myself away to make my hourly phone call to Daniel. Still no answer.

After the seven days of shiva ended, people stopped coming to our house and I stopped calling Daniel. My mother gave Neil my dad's car, and they agreed that I'd return to Madison with him for the summer. He'd take organic chemistry, and I'd acclimate myself to the town and start college in the fall. Neil came up with the plan. Leaving Milwaukee and my mother made sense. I needed to heal elsewhere.

The morning we were scheduled to leave, the sun filled our kitchen with lovely light. It was finally growing warm outside, and my mother came downstairs in her Door County outfit, slacks and a short-sleeved blouse, clothes she wore when she left the Schines' world. She fussed over our breakfast as if we were houseguests. Toast or bagel? Butter or some of the jam Mrs. Fried brought over? Orange juice or milk? Neil and I watched her stack a plate with more toast than we could eat in a week. I knew she was leaving with the Shabbos goy.

"So when is he picking you up?" I asked so she would respond by telling me that of course she was staying right here. How ludicrous! I'd feel guilty for posing such a question, and she'd tell me to stay a few extra days in Milwaukee and the rebbetzin would stop by and make us a nice cup of tea. Instead, she stood at the counter and buttered a slice of toast for Neil.

"Neil is capable of buttering his own toast. When are you going?"

She dropped the knife on the floor, and Neil scurried to pick it up for her.

"After breakfast." She looked down at the tiles.

"Is the Shabbos goy picking you up in the alley or out front?" I asked as dispassionately as I could.

Neil studied his toast and took a large bite.

She sat down at the table and put her hands over ours. "I'm just taking a little trip to get some rest." She'd never looked more rested.

Don't you want to know what I did? I wanted to ask her, so she'd stay and try her best to make me feel better, as she'd done so many times. Another part of me wanted to spit in her face for bailing on us right after our dad died.

"I need to get away from here for a little while," she said.

"I was *inappropriate* with Ollie's dad."

Neil started chewing vigorously as if his crunching noises could drown out our conversation.

"A change of scenery will be restorative for all of us." My mother smiled as though she'd just told us that we were about to pile into the car for a visit to the Domes.

"I sat on his lap and made him hold me, and Simone caught me, so she went out into the storm," I said over Neil's damn chewing. I was desperate to confess my sin to someone who might understand a flight urge strong enough to make me do what I'd done.

She cut me off before I got to the good part. "And then I'll come back, and we'll sort everything out." She was that coyote again in the mikveh, more determined than ever to chew off her arm to escape us.

She walked over to Neil and kissed his cheek, mid-bite. I lunged at her and held on so tightly that she let out a little gasp, and then she peeled me off her limb by limb. I followed her out the front door. The Brisket Ladies were walking up our driveway carrying shopping bags full of food. My mother went right by them, taking nothing of her old life, not so much as a scarf or a hairpin. They watched her climb into the front seat of the blue Dodge and kiss the Shabbos goy on the mouth.

Neil finally stopped eating.

I was too stunned to chase after her. I went upstairs and packed my suitcase with my clothes and a few photos of my father. I went into my parents' bathroom and took his metal comb from the vanity, and then I opened my mother's closet, nearly empty except for her hatbox. I opened the lid, tossed her Shabbos hat and the surrounding tissue paper on the floor, and returned to my room for my letters to Tzippy. I stuffed them into the box and held it to my chest while Neil carried my suitcase and led me out of the house. We left fast, as if we'd received news that the Cossacks were raiding the next village over, not bothering to wipe the toast crumbs from the counter.

"We should put away the butter," I mumbled as Neil helped me into my father's car. He held my sweaty hand the entire drive to Madison, and when we arrived at his apartment he gave me his room.

"The butter is going to spoil," I said, and then I crawled under his covers with my clothes on and stayed there for three months.

I gave Neil Marci's card, and he called her for me. Simone had suffered injuries to her leg, but she was recovering. That was all Marci would tell him. When I slept, I dreamed of Simone. She sidled up to my father's coffin, her Mexican sweater draped over her mangled leg.

I curled up in a fetal ball with my hands over my ears and slept away the days. When I couldn't doze off, I soothed myself by digging the metal teeth of my father's comb into my forearm. When that pain became too predictable, I took to ripping out clumps of hair, comforted by the exquisite tenderness in my scalp. When I was almost bald, I yanked out my pubic hair, five and six at a time, and then I moved on to chewing the insides of my cheeks and spitting out the blood.

The pain muffled all of it: the guilt over what I'd done to Simone, the hurt of my mother's leaving, the loss of the shul, the fear of being alone in the world. It numbed everything except my longing for my mother, the mother who had taken care of me for so many years. I hadn't forgotten that mother.

Every night, Neil sat me in a chair while he rolled a lint brush over the sheets, collecting my day's work. I bathed rarely, and I didn't talk, and I grew so thin that my bones stuck out of my skin. I wanted to disappear.

Neil was getting skinny too. One night, he came home with a paper bag full of cherry yogurt. I loved cherries. He opened a carton and sat down next to my bed.

"All right, Barbara. You need to eat this." He handed me the yogurt and a spoon.

"Can't," I said.

"Come on, Barbara," he said. He filled his own spoon with yogurt and held it to my lips.

I opened my mouth, but I was afraid that I'd choke on the lumpy cream. "I don't think I can do this."

He set the yogurt down and put his head in his hands. "I don't think I can do this either."

I sat up and emerged from my grief long enough to look at my brother closely. He was just a kid. "I'm sorry."

His eyes were full of tears. "I'm trying here, but I don't know how to take care of you."

I wanted to tell him that we should call Mom. We never spoke of her, but occasionally I'd hear him talking to her on the phone. He told her about his classes and the weather, and that was it. I looked at him again. "Should we call someone?"

"Who?" Tears were running down his face. I'd only seen him cry twice: once when he got hit in the face with a baseball, and once when my father punished him for lying about eating cheeseburgers with his friends.

"The rebbetzin?"

"We can't go back there," he said, and I felt his sorrow in his words, even though he'd rebelled against the Schines in his quiet way. The weight of what we'd lost bore down on me.

"Mom?" My voice was tiny.

"We can't go back there either," he said softly.

He was right. If we did, we could never tell ourselves later that she would have shown up if we'd asked. Too risky. We'd already lost one parent.

I patted his shoulder, a hard ridge of bone under his T-shirt. "Give me some of that yogurt."

He handed me the carton. "There you go, Bunny."

I swallowed a spoonful and gave the "Aren't you proud of me?" smile I'd reserved for my father alone.

The next week, I stopped dreaming, and then I stopped feeling anything at all. That was when I quit hurting myself. One night toward the end of July, Neil stood at my door with his arms folded over his chest and reported on his day, as he always did. He told me about his organic chemistry partner's stolen bike and the number of sailboats he'd counted skimming along Lake Mendota that afternoon, and for the first time I really saw what I'd done to him. He was pale and drawn, with a new tic in his left eye.

"Will you show me those sailboats?" I hoisted myself out of his bed.

He closed his eyes and looked up at the ceiling. "Thank you," he said.

I didn't know if he was talking to me or to God.

21

November 2009

The rebbetzin held my palm between her cold fingers while I told her my story, as if her touch could heal the skin that I'd once punctured with the steel teeth of my father's comb. The self-loathing came back as I spoke; it all sounded even more pathetic in the telling. The thing about suppressing personal history is that it becomes a part of your biology, changing your gait and breath and voice. Lili didn't have to drink my breast milk to suck down my poison.

"That was fun." I laughed bitterly, sadness filling my body. That awful pulsing returned, so loud that I wanted to put my hands over my ears.

"I won't make excuses for your mother's choices," the rebbetzin said, and I guessed that she'd had to do a lot of this during the years of my mother's affair.

"Who would do something like that to her kids?"

The rebbetzin shifted in her chair, and we sat in silence until she said, "Did your mother ever tell you about her mother?"

"My mother told me nothing about anything."

The rebbetzin touched her lips before she spoke, as if she were contemplating her next words. "Your grandmother died while giving birth to your mother."

This piece of information landed in my lap with a thud. I sat with it for a good while, trying to absorb it.

"That explains at least some of her actions," the rebbetzin said.

"It does." I told her about my ruptured uterus and my mother's unexplained disappearance after Lili was born.

The rebbetzin pulled a tissue from her sleeve and wiped her nose. "She may also have been scared. Your mother lost a lot of blood, too, during her botched ... procedure." She told me how a "fast girl" from my mother's high school had taken her to Chicago. "She was frightened, this girl, and she didn't know what to do when things went wrong. She left your mother, fevered and hemorrhaging, at the door of the emergency room."

I let the words swirl around in my head. The palpable melancholy that was always just below the surface even at my mother's best times pooled in my chest. "My mother gave hundreds of dollars to Planned Parenthood."

"Yes." The rebbetzin was smoothing her hand over her kitchen table as if wiping up invisible crumbs.

"Can I get myself a glass of water?"

"Of course, Barbara."

I went to the sink and fiddled with the stubborn faucet. "It sticks," she said, and got up to help me. We stood next to the old sink, and she patted the worn countertop. "We've never touched anything in this kitchen. Do you know why?"

I'd assumed that they didn't have the money to remodel, and it occurred to me now that it must have been hard for the rebbetzin to cook for tables of Shabbos guests in this run-down kitchen. "Why?"

"Did you ever notice how peaceful your mother seemed when she was here?"

"This was her happy place." Her mood changed radically when she visited her Rivkah.

"She told me very little about her childhood, but I do know that this was the maids' suite, and she used to sneak up here and visit them."

"There was more than one?"

"Well, yes, but there was usually one who took care of your mother and her brother."

I considered what it would have been like if Lili had been

raised without me.

"None of them lasted more than a year. There came a time when they wanted to start their own families, no matter how hard your mother smiled at them."

"The June smile," I said, and the rebbetzin nodded her head in recognition. Maybe that was how she developed it, to keep the maids around. I felt my mother's aloneness cloak me.

"Barbara, I've been wanting to ask you a question." She paused.

"You can ask me."

"Do you think you might be ready to go back to the mikveh?" Her voice held a hint of pleading, as if she had as much to gain by my return to the mikveh as I did.

"I think so. Yes." I stood and followed the rebbetzin out of her apartment. My breathing quickened as we neared the pantry, but this time we didn't stop. She continued down the special stairway and stopped outside of the heavy wooden door. The room was pitch-black. I half expected to smell my mother's cigarette smoke, but only the scent of rainwater filled the air. "Will you please turn on the light?" My voice trembled like a child's.

"Of course."

The rebbetzin flipped the switch, and a weak yellow light illuminated the pool, which was the size of the men's section of the sanctuary, a space big enough to fit its sixty-seven folding chairs. The pool reminded me of the kidney-shape pools on the top floors of cheap motels. At the far end were two chairs. My mother must have been smoking in one of them. The ember had seemed close to me and far away at the same time. The water was as smooth as a freshly made bowl of my mother's grape Jell-O.

The rebbetzin led me to the changing room, a large bathroom. She took my hands and examined my nails. "There's some nail polish remover over there. You'll have to take off your jewelry and makeup, too." She handed me a pair of clippers. "To clean your fingernails and toenails."

My mother had told me that before you entered the water,

the mikveh lady would pluck any stray hairs from your back, inspect your nail beds, look between your toes, and ask you to check your own belly button. I thought of how we'd cleaned under Mrs. Kessler's nails.

The rebbetzin handed me a cotton robe. "When you finish, I'll be outside waiting."

I dipped a cotton ball in the nail polish remover and wiped the clear shellac from my fingers. I washed my face and scrubbed my eyes with the gentle soap until my mascara came off in clumps that speckled the basin. I undid my tiny silver hoops and removed my black jeans, green turtleneck, and bra and panties. Lastly I slipped off my wedding ring, a band of white gold with a handsome emerald-cut diamond. I never cared much about jewelry, but the ring had been handed down from Sam's grandmother, and it meant something to him.

I filled the bathtub and soaked for as long as I could, but I was too jumpy in such close proximity to the mikveh, so I turned on the shower and scrubbed every part of my body clean. I rinsed my hair of the remnants of shampoo and conditioner from early this morning, I cleaned under every nail twice, and I swirled a Q-tip around the inside of my navel. I checked my shoulders for stray hairs, and then I put on the robe and walked out to the mikveh, where the rebbetzin sat waiting for me on one of the chairs. She put her arm around me and prayed into my ear.

"Before God shall you become pure of all your aberrations. Whatever your past may have been, no matter where, when, and how you may have strayed before God who owns and dispenses all of the future, you can and shall rise up to a new future of purity. You shall rise again before God with a new spirit and a new heart, with a pure new mind receptive once again to all things godly, joyously going out toward all that is good and pure."

I absorbed every word as though it had been spoken just for me. I walked toward the mikveh, turned my back to the rebbetzin, and removed my robe. The humid air felt good on my damp skin, but I was breathing hard. These waters terrified me. My mother had drowned in them.

"I'm here, Barbara," the rebbetzin assured me. "Now dip your entire body three times so that you have immersed every strand of hair in the water. We'll say a prayer after the first immersion."

The water was cool. I shivered as I waded in and felt it travel up from my toes to my thighs to my waist. I turned around and faced the rebbetzin, who stood at the lip of the pool. I was not conscious of my nakedness, though my every blemish and loose fold of skin was exposed. I looked directly into her eyes, and her love fell around my body like a silk sheath.

"Repeat after me," she said. "*Baruch atah adonai ... asher kideshanu bemitzvotav vetzivanu al hatevila ...* Blessed be He our God who has sanctified us with His commandments and commanded us on immersion."

I repeated the prayer, my voice caressing every syllable. I breathed in, filled my lungs with air, and emptied them so that I wouldn't float to the top of the water. I sank into the pool a second time, letting the water wash over me. I immersed myself again and then floated on my back, staring up at the ceiling, my arms outstretched.

The rebbetzin repeated the last line of the opening prayer. "You shall rise again before God with a new spirit and new heart, with a pure new mind receptive once again to all things godly, joyously going out toward all that is good and pure."

"A new heart," I murmured and a few more fingers of that fist uncoiled.

I lingered in the mikveh, inviting the holy water to wash away the dead parts of me. I asked God to help me love my mother as I had when I was very young, before her mists and wanderings. Since I'd caught her here in the mikveh, my elbow had been locked in hers, me holding on for dear life, her desperate to flee. I'd alternated between hope that this time she would stay and hurt when she inevitably didn't. It hadn't occurred to me that her absences were a part of her, like negative space in a painting, or that they'd become a part of me. I knelt down in the water and folded my arms over my breasts. I wanted to settle every score, to rinse away every old hurt.

"Why didn't you come and find me after my father's funeral?" I knew my question would pain the rebbetzin, but I had to ask.

She winced. "Your mother begged me to leave you alone. She didn't want you anywhere near these waters and the shul."

"What?" I was stunned.

The rebbetzin spoke quietly, as if my mother could hear. "Her ghosts had taunted her, and she didn't want the same for you."

"I thought it was you who didn't want me here," I said like a hurt little girl.

The rebbetzin put her hand over her heart. "Never," she said, her voice vibrating with love. "Your mother knew you'd build a good life for yourself outside the shul. And you did."

"Yet here I am." I felt my nakedness before her.

"Strong enough to face down her ghosts. And yours." The rebbetzin wore years of remorse on her face. "It's not too late. She'll have more lucid moments. People live for years with Alzheimer's."

"I forgive both of you," I said, and dunked back under the water.

THE FINAL WASHING

If we cannot name our own, we are cut off at the root,
our hold on our lives as fragile as seed in the wind.

—Dorothy Allison, *Two or Three Things I Know for Sure*

22

I floated home, relieved that I wouldn't have to face Sam or Lili for another hour and that they'd return fed.

Lili was in good spirits when she got home from a babysitting job. She hadn't had time to babysit when she was training hard, and she enjoyed being with kids. The Adderall was helping, too. Sam came in and kissed me on the cheek before he went through the day's mail. I was content not to ask him about new clients or fish around for information that would assure me that the engine of our home was running smoothly.

"You're quiet tonight, Barbara," Sam said.

Lili examined me. "And a little spaced out."

"Just tired," I said.

Neither of them asked why, and I certainly wasn't going to tell them that I'd spent the afternoon at the mansion or that I'd stood naked before the rebbetzin.

"But I'm ready to think about Thanksgiving," I said. All my senses were alive. I could smell Sam's aftershave and feel Lili's calm. Tonight she wasn't jiggling her foot.

I was so fond of a holiday that forced you to be grateful that I'd begun keeping a Thanksgiving journal when I started teaching. The idea stemmed from the turkeys I cut out of brown construction paper, each with a line for children to list something they were grateful for. I put a halt to this exercise when a smart little girl pointed out that we ate turkeys and were therefore eating the bearers of our thanks, with cranberry sauce, but I still kept the journal.

"Over the river and through the woods," I sang to Sam when we were in bed. Our tradition was that a week before we drove down to Deerfield to spend the holiday with Grose and Artie, I'd open to an old entry, complete a new gratitude list for the year, and read both to Sam.

He looked up at me from his *Newsweek*, which he read religiously. He loved me and indulged me this exercise that I knew he found goofy. I unsnapped the little gold lock on the journal and opened it to a random page.

"Ew, November 2005," I said.

Sam removed his reading glasses. "That should be interesting."

It was the year Lili combusted. "Okay, here goes." I inhaled dramatically.

"Number one, Lili's discovery of her gift for running."

"Yes, the swing."

"Now it's the Adderall," I said.

"Let's move on to item number two."

"Number two, Sam's foot rubs." I put the book down and turned to him.

He kissed me on the mouth.

"None of that until we're done. Three, Jenny's Kitchen Aid mixer." I snorted.

"Are you still angry with Jenny?"

"Never mind. Number four, the arrival of Theresa in my classroom, and number five was your new office space."

"Let's go back to number two." Sam reached for my foot.

"After I finish my new entry," I said, pulling out the Cross pen I used exclusively for this task. It had belonged to my father, and he'd used it to sign the New Year's cards we sent out to the families we'd hosted for the Schines.

I smoothed the pages and wrote "November 2009."

1. Lili's physical health.
2. Sam's success in weathering the financial shitstorm, as he calls it.
3. My Educator of the Year award.

The next two items felt like they came straight from my heart to the pen to the page.

4. The rebbetzin.
5. My mother.

I closed the journal, twisted the pen shut, and returned both to my nightstand.

"What? You're going to keep me in the dark about your 2009 list?" Sam asked, a hint of mockery in his tone.

"Tomorrow, honey. I'm really tired."

Sam returned to his *Newsweek,* and I tried to go to sleep, but a torrent of gratitude for him overcame me. I took the magazine from his hands and removed his reading glasses. He asked me what I was up to, and I showed him. He was a magnificent kisser, and we made out like teenagers at a drive-in. And then we made slow love. I was ready for him. I'd been to the mikveh.

The next morning I was thrilled to find that my new calm had not vanished overnight. I had more energy than I'd had in weeks as I cleaned Daphne Meckleman's vomit from the hallway and sang ditties about turkeys. "You sure have some pep in your step this morning," Theresa commented. Poor Theresa had been carrying the class for me these past few months. I made a mental note to pick up a gift certificate to Kohl's for her as a little Thanksgiving token of gratitude.

After I finished teaching, my car practically drove itself to Neil's office. I was ready to see my mother, and I was still peeved that I had to plead my case to Jenny and Neil to visit her, but less so. Before I entered the building, I kissed the gold letters of the old black Pupnick Orthodontics sign as I would a mezuzah. God, I missed my father. It struck me that Neil was like my mother in a way; he'd chosen to return to his father's home.

Neil's office manager, Donna, greeted me with a big smile. "Oh, hi there, Mrs. Blumfield. Dr. Pupnick's finishing up his last appointment before lunch. Is this an emergency?" She was a ferocious protector of his schedule.

"It kind of is," I said apologetically.

"Hold on a quick sec." She went off to find Neil.

He greeted me with a dental wire in his gloved hand. "Is everything okay?"

"We need to talk."

He cleared his throat. "Follow me."

He took me to his office in the back of the building. My dad used to bring me here on Sunday mornings, and I'd wheel around on his squeaky gray stool or make blizzard scenes with cotton balls I found in his supply room. Neil had kept the stool.

He removed his gloves and threw the wire in the trash. Instead of sitting behind his sleek new desk, he took the easy chair next to mine, as he probably did with parents of children in need of college-fund-draining orthodontia.

"I need to see Mom."

"I have a patient waiting for me with twelve wires sprouting out of his mouth. Can we discuss this tonight?"

"No. This is a private conversation." I didn't have to say that I didn't want to include Jenny.

He paused. "Let me see if Jack can finish up for me."

"Okay."

Neil came back and sat down at his desk. "Barbara."

"Just hear me out," I said.

He nodded, and proceeded to receive my story of the tahara and what I'd learned about our family history with a look of wonder and love etched all over his face. By the time I finished, the room was so still that I could hear the faint ringing of his phone in the reception area. Neither of us said anything for what seemed like hours.

Then I told him about the mikveh, and how some of the water must have seeped into my chest and made my heart expand like a sponge, because I wanted to understand every part of my mother, even the parts that had hurt me.

"You sure you're okay digging all this up? I'm not just worried about Mom."

"You can say it. You're scared that I'll go loco again." I tried to make a joke of it, but he didn't laugh.

We'd carefully constructed a moat around my breakdown, both of us too afraid to examine it through the lens of our adult selves or as parents who would never desert a child, sick or healthy. Neil was still the boy who had fed me yogurt, and my rooting around in our past frightened him.

"I know it wasn't an easy time for you either," I said.

"It wasn't. Why can't we just let it all go, Barbara?" He sounded tired and exasperated. He couldn't meet my gaze.

"Don't you see? I can't let it go now. It was Mom who wanted us to leave the shul."

"I do see, and maybe she was right, but it felt awful." He looked like a little boy whose feelings had just been hurt for the first time. I'd always seen myself as the only victim in all this.

I wasn't angry with him anymore for keeping me from my mother. "You were a good brother, Neil. The best."

He pulled a wire from his pocket and fiddled with it.

"I want to go back to the mikveh." Our code word for my mother's absence.

"Well, don't fall in," he said, and now he was trying to be funny, and we both strained to laugh.

"I have to do this."

Neither of us had to say, "before it's too late."

"Go see Mom," he said, his eyes beginning to tear.

I stopped by Sendik's to buy my mother a pumpkin pie on my way to Lakeline, a U-shape building with a big circular driveway lined with pale green gourds shaped like swans. A fall motif, no dead summer flowers. Nice.

Sunlight streamed through the skylights above the lobby, and the scent of freshly baked cookies and Lysol filled the air. A large woman in a long blue smock greeted me at the front desk.

"How can I help you?"

"I'm Barbara Blumfield, and I'm looking for my mother. June Pupnick." I glanced around the lobby, wondering if I'd spot her.

"You know, I was going to ask if you were Mrs. Pupnick's daughter. You favor her, so pretty and petite you two are."

I blushed. "Thank you."

"I'm Bonnie, by the way. I'll take you to see your mama." Her polyester-clad thighs rubbed together as she led me down the hall. She swiped her badge against the side of a large door and waited for a click.

Why was my mother in a locked facility? Hadn't she just been diagnosed? God, how awful.

"You know, your brother and his wife are real honeys." Bonnie turned to me and smiled.

"They're good people." It was true.

I followed Bonnie through the lounge and dining area, which smelled like old people's waste. The lounge area was almost empty except for a hunched woman engaged in an animated monologue and a distinguished-looking man in a Brewers cap shuffling to a chair.

"Good work, Mr. Kuper." Bonnie gave the man a thumbs-up.

Mr. Kuper saluted her.

"Mr. Kuper was a Green Beret," she told me as we approached a wooden door with a small white sign: June Pupnick. My mother had a room in this ward? "Thank you, Bonnie. I'm okay from here," I managed to say.

"Doesn't work that way, hon." She lowered her voice and tapped my wrist. "I have to announce you to the patient first." She opened the door and stuck her head into the room. "Yoo-hoo, Mrs. Pupnick, your daughter's here."

My mother sat in a chair that nearly engulfed her, like Lily Tomlin's Edith Ann character on *Laugh-In*. My father loved that bit. She'd lost weight in the weeks since I'd seen her, and the fit of her blouse reminded me of when Lili wore Sam's old shirts as smocks for her kindergarten art class. Over it, she wore her old pink cardigan, which Jenny must have had dry-cleaned, because the coffee stain was gone. Gray infiltrated the roots of her hair, now an even brassier red than Jenny had dyed it. She looked well cared for, but the mother I knew would never have left the house without her lipstick.

"I'm glad to see you," she said in a thin little girl's voice, but her eyes were clear and focused.

I sat down next to her in one of her plastic chairs. "Me too," I said.

"We're all having good fun in the dining room. Would you ladies like to join us?" Bonnie inquired cheerfully.

My mom got up. Maybe she was afraid to be alone with me. I couldn't blame her after our last visit. We made our way down the hallway, and I noticed that she still walked at a good clip. A woman who looked much older than my mother sat in a hard chair humming Mozart and kneading her forearms.

"That's Mrs. Noonan. She used to teach piano over at the conservatory," my mom told me.

The tables in the dining area were filled with groups of people, some talking, some coloring, some hooking rugs. My mother sat down at an empty table and began making a chain out of orange and brown construction paper. I sat beside her and spoke to her in the tone I used with my students.

"Look at the pattern you've created!" I picked up her chain. "Orange, orange, brown, orange—"

She cut me off. "Barbara, I'm not an imbecile." Her eyes sparkled as brightly as a Door County lake. "Well, sometimes I'm an imbecile."

We both laughed at the preposterousness of the situation.

"Some days are better than others," she said.

I picked up a sheet of construction paper and ran my fingers over it, soothed by the familiar texture. "I'm sorry I upset you during our last visit."

"You and I go way back, don't we?" she said. She put her shriveled hand on mine.

"I've been so mad at you."

She sank into her chair and started playing with the button on her sweater. "I've noticed."

"I brought you a pumpkin pie."

"You remembered," she said with irony.

Part of the reason I loved celebrating Thanksgiving was that it was such a non-event when I was growing up. I had no living grandparents, and my parents focused most of their social efforts on entertaining the Schines' Shabbos guests. My mother would overcook a kosher turkey, and we'd eat it for days, but for dessert she'd serve a homemade pumpkin pie, and the two of us would polish off half of it in one sitting and have the rest for breakfast the next day.

"The boys didn't much like pie, did they, darling?" she said.

"No, Neil and Dad would eat strawberries topped with nondairy, pareve Cool Whip instead." I wrinkled my nose.

"Of course, pareve," she repeated.

"Nondairy because we'd eaten meat," I said.

"That's right, pareve." She looked pleased with herself.

"Did you have big Thanksgiving dinners when you were little?" I asked, hoping to prompt a memory that might open a door to her childhood in the mansion.

"No. Just Norman, Daddy, and me." She still looked lucid, but she was struggling for words, as if she were trying to tell me something before the veil lowered over her brain. "And Andy and his dad."

I grabbed my purse and pulled out the photo. "Did Andy know you when you were a child? Is that why you had this?"

My mother took the photo and smiled. "That's Norman," she said in her little-girl voice. I was losing her, but I tried to stick to my childhood instinct to sit tight and let her retreat, knowing she'd come back to me.

"Norman's so busy now. That's why he hasn't come to see me." She smiled proudly. "He's writing a big paper on the Spanish-American War."

"Do you miss him?" I asked, aching for her.

"Oh no, dear. We're going to go for a splash tonight after he gets done with his paper. Big paper. He's writing about the Spanish-American War."

I wanted to crawl into her broken brain and hold up the veil with my bare hands. I wanted to know everything. "What about Andy?"

She looked at me, her eyes clouding, the veil dropping, dropping.

"Let's have some pie," I offered. "I'll go get a knife."

Her face slackened as if someone had flipped a switch. The mechanics of opening the pastry box and removing the pie baffled her, so I glided my finger along the flap and lifted it, releasing a burst of cinnamon and cloves. I set the pie in front of her and handed her a fork. My refined mother gobbled up most of the custard in four bites, orange goo smearing her mouth. She pointed to the crust, giggled, and scooped out a little more pumpkin filling with her finger. Then she shoved her finger in her mouth, licking it clean like one of the beaters she'd doled out to Neil and me when she was baking our birthday cakes.

"Oh, we can salvage this," Bonnie announced as she walked over to us. She reached into her pocket and retrieved a packet of wipes. She blotted the damp square against my mother's chin and upper lip, which was sprouting two coarse gray hairs. She cleaned the creases around her mouth as she stared up at me, her eyes not quite vacant, her sticky hands clutching my knee as if we were sitting together at the Downer Theater watching the scariest movie of our lives.

23

I'd never missed my mother as profoundly as I did after I visited her at Lakeline. I hungered to learn every detail she'd buried about herself. Then I could go back to the Shabbos goy and ask him who he had been to her. And he'd tell me. He'd wanted me to open my heart to her, and I could. I'd go see her again. I'd catch her on a better day. She'd have more lucid moments, and I'd wait for them. I wasn't giving up. Now it was time for me to dispose of my letters to Tzippy. I'd held on to this documentation of my resentments long enough.

I went home and headed straight downstairs to the basement. I hesitated for a second before I opened the cedar chest and retrieved my mother's hatbox from under a mountain of linens. As I was refolding the linens, a joint fell to the floor. My brain slowly absorbed the information in front of me. I knew Lili and her friends had tried pot. Kara's mother had called me in a snit after she picked the girls up from Summerfest last July and she'd smelled it in their hair. She headed up the D.A.R.E. program at the high school and had a good deal invested in the issue of drugs. Dawn and I had assured her that they were good kids, and they were all contrite when we confronted them.

I put the joint in my pocket. The idea of Lili smoking pot in our house felt like a violation of the nest I'd worked so hard to create, particularly if she'd been smoking with that horrid Taylor. Then a more alarming thought entered my consciousness, shoving aside my Taylor worries. What if Lili had read my letters? I should never have kept them.

I took the letters upstairs and pulled out Sam's paper shredder. I dropped in the first letter, mesmerized as it devoured my words and spit them out in shards. When I'd shredded the last letter, I went back downstairs and looked into the bottom of the hatbox, hoping against hope that I'd find a few strands of my mother's hair, colored the way she liked it. I fished the joint out of my pocket and brought it to my nose, sniffing in the sweet smoky scent. I considered taking a big hit.

On my way to pick Lili up from school, I called Dawn and told her about the joint. She was jammed up at work and asked me to call back later.

"So you're not worried?"

"Not about the joint," she said.

"What do you mean?"

"God, this is awkward, Barbara."

"Just tell me."

"Megan says that Lili hasn't been herself."

My mind raced directly to the hospital bed where they would hook Lili's brain to electrodes. "What do you mean? That she's depressed?"

"Don't let your imagination run away with you. Listen, honey, I can call you in thirty."

"Please call me."

Lili was waiting for me outside school. She was standing with Taylor and Amanda, another new friend I didn't like. Lili was spending her babysitting money at the mall, buying skinny jeans and blousy shirts that rolled off her shoulder. She was no longer wearing the boot, but her gait hadn't returned to normal yet. I rolled down the window as my blood warmed. The thought of her reading my letters, my diary, shamed me. So much for my new calm.

"How about if Daddy grills some steaks for supper?" I asked as she shut the car door. I was trying to figure out how to talk to her about the pot.

She shrugged. "Sure."

"We need to stop at Sendik's then."

"Okay with me."

"How'd your math test go?"

"C-plus." It was an improvement.

"That's good. Maybe the medicine is working?" We never called it by its name. I hadn't noticed much of a change in her in terms of her focus, and she was growing more distant every day.

"Yeah, I lost the bottle, though. Can we get some more?" There was no apology in her voice.

"Lili, you have to be careful with that stuff."

"What, like do you think some kid is going to steal it and sell it on the black market?" She cackled.

"That sounds a little extreme, but it is an attractive drug to people." I told her I'd call the pharmacy.

I failed three times at parallel parking the car because I was so distracted by my drug worries and those letters. What if Lili asked me about them? How would I ever begin to explain everything about my mother? I was just beginning to grasp the story I would someday share with her.

Mindy Hecht spotted us pulling into the parking lot at Sendik's. When I got out of the car, she hugged me so hard that my earring got caught in her tennis visor. "I can't wait to tell Ian who I ran into!"

I didn't get paid much as a preschool teacher, but I did enjoy my rock-star status. "I can still see Ian sloshing around the playground in those alligator rain boots."

"He's reading Harry Potter." She lowered her voice, as if protecting the ears of a parent of a less precocious reader who might be passing by.

"Harry Potter? So young?" I asked with sincere awe. Making Mindy feel proud of her son restored my sense of equilibrium. "I'm not surprised."

Mindy smiled at Lili across the roof of the car. "She's gorgeous," she told me.

I said to Lili, a little belatedly, "You remember Mrs. Hecht, don't you?"

"I think I met you here once. Nice to see you again," Lili answered respectfully.

"I had a third child just to be a part of your mom's classroom again. She's the guru!" Mindy glanced at her watch. "Oops, gotta run."

We were pushing our cart down the cereal aisle when Lili said, "Mrs. Hecht is like stalker into you."

"Lili, she's not a stalker."

"Is she your friend, then?" Lili tossed a box of Pepperidge Farm Lido cookies into the basket.

"We're friendly." I ignored the bag of potato chips she grabbed.

Lili limped along through the produce section and put a four-dollar box of raspberries in the cart.

"Would you please ask first?" I snapped. "These are out of season." I put them back.

"Well, like what does friendly mean? Do you like have lunch or go shoe shopping?"

"Why are you asking me this?"

"I'm just trying to figure out who your friends are."

"You don't think I have any friends?" And then I flashed on Dawn and her high school buddies yukking it up at Oktoberfest. "I do. Your aunt Jenny, Sheri Jacobstein, and the 4th of July gang—"

"Your sister-in-law and Mrs. Jacobstein, who's, no offense, way more into you than you are into her, don't count. Neither do your teacher friends and Dad's business friends," she said officiously.

"They are my friends, Lili, and then there's Mira."

"Who's Mira?"

"An old high school friend. We see each other for lunch sometimes." The last time I had lunch with Mira was when Lili went off to kindergarten and my afternoons freed up. We'd lost touch after high school and run into each other when she was looking for a preschool for her daughter. She'd become a prominent divorce attorney, and I met her downtown at a restaurant where all of the men and women were wearing power suits and talking on their cell phones. I tried too hard to sell Mira on the new and improved version of myself, and the whole lunch was an uncomfortable affair that I wanted to end quickly.

"Mrs. Hecht seems nice. Maybe you could have lunch with her."

"Why are you so worried about my friendships?" I asked, aware that I had just been scrutinizing hers.

"Everyone should have a best friend," she said with conviction.

I had a best friend once, I wanted to tell Lili. I wanted to drive her to the mansion and take her on a tour of every spot where Tzippy and I had played when we were growing up. Another wave of loss lapped against me.

She picked up a bunch of bananas. "These in season?"

I looked at her, amazed at how she'd gone from bratty to compassionate to impish in the span of the last ten minutes. "Yes, smarty-pants."

Back in the car, I took a deep breath and said, "I found your marijuana in the basement."

"I'm sorry," Lili said after a fraught silence. She looked just as she had when she was seven and I made her return a handful of sugar cubes to Benji's Delicatessen. She held out her little hand, coated in white granules, and apologized to Benji remorsefully.

"Were you getting high in our house?" I asked, remembering how smug I felt when I assured Dot that this was just a phase.

"Just once with a couple of kids from Summerfest, swear. When you and Dad went up to Elkhart Lake." Lili had sold lemonade at Summerfest and met some college kids.

"You mean you weren't doing it with Taylor?"

"You hate her, don't you?"

"That's not the point, Lili. I'm concerned that we can't trust you and your friends home alone anymore." I shuddered thinking about the four girls in her class who only a few months ago died in a solo collision.

"It was ages ago, Mom. I hid the pot in the freezer, and I was going to throw it out, but I forgot."

The freezer? "But I found a joint in the cedar chest."

"This guy Ned must have stuck it in there," she said quickly, gulping down her words as she did when she was nervous. "I didn't."

She sounded convincing, but I was afraid to read her face. I needed to believe that she'd in fact hidden the marijuana in the freezer and had never opened my chest or found my letters to Tzippy.

"Is there anything else you need to tell me?"

"No." Lili looked down at her lap. "Swear."

Sam would not be grilling steaks for us that evening; I'd failed both to buy them at Sendik's and to remember that he had a client dinner. I'd also been so tied up with Lili that I hadn't picked up Dawn's return call. I dialed her number three times, but my calls went through to voicemail. I microwaved a few burgers for Lili and me, and she was sweetly contrite as she slathered on mustard, volunteering all sorts of newsy tidbits about her day. After dinner, she went upstairs and did her exercises.

When Sam called me on the way home from his dinner, I told him about the pot. He was willing to accept Lili's explanation and move on. He walked through the door with a big smile, changed into jeans, and made one of his enormous bowls of freshly popped popcorn—no microwave bags for him. The three of us sank into the soft brown cushions of our sofa and let the buttery kernels comfort us. I couldn't have told you what was on or how we managed to polish off the entire bowl. But for that moment, with Lili's body curved into mine and Sam's arms around us, I felt like a bird who had returned from a dangerous migration. For tonight, life was sweet, maybe Splenda-sweet, but I'd take it.

A few days later, we made our annual Thanksgiving trek to Deerfield. Traffic was predictably heavy, and the drive took us two and a half hours. Lili slept most of the trip; she'd gone over to Megan's the night before and hadn't come home until midnight. For the last couple of days, she'd been doing her exercises diligently, and soon she'd be running again. Sam and I were elated that she was already falling back into step with her old friends and her old self. She'd decide that Taylor was bad news, if she hadn't already.

Lili only woke up during our ritual pit stop. Sam bought her a package of watermelon Bubblicious, as was our tradition, and for me a can of diet soda, my road trip indulgence. He didn't buy anything for himself. Sam rarely ate between meals, one of the many good habits Rose had instilled in him.

I caught a glimpse of Lili in the rearview mirror, blowing a big pink bubble. She looked about ten years old.

"Did you have fun at Megan's last night?" I asked.

Her bubble popped. "Total blast. Mrs. Travinski took us to Kopp's when she got home from work."

Dawn was fun like that, the kind of spontaneous mom who would pile a gaggle of teenagers into the car and take them for custard in the dead of winter. "What was the special flavor?"

"Cranberry Medley." Lili wrinkled her nose. "Gross. I got chocolate," she said, and blew an enormous bubble.

"They usually have pumpkin this time of year," I said as the bubble popped. We all laughed as she peeled sticky pink gum off her eyebrows.

Rose and Artie met us in the driveway and gave us a warm hello. Rose held out her hands and squinted at me. "You look svelte." It was the highest form of compliment from Rose Blumfield. I had lost weight over the past few months, but not enough for anyone else on this planet to notice.

She slipped her arm through mine and pulled me to her. "I've lost a few pounds too. Had to. I'd nearly gone over my Lifetime." Rose needed to maintain a certain weight for the privilege of inspiring her rather cultish Monday-morning following.

"We'll have a little brunchy and then leave these boys to their football," she said, although she didn't need to tell me the plan; we'd been following the same routine for years.

Rose kept an immaculate house that always smelled like fresh air. This sense of order was important to Sam, so I kept our house clean too, although I'd always been a bit of a slob as a child. Rose had already set the dining-room table for Thanksgiving. "We'll be eighteen tonight," she told me, and reeled off the guests she'd invited. The Blumfields had been celebrating Thanksgiving with the Hirshes since Sam was in diapers. The group expanded and contracted based on which of each family's children were able to make it. Neil celebrated Thanksgiving with Jenny's family.

The kitchen table was set with pretty yellow plates and a matching tablecloth decorated with sunflowers. Rose had put out a basket of muffins, fruit, and turkey-and-cheese sandwiches, sans the crusts.

"Come, let's eat," she commanded.

We all sat down, and Lili took a muffin. "Looks delicious, Grose."

Artie asked, "So, Lil, when's that ankle going to heal up?"

Lili smiled at him brightly. "Soon, Grandpop."

I hadn't seen her so optimistic about her injury in months.

"Good girl. Grose and I know you're going to get back into tip-top shape."

After lunch, Sam and Artie went off to the den to read the paper together, both grumbling about the Tea Party's latest antics. Lili and I cleared the table while she chattered on about the stores we'd hit tomorrow afternoon. These shopping expeditions had begun when Lili was six and we took her to the American Girl store, and they'd evolved into a whirlwind tour of her favorite shops, where Rose would treat her to something I would never buy for her. Grose and Lili enjoyed the frenetic energy of Black Friday, and I enjoyed watching them enjoy each other. I wondered about the rituals Lili and my mother might have shared had I allowed them the freedom to do so.

I was on my way to freshen up when my cell phone started to vibrate. I discovered two messages from Neil. In the first, he was trying hard to sound casual when he asked me to phone him. In the second, he said, "It's about Mom. Please call."

I dialed Neil, but his voicemail picked up, so I tried Jenny. No answer. Now I was growing frightened. I went downstairs to get Sam. He and Artie were watching the Bears play the Lions. "What's the matter, honey?" he asked.

Rose and Lili emerged from the kitchen as I was explaining. "Why don't you try the nursing home?" Rose said.

"Thanks, I will." After a few minutes of waiting for Bonnie to pick up, I learned that my mother had been taken to the hospital. As I dialed Neil again, my fingers shook so hard that I could barely punch the numbers on my phone.

"Neil, what's up?" I asked, trying not to sound panicky.

"She had a heart attack."

"Do they need to operate?"

"Let's just wait for the test results," Neil said soothingly.

"I'll be there as soon as I can." I hung up and slouched into Rose and Artie's couch with the phone in my hand. I knew that my mother had high cholesterol, as did half our friends, but she was taking medication. Unless she'd forgotten. "I need to go to the hospital to see my mom."

Rose's lips curled into a smile that barely masked her disappointment. "Of course, dear."

Surely she must think I should go see my mother. It had been Rose who'd convinced me to invite her to our wedding. She said I'd regret it for the rest of my life if I didn't.

Sam jangled the loose change in his pockets.

"Why don't we wait until after dinner?" He was trying to be practical and appease both his mother and me.

"Well, I could go alone and come back and pick you up after things settle down," I offered.

"Come on, Barbara. That doesn't make sense," he said. We were heading into dangerous territory, the place where he didn't want to accept that we had a crisis on our hands.

"Those are your options, honey." I spoke slowly and without emotion.

The person who handled the aborted holiday feast with the most maturity was Lili. She looked at me with an expression I couldn't read and said, "Mom, I'd come to see you right away if you had a heart attack."

Her words, so simple and beautiful, made me forgive her for months of snottiness. "Oh, Lili."

"Why don't I stay with Grose and Grandpop, and Dad can take you home and pick me up tomorrow?"

We all looked at one another with a *Why didn't we think of that before?* expression. Lili had a knack for knowing what needed to be done.

24

Sam and I walked through the front entrance of St. Mary's Hospital together, our arms touching slightly. Neil had given us my mother's room number, and I followed Sam while he figured out the proper elevator to the cardiac unit. We were waiting for it when I spotted Dawn. Maybe it was her walk, youthful and confident, or the appeal of her otherness or her vocation, but something about her had always felt familiar. She reminded me of Simone.

"Everything okay?" she asked, looking worried.

I felt like I'd been traveling in some exotic country and finally encountered someone who could speak English—that's how grateful I was. "My mom had a heart attack."

"Oh, crap."

"We'll be on the fifth floor."

"I'll let you get settled, and then I'll sneak up to see you on my next break." She massaged my shoulder for a second. "Now, you hang tough, honey."

"Thanks, Dawn."

Neil met us outside my mother's door as if he'd been keeping a lookout for us. Jenny was home with her brother's family, all in from St. Paul for the holiday, so he was alone. He put his hand on my forearm. "They're running tests now."

"When did they take her?" The hall felt stuffy, and I was having trouble breathing.

"Just before you got here. Could be a while."

I wanted to see her now.

"Go stretch your legs a bit," Neil offered. "Nothing you can do in an empty room."

"Can I get you something?" I asked.

"Nope, I'm fine." He didn't look fine. His eyes were tired and puffy, and he was frowning.

Sam and I found Dawn waiting in the lounge around the corner. We sat down across from her. She'd brought us coffee and a Styrofoam plate with a slab of pumpkin raisin bread. "We've got a baker in our unit," she said.

"You're a sweetheart, Dawn." I didn't have much of an appetite, but Sam popped a piece of the bread into his mouth.

"So how's Lili doing?" she asked.

Her comment washed over me at first, but then it registered. "You just saw her last night."

Dawn looked at us both. "No. We were down in Kenosha having an early Thanksgiving dinner with my brother."

Sam clenched his jaw, and the tiny muscles around his mouth moved under his skin.

"What did you mean when you told me that Megan said Lili wasn't herself?" I asked.

"Well, I think she's been hanging around with some girls who push the envelope a little more." Dawn was not the type of mother to stick her nose in other parents' business, which made her observation more reliable.

"Don't get Barbara started on Taylor Miller," Sam said, trying to lighten the conversation.

"Look, let me go and see if I can do some recon on your mom." Dawn excused herself with the skill and experience of someone who knew to leave a family alone to digest bad news.

I dug my nails into the lip of the Styrofoam plate, making waves of half moons. "Pushing the envelope. I don't like the sound of that. And Lili lied to us again."

"We'll talk to her." Sam flashed the smile that went with his comforting tone while he dusted crumbs from his sweater.

I looked toward my mother's room and back at Sam. I wanted him gone as I only had one other time in our marriage, during Lili's sonogram. I wanted him to leave me to face the mess and glory of my past. I understood my mother's drive to retreat from all of us and sit in the mikveh, alone and in silence.

I slid my chair close to his. "Sam, honey, thank you for being here."

"Of course." He put his arm around my shoulder.

I rested my head against his chest. "But I need to do this solo."

Dawn came hurrying toward us. "They're bringing your mom up right now."

He pulled me toward him, and the arm of the chair dug into my waist.

"Go back to Deerfield Sam, please," I whispered.

"But Lili's fine with my parents, and you need me here." He looked frightened, a rarity for Sam.

"Drive safe." I caressed his cheek. I was hurting him, but I couldn't think about that now. I got up and walked toward my mother's room, away from Sam and the befuddled look I could feel on his face.

I stood next to Neil as two nurses wheeled my mother into her room. Long tubes streamed from her nose, and her body occupied a sliver of the mattress. Jenny had colored her hair with the proper auburn rinse, but the veins beneath her translucent skin resembled roads on a city map.

Neil and I zoned out in front of back-to-back episodes of a reality show about hoarders. After a few hours, the nurses told us to go home. My mother was sleeping comfortably, and her condition wouldn't change overnight.

Neil offered me a lift, but I sent him on his way and took a cab. I phoned Sam. I could hear the sadness in his voice when we talked about trivial things like the traffic just south of Racine and Mrs. Hirsh's newest dietary issues.

"You're hurt," I said.

"I'm supposed to be your rock." I could hear CNN blaring in

the background.

"I need to be my rock for a while."

"Lili just came upstairs, why don't you say hello," he said and put Lili on the phone.

"Hi, Mom"

Her voice was warm, and I had no intention of confronting her about the ice cream lie, but the cab was approaching Kopp's, the site of her fictitious custard run. I peered at the marquee that posted the new flavor of the week.

"I'm just driving by Kopp's, and guess what! This week's flavor is actually *not* Cranberry Medley. It's pumpkin! How about that?" I couldn't rein in my sarcasm.

"I knew you'd throw a hissy fit if I told you I was going out with Taylor and Amanda," she muttered.

"Well, you were right. You're grounded."

She hung up.

I redialed Sam. "Your daughter just hung up on me."

"I'm going to talk to her about that, believe me."

"Listen, the cab is in the driveway. I'll call you in a few," I said wearily.

The cabdriver, an older man with a European accent I couldn't identify, pulled up to my house. I handed him a fifty-dollar bill, and he looked at me with such sympathy in his tired eyes. "Kids, husbands," he said. "They make you crazy."

"Sure do. Keep the change."

The house was cold and empty. I heated up a can of minestrone and called Sam back.

"Are we okay, Barbara?"

I thought of my mother lying in that hospital bed, sick and alone, and Sam sitting in his childhood bedroom, CNN blaring, alone, while Lili was likely texting manically in the room across the hall, alone. And me, freezing in our ice-cold happy nest. Alone. And for now, I couldn't see how it could be any other way. "Nothing feels okay to me right now."

"I love you," he said feebly.

"I love you too." Before he could reassure me that we'd all be just fine, I wished him good night and hung up.

I fell asleep as soon as my head hit the pillow. I dreamed of the mikveh. Through a haze of smoke, I could make out my mother sitting on a chair, her wrist delicate and lightly freckled, half covered by the tattered cuff of her blue coat, her fingers pinching a lit cigarette.

I woke up early the next morning and showered quickly. Soon the roads would be busy with shoppers, but for now nobody else was driving. The sky was gray, and it was snowing lightly. I phoned Neil from my car to tell him that I'd be at the hospital shortly and drove straight to the Shabbos goy's nursery.

He set down a tree he was planting and walked toward me. "Is your mother okay?"

"Her heart is failing."

"Where is she?"

"St. Mary's." I pulled out my checkbook and scribbled my cell number on a deposit slip.

He looked around the lot. "I'll be there as soon as I can."

"So I haven't scared you off?"

"I don't scare easily." He smiled.

"My mother told me that you were a part of her childhood," I said.

"Is that all?"

"I think that's all she was capable of telling me."

"I'll tell you what you want to know, but not this second." He pulled his collar up around his neck. "At the hospital."

I felt such a strong wave of relief that I almost cried.

When I arrived at the hospital, Neil was already sitting in my mother's room. "What took you so long?" he asked.

"I had to make a stop." I handed him a Starbucks grande.

"Thanks. The hospital joe tastes like battery acid. Since when did you start drinking coffee?"

"About a month ago, and now I'm addicted." I took a gulp of

my latte. "How is she?"

"Still zonked out."

Just then my mother opened her eyes and turned her head toward me. "Barbara," she said, as though speaking my name demanded all her strength.

"Hi, Mom." I kissed her forehead. Her skin felt papery against my lips. "You feeling better this morning?"

She nodded weakly and stared at the television while I stared at her. I was that little girl curled up on the chaise longue, waiting for my mother to wake up, wondering what I could possibly do to rouse her. She dozed off again, and Neil and I watched an ESPN highlights special and talked about trivial things such as Tiger Woods' fall from grace and Aaron Rodgers' last game. I checked the door every few seconds for signs of the Shabbos goy, but a watched pot truly doesn't boil. Maybe he wasn't going to show.

I went downstairs to call Sam, but he didn't answer. I bought a bag of Fritos, Neil's favorite, and went back upstairs. Neil was waiting for me outside my mother's room. "Before you go in, I need to tell you something."

He was scaring me. "What? What?"

"Mom has a visitor. I wanted to prepare you."

"I know who it is."

Neil looked down at his shoes. "I don't think you do."

"How do you think he knew where to find her?" I asked and stepped past him into the room.

The Shabbos goy was sitting with his back toward me, his lumber coat slung over his chair. I sat down on the other side of the bed. Now he was not the bogeyman in the blue Dodge, he was an old man watching a woman he loved slip away. My father had worshiped my mother, and if he were alive, he would be sitting in that chair next to her withering body, but he wasn't. We listened to the faint sound of her breathing and the periodic buzzer preceding the opening of the heavy locked doors to the critical care wing. Words would come later.

Neil sat down next to the Shabbos goy and patted him on the

shoulder as if he were an old friend. They'd played hours of basketball in the Schines' driveway, something that never had interested my father. Neil had muted the television, and I pointed to a weather map on the screen. "Looks like a cold snap is coming our way."

"Looks like it," Andy said politely.

"It was nice of you to come," I said. It seemed both strange and natural to be sitting here with him.

"She was my best friend," he said simply.

Neil and I looked at each other. "How did you two become best friends?" I asked.

"My father was the groundskeeper at the mansion." His eyes grew foggy. "I grew up in the carriage house."

My mouth opened, but no sound came out. Neil seemed shocked too. "The Schines' mansion?" he said.

The Shabbos goy told his story, and we spoke to each other over my mother's body, as if she were a table at Pandl's upon which a waitress would arrive and plunk down a German pancake. He spoke steadily and without interruption, as I had during my Mexican lunch with Simone, and although he hadn't been smoking pot and drinking margaritas, I suspected he was just as tired from shouldering too many secrets. He said that when my uncle Norman died, my grandfather's heart went bad, and he died of a massive heart attack.

"Bad heart." I pointed to the monitor above my mom's bed. "But where were you when she had her first breakdown, when the Schines found her?" I asked, avoiding mention of the abortion.

He took my mother's hand. "Up at Oshkosh at college. I stuck around for a while, but she asked me to leave after your grandfather's funeral."

My mother fluttered her eyes, and the Shabbos goy leaned toward her.

"She's been doing that all day," Neil said, reminding us all to not get our hopes up.

I waited for my mother to move again even if it didn't mean

anything, and then she opened her green eyes and looked at us all with a clarity I hadn't seen since Neil moved her to Milwaukee.

"Andy," she murmured. "You're my best friend too."

"How ya feeling, Junie?"

"Did you bring Norman?"

"Not today," he said softly.

"Hi, Mom," Neil and I said at the same time.

"You're all here." She smiled peacefully as her eyes traveled to each of us, and then they lost focus and she closed them.

Wait, don't go, I wanted to say, but she fell back into slumber.

The Shabbos goy extended his hand, and I took it. "Thank you, Andy." His proper name came through my lips like a faint breeze. We stayed like that for a minute, our arms forming a bridge across my mother's body.

Neil left the room to make a few phone calls, and I was alone with Andy. Since I had accepted the invitation to wash Mrs. Kessler's body, I felt like I'd fallen back down the rabbit hole, and now it seemed that Andy was standing at the bottom, arms outstretched, waiting to catch me.

"Can I ask you a personal question?" I was looking at his ringless finger.

"Sure."

"Did you ever marry?"

"Yup, but it didn't last long," he said matter-of-factly.

I didn't ask for the details. He didn't need to tell me that his heart belonged to my mother. "I'm sorry."

"So it goes. What else did you want to know about your mom?"

I wanted to know everything. I asked him about the fancy balls my mother had once described to me.

"Come again?" he said.

"At the mansion, when my mom was a little girl."

"By the time she was born, the Depression had hit, and there were no parties."

"But my grandfather was very wealthy, wasn't he?"

"He was. He manufactured shoes, made a lot of money in the First World War, socked it away in gold."

"Were there ever parties?" I asked wistfully.

"Maybe before your grandmother died, but I can't say for sure."

I felt like a kid who had been told that there was no such thing as Santa Claus.

"There were small dinner parties, though. Your mom and your uncle Norman would greet every guest."

I pictured the two of them prancing about in thick cotton pajamas after their baths, my uncle carrying my mother piggyback.

Neil interrupted my fantasy by returning with Dr. Newton, a youngish man with thinning red hair and a prominent chin. While he examined my mother, we stepped into the hallway.

"Andy and I have been talking about our grandfather," I said to Neil.

"What was he like?" Neil asked.

Andy gazed toward my mother's door as if Joseph Fischer might appear on the other side. "My dad said that before your grandmother passed, he was always telling jokes. Liked to get in the kitchen on Sunday mornings and make his own pancakes, too."

"What else do you remember about him?" I asked.

Andy kept staring at the door. "He was social enough when business friends came to the house, but he was mostly quiet, especially after Norman got sick. He worried about your mom and Norman a lot, always had doctors coming to the house to check one thing or another."

Dr. Newton opened the door. "I'd like to talk to you two alone," he said to Neil and me.

"Andy can stay," Neil said.

"He's her best friend," I added.

Dr. Newton hugged his chart to his chest. "All right, then. Her aortic wall has been severely compromised, and her arteries are clogged."

I stared at his lips as they moved up and down. They were

chapped. My mother's condition had clearly gone untreated for months.

"What about surgery?" Neil asked.

Dr. Newton shook his head sadly. "She's not a candidate. Her heart is too damaged."

"So what does that mean?" Andy asked.

"It means that we try to keep her comfortable," Dr. Newton said.

"And pray." I wasn't about to give up on my mother.

"Why don't you all go home and get some sleep, maybe in shifts?" Dr. Newton suggested.

We nodded, but nobody made a move to leave. We were waiting for her to wake up. She'd open her eyes and look around at Neil, Andy, and me, and her lips would flower into my favorite of her smiles, not the June smile, but the one that lit her up from the inside out. I'd feel that old childhood rush of relief. Our patience would pay off. She'd come back to us, however fleeting her return. We were her family.

Sam and I fought when he phoned that night to tell me that he and Lili were coming straight home to help me take care of my mother.

"No need," I said.

"Jesus, Barbara, you're not letting anyone in."

He was wrong. I'd let Andy in, and I'd begun to let my mother in, too. I thought of the clients for whom I'd cooked soufflés and chicken dishes and the tennis game I'd mastered so that we could play doubles every summer. "I trot well. Isn't that what matters?"

"That's a crappy thing to say."

"I know," I murmured. "I'm just wrecked."

"It's like you're going AWOL on us."

That stung. AWOL was the term I'd used to describe my mother's disappearances. "Listen, I'm sorry. We can't start fighting now," I said.

"A little fighting might do us good."

"You think so? What do you want to fight about?"

"Lili needs you right now," he said.

The vulnerability in his voice broke me in two. "Just give me a little more time here, Sam. Come home on Sunday."

I wanted to explain about the hole I'd fallen into when I'd allowed the rebbetzin and my mother back into my life and perhaps give him the coordinates. I couldn't. I wasn't finished with whatever I'd started. If Sam and Lili came home tomorrow I was afraid I'd get stuck down here, separated from them for good. And somewhere deep inside, I knew that if I didn't figure this out, Lili would end up here one day too.

Neil phoned first thing in the morning to tell me that since there was nothing to be done for my mother, Dr. Newton had sent her back to Lakeline for hospice care.

Bonnie was there to greet me when I walked through the front door. "I'm awfully sorry about your mom. Such a nice lady. She's not back yet, but she'll be here soon."

"I'll wait."

"Fresh-baked cookies in the dining hall!" She pointed to her left. "Come on, I'll walk you," she said as though I might leave before my mother arrived.

"I'm not a flight risk, Bonnie."

She grinned at me. "Of course you aren't."

In fact, I was a flight risk. I'd been running from my mother for years. Bonnie settled me in a comfortable chair and handed me a snickerdoodle.

A woman who looked to be a little younger than my mother sat at a table playing solitaire. Her hairstyle reminded me of Sally Rogers from the *Dick Van Dyke Show*. Fake Sally Rogers looked up from her cards and smiled in recognition of a handsome man in a suede jacket and a young woman, probably his daughter, with a mane of wavy brown hair and a diamond stud in her nose. She was about Lili's age, and her loving smile revealed a mix of loss and relief that Sally was having a good day. She pointed to a play that Sally could make, and the old woman clapped her hands, and in that moment I knew that I needed to bring Lili to visit her grandmother. I went out into the cold, grateful for the fresh air, and called Sam.

"I'm sorry about last night," I said.

"Me too."

"What are you guys doing?"

"Well, Lili is sleeping, and Rose is on the treadmill, earning some activity points."

I laughed. "Why don't you come home tonight?"

"Seriously?" he asked eagerly.

"Yes, I want Lili to visit my mom."

Silence.

"My mother's dying. Lili needs to say goodbye to her."

"I know," Sam said, and then he gave me a speech he must have been rehearsing in his head. "Call me a shit for saying this. I want to be there for you, but I'm in no hurry to show up for June."

"Sam, please. Not now."

"I was *there*, Barbara, in the hospital after Lili was born. I watched you wait for her to show, and I held you when she didn't. And I saw the phone bill and the calls to Stevens Point. Thirty seconds, long enough to hear her voice on her machine."

"Sam, stop," I said as if he were physically hurting me.

"And what about Lili's bat mitzvah, when she showed up like some distant cousin? Or when she put on her coat immediately after those brunches you made us endure?" His voice shook with a pent-up rage I never knew existed.

"Sam!"

"Your daughter is veering off the rails, and I know you want me to give her a good talking-to, and I will, but where the hell are you?"

"You're right, Sam. You're a shit for saying all of this."

"It had to be said."

"Not really." My voice shook. "After years of pain that you've clearly been documenting, I'm finally finding peace with my mother, and you, my supposed best friend, are resisting me? What the hell is wrong with you?"

A thick silence hung between us before he answered me, his voice full of remorse. "I don't mean to get in your way, but you've been scaring the hell out of me these past months."

"I know."

"Come back," he begged. "From wherever you are."

"I'm trying, baby. I'm trying," I said, and hung up.

I was about to go back inside when Andy appeared. His breath smoked in the cold as he told me that he'd just come from the hospital, and that Neil and Jenny were following the Lakeline van that was transporting my mother.

"It's going to be a few more hours," he said.

"Oh."

"You don't look so good."

I waved my hand in front of my face as if I were shooing away a fly. "My husband and I just had the roughest fight in our marriage." My eyes burned from lack of sleep.

"I'm sorry. Is there anything I can do?"

I knew exactly what he could do, and just thinking about asking for this favor made the nerve endings in my body dance as they had when I called Daniel or saw the rebbetzin after all these years.

"Yes. Take me to the mansion."

Since Mrs. Kessler's tahara, the surreal had become normal, and minutes later I was sitting in the passenger seat of Andy's truck. The cab was as spotless as a rental, but this car was too old for a rental, and there was a cassette of *Blood on the Tracks* in the well under the tape deck. I put on the tape and listened to Bob Dylan singing "Simple Twist of Fate." Andy thumped his hand on the steering wheel and concentrated on the road. He clenched his jaw as we approached the last flat stretch before the mansion.

"It's okay." I wanted to reach over and touch his arm, but I didn't.

He pulled into the driveway and parked in his old spot. It was Sunday, and the house was quiet. I wondered if the rebbetzin would find us, but it didn't matter. I thought she would understand how I'd come to this place. She'd directed me here.

Andy turned off the engine and pointed to the basketball hoop, now a bare, rusted rim. "Your uncle Norman, he was quite a ballplayer. Strong legs. Quick." He shuffled his feet like a boxer.

I imagined the boy in the photo and a younger version of Andy playing one on one out here in the cold.

Andy shook his head. "Damn shame. He taught me how to shoot."

Tzippy and I used to watch Andy giving Neil pointers on shooting free throws. Back then, the rim was bright orange and the white net intact. "And you taught Neil," I said.

"Sure did."

We got out of the car without discussion and walked along the bluff. Gray clouds filled the sky, and the wind howled along the lake, chopping up the water into little waves. The lake stirred something inside me as it always had, making me feel once again like anything was possible.

Andy's jacket was open, but he wasn't shivering. He picked up a rock and hurled it toward the water. His voice shimmered with a sweet nostalgia when he talked about playing on the bluff with my mother and Norman. "They called us the Three Musketeers," he said. "Of course, we were quarantined because of the polio epidemic, so that made us even tighter."

I stopped walking. "This is where my mother posed for the photograph." It was also where I'd spotted her, years later, emaciated and smoking in her baggy blue coat.

"I took that picture with the camera Norman got for his sixteenth birthday, just months before his polio hit."

As we walked on, the cold dead grass crunching under our feet, I asked Andy how he and my mother found each other again, and he told me that she showed up at his father's funeral. She'd begged him to take the job as the Schines' caretaker because he was the only thing she had left of her past. I hugged my coat tightly around my body. The rebbetzin, my father, her neighbor in Stevens Point, Mr. Beckerman—nobody could resist taking care of my mother. Her smile had won me dozens of Mrs. Beckerman's special rolls and hours of special attention from my teachers.

"Let's go inside," I said.

The back door of the mansion was open, and Andy followed me into the kitchen. We stood in the pantry, and I listened for his breathing, praying that he would come downstairs with me.

"I'm not sure we should do this," he said. "This is private property."

I imagined that my mother had led him to this very place, and that he'd spoken the same words to her. "This pool belongs to my family," I said.

I opened the pantry door, and the steps, more swollen than ever, groaned beneath our weight. I didn't care if the rebbetzin heard us. She would understand. Andy reached for the key to the mikveh and handed it to me. I unlocked the door. I was about to turn on the light when Andy stopped me. "Please, I want to be in the dark."

We stood in the spot where I'd seen my mother's cigarette ember, only a few feet from the water. It was too dark to see Andy's face, but I could feel him next to me.

"You asked what was between your mother and me." His voice was raspy.

I waited for him to go on.

"Your mother and your uncle used to come here together."

"Without you?" I stared at the still black water.

"My job was to carry your uncle down the steps."

"You didn't swim with them?"

"No. This was where your mother talked to the dead."

I remembered the whispering. "Do you mean to her mother?"

"Yes. She convinced Norman that your grandmother was watching over them and could heal him."

"I always knew there was more to the story."

Andy didn't speak for a few minutes. The room was so quiet. And wet. I unbuttoned my coat.

Finally he said, "The night your uncle Norman died I came down here to look for your mother."

My breath caught in my chest.

"We swam here every night between Norman's death and your grandpa's."

I pictured my mother and the young, beautiful Andy, naked in these waters, holding each other.

"This was where we made a baby."

His words sliced through me. I remembered the look on my

mother's face when she went away from us, when she smoked, when I found her here in the mikveh.

"She came to my dad's funeral to say she was sorry about the baby." Pain laced his voice.

The baby.

When he didn't go on, I asked gently, "Was this where you'd come on your Tuesday nights?"

My eyes had adjusted to the dark enough to see that he was looking right through me. "No. This was where your mother came, by herself, to talk to her mother, Norman, and the baby."

So he hadn't been in the mikveh the day I found her. She'd been talking to her ghosts. Andy must have mussed her hair and lipstick someplace else, maybe the pantry.

My mother's grief rolled through my body in waves. "She always seemed to be roaming with her ghosts."

"That's true," he said.

My question came out before I knew I would ask it. "Then why in God's name would she leave her own family?"

He sighed. "She thought that if she could put the pieces of herself together, then she could make things better for you."

That was exactly why I was standing in this cellar with Andy, so I could rescue my troubled daughter. I walked toward the water. Andy reached for my elbow. "Don't go in there," he whispered to my back. He pulled me away as I had tried to pull my mother away, and I resisted him with a force that took both of us by surprise. The ghosts were winning the tug of war.

"I need to touch the water," I said.

"Your mother wouldn't like that."

"She would understand."

"She didn't want you anywhere near here, Barbara. Your mother got trapped between that"—he moved my arm toward the mikveh—"and you."

I could see the loss in Andy's face. He would have loved to have built a life with my mother. His jacket was worn, his body weakened, yet I could see a trace of the boy who had been kind to my mother as a child and who had helped Norman in and out of his wheelchair. My years of anger toward him shamed me.

I sat down, removed my shoes, and dangled my toes in the water. I listened for the voices of my grandparents and my uncle Norman, beckoning them to appear in front of me, as Mrs. Kessler had the night before her tahara. I shut my eyes until I could hear only the whooshing of the water and Andy's breathing. There behind my eyelids, behind the blackness, I saw an image, blurry at first, but the harder I closed my eyes, the more it came into focus. My mother was sitting next to me, in her pink cardigan, knees cradled to her chest, visiting with my grandmother and her brother. And my sibling.

I opened my eyes and turned toward Andy. "It's time to say goodbye," I said.

26

Sam and Lili came home Sunday evening after I'd spent the day at Lakeline watching my mother sleep. Our fight made Sam and me cautious around each other at first. We were all treading lightly, trying to regain our footing. I put up a pot of barley soup, and Lili baked her famous lemon cake, and we ate the first family meal we'd shared in more than a week. We stayed away from touchy subjects like my mother and Taylor, and then Sam made us a big bowl of popcorn and we settled in front of the television and watched *Airplane*. Lili retrieved the afghan Rose had knitted, and we cuddled up under it and laughed. Halfway through the movie, Sam grabbed my hand, and I held it hard.

I poked my head into Lili's room on my way to bed.

"I missed you," she said shyly.

"Me too." I sat on the end of the bed and rubbed the arch of her foot like my mother used to do for me.

"That feels good, Mommy."

I took her other foot in my hand and rubbed it too.

"You know, Kara's grandmother was in hospice, and then she got better."

Her sweetness made me want to cry. But then, just about everything made me want to cry these days. The doctors couldn't predict how much longer my mother would survive. Weeks, maybe a month, but she wasn't going to recover.

"She'll get better," Lili said. "Pinkie swear."

"No, Lil, she won't," I said. "She's in hospice."

"Maybe she'll have a great day, and we'll invite her back here, but we'll have a *good* visit."

"I like that plan." I stroked her face and kissed her good night.

The next morning, Lili surprised us by getting up early and going for a run. I was making pancakes when she came through the back door, her cheeks red from the cold.

"How's the ankle?" I asked.

"Still hurts."

"I'm sorry, sweetie. Give it more time."

"Running is the only thing I'm good at."

"That's not true."

"I'm perceptive, you're going to say."

"Case in point. That is exactly what I was going to say."

She let out an exasperated breath and went up to shower.

Lili was always a little grumpy when she had to return to school after vacations, but she was particularly sullen on this Monday morning.

"What's the plan for after school, Lil?" I asked casually. Anything could set her off when she was in one of her moods.

"Dunno."

"Want to come with me to visit Grandma?"

She started texting, ignoring me completely; her warm feelings from the night before had vanished.

"I'll take that as a no," I muttered.

Her fingers continued to dance across her keypad.

"I have a planning meeting this afternoon, and then I'm going right to Lakeline. I should be home by five."

"Okay." She barely acknowledged me.

Sam busied himself making coffee, but I could tell he was listening, and when she left for school, I went over and rubbed his shoulders.

"Can we not fight again like that?" he said.

I reached for him, and he held me so tightly I thought he'd crack a rib.

Not even my students could distract me from worrying about my mother. I let Theresa take over leading the lesson, and she rallied as always. After finishing up in the classroom, I sat through a meeting about hiring a new music teacher, not hearing a word that was said. When the meeting was over, Sarah pulled me aside and asked me if I was all right, and I told her yes, but she knew I was lying. "Whatever you need, Barbara," she said.

I stopped at Starbucks to pick up my latte fix and spilled the whole cup down my shirt on my way to the car. "Shit," I muttered. I was anxious to see my mother and relieve Neil, and now I'd have to stop home to change.

Perfect. Taylor's car was in our driveway. There were two other unfamiliar cars on the street, one with a University of Wisconsin decal.

I huffed up the front steps, furious that Taylor had the audacity to park in the driveway. When I opened the door, I heard loud music, and the foyer smelled like cigarettes and beer. I rushed to the back of the house.

"Hey, Babs," Taylor said. She was lying on our couch, one elbow behind her head, her boots planted on the cushions, her eyes cutting into me. Our afghan was on the floor, and there was a keg on my coffee table. Lili's Adderall bottle, the second one she'd asked me to replace, was lying on top of Taylor's purse.

I snatched the bottle. "What the hell?"

Taylor smirked. "Oh, I was just holding this for Lili."

"Where's my daughter?" My voice trembled.

She shrugged and took a drag of her cigarette, scattering ashes on the carpet. I stormed into the kitchen, where two girls were eating Lili's apology cake with their fingers. I marched over to Sam's iPad and turned it off. The house quieted, and a dozen kids stared at me. "Where is Lili?" I asked in a tone Sam called quiet crazy.

"I think she's in her room," said one of the girls, who looked older and a little drunk.

Christ. I thought of those girls who had just been killed in a car accident. These kids could wreck their cars after drinking in our home. I felt dizzy.

"All of you sit down, and don't move until I come back," I barked, and ran upstairs to find Lili.

I heard retching sounds from the bathroom. I went in and found Megan holding Lili's hair while she vomited.

"Christ, Lili." Her eyes were closed, and she was moaning. Seconds later, I heard footsteps and turned around to find Dawn standing there in her scrubs.

"Lili called me, and she didn't sound right, so I called my mom," Megan said apologetically.

"You did the right thing, sweetie," I assured her. "I've got it from here."

Dawn walked over to Lili and examined her. "Lil, can you hear me?"

Lili nodded her head.

"How much did you drink, sweetie?"

She answered by throwing up.

Dawn wiped Lili's mouth and checked her eyes and took her pulse. "Okay, she's going to be fine. You stay with her while I go collect those brats' keys and make sure nobody drives home drunk."

Megan lingered in the hallway. Lili was literally hugging the porcelain bowl. She wore an off-the-shoulder sweater I'd never seen before and jeans so tight I wondered how she got them on. When she looked up, mascara streaked her face.

"I'm so sick," she groaned. I ran the water, wet a washcloth, and wiped away the mascara and liquid eyeliner.

Dawn's voice drifted upstairs. She was calling parents to come and pick up their kids. Every time my doorbell rang, I cringed. The timing of Lili's caper meant everything. You didn't have to be a parenting guru to figure out that she was screaming for my attention.

When Lili finally finished throwing up, I stuck her in the shower to rinse off the vomit. I helped her into a clean pair of pajamas and tucked her in bed, a wastebasket at the ready.

"I'm so sorry, Mommy," she mumbled over and over again.

Dawn came upstairs with a big glass of water. "Drink this, Lil. Slow sips."

I went into the hall and Dawn followed. "God, this is so awful. She's been supplying her little friend Taylor with Adderall," I said.

"You can deal with that later. For now, they're all gone."

"Where is Sam?"

"On his way."

The phone rang. "Just a second." I ran into the bedroom to answer it.

"It's Mom," Neil said. My knees went weak because I knew what he was going to say next. "Her organs are starting to shut down."

"Oh, God." I told him about Lili. "What should I do?"

"I don't know what to say, but it's bad."

"What do you mean? I thought she had a few weeks or days at least."

"I'm sorry, Barbara."

I hung up the phone and sat on my bed. I couldn't leave Lili when she needed me most, but if I didn't, I might miss the chance to say goodbye to my mother. I didn't want her to die without me there to hold her hand. I felt the profound pull of her need, as a dying woman, as a motherless child alone in the mikveh talking to the dead.

"Barbara." Dawn was standing in the doorway. I pictured her in some hospital room, guiding a family through an impossible decision.

I told her about my mother's condition. "What should I do?"

"That's your choice, but know that I'll stay and take care of Lili."

"Where the hell is Sam?"

He appeared behind Dawn. "Right here."

"Tell him," I said to Dawn, and she relayed the facts of the situation.

He walked over to the bed and sat next to me. I was being

sawed in two. There was no good choice. I got up and went into Lili's room. She usually slept on her back with her arms slung over her head, but she was curled under the covers in the fetal position, her hands over her ears. I'd assumed this exact position when I'd had my breakdown. Now I only slept on my stomach. I wanted nothing more than to wrap my body around hers and hold her.

"I'm going to the hospital," I told Dawn and Sam.

He leaned over and whispered into my hair, "I got this, sweetie."

Dawn looked at me like she wanted to say something.

"You think I'm doing the wrong thing?"

She shook her head and pointed toward my coffee stain.

"Oh. I owe you."

"You'd do the same for me," she said.

I would, but up until now, I'd never been able to ask for help. When this was over, I'd tell Lili that I did have a friend. Dawn.

I put on a T-shirt and yoga pants. It took every ounce of strength I had to walk past Lili's room and go to my mother's side.

Bonnie was trained as a hospice nurse, and she'd been assigned to my mother's care full time. My mother probably weighed no more than eighty pounds. She'd been shrinking since her heart attack, and her breathing was labored. Bonnie had dressed her in one of her favorite nightgowns and put a clip in her hair. Seeing her that way made every bone hurt, as if I had the flu.

Andy sat on one side of the bed, and Neil and I on the other. We stayed with her for the next twenty-four hours. This time we were not waiting for her to come back to us.

I held her shrunken hands, the hands that had braided challah dough and put a candle to the fine hairs of the kosher chickens she bought for Shabbos. The hands that had stitched my Purim costumes and shampooed my hair when I was too young to wash it myself. The hands that had given and received love from Andy, the Schines, Neil, my father, and me. I could see her in her entirety. I prayed for peace, hers and mine. She squeezed my fingers so slightly that I barely felt it. Neil had been surviving on Diet Pepsi and hospital food, and his face looked bloated. And very sad. His relationship with my mother had been less complicated and painful than mine. She'd played a role in his adult life. While I mourned lost opportunities, he was grieving over something real. She knew his kids, and they knew her.

"Do you want a minute alone with Mom?" I asked.

"Thanks, Barbara. You go first, though. I need to check in with Jenny."

Andy followed Neil out of the room. I had so many things to tell my mother. I scooted my chair up to the bed, until I was only a few inches from her. She no longer smelled like lavender or Chanel, she smelled like hospital and death. I leaned over and whispered to her through the dirty gray strands that covered her ears. I whispered our secrets as if the naming of them could close the distance that had grown between us over the years.

"I know who you are and who you were, Mom. You were a good mother for a long time. You taught me how to write a proper thank-you letter, and you rubbed Vaseline into my feet during the harsh winter months. You listened carefully to Neil and me when we told you about our playground scrapes, and for a long time we knew that we mattered most to you. I know this to be true now, too—it was you, not the Schines, who cast us from the mansion, and I understand why only now, only after I have left my own family when they needed me. I know why you loved Andy and that you didn't pick him over us. I have felt the powerful pull of our family history. History, you always loved history, yet it kept you from the present. There is no shame in the desperate sorrow of a motherless girl, Mom. Please forgive me. Please forgive yourself."

I put my head on her chest and listened to her addled heart. She would go soon, I could always sense her impending absences.

The door opened and closed. "I just heard the death rattle," I told Neil and Andy, and rose from my mother's death bed. Neil,

Andy, and I sat next to her, afraid to leave for a second, while Jenny came in and out with offers of coffee and vending-machine food.

My mother died shortly before midnight, one week shy of her seventy-ninth birthday. I felt her spirit leave her body before Andy told me that she was gone.

Neil swung into action. He called the nurse, a youngish dark-haired man in scrubs who offered his condolences and explained the procedure for transporting my mother to the funeral home. Andy and I sat with her until the orderlies arrived. They pulled the curtain around her, so we couldn't see them removing all the tubes, and then they wheeled her away.

Neil came back to the room. "Go home and get some sleep, Andy."

"Can I have a moment with your sister first?"

"Of course. I'll be outside."

Andy stared at the floor and collected himself. "I want you to know something, Barbara."

"Andy, you don't have to explain anything—"

"No, that's not it." He gave his nervous cough. "You were her Sweet B."

My nickname on his lips pierced me.

"And she loved you with all of her heart." Andy reached out his ropy arms, and held me, maybe pretending for a second that his Junie had come back to him. I wished my mother had married him.

I was happy to offer Andy this small comfort. I was grateful to him for relaying a message from my mother, and to the rebbetzin for guiding me back to her. They helped me see that my mother's absence was a part of her, like a rest in a piece of music, beautiful notes followed by unpredictable silences that made you wonder if the song had stopped playing for good. Now I knew that her music pulsed through the silent notes.

27

I designated myself as my mother's shomer; I would watch her body until the funeral.

Neil didn't dare ask the Abromowitz Funeral Home to accept a dead Jew who had had an affair with a Shabbos goy, so he chose a nondenominational funeral parlor in Mequon. I drove there alone to wait for my mother's body to arrive. Mr. Gorzon, the funeral director, a middle-aged man in a nice-fitting suit, offered me tea. His easy smile soothed me.

After we finished discussing the details of my mother's burial, he showed me to a comfortable bench in the drafty corridor outside the preparation room. He offered me a siddur, the same prayer book we used in Temple Micah, and then he patted my shoulder and disappeared. He returned a half hour later, wheeling my mother's gurney into the preparation room. Her body formed a small mound under the sheet. I lowered my eyes and turned the pages of the prayer book until I located Psalm 51.

Have mercy on me, O God
According to your unavailing love;
According to your great compassion
Blot out my transgressions.

Wash away all my iniquity
And cleanse me from my sin ...

Create in me a pure heart, O God
And renew a steadfast spirit within me ...

I read it over quietly, in a whisper, and then again and again in full preschool-teacher voice until I was hoarse.

Hot air started to blast out of the old radiator across from me, and soon it lulled me into a nap. I woke up when I felt a presence in the corridor. The basement light was dim, and my eyes were bleary from exhaustion and reciting the psalm without my reading glasses. The rebbetzin walked toward me as if she were emerging from an old black-and-white movie. She put her hand on my cheek. I bolted up in my chair.

She was not alone.

Tzippy stood behind her in a sheitel and a long skirt. I recognized her instantly. My mouth could barely form her name.

"It's me," she murmured. She sat herself on my left, and the rebbetzin sat on my right. Tzippy put her hand over mine, and we sat together for a minute or two in silence.

"Your letter was beautiful," she said.

I took her face in my hands and touched my forehead to hers, and we stayed like that for a time, talking without words. I didn't need to tell her how much I'd missed her, because I knew she felt the same way, and for now that was enough.

I sat back. "I want to pinch you to make sure you're real."

"I know, I know." Tzippy laughed through her tears, and the sound carried me back to all the nights I'd slept at her house, lying on her trundle bed, holding my eyes open with my fingers so I wouldn't drift off while she was talking. I didn't want to miss a word.

"Look." The rebbetzin pointed down the corridor.

I squinted at an approaching figure. Kinky hair and wiry limbs. Lili. She was wearing a modest sweater, a long skirt, and boots. I stared at her, and then I stared at the rebbetzin and Tzippy. "How in the world?"

They got up and started down the hall to leave me with my daughter, but she grabbed their hands. "Please stay."

"We'll be right around the corner," the rebbetzin said and stroked her arm.

Lili knew them! I looked at them, trying to wrap my head around the absurdity of this threesome. "How?" I asked dumbly.

"You're not going to like this," Lili said.

"What? What will I not like?"

She played with the buckle on her purse and then swallowed hard. "I know them from the letters."

"Letters?" I felt ill.

Blood rushed to her cheeks. "In the cedar chest, please don't kill me."

"Lili, those were *private*."

She looked down at her boots. "I know." She pinched her eyes shut the way she did when she was trying not to cry.

I was scanning my memory for all the embarrassing and taboo things in those letters when Lili came over and sat on my lap. I stopped scanning and held her. On some level, I must have known that an old cedar chest would entice a scavenger like Lili.

"When?" I asked.

"Last summer, a few weeks before my injury. Mom, those letters are so sad." She told me that my falling-out with Tzippy broke her heart and that she wanted to get us back together, like the sisters scheming to reunite their divorced mom and dad in *Parent Trap*. She'd always noticed my look of longing when I saw her with Meghan or Kara, and she wanted that for me, too.

I rested my cheek against the itchy wool of her sweater.

"And then there was the mysterious Grandma June," she said. "I couldn't imagine you leaving me like that. I hated her, and then I felt guilty when she stayed with us after my surgery, because I could see why you loved her, and that made me feel even worse."

"Oh, Lil. This must all have been so confusing for you."

Her voice grew shaky. "And then you started to get all distant and weird, and I worried that you were going to run off with some Shabbos goy."

I almost laughed. "No danger there."

"Annette," she said, recalling the name Tzippy and I had given the Shabbos goy's imaginary dead wife. "After I discovered the letters, I went on the Schines' website and found Tzippy."

"Come," I said. I helped her up, and we walked down the hall to Tzippy and the rebbetzin.

Tzippy put her hand on my arm. "My mother and I found a way to reach out to you."

"We knew Mrs. Kessler's tahara would help us bring you back," the rebbetzin said.

"But why didn't you come to me?" I asked Lili.

She pointed to the room where my mother's body lay. "I thought about it a hundred times, but there are certain topics I know to stay away from. And you got so mad around Grandma when she visited that it freaked me out."

I took her hand in mine, and I thought of how she must have felt lying in her bed, ashamed and afraid when I went to the hospital for the last time. I remembered how I felt in Madison, and how I couldn't leave Neil's bed. I had walked in my mother's shoes. I had left my child in a moment of need. But Lili had risen from her sick bed, and here she was beside me.

"I wasn't sure I'd done the right thing," she said. "You've been so, I don't know...."

"Distracted."

She smiled. "Kind of."

The rebbetzin put her hand on her chest. "When Lili cried out for help, I had to face the fact that I'd made a terrible mistake by abandoning you so many years ago."

"It's what my mother wanted."

"It doesn't matter. It was wrong."

I felt as though she had unclogged an artery and my blood could now pump freely through my heart. "Did my mother know that we were back in touch?"

"Yes, but I'm not sure she understood." I pictured the rebbetzin visiting my mother at Lakeline, chatting with Bonnie. "You and your mother. You both carried so much inside. And you, Barbara, you carried your sins and hers. It was time for it to stop."

We all looked at Lili, not having to say that our demons had found her, too.

"Your daughter is a brave one. She asked for help," the rebbetzin said.

"You set this all in motion, Lili. Incredible." She had felt the holes inside me, and despite her own struggles and resentments, she had summoned Tzippy, the rebbetzin, and my mother back into my life. Lili's "subliminal awareness," a term I'd never fully understood until now, assured her that they would accept her invitation. Perhaps it was ultimately my mother's unearthing of Lili's gift that had brought us here to the funeral parlor where her daughter and her granddaughter would watch over her soul.

"Yeah, I guess I did," Lili said. She gave me the smile I'd seen when she won her races, half embarrassed, half proud.

Last summer, I couldn't have imagined the possibility of Lili reading my letters and still loving me afterward. She knew more about acceptance than I had the capacity to teach her.

The rebbetzin stroked my daughter's cheek as she'd done mine so many times. "We have another tahara, Barbara, if you'd like to help."

"We're going to wash my mother's body?"

"Yes, Tzippy and I are going to prepare. You take your time with Lili."

"But there are only three of us," I murmured. How would we lift her body? I supposed we had no choice; the rebbetzin never would have put Chana and her crew in the awkward position of performing the tahara for my mother.

"Can I help?" Lili asked.

"No, Lili. You stay outside. You are the shomeret," the rebbetzin said. Lili had always been the shomeret, the one who watches.

I turned to the rebbetzin. "Are you going to get into trouble for this? My mother is far from kosher."

Tzippy smiled. "It's okay, Barbara."

"But I shouldn't be here either. You're not allowed to wash the body of a relative." I was worried about their souls.

"We owe you this, Barbara," The rebbetzin touched my sleeve. She spoke not as the wife of a rabbi, but with the humility of an old woman seeking forgiveness.

"Thank you," I said.

"When you're ready, come inside." Tzippy kissed the top of my head, and the rebbetzin picked up the large canvas bag she'd brought with her. Tzippy followed her into the preparation room.

I turned to look at Lili, sitting primly in her respectful attire. Her hair was streaked with strands of my mother's auburn and a faded gold left over from the summer. When she looked up at me, I saw that her eyes were blue-green like my mother's and mine, but they were also rounder and more open, like Sam's. I opened my siddur and handed it to Lili. She couldn't read Hebrew fluently like me, and she didn't recite the words with my mother's Ba'al Teshuvah born-again fervor, but she read proficiently and without affectation.

Less than a few days ago, she had wrecked our house, and here she was the mastermind of this enormous act of redemption. I'd always thought I could read her, but she was a collage of fragments that would continue to surface from the cropping and slicing of everyone who touched her life. I blinked, and she appeared in her entirety. Lili. We were all such collages.

"I need to go help now," I told her. I kissed her and walked toward the tahara room.

Tzippy met me outside.

"I knew you'd show up again," I said. "I just never knew that I was still waiting for you." I had tried to comfort her before she married a stranger, and now she would walk beside me while I buried my mother.

She shook her head. "I'm a few years too late."

"Never too late." I saw now that time could not reverse itself. Nothing could have stopped my mother from having an affair with Andy. Like us, he was a lovely apartment she'd rented. The mikveh would always be her home.

I thought about the stillness I'd felt floating in that water, all of it fortifying me for this moment. Everything that had happened since I left the Schines' shul had led me here. Maybe my mother had pushed us all in the right direction after all. Maybe she trusted that we'd find our way home. This perfect spot.

"I'm ready."

As soon as I entered the cold room, I smelled death, as I had when I washed Mrs. Kessler. The rebbetzin handed me a pair of latex gloves and sent me back to the day at Mr. Beckerman's when my mother sacrificed her brand-new gloves for the rebbetzin. I was only beginning to understand the courage it took to accept an object of warmth from someone who had disappointed you in the most profound way, to love a person with all her imperfections. My fingers grazed the rebbetzin's as I accepted the gloves.

We washed our hands, and then the rebbetzin said the Chamol prayer. "Master of the universe! Have compassion for June Pupnick, the daughter of Joseph Fischer, this deceased, for she is the transcendent of Abraham, Isaac, and Jacob, Your servants...."

Tzippy put an arm around me, and we rocked gently back and forth to the rebbetzin's words.

"Blessed are You who gives great mercy and abundant grace to the departed of His people Israel. Amen. So may it be His will."

"Amen," I said loudly, repeating to myself an earlier part of the prayer. *Through mercy hide and disregard the transgressions of the departed.* Mercy and abundant grace, these were things I wanted for my mother.

Tzippy handed me an apron, which I remembered from Mrs. Kessler's tahara. Today was different. I was not afraid or angry. The celebration and memorializing of Mrs. Kessler's role in my life had been an excruciating reminder of my mother's absence. Today, my mission was pure.

The rebbetzin removed the sheet from my mother's head. She stood still for a few seconds before she reached down and smoothed back my mother's hair. She didn't have to explain the hefty price of loving June Fischer Pupnick.

I stared down at my mother. I didn't compare her slack gray

face to the beautiful mother I'd watched blot her lipstick in one of her pretty slips. Her bones and skin were just a suit of clothing. Her soul lived inside me and Lili.

Before I put on my gloves, I held my hand up to the light and looked at my heart line. I had more wrinkles now, but I knew that the big split represented the gap between my mother and her mother and Lili and me. The smaller ones branching out from the trunk were Andy and the Schines and Neil and Simone and Daniel and everyone who had fallen into the chasm we'd created with our secrets.

Tzippy handed me a toothpick, and I took my mother's hand and cleaned under her nails. When I was finished, I rested her heel against my belly and ran my fingers over her arches, wishing she'd laugh. She was always ticklish. Her skin was rubbery soft, and she no longer had thick calluses on her feet from the high heels she wore to walk to the Schines for services.

The rebbetzin dipped a rag in a bucket of water, and I leaned over and tested the temperature with my wrist before I accepted the cloth. Tzippy stood on my mother's left side, I stood on her right, and we worked as a pair, cleaning her body. We began with her face: her eyes with their delicate blue veins, her sunken cheekbones, and the lips that made a smile nobody could refuse. I washed behind her ears and in her nostrils. I washed her neck, her right arm, her right hand, and her armpit, nearly bare. Tzippy and I uncovered only one part of her body at a time. We swabbed her thighs and her bony knees and between her toes, and when we were finished, we turned her on her side and cleaned her back and wiped her bottom like a baby's.

When we finished bathing her, we poured three buckets of water over her body. The water was cold, and I shivered for her. The rebbetzin closed my mother's mouth, and we poured continuously, moving like ballet dancers, quickly, efficiently, never getting in each other's way. The rebbetzin said another prayer, and then we patted my mother's body dry with a towel before shrouding her.

The rebbetzin removed the tachrichim of white linen from a plastic bag. She laid out the head covering, pillow, and veil on a small table first. Then she pulled out a pair of white trousers, loose-fitting, almost like hospital scrubs, and placed two ribbons and a shirt next to them.

I remembered my mother and the rebbetzin sitting on the Schines' living-room couch with this white fabric covering their legs. I had no idea what they were sewing. They made these shrouds without fanfare, just as they showed up at the houses of the sick and stocked the fridges with roasted chickens, eggs, and milk.

The rebbetzin placed the veil on my mother's forehead, as Tzippy and I had done with each other so many times when we played with the yellowed cloth we found in the brides' room at shul. The rebbetzin tied the veil and positioned the headdress while I slid my mother's feet through the legs of the pants and pulled them up to her waist. We wrapped bands around her knees and fastened them with slipknots. The rebbetzin laid the blouse on top of my mother, face down with the neck toward her feet. Tzippy and I drew her arms into the sleeves while the rebbetzin guided her head through the opening and slid it over her body. We tucked the edges into her pants.

The rebbetzin and Tzippy wrapped the final band around my mother's waist nine times while the rebbetzin recited the first nine letters of the Hebrew alphabet, except for Yod, which stands for God; the body itself was significant of the letter. They wound the belt around thirteen times. Aleph, twist. Bet, twist. Gimmel, twist. Daled, twist. Hay, twist. Twist, twist, twist. When she finished, she took the band and made three loops, forming the letter shin, an abbreviation of Shaddai, a name for God.

"As he came, so shall he go," I read from Ecclesiastes, and then I reached under her arms and cradled her to my breast, washed and swaddled, as she must have done when the delivery nurses placed Neil and me in her arms, as she'd never had the chance to do with Andy's baby. My mother would leave this world clean.

And loved.

Only Tzippy would have known the precise moment when I was ready. She appeared at my mother's feet, and we managed to lift her body and lower it into the pine box the rebbetzin slid toward us. The rebbetzin handed me a bottle of egg white mixed with white vinegar, and I put it in the casket, to hasten decomposition and lessen the anguish suffered by the soul. This soul had suffered enough. I put two pieces of wood the size of ski poles in my mother's hands to help her spirit rise from the grave. I sprinkled dirt from Israel over her body, over her face, over the white shrouds. We picked up the lid and sealed it over the pine box, and then we kissed the coffin before we left.

Lili was still reciting psalms outside the room when we emerged from my mother's tahara. I didn't want her touching my hands until I'd washed them, so I crooked my elbow, and she slipped her arm into mine.

The four of us walked out the basement door of the funeral home into the bright winter morning. The sky was cloudless. The rebbetzin put a fresh rubber glove on her hand and retrieved a plastic baggie and a bottle of water from her purse. She unscrewed the cap. I held out my palms, and she poured water over them, three splashes on each, alternating sides. She set the bottle on the ground, and I picked it up, holding it where she hadn't touched it. I washed her hands. We repeated the ritual with Tzippy.

We all stood together, letting the cold air dry the droplets beading our hands. It is said that the water represents the tears of our people. Only God can dry those tears.

THE END

ACKNOWLEDGMENTS

My gratitude to Prospect Park Books, specifically Colleen Dunn Bates and Patty O'Sullivan, for believing in this novel and offering their editorial genius and gentle prodding to help it reach its potential. They've worked tirelessly and with great passion, and I couldn't have dreamed of a better home for my book.

To my agent, Jill Marr, for picking this manuscript out of the slush pile and finding the perfect publisher via her unrivaled savvy, editorial instincts, and tenacity. Without Jill this book would be sitting in a drawer, plain and simple.

To my writing communities, past and present, beginning with The Johns Hopkins MA in Writing Program, including Mark Farrington, David Everett, and Ed Perlman. I am indebted to the George Washington University Creative Writing Program, the DC Women Writers, the DCJCC Writer's Group, with a special shout-out to Jean Graubart, and to every single one of my students. I learn more from their literary offerings than they will ever learn from me.

I am grateful to the Congregation Beth El of Montgomery County Chevra Kadisha, specifically Sara Greenbaum, who taught me how to perform a tahara, as well as the deeper meaning of the ritual. Special thanks to Rabbi Greg Harris for providing spiritual sustenance and Melissa Goldman for planting the seed for this book.

I relied heavily upon the following publications: Rochel U. Berman's *Dignity Beyond Death: The Jewish Preparation for Burial*; Rebecca Brown's *The Gifts of the Body*; Hope Edelman's *Motherless Daughters*; *Her Face in the Mirror: Jewish Women on Mothers and Daughters*, edited by Faye Moskowitz; and the website Kavod v'Nichum: Jewish Funerals, Burials, and Mourning.

These early readers provided the smart questions and belief needed to carry me to the next draft: Bill Loizeaux, Susan Stiglitz, Julia Wilson, Maire Hewitt, Marci Kanstoroom, Beth Lynch, Lois Hauselman, Lisa Friedman, Rebekah Yeager, Jim Grady, Shannon

O'Neill, Tammy Greenwood Stewart, Jeff Kleinman, Gail Hochman, and Wendy Sherman. To my last readers and fact-checkers: Mary Wallace, Kathie Bernstein, Sheila Elana Jelen, and the generous Caren Sadikman for reading early and late drafts.

Several of my many fine teachers guided the writing of this novel: Faye Moskowitz reminded me that the bridge is always love, and Margaret Meyers midwifed this story over dozens of Mon Ami Gabi salads. David Groff directed me to the heart of this book, and Joy Johannessen sprinkled her fairy dust over my prose.

Warm thanks to Richard Peabody, also my teacher, for publishing the short story "Washing the Dead" in *Gargoyle* and nominating it for a Pushcart Prize. And to Leslie Pietrzyk for republishing the piece in *Redux: A Literary Journal.*

To my literary *landsmen* for the coffees, phone calls, smart reads, and general hand-holding through every step of the process: Susan Coll, Dylan Landis, Melinda Henneberger, Cathy Alter, and Jamie Holland. An extra helping of thanks goes to Mary Kay Zuravleff for her advice, proofing, and faith.

I am indebted to my stalwart supporters and sages who hung with me from word one: Miriam Mörsel Nathan, Kathy Stokes, Priscilla Friesen, Rachel Wollitzer, Lori Baird, and my MacArthur Boulevard buddies who have spent miles walking and talking this book with me. More thanks to numerous friends and believers for their support during subsequent parts of this journey.

To Molly Mikolowski for spreading the word far and wide and Maggie Vlahovic for her behind-the-scenes efforts.

To my dad, Stuart Brafman, who taught me how to tell a story, my mother, Lotta Brafman, who taught me how to listen to one, and my brother, Lester Brafman, who always makes time for mine. To my children, Gabriela and Gideon, for stretching my heart wide enough to write this novel, and finally, to my husband, Tom Helf, my first, middle, and last reader, my metronome and best friend.

ABOUT THE AUTHOR

Michelle Brafman has received numerous awards for her fiction, including Special Mention in the *2010 Pushcart Prize Anthology*. Her fiction has appeared in *Fifth Wednesday Journal, the minnesota review, Blackbird, Lilith Magazine*, and other journals, and her essays have been published in *Slate, Tablet,* the *Washington Post,* and elsewhere.

Michelle teaches fiction writing at The Johns Hopkins MA in Writing Program. She lives in Glen Echo, Maryland, with her husband and two children. Learn more at www.michellebrafman.com.